MERONA GRANT AND
THE ISLAND OF
DEVILS

LOST FRONTIER

MERONA GRANT AND THE ISLAND OF DEVILS

BRINA WILLIAMSON

cover & illustrations by
Brina Williamson

All characters and situations portrayed in this work are
purely fictional and any resemblance to events or persons,
either living or dead, is entirely coincidental.

To my sweet, fluffy, faithful companion, Luah. The original inspiration for my leading lady's loyal Argos. You were the best dog a girl could have, and losing you amid writing this book made it that much harder to finish. But finish it I did, with you in my memory for every step. I wish you could have finished this adventure with me. You will be forever missed.

And to my new, fluffy sidekick, Pixie. Thank you for being my emotional support while I finished this book. You give the best cuddles.
You're a little crazy, but that just makes you extra lovable. I look forward to my ongoing adventures with you stuck to my side like glue.

NAVIGATION

ILLUSTRATIONS

CHAPTER I

DEBTS OVERDUE

A coiled lasso hung over a rumpled green scarf on the arm of a chair, silently awaiting further adventures upon its devil-may-care owner's belt. It had been a long and arduous day among the sand, and the lasso's aforementioned owner, Merona Grant, fell back into the shallow waters of her freshly filled bathtub, immersing in the liquid as it infused her aching muscles with its soothing heat.

The Grant sisters' work out at the dig site, unearthing tombs and disabling traps for rich men, who paid little, had lasted nearly three weeks already. This trip into town to address their sorely neglected hygiene seemed a well-deserved reward after the endless days of ducking darts, sidestepping spears, and near misses with bothersome blades.

The half-filled tub sat in the center of the cramped bathroom as Merona plunged back into it, the once clear water growing murky as dirt and dried blood lifted from the adventuress' filth-encrusted form. Merona felt the flood of water wash over her face and tightly shut eyes, tickling up her nostrils as her head sank down into the bath.

Her long days of toil were washed from her thoughts like the grit from her body, and she lay submerged at the bottom of the tub, fully absorbed in the moment. Though this particular moment didn't offer the kind of relaxation she had anticipated, partly because she was still half dressed in her slacks and undershirt, and partly because of the six-foot-two, bearded individual who stood over her, holding her head forcefully beneath the water with stumpy fingers clenched around her throat.

Luxuries, like the ability to breathe, rapidly superseded any such frivolousness as bathing or relaxation as Merona frantically kicked out, landing a hit to her assailant's thick jaw with her one remaining boot.

Staggered only a little, his grip on her neck loosened just enough for Merona to twist free before grabbing hold of his wrist and slamming her palm into the back of his elbow. A loud pop echoed off the walls, followed by a scream from the man, who's elbow she'd just dislocated.

Free from his grip, Merona pushed up, breaking the surface of the water with a gasp as she rolled from the tub, toppling onto her hands and knees, water spilling from her mouth and nose in retching, sputtering coughs.

Clenching his jaw in livid pain, her attacker rounded the undersized tub in three steps before grabbing hold of Merona's dripping, blonde hair, with his one good arm.

Jerking Merona from the floor with a sharp tug at her scalp, the man twisted the matted clump of hair in his fingers as she staggered to her feet.

He grinned with a mouthful of yellow teeth. "Time to pay up, little missy."

Merona grunted with the next tug to her hair. "Pay up to who, exactly? I owe quite a few people money, so you'll have to be specific."

The thug snarled, jerking her hair again. "Mr. La Roche wants his money!"

"Oh? Mr. La Roche, huh? Well, in that case…"

Merona's elbow shot back, jabbing sharply into her

assailant's sternum as she simultaneously ground her heel down on his foot.

Air forced from his lungs as he tried and failed to voice his pain, and with her hair finally relinquished, Merona dropped out of reach, snatching up the floor towel with one, forceful jerk.

The thug lurched back, slamming his head into the sink in a shatter of porcelain and teeth on his way to meet the floor. Hitting the tiles with a pitiful slap, his unconscious face abruptly settled into a soapy puddle.

"You got the wrong girl, pal," Merona continued. "I don't know any La Roches."

The thug lay motionless on the floor, bubbles gurgling from his nose into the puddle that partly submerged his face, and Merona shut her eyes, her head falling back as she let out a long overdue sigh. But her moment of relief was premature, as a seething groan echoed off the floor.

Rising to his feet, her attacker turned, bathwater and hatred dripping from his face.

Merona sighed again. "Haven't had enough, huh?"

A clenched fist plowed toward her face and Merona's arm rose to meet it, deflecting the blow only enough to catch his rough knuckles across her cheekbone.

Staggering back to avoid his next blow, Merona's calves hit the toilet rim behind her and she ducked low, spinning to the side to avoid his right hook.

Rising up, Merona threw a solid kick to the thug's head, plunging him face-first into the toilet bowl. Slamming her knee into his neck, she trapped his head inside the bowl with her full body weight as she locked his injured arm behind his back.

Bubbles surged up in a gurgling froth as he writhed beneath Merona's knee, fighting to remove his head from the foul water. Struggling to grab hold of his free arm, she felt him pushing off the seat, and even with the use of only one arm, his strength soon overpowered her own. In a flood of toilet water and rage, he rose up, knocking Merona backward off of him.

In an instant, his fist plowed into her eye, sending the room spinning around her. Again, his coarse, stumpy fingers seized hold of her hair, and with a hard jerk he wrenched her from the ground, plunging her face-first into the murky water of the toilet. Eyes and mouth clenched shut, Merona pushed back against him, escaping the water once, then twice, only to be forced back under with each effort to break free.

Water and filth filled her nose, scraping her airway as it seeped down her throat. Struggling to break free, the disheartening thought that this might actually be how she met her end, face down in the soiled water of a toilet bowl, pricked her resolve.

Her arms grew weak and, as she pushed against the rim, a distant sound of breaking glass brought all force and strength upon her head to a halt, and she jerked free from the water for the third and final time, gasping for air and the small scraps of dignity she had left.

Falling back, Merona slumped against the tub in relief. Looking up through the murky water which clouded her vision, fiery red hair framed the familiar face who now stood over her, casually discarding the shattered remains of the bathroom mirror which had been her assailant's means of defeat.

With fists planted firmly on hips, the redhead looked down toward Merona. "Well… care to explain just what in the devil's name is going on in here, little sis?"

"Oh, Liora, how nice of you to stop by," said Merona through dazed and stifled panting. "I was just explaining, to this gentleman on the floor, that I'm *not* the same broad who owes his boss money."

"Yes, you seemed to be *explaining* things very well."

"Hey, I was doing just fine before you came in. The toilet was... my low point of the fight."

"I'll say." Liora extended an arm to assist, and the Grant sisters locked hands, raising the still-dripping Merona to her feet.

Glancing toward the motionless heap on the floor, Merona blew the remaining water from her nose. "Think he's still breathing?"

Liora knelt and felt for the thug's pulse. "Sadly yes. But he should be out for a while."

"I suppose that's something."

"Just how much did he claim you owed him?"

"Oh, who knows. Presumably hundreds. Said he worked for..." Merona snapped her fingers. "A La Roche somebody or other."

Liora's eyes grew round. "Mr. *Lionel* La Roche?"

Merona's gaze narrowed at her sister. "I wouldn't know, but *you* sure seem to... and just how *do* you know that name?"

Liora bit her bottom lip tightly, her calm poise rapidly dwindling.

"Liora?" Merona growled through clenched teeth.

"Yeah... sorry about that. I think that black eye and toilet dunking were meant for me."

"Wonderful! So, *you're* the one who owes this La Roche guy money? How much do you owe him? And exactly when were you going to tell *me* that we had debt collectors, of the violent variety, on our backs?"

"It slipped my mind, okay? And it's only a thousand or so."

"*Only* a thousand!" Merona's palm met forcefully with the back of Liora's head. "Are you out of your ever-loving *mind*?"

"Ow! I've got it under control!"

"How is *this*, in any way, having things under control?"

"Because I have a meeting lined up for tonight. A good job, making good money."

"We're already working a dig."

"That's pennies, and we're nearly finished that job anyway. If we can get in on this new job, I can go on ahead while you wrap things up at the dig."

"Why should I stay behind so more of *your* debt collectors can track me down and finish what Ugly over there started?"

"Okay… *you* go on ahead while *I* finish up at the dig."

"That's better."

Liora's lips rose in a hostile smile. "It's nice to know you care, little sis."

"Hey, I already took a black eye and a mouth full of toilet water for you. The next one is *all* yours."

~

The Grant sisters strode through the narrow bar door, Liora's chin raised high as she searched the room for their client. Merona slouched up behind her, hands in her pockets as she glanced from behind the tangled strands of her messy blonde hair, scrutinizing the ragged faces in the establishment.

"So, who's this client we're meeting with, and what exactly is the job?"

"I told you, he's well-known amongst top archaeologists, excavationists, and ancient history experts, and I'm not sure of the job's specifics, but I know it's big, pays well, and is here in Cairo."

"Right… and his *name*?"

"Who's name?"

"The client…"

"I already told you, didn't I?"

"Nope. As a matter of fact, you've been pointedly avoiding saying it. Which makes me suspect it's a name I *know*, and won't like."

Liora smiled through pursed lips. "You know me too well."

"And yet you still bother trying to be clever."

"It's one of my principal talents."

"True. Because even now, you're still avoiding the question."

"You noticed that, huh?"

"I notice little things, it's one of *my* principal talents."

"Yeah, you are annoyingly good at that sometimes."

Merona stared at her sister, expectant and unblinking. "The name?"

With a defeated sigh, Liora relented. "It's Max Von Trent."

Merona's mouth fell agape. "Von Trent? Are you *nuts*?"

"It's good money!"

"It's a good way to get *killed*. You know that guy's as shady as they come. There were six names uncle Quincy told us never to tangle with, and he was the third!"

"Okay, okay, I know it's not ideal, but it's not like we have much of a choice."

"Ha! I thought *I* was the negative sister! There's always another option. We're *not* having this meeting, Liora."

"Merona, just hear him out."

"Not a chance. Do I need to remind you of that man's track record?" Merona instantly began counting off fingers. "Sent Fraser and his crew completely ill-equipped, into a trap-ridden tomb, just because he wanted to be first inside. Result: two men dead, and three more injured… and by injured, I mean one of them got lucky and only lost a finger. Then there was that renowned archaeologist he tipped off about a valuable find, so the poor sap would do all the work, risking his own neck to get ahold of that golden idol, meanwhile Von Trent is waiting just outside to literally stab him in the back and take possession. And of course, we can't forget about that highly illegal museum heist he was involved in, where—"

"Okay, okay, you've made your point. But you and I both know that those are *all* hearsay."

"No… no, I'm pretty sure we don't."

"Look, do you want to deal with another one of La Roche's goons?"

"Better than working with one of the most infamous names in the industry."

"Ladies," said a slithering voice through the smoke of the room. "How nice of you to show up."

The sisters turned to the congenial, smiling face of Max Von Trent as he approached.

Merona snarled. "Well, speak of the devil."

Stepping forward with a bright smile, Liora was quick to talk over her sister's ill-manners. "Mr. Von Trent, so good to finally meet you."

"And you," said Von Trent, shaking Liora's dainty hand in a cordial greeting. "It seems I can't go a week these days without hearing about the Grant sisters and their daring exploits. You ladies are quickly building quite the name for yourselves."

"Thanks," said Merona with a hostile smile, "And we didn't even have to stab anyone in the back to get here."

"*Merona*," Liora hissed.

"That's alright," Von Trent interjected. "My reputation is less than desirable, if woefully exaggerated.

I can assure you, I never stabbed anyone in the back, literally or metaphorically. And I'm sure bright young up-and-comers like yourselves can afford to be a bit choosy about who you work with, but I wouldn't be speaking with you if I didn't have the greatest respect for men like your uncle, as well as for what you've accomplished on your own, in such a short time."

Liora smiled politely at the compliment, as her sister merely scoffed at the idea such a man had any respect for anyone but himself, or thought their meager reputation was all that impressive. It had been a long road building up their name and reputation so that even a few might know them, let alone give them any kind of consistent work in spite of their Jewish heritage.

As Von Trent continued, doing his utmost to charm and butter up the sisters, Merona's thoughts remained on their financial situation. The simpering backstabber before them was exactly the sort of individual they had always avoided getting involved with, but Merona had to admit, their offers for good money weren't exactly thick on the ground just now. If they were going to eliminate the looming threat of deadly debt collectors, they'd have to take whatever work they could get. She had always been a pragmatist, and as much as she detested the idea of going against her favorite uncle's advice, as well as her own gut feelings of the man, she had to at least consider what he was offering.

Von Trent stood, still exchanging platitudes with Liora, and Merona grumbled at her own resolution before cutting in. "Right, well, why don't we cut to the chase, and you tell us just how much you are offering, and what the job is."

Blinking back with a wince, as though her sister's curt words were the screeching of a knife and fork on fine china, Liora did her duty to reintroduce civility to the conversation.

"Yes, quite. We wouldn't want to waste your valuable time with endless chit chat."

Von Trent smiled, turning and guiding the sisters toward his table.

Leaning toward her sister, Liora whispered into her ear. "Thank you for going along with this."

Merona shrugged her hands into her baggy slack pockets and replied in a much louder tone than her sister would have preferred. "Don't think this means I've made up my mind to take the gig. I've agreed to hear him out, but he's still a no good grifter."

"Do lower your voice, please."

"Why?"

"He might hear you."

"Good, then maybe he won't want to work with us."

Taking their seats across from Von Trent within a spacious booth, Merona's arms crossed over her chest. "So, Von Trent... dazzle us. What's this job of yours?"

"I like your style, Miss Merona. You take no nonsense and cut to the chase. Just the sort of thing I like to see in my women. Now, why don't we talk numbers first, since I think we both know that *money* is what any self-respecting adventuresses like yourselves should really care about. So, how would five thousand, *each*, sound to you two?"

The Grants' mouths threatened to gape, but Merona's cynical side kept a tight clench on her jaw.

"What's the catch?" Merona shot back, her eyes slivered in apprehension.

Liora shifted in her seat, instinctively eager to maintain civility, but in truth, beginning to share her sister's apprehensions. "I'd have to second my sister's question here."

"Why would there be a catch?"

"In our limited experience," said Merona, "whenever a fellow starts with a number *that* high, there is always a catch hiding behind those zeros."

"And what if I swear there isn't?"

"With your reputation, it wouldn't do much."

"If you could just give us some particulars on the job," Liora interjected, "that might help things."

"I'm afraid I can't at this juncture. The expedition is highly sensitive just now, and I can't risk any details getting out. It's a big find, and rival parties are as eager as I am to be the first to uncover it. I hope you understand."

"Then how do we even know we would be the right fit for the job?"

"Oh, I'm quite familiar with you ladies' past work... I'm sure you will be just the right fit for my expedition." His gaze trailed down Liora, taking in her figure with clear interest. "As well as *excellent* company."

"We hire out our brains, guns and *fists*, Von Trent," Merona snarled. "I see you eyeing anything else, and you'll get both fists for free."

Von Trent chuckled in amusement. "Fair enough, I'll be on my best behavior, just for you."

"Is there *nothing* you can tell us about this expedition of yours?" asked Liora.

"It relates to mythologies I know you two to be experts in, and to put it simply... it's going to be *big*."

Merona squinted. "How big?"

"World changing, Miss Grant. Do we have a deal, ladies?"

"Let me think... you offer us a suspiciously obscene amount of money, answer none of our questions about the job, and eye up my sister like a freshly marinated leg of lamb. Yeah... I think we'll pass."

With that, Merona rose from her seat, dragging

Liora from the booth by her waistcoat.

"You can't be serious?" Von Trent spat.

"When it comes to who my sister and I work with, I don't get more serious."

"But you *need* this money."

Merona froze in her tracks, turning toward the ever-growing crooked customer.

"And how do *you* know we need money?"

"I have my connections."

"You've been *watching* us?"

"I wanted to get to know my new employees better."

Merona's gut instinct took over. "And did you convince La Roche to call in our debt so we would be sufficiently *desperate* for you?"

Liora gripped her sister's tensing shoulder. "Merona, there's no need for unfounded accusations."

"You're right. There's no need to talk anymore *at all*."

Without even a nod, Merona stormed through the crowded bar and out the door, Liora following quickly behind her.

CHAPTER II

THE HAND OF FATE

IT had been five days since the failed meeting with Von Trent, and the Grant Sisters' situation had not improved. Their pay at the dig had decreased to extend the dig's limited funds through the next several weeks, as the crypt had proven to be much more extensive than anticipated. And though they knew it was likely an erroneous excuse, they could do little to argue it.

"You know, if you would just uproot your stubborn feet for half a minute, I could book another meeting with Von Trent, and we could get out of these flea-ridden tunnels." Liora said, striding out in front of her sister, torch aloft to fight back the shadows of the newly opened crypt.

"Why," replied Merona, "so I can spend the next month watching a filthy lech give my sister the eye?"

"I can handle myself."

"I'm sure you can, but what's the point in taking a job we're just going to lose when my temper gets the better of me and I give old Von Creep a black eye, fat lip, broken nose and arm, fractured pelv..."

"Okay, okay, point taken."

"I wasn't finished..."

"*Shush*," Liora snapped. "Did you hear that?"

"No."

"Then shut up and listen."

"Okay, miss grouchy."

"Merona, *shhh.*"

The sisterly bickering fell abruptly silent, and Merona and Liora stood motionless, their ears pricked to their surroundings. The flame of Liora's torch crackled overhead, its faint noise raising to a din along with distant voices of the impatient archaeologists murmuring down the tunnel at their backs, but pushing past these clearer sounds, Merona soon isolated a soft tapping, resonating from beneath the cavern floor.

"It sounds like… a clock," Merona whispered.

Liora raised an eyebrow. "Right, because all ancient burial chambers have clocks."

"I thought I was supposed to be the snarky one?"

With each step forward, the muffled ticking grew faster, and sister looked to sister for an answer neither had.

"Why is it getting faster?" Merona said, squinting.

"How should I know?"

"Well, *you're* the one who likes to read."

"Right, of course, that academic journal I was perusing the other day was all about ancient Egyptian *clocks*, they liked to keep under the *floors*."

"Okay, enough with the snark. You don't do it well at all."

Liora acknowledged her sister with a fleeting eye roll before shifting her attention and torch from side to side in search of the culprit of the unnerving noise.

"What *is* that?"

"How should *I* know?" Merona snapped. "I mean, you're the self-proclaimed brains of the operat—*duck!*"

Without hesitation, Liora obeyed her sister's command and dropped low, knowing that even a second's delay might mean death. Their personalities hadn't always blended in the most congenial way, but through their years of adventuring together, the Grants had built an unbreakable trust in one another's instincts which kept them alive. They may have questioned or disagreed on nearly everything else, but when it came to split second, life and death scenarios, they seemed nearly telepathic.

Dropping to one knee, Liora felt trembling air brush her neck, as a massive blade spun out from the wall overhead, missing her by mere inches. But with her escape, her new eyeline now sighted a second danger: a glint of steel slipping from a crack in the stone, and this emerging blade was peeking from the wall just behind Merona's knees.

"*Jump!*" Liora called, and in a flash, her sister sprang up, tucking her legs beneath her as a second saw spun out. Merona's body flew just over the danger, narrowly avoiding the spinning razor's edge before she hit the ground in a roll and sprung to her feet.

More blades glinted in the walls with a click, setting themselves into place before fully emerging.

Liora shouted again for her sister to veer left, then duck right, as she sped after her. Reaching the end of the series of razors, Merona glanced back, bellowing for Liora to stop as a blade lurched up from the floor just in front of her.

Leaping from the ground, Liora planted her foot on the wall, bouncing off and sailing over the blade to at last join her sister. A short ways off, the light of their torch illuminated a stubby lever in the ground, and without a word, the Grant sisters charged forward, their eyes and ears already attuned to the telltale snap and glint of the emerging blades.

Worn boots and flat heels hit against floor and walls in a synchronized flurry of well-practiced athletics, the sisters' hair, sleeves, and boot laces proving the only casualties claimed in the ordeal.

Taking hold of a lever at the end of the hall, Merona pulled back on the ancient mechanism, feeling the long-dormant cogs fight against her efforts. Stepping up, Liora pushed against it, the two sisters' combined strength grinding loose the centuries of dust and debris which clogged it.

Looking back at the hall of blades, they waited for the danger to come grinding to a halt, but with the pull of the lever they had only awoken further horrors. Long spears jutted from the roof, stabbing toward the ground in haphazard intervals, as flames belched in rows on the floor.

The sisters stood blinking, watching the chaos before them in awe. Without speaking, Liora stepped toward the lever, slowly pushing it back into place until the new implements of death had fully retracted back from whence they had come, leaving only the slicing blades remaining.

"Let's just... not touch that one."

Merona stood rigid. "Good plan."

"Now how do we stop the blades?"

"Shoot them?"

"Is that your solution to everything?"

Merona shrugged her rifle strap over her head. "Why not? It usually works."

With a reluctant sigh, Liora plugged her ears as Merona lined up her shot, pelting a slug into her mark.

The hall echoed with ringing reverberation, and the sisters watched as the disrupted saw blade began to wobble loose. The old stones cracked around it as the blade was flung with immense force from its perch, launching into the opposite wall and simultaneously dislodging several other blades.

The hall erupted into chaos.

Outside, plumes of dust rapidly belched from the catacomb's small opening, sending the awaiting workers and archeologists scattering for cover, but a moment after the turmoil, as the dust began to settle, the Grant sisters finally emerged.

"It's all yours." Merona called, pulling her heavy green scarf from her nose. "Just make sure no one touches the lever."

"What lever?" called a bespectacled archeologist.

"The big one... on the floor at the end of the hall," said Liora.

"Can't miss it," continued Merona.

"Don't worry, professor, we've cleared away the most dangerous obstacles, but I can walk through things with you and your men, so you know what *not* to touch."

Leaving Liora to play tour guide, Merona made her exit with a parting salute before trudging off toward the Grant sister tent, happy to be free of the claustrophobic and stifling heat of the crypt.

Pushing back the tent flap she slumped immediately on a cot and snatched up her canteen to gulp back its remaining contents. Tiny rivulets of water trickled down the side of her cheeks before being wiped away by her dusty sleeve. Pulling off her scarf, Merona mopped across her face and neck, new beads of sweat pricking up where the old had been cleared.

Outside, a timid, youthful voice called out. "Miss Grant?"

"Enter," Merona called back, and a boy's dirt-smudged face popped into sight between the tent flaps.

"A letter for you, miss Grant."

"Well, bring it in, kid."

The boy's dusty, white robes danced around his tanned, scrawny legs as he trotted inside and handed over the letter. Ripping at the envelope, Merona scanned across the paper, quickly recognizing the handwriting of her favorite uncle, Quincy M. Grant, who's scratchy scrawl she and Liora had long since agreed was on par with deciphering hieroglyphics.

Squinting at the writing, Merona's jaw abruptly dropped, as she spotted the words, "job opening" "excellent pay" and "how soon can you be here?". Immediately Merona began reading back over the scribblings, deciphering yet more information about the job and its demands. It seemed too good to be true, but with all they had stacked against them, who was she to question such timely good fortune.

Not a half hour later, Liora entered the tent to find Merona sorting her things and packing her bags.

"That sick of the job already?" Liora asked.

"Just got a letter from Uncle Quincy. You know how he's been working on that job over at the Azorean Islands? Well, sounds like one of the men just got... taken out of commission. So, now there's a nice, handy job opening for one of us."

"And by one of us, you mean you?"

"Naturally. You're better at talking with the academic stiffs anyway. So, you can finish up here and I'll send enough back to pay off your friends as soon as I can."

"So, I'm just supposed to tell them, don't worry darlings, the money is coming?"

"Don't be stupid. We are way past talking things out. They want to kill you, remember?"

Liora rolled her eyes. "Thanks for reminding me, I'd forgotten that detail."

"Don't worry, I'm sure Sasha will be more than happy to let you stay with him for a while until I can get you the money."

"Ahh, yes, dear Sasha. How is he holding up?"

"Got a pretty good gig flying around stale, rich sightseers. Trying to save up for a hangar and runway of his own."

"That'll be a long way off."

"Well, who are we to shatter his dreams. But speaking of Sasha, he owes us a couple favors each, so that should make this flight a little *cheaper*."

"Cheaper? When has Sasha ever made you pay *anything* for a flight?"

Merona smiled. "Exactly."

~

The red sun hung low in the sky as the silhouetted biplane glided forward, a sturdy Vickers Viking IV, amphibious model, with retractable wheels that allowed for both runway and water landings. It was Sasha's pride and joy, and he'd spent all his savings on it the prior year, lovingly naming it Katya, which he had painted across the side in bright red.

Drifting lower, the biplane soared on toward the two sisters who stood awaiting its arrival on the runway below. A strong wind rushed in from the east, the remains of a violent sandstorm which had just passed through, but in spite of the winds, the plane held steady on its path. In the next moment, its wheels smoothly touched down, rolling to a halt on the runway, just a few yards from the awaiting Grant sisters.

The door swung open and three passengers scampered out, clearly relieved to be on solid ground after the gale they had just escaped. A moment or two after their departure off the runway, the pilot emerged, angling sideways just to fit his broad shoulders through the not-remotely-narrow opening. His long white scarf caught in the breeze as he stood to his full, towering height beside the plane, and one had to wonder how he could have fit in it in the first place.

Slipping his goggles from his eyes, he turned to see the sisters striding toward him. "Merona! Liora!" He called out in a booming voice, spreading his arms wide in readiness for an impending bear hug.

"Sasha," Merona called back. "Glad to catch you in such a good mood."

"*Da*! Of course!" He said, his resonant voice drenched in a thick Russian accent. "Me and Katya just make it through great sandstorm. Any other plane be tossed from sky, but not us!"

Sasha patted the side of his aircraft, proud of the old bird's tenacity. Turning with a broad grin beaming out beneath his thick mustache, Sasha scooped up the two sisters into a giant, crushing hug.

"So, what bring my two favorite sisters to my runway?"

"I need to call in one of those favors you owe me." Merona said bluntly.

Sasha's shoulders drooped in disappointment. "*Da*, of course you do... I not know why I remain friend with you two. You only come to ask favor."

"Because you secretly love us," Liora said smiling.

Sasha sighed. "Alright, what it this time?"

"I need a flight out to the Azores."

"When?"

"Right away."

"*Nyet*."

"What do you mean, no?"

"I mean I not free to fly you." Sasha folded his arms across his barrel chest. "I busy with real, *paying* job until..." he counted out on his fingers, "end of month at least."

"The end of the *month*? We can't wait that long!"

"I sorry, you know I fly you if I free, but I not. Word get round that I best pilot on roster, so I quickly get booked up." He said with an immense smile.

"Congratulations Sasha!" said Liora, with genuine pride.

"Yes, fantastic," said Merona, concealing her disappointment and trying to be happy for her friend's success. "But it's just a short flight, Sash, can't you postpone them just a few days?"

"*Nyet*, I do that, and I lose job."

"Not even as a favor for an old friend? If I recall correctly, you owe me at least one."

Sasha winced. "I know, I know, I owe you three, and Liora five. But I not just able to fly you anywhere at drop of cap! I have job obligation, and *bills* to pay, same as you!"

"I doubt yours are *quite* as extensive or pressing as ours," Merona muttered under her breath.

"Besides," Sasha continued, "I need find different way to pay you back. I owe you both so many favor, every flight is for *free* these days."

"Tell you what, I'll *pay* this time."

Liora cleared her throat. "Merona... *debts*."

"Oh... right. Okay, well I can't pay *this time*, but I can pay you back later."

Sasha squinted. "Debts? What debts? Merona, what you do?"

Merona's fist fell on her hip in protest. "Why do you always assume it's me?"

"Because *always* it you."

"Well, this time it's not. This one's Liora's fault."

Sasha let out an audible gasp. "Liora, I thought you were smart sister."

"*Hey*," Merona snapped. "I'm standing right here."

"It's not important whose fault it is," Liora interrupted. "The point is our uncle has a job opening on his team, and if Merona can't fly out there in time, they are going to find someone else to fill it."

"I want help you both, truly, but I not afford to give up this job."

A true look of remorse fell over Sasha's face, and Merona patted the pilot's hefty arm. "It's alright, we understand. It just means I'll have to find another pilot... and fast."

~

The biplane's propellers sputtered to life on the distant runway as Merona slung a hefty pack over her shoulder, her thick green scarf rippling in the strong winds as she turned to Liora and Sasha to say her goodbyes.

The towering Russian clutched the last piece of Merona's luggage in his massive hands, an expression of apprehension resting on his face, brought about by the ever-present fact that he would not be the man in the pilot seat.

"I not like it," said Sasha, hesitating to relinquish his hold on the bag. "The man is not reliable pilot."

Merona smiled. "Yes, yes, Sasha, so you've told us... about twenty times over. But I don't have time to be picky, pal. We need the money this job can offer."

"*Da, da*, so you tell me," said Sasha dismissively. "But what good is all money in world if you dead before you land? The man is not of sound mind!"

"He could be worse." Liora Interjected.

"His copilot is dog!"

"I didn't say he couldn't be better," replied Liora, knowing full well the Russian was not wrong.

Their chosen pilot was, to put it kindly, a bit of an eccentric, who did in fact insist on flying with his pet dog as his copilot. In his own words, the mutt brought him luck, and though this was the sort of thing which discouraged most logical individuals from flying with the man, Merona couldn't be bothered to give such idiosyncrasies much notice, since Cornelius Carver was the only pilot available on short notice that wasn't charging an arm and a leg for his services.

"This flight will end in ball of wreckage, I tell you," Sasha insisted. "Please Merona, let me finish these jobs, and then I fly you, no charge!"

"Sasha, someone tried to kill us a week ago, remember? I can't just sit around waiting for you. We caught a break with this job. I've got to take it before it expires, and before another associate of Mr. La Roche shows up."

"I already tell you, you can *both* stay in my spare room as long as you need! And if any more men come looking for you, I deal with them, no problem."

"The offer is appreciated, it really is," replied Merona. "And I'm sure Liora will be happy to take you up on it when she's not needed at the dig, but it's a short-term solution, and I've *really* got to board now, pal."

"You'll let us know when you land safely?" Liora reminded, hooking one arm around her sister's shoulder in a partial hug.

"I'll try to remember," replied Merona, returning the half-embrace.

"You always say that, and then never do," Sasha muttered. "Why you like to let us worry so much?"

Merona slapped him across the arm with a chuckle, taking hold of the luggage held hostage in his hands, and started off towards the plane without answering.

"Don't worry Sash," she called back. "I'll be just fine

out there on my own. I usually am."

With a smile and salute, she reached the westerly bound plane and climbed aboard, leaving Liora to calm the Russian's nagging fears.

"I not like it," Sasha muttered once again.

"Try not to worry about her," Liora said, patting their friend's wide back. "This is Merona we're talking about, she can handle just about anything bad luck throws at her."

"And as someone who know you both for lot of year now, I also know how much you both dance on edge of cliff with your luck."

"Fair point. But I mean, come on, it's not like she's *your* sister. If I'm not worrying, neither should you."

Sasha looked down at her with disappointment in his eyes. "That hurt. I thought over this last year we all become like brothers."

"You mean we're like your sisters?"

Sasha shrugged. "You more like sister, perhaps, but Merona feel much more like brother."

Liora smiled. "She has that effect on men."

~

From her cramped seat behind the pilot, Merona eyed her surroundings of rusted bolts, mismatched wicker chairs, and several crates of cheap whiskey. Her only passenger companion matched the craggy interior of the plane rather well, being an elderly gent, in a patched-up jacket, reeking of booze. Though whether the smell came from him or the cargo, was uncertain. Eyes shut, and head drooped, her fellow passenger snored loudly in competition with the growling engines, as the plane's pilot looked back from his cockpit to greet his passengers.

"Welcome aboard!" said the cheery pilot through curled whiskers. "I hope you're both comfortable and ready for takeoff."

Merona flashed an unconvincing smile in reply, sinking low into her rickety wicker chair and dreading the next several hours trapped in a plane with such a chipper mustache.

Sliding his goggles down into place, the pilot tossed his crisp white scarf over his shoulder. "My name is Cornelius Carver, and I will be your pilot for this flight."

A flourished hand-gesture directed Merona's attention towards the gray, scraggly dog sitting next to the pilot, dressed in matching goggles and scarf, and sporting an identically cheery expression.

"And this is my dog... or should I call him my copilot!" Carver continued. "If you need anything, I'm sure he'll be happy to help, in any way he can!"

The mutt barked excitedly, and the pilot let out a hearty laugh at his own joke before at last settling into his seat to get underway.

The takeoff was a relatively smooth one, but as they glided into the air, Merona slipped her lighter from her jacket, fiddling with it briefly to ease her nerves.

She'd never show it, but Sasha's words hadn't left her with a great deal of confidence for the flight ahead, but the plane was in the hands of the pilot, and she was locked within the plane. No part of the journey ahead was within her control, and so she resigned herself to her fate, pocketing her lighter once again and following the example of her snoring fellow passenger. Sinking back into her cramped chair, she shut her eyes, taking in a deep breath and hoping to pass the time with some much-needed rest.

Unknown minutes or hours passed and Merona woke more than once during the flight to the gleeful, though off-key singing of her pilot, as well as his copilot's accompanying howls of merriment, or possible protest at his master's wailings. Merona found it necessary to bundle her scarf over her head and around her ears to muffle all future cheerfulness that sprung from the cockpit.

Upon landing in Morocco to refuel, Merona awoke again and decided to stretch her legs by spending the few hours of their sojourn in hunting down a bar near the airstrip and treating herself to a hot meal. The meal turned out to be the highlight of the trip, and Merona regretted returning early, to not hold up the flight, when she found her fellow passenger eager to chit chat to pass the time during the remaining hours.

Thankfully, his excessive drinking habits soon took hold and the man fell once again into a happy slumber. Merona took advantage of the relative calm, and once again sank back into her own precarious sleep. But it was a rest that wouldn't last long.

Bolts and brackets rattled with the sudden jolt that pitched Merona upright as her eyes shot open.

They were back in the air, and the pilot's chipper voice drifted back over the screeching winds outside. "We seem to have hit a bit of a storm, folks."

Blinking past foggy eyes, Merona took in her surroundings. To her right, her fellow passenger still slept, shifting in his seat and muttering to the minor disturbance of the roaring storm. Looking out into the blackness of the night beyond her window, she squinted past the rain which pelted the glass, spying a faint hint of waves crashing far below the aircraft.

"Where are we?" called Merona over the din.

"Not sure," called back the pilot. "Somewhere over the Atlantic."

"You don't know?" Merona snapped.

"The storm pushed us off course!"

Merona sighed. "Oh, fantastic."

The plane quaked around them as Carver attempted and failed to regain control of his aircraft. With intense panic in his no-longer-cheery voice, Carver barked at his passengers to, "Hold tight!" amidst curses toward his unruly plane.

Merona gripped tight to the sides of her undersized wicker chair, before realizing it, like most everything else around her, was neither secured to the floor, nor very well held together itself. The tremors intensified and Merona scrambled to find something worth holding onto.

Grasping to the crisscrossing rope which held the luggage in place near the back of the airplane, Merona could hear the pilot shouting unrelenting curses and warnings of impending impact from his cockpit, but all his words seemed to drift back, as Merona caught sight of a looming blackness beyond the windows.

She had seen the distant waves crashing below when first she had awoken, but now they were growing; rising from the sea in an unnatural wall, which twisted and writhed towards them. Surging up, the pitch-black wave rushed closer, growing and twisting as long, sharp strands broke away from the black, liquid wall, stretching up and curling towards the plane, like immense, unnatural claws.

Merona looked on, anticipating the impending impact as the wave continued to take shape, shifting from a faint hint of claws, to a clear, gigantic black hand, rushing to pluck the struggling plane from its tenuous place within the sky.

The hand neared. The plane quaked. All went black.

CHAPTER III

THE ISLAND

MERONA's head pounded. Willing her stinging eyes to open, she found herself wedged in a crumpled heap at the back of the plane, and painfully forced her aching limbs out from under her body.

Having acquired many injuries in her short but adventurous past, such as broken bones, torn muscles, dislocated joints, gashes and gun shots, Merona was familiar with the various sorts of gnawing or stabbing pain which accompanied each kind of injury, and though her body ached in every imaginable place, she knew the throbbing pain of her limbs as she got to her feet and staggered forward, was only the ache of more or less insignificant bruising.

Blinking past the glare ahead, her eyes were met with the sight of twisted metal and shattered glass. One side of the plane was all but caved in, and beneath it lay the bloody body of her former fellow passenger. The old man without a name, who, for all she knew, had died in his sleep upon impact.

Checking his pulse to be sure of his fate, Merona once more forced herself forward, scrutinizing the plane for other survivors, which, to her surprise, there was no sign of. In the cockpit she found neither pilot, nor copilot, but only a bright spattering of blood across the seats, punctuated by smeared handprints in the same bright red.

Following additional marks of blood, Merona pushed back the crumpled side door and recoiled from the stinging sunlight that assaulted her sore eyes. Stepping from the plane, she let out a weak cough, expelling the debris in her lungs before gulping back some much-needed fresh air.

Her eyes adjusting to the once harsh light, Merona found herself surrounded by jagged rocks and lush green ferns. The front of the plane was wedged solidly into the jagged base of a rocky slope, and as Merona stepped back from the aircraft, a steep cliff revealed itself below her and the plane, jutting down harshly into a great, foggy expanse, the aircraft's left wing hanging far out over the precipice.

The plane had crashed on the high point of a low mountain, and Merona could see hints of distant beaches in every direction, through the thick fog which engulfed her.

For the first time since waking, Merona noticed a lack of weight at her hip where her machete always hung, and reached for the blade. Naturally, it was gone, sheath and all. Anxiously she checked her pockets, finding both the lighter and compass which were kept there, also missing.

Returning to the back of the plane in haste, Merona dug into what remained of her luggage, finding the bags too had been fully picked through like her own pockets. No sleeping bag, no rifle nor spare ammunition, no tinned food or water canteen. All her carefully packed supplies had been utterly ransacked.

Hissing out a curse, Merona struggled to her feet, pocketing a packet of broken crackers forgotten nearby on the floor, and checking her boot for the multiplex knife she kept there, which had thankfully been missed. Grabbing one of her empty, left-behind backpacks,

Merona began scavenging anything and everything of use into it that was left behind; spare shirts, the netting which once held the luggage in place, and so on, until her pack was full.

Tossing her pack of supplies on the floor nearby, she then reluctantly returned to the body of the old passenger, and spied his remains for anything useful.

Kneeling down, Merona began pulling the laces from the old man's boots, letting out a heavy sigh. "Sorry about this, old fella. Wish I didn't have to do it, but if it makes us even, my carcass was already scavenged, and I wasn't even dead yet."

The old, dead man made no reply, to no one's surprise.

As she continued in her pragmatic search, it seemed clear that the pilot who had so kindly pilfered supplies from her own unconscious body, had neglected to search the deceased old gent altogether. Most likely because Merona had looked the sort to possess more useful equipment. But whatever the reason, Merona was thankful for her robber's negligence as she rummaged through the dead man's pockets, appropriating a handkerchief, a small, unopened tin of "Bush's Best Pork & Beans", a half-empty hip flask, a tin of mustache wax, a packet of chewing tobacco, and whatever pocket lint she could scavenge.

"Of course," Merona muttered, "of all the men, in all the world, I had to fly with a nonsmoker. Not a lighter or a solitary match to be found."

Securing her new provisions safely behind the button-down flaps of her coat pockets, Merona made up her reluctant mind to do the decent thing and give the poor old fellow a semi-proper burial, as a "thank you" for the donation of his few useful belongings, if nothing else. But as she bent down to extricate him from the mangled portion of plane he was crushed beneath, a deep moan emanated from the walls of the plane, followed by a loud crack. Merona's feet were jolted out from under her as the aircraft pitched to one side. The metal groaned in complaint, creaking and twisting as the whole plane began to dislodge from its place in the rocks.

Scrambling towards the exit, Merona darted up the rapidly inclining floor and grabbed hold of the sides of the door. Pushing up through the opening, she sprang from the aircraft as it rushed out from under her feet, screeching metal gouging against the rocks as it tumbled down the steep, jagged mountainside and vanished from sight, taking her bag of supplies with it.

Grasping for a hold of stable ground, Merona heard the aircraft as it dropped out of earshot behind her, into the foggy gulf below. She gulped back a breath of shaken relief, and got to her feet, gazing out towards the misty greenery of the island she must now call home.

~

Weaving through dense greenery, Merona found her descent down the mountain side continually inhibited by the suffocating mist and residual slickness it left behind. Fog closed in around her with every step, and Merona's once lush green surroundings soon fell into an overwhelming gray haze. It was quickly growing difficult to find her footing, or even her own hand a mere arm's length from her face.

With the fog increasing, night quickly descending, and her battered limbs throbbing all the more, Merona made her decision; she would set up camp where she stood, as she had no interest in forgoing a much-needed night's rest to instead blindly grope through the fog, down a treacherous mountainside.

Cursing her failure to acquire any means of a tent or cover from the aircraft before its regrettable tumble down the cliff, Merona set about snapping off what bushy branches she could find of a reasonable softness to form her bed for the night beneath the shallow overhanging of a nearby jutting rock.

In a subtropical environment such as this, she hadn't anticipated needing a fire to keep warm in the night, but as the darkness grew, so did an unnaturally cold wind, and she set about gathering any and all drier branches or twigs that could be found, but with the dense mist soaking so completely into the environment, this simple task was made nearly impossible. Hours passed, the darkness closed in, and Merona clutched the scant collection of kindling she had managed to procure, as she groped through the blackness for the last component that alluded her: a striking stone to light her tinder.

It needed to be hard enough to make a sharp striking edge, so quartz or jasper seemed her best bet to spot in the growing night. And with little other tools to hand, her pocketknife would have to serve as a metal sparking tool. As she pushed forward through the vines and trees, one hand outstretched in the darkness as branches continually snapped back against her face and shoulders, her eyes adapted as best they could to the dark.

Scanning the ground, Merona found herself bending low to see past the denseness of the fog. Countless stones littered the rough terrain of the mountainside, but even with her vision adjusted, she found it difficult to spot a favorable rock. Stooping and snatching stones from amid the rocks, Merona brought each pebble before her eyes, struggling to identify much more than its shape and vague color.

She needed light to see the rocks by, but she needed a rock to create light. Breathing back in frustration, Merona bit the finger of her glove and pulled it from her hand before shoving it into her pocket. With her eyes failing her, she would have to aid her search by touch.

Taking up a stone, she rolled the rock in her fingers, feeling across the surface and assessing its roughness before placing it into her pocket or discarding those which didn't meet her needs.

As the cold began to bite into her exposed fingers, numbness threatened, and her ability to assess by touch rapidly started to dwindle. Soon Merona resorted to striking her findings against larger boulders to test their hardness, but most only shattered into pulverized chunks.

With several potential stones now filling her pockets, Merona returned to her partial shelter and huddled into her bed of foliage to begin her work. Retrieving her pocketknife, and the pocket lint she had scavenged, she flipped out her blade, and set to work slicing the edge of her green, wool scarf until she had collected the bits of shredded fiber into a small, fluffy ball at her feet.

Her tinder ball collected, Merona immediately began pulling the stones from her pockets and placed them at her side. Flipping her knife around, so as not to dull the blade, she shielded her delicate tinder ball from the howling winds with her body and began striking the steel against her first stone, quickly casting the stone aside after her numerous attempts failed to produce a single spark. Stone after stone was discarded in failure, and Merona found herself down to her last three gathered rocks.

Raising her tired arm, she struck steel against stone, and in a startling burst, sparks showered out, tapping and fizzling out at her feet. Merona blinked, pausing for a moment in disbelief before moving her tools into position near the tinder ball. Another strike and more sparks rained down, catching in the wool and pocket lint, igniting the fluffy fibers in the darkness like a beacon. Immediately, Merona began to blow against the unstable embers before a bright flame took hold and she rapidly worked to feed the fire, building her meager supplies around the bright, unstable flames.

The fire grew and Merona was soon splitting large branches into a suitable size to stack them into position, leaving plenty of room amid the branches for her fire to breathe and grow. The bright flame quickly broke the surrounding blackness and fought back the cold as the adventuress huddled near her precious fire.

Her work now done, Merona slowly removed her boots, pushing her feet towards the flames to begin drying her damp, woolly socks. Despite the overhanging stone wall at her back, cold winds still bit at her exposed sides, as her hands, feet, and face enjoyed the scant glow of heat before her.

Reaching into her pocket, Merona allowed herself to plunder the paltry supply of food available to her, knowing it was useless to hoard her provisions, as she would eventually have to find another means of sustenance, and would need all her strength to do so.

Tapping into the can of beans with her pocketknife, Merona placed it near the fire to warm as she pulled the flask from her pocket and unscrewed the lid. Sniffing the spout with hesitance, Merona hoped, but doubted she might find the decanter filled with water which might quench her thirst, but as she failed to scent any odor over the smoke of the fire, her hope rose, and she gingerly tipped the flask to her lips.

Her features crinkled in disappointment as the burn

of vodka hit her tongue, and she instantly replaced the cap, muttering to herself as she returned the flask to her pocket.

"All right then, guess I won't have a drink to go with my dinner, but at least I have a disinfectant at hand."

Her beans soon warmed, Merona decided to add a cracker or two to her meal, as a means of scooping the beans from their tin before resorting to the use of a wide blade from her pocketknife to reach the last remaining bites.

Periodically tossing sticks atop her fire, she finished her meal with great enjoyment, and found her weary mind and limbs drifting off. To the best of her knowledge, hunger, shelter and warmth would be the greatest challenges to her survival, and with hunger, warmth and at least a partial shelter met for the night, sleep became Merona's top priority, as she would need all her energy and strength to face the coming days. But her knowledge of the island she now found herself stranded on, was limited, and had she known what lurked within the shadows nearby as her eyelids flickered shut, sleep would have been the furthest thing from her mind.

CHAPTER IV

A WARM WELCOME

The back room of Sasha's lodgings was cramped, to say the least. Filthy plane parts were crowded onto a rickety shelf in one corner, and grease stains still remained atop the table, and other available surfaces where the parts used to rest.

But it was clear that the pilot had done his utmost, on such short notice, to prepare the room to be as comfortable as possible for his guest. A small bed was neatly spread and situated in the only available floor space, and a worktable had been moved into position alongside it to act as a nightstand. A small tin mug, with fresh flowers sat on the "nightstand" but watering had clearly been neglected, as the flowers were already withering.

"Thank you, Sasha, this will be lovely," said Liora, politely, appreciating his efforts in spite of the outcome.

"Truly? You sure you have everything you need?"

"I have a bed, a roof over my head, excellent company, and a bodyguard to fend off debt collectors: what more could a girl ask for?"

"No debt collectors?"

"Mmmm, one can dream."

"How you get mixed up in all this, anyway? You usually sensible one."

Liora sighed. "I know, it was just... I wanted us, Merona and I, to make a name for ourselves, you know?

We were still just known as Quincy Grant's nieces. Sure, we've been doing jobs on our own for a while, and were doing pretty well at it too, but to make our mark we needed something big... that first big venture of ours and ours alone. During one of our jobs I stumbled onto a lead to what could have been one of the biggest finds in recent history, something almost no one else would have the guts to go after, but with all I'd been spending to get our names out there, there was just no way we could fund it with what was left in our savings, so I had to borrow. We got so close to finding it, but then when things didn't pan out... the interest has just been growing ever since, and these little jobs we've been getting just haven't been enough to pay it off."

"If I known, then I not let you pay me for flight on that job. Then maybe you be in less debt and danger now."

"We didn't pay you for that one, Sasha... we almost never do."

"Ahhh, yes. I remember now. You two really take advantage of friendship."

Liora bit her lip. "Yeah, sorry about that."

"It alright. You pay me back later when you both famous adventurer."

Liora laughed. "Famous? We aren't even capable enough to go it on our own for a year, before we're running back for work with our uncle again."

"Not capable enough?" Sasha scoffed. "No one who know you can doubt Grant Sisters' capabilities. You two of the most capable, resentful woman I know!"

Liora smiled at the brotherly pilot's failed attempt at encouragement. "I think you mean resourceful."

"*Deystvitel'no*? As in *nakhodchivyy*?"

"Yes, resourceful is the word you're looking for there, Sash."

"What is resentful?"

"I believe it would be equivalent to *obizhennyy*."

"Oh! *Nyet*, not that… well, Merona is sometimes."

"She's just prickly in general."

"You sure you sisters?"

"Pretty sure… though there was this one time when we were working one of our first solo jobs, and there was this big old door we just could not open. No signs of a key hole, nothing, but I found these symbols in the center of the door that matched up with some hidden around the room, and was sure it was a puzzle of some kind. Anyway, while I was occupied trying to unpuzzle it all, and marveling at the ingenious mechanism that must be behind it, what do you think Merona was doing? That's right, she was rigging the thing up with dynamite to just blow it!"

Sasha laughed heartily.

"I was furious, Sash!" Liora said, insisting on her anger while holding back laughter at the memory. "And do you know what she had the gall to say to me after? She said 'if a puzzle takes longer to solve, than it takes to set explosives, it's not worth the trouble.' I'm telling you, I sometimes wonder who raised her!"

"*Da*, you definitely not related."

Liora shook her head, still laughing. "You might be right. Still, her bulldozer ways can come in handy sometimes. Plus, she's grown on me over the years… so, I think I'll keep her around, all the same."

"*Da*… I suppose so. She good in a fight anyway," Sasha said with a wink.

"You should know, she's saved your hide more times than she's saved mine."

"That not true!"

"Oh, it absolutely is! Remember that raven-haired beauty in Bangladesh? She would've absolutely fed you to those snakes if Merona hadn't stepped in."

"That only because she was woman and I have rules."

"Sasha, I admire that you have limitations when it comes to fisticuffs with the fairer sex, but you've got to learn to make exceptions when the skirt is actively trying to kill you."

Sasha grumbled, unwilling to compromise his morals or discuss the question further.

"All right, I'm sorry I said anything," said Liora, before gracefully turning the conversation to happier topics of one of the many times Merona's reckless risk-taking had landed them all in yet another tight spot, and only Uncle Quincy could get them out of it.

"I just hope Merona not get herself into even more trouble with reckless choice of pilot," said Sasha.

"I'm sure she'll be fine Sash, stop your fretting. It's just a short flight, what's the worst thing that could happen?"

~

Merona's eyes shot open to an unnatural noise.

Her body awakening just behind her fully conscious mind, which recognized the distant crack, yet couldn't quite place it. It was neither a snapping twig, nor breaking bone, yet was so distinctly familiar she knew she had heard it a hundred times before. Once again it sounded, a sharp cracking in the distance, and she knew in the next instant where she had heard the sound before.

"That's my rifle!"

Merona darted up, enraged at the sound of her stolen weaponry in someone else's hands, but before she could begin to even consider her next course of action, a faint, looming figure moved in the blackness, the glint of his rushing spear catching her attention as she rolled to her left.

A rush of pain pierced her flesh as the spear ripped down the side of her thigh, plunging into the dirt behind her leg. Her instincts to roll clear had left a jagged tear along her outer muscle but spared any major internal damage.

Sucking back the pain, Merona's eyes locked on her inhuman attacker as he tore his bloodied weapon from the dirt. Though his body was that of a skeletal, gray man, his face resembled an animal with a scraggly mane, tusks protruding from beneath a pig-like snout, and black pits where his eyes ought to have been.

Snorting out a snarling grunt, the boar-headed beast lunged for her once again and Merona twisted to the side, grabbed hold of the spear as it sped past her abdomen. With a sharp elbow to its face, his horrifying head was knocked off, revealing her inhuman attacker to be nothing more than a man.

Wrenching the spear from her attacker's hands, Merona spun it up, driving the stone point into his throat with a single thrust.

Merona's gaze locked with his, her tanned face mere inches from his dry, gray features. His was a face unlike anything she had seen before: no emotion, no color, human, yet inhuman. His body was lean, starved of all fat and nearly all muscle, leaving nothing but sinew and bones beneath a coating of gray, dry mud.

As he slumped forward, his once determined stare growing vacant and weak, Merona felt the last exhale of his hot breath across her face before his limp body toppled abruptly to the ground.

Drawing the spear from the corpse, Merona caught a hint of movement passing at the edge of her field of vision, as more gray-skinned men approached from the shadows. With the sight of their fallen comrade, the three men snarled at her, chattering their teeth in animalistic fury as their heads arched back in repeated jerking movements.

A guttural cry sounded from the forward warrior, and the three men charged.

Whipping her spear out in a wide sweep, Merona slit the gut of the forward attacker, dropping him to the dirt in a heap of gore.

The remaining two men lunged towards Merona, forcing her backward as she staggered to keep them at bay with each wide arc of her weapon. Merona was rapidly losing ground, and soon they would have her in a position to finish her off. With each swing of her spear, each foot of ground she relinquished, the slimmer her chance at victory became.

In the next moment, Merona's weapon was hooked by the barb of her enemy's spear, wrenched from her grasp, and sent spinning through the air. She ducked beneath the sweeping attack that followed, rolling past her foe to escape her cornered position.

Finding herself up against her second opponent, Merona was swift to duck the warrior's attack, slipping under his dagger to step face to face with him and slammed her head into the bridge of his nose.

The warrior toppled back, relinquishing one of his daggers into the air as he fell. Snatching the knife mid-air, Merona drove it into the startled warrior before turning toward her final enemy.

She felt the sting of his spear as it ripped through her sleeve, slicing open her shoulder in a long, jagged cut. Diving clear of his next attack, Merona rolled out of reach and reclaimed her lost spear from the dirt.

Forcing him back with a swing of her spear, Merona

and her assailant stepped slowly in opposing circles, each eyeing the other with predatory instinct. Blood trickled down Merona's arm and leg, as sharp rocks gouged into her still-bootless feet.

Assessing her opponent and looking for openings in his defensive posture, Merona could hear one of the men on the ground nearby as he spat up blood, pulling the knife from his side as he staggered to regain himself. It was only a matter of moments before he rejoined the fight, and waiting for the perfect opening was a luxury Merona couldn't afford.

Taking her chance, Merona lunged in with a mock high thrust to her opponent's face. His weapon rose in anticipation, but her spear dropped low, weaving beneath his defense with an abrupt turn up into his ribs.

The gray man's blood seeped out across the weapon as Merona buried its spearhead deep into his torso. He spat out, sending blood and spittle across her face and shoulder. Again, she felt the last breaths leave his body, saw the life flicker from his eyes, and felt the jerk on her weapon as he drooped limply to the ground.

Merona was not unaccustomed to taking a life in self-defense, but in the past, she had nearly always had her rifle to hand, defending herself from cover as the bullets sped by. It took a certain kind of mettle to keep your head in a gun fight, but this; impaling one's opponent a mere breath away, this took a kind of ruthlessness she hadn't known she harbored. A ruthlessness she instinctively disliked in herself, and yet was glad she possessed.

With all but one attacker dead, Merona turned to face her final opponent as he rose from the ground, eyes livid, and blood seeping from his mouth like a feasting lion rising from its latest kill.

No words would halt him, could they even be

understood, his eyes made his intentions clear.

Keeping her gaze on her opponent, Merona jerked on her spear, trying and failing to wrench it from its place between her fallen foe's ribs. Then, in that moment, the gray man showed the first hint of human emotion since the encounter, an emotion Merona didn't like one bit.

His thin, cracked lips parted in a wide grin, exposing blackened teeth and a pink tongue as his eyes turned toward the spear protruding from his fallen brother who lay on the ground, mere feet from him.

In a wild dash, each lunged for the weapon, colliding with each other as they hit upon the shaft.

Fingers clutched around Merona's throat as she felt her body forced to the dirt, the gray man landing on top of her in a frenzied bloodlust. His gaze burrowed into her own, as though he relished the impending second when he would see the last wisp of life leave her eyes.

Merona struggled, gripping at his hands around her throat, yet helpless to push him from his place of power. That same grin still rested on his face, and in the next moment he lunged, sinking his teeth into her arm with delight.

Unable to scream past the pressure on her neck, Merona let out a constricted grunt of pain. In the next moment she gripped tightly to his wrists so he couldn't catch himself, then forced her hips up, throwing the gray man off balance and face-first into the dirt above her.

Rolling free in his moment of disorientation, Merona leapt to her feet, gulping back air into her once-strangled lungs before she landed a swift kick to her assailant's crotch before he could stand. The Gray Man winced, letting out a stifled yelp, showing a second sign of human emotion which Merona liked much better than the first.

Still on the ground, the Gray Man's eyes glinted like a reptile in the darkness as he clawed at the dirt in pain, and Merona reached for the nearest spear, wrenching it loose from her last kill and without the luxury of hesitation, plunged it cleanly between his shoulder blades. She knew she must ignore all humanity which might come naturally to her and embrace her animal instincts if she hoped to survive amid her newly discovered neighbors.

CHAPTER V

SURVIVAL

MERONA slipped her boots over her gouged feet, her hands shook with lingering adrenalin as she worked to reignite the fire.

Blood seeped from her wounds, soaking into her slacks and shirt as she tossed her last sticks upon the extinguished fire's remains, soon building it into a bright blaze once more.

The flames' glow fell across the bodies that littered the once-peaceful campsite, at last giving enough light for Merona to properly tend her injuries by. But how she would do so with almost no supplies at her disposal, became her next obstacle.

Merona rose, limping as she searched her surroundings and the lifeless men at her feet in a hopeless attempt to procure something useful. But it seemed she had run through her good luck for that day.

It was clear that the gray men were a people whose lifestyle had left their bodies rife with all manner of filth, and even a scrap of fabric from their scant coverings would be a sure path towards infection. Merona would have to find another means of stemming the flow of blood and dressing her wounds.

Retrieving her pocketknife, she slipped her jacket from her shoulder and carefully sliced along the tear in her sleeve. Soon, Merona had removed the sleeve entirely, leaving only a short scrap covering her shoulder, and the raw tissue now stinging from exposure to the wind.

Slicing her old sleeve lengthwise into long strips, Merona was left with four long bandages to mend her injuries. But as she glanced at the deep gash oozing down her arm, and her other jagged wounds, it was clear that these meager bandages would do little to nothing to halt the flow of blood.

Merona gritted her teeth at the thought of what she must do, before placing her blade at the fire's edge to heat. Limping from the fire toward a nearby tree, she struggled to ignore the memory of her first attempt at the, now imminent, procedure. Back then, she'd had no idea what pain she was in for and her ignorance had made the first searing almost easy, but now, as she snapped a branch from a tree, her mind reeled at the thought of what she was about to do. Yet she had no other options.

Placing the branch between her teeth, Merona pulled the flask of vodka from her pocket, disappointed she would have to tap into it so soon. With a twist of the cap, she gingerly tipped its contents out across her wound, grinding the branch in her teeth as the pain shot through her limb. Her body shook as she held back the instinctive urge to apply pressure to her stinging injury, undoing the painful work of the cleansing vodka.

Merona gasped out in relief as the pain retreated, dropping the stick from her lips with a heavy breath. But that had been only one wound, and the cauterizations were still to come.

She gingerly drew up her other sleeve, careful to avoid contact with the gnarled, raw and bitten flesh of her wrist. Her mind returned to the moment the gray man had sunk his black, rotting teeth into her arm and she shuddered to think of what filth must have resided in his mouth. Once more, she repeated her process, dowsing her flesh and clamping the stick in her teeth to fight the pain.

Vodka and blood dribbled from her skin, dripping to the dirt in a steady trickle as she struggled to focus on the repetitive, drip, drip, drip as a distraction from the pain. Vodka: the word reminded her of her old friend, Sasha. She'd once offered him a glass, assuming all Russians enjoyed the liquor, but found herself wholly refused. He had, and always would detest the foul drink.

"It good for nothing but melting brains and killing honor."

Merona laughed to herself, remembering his words as she tried to ignore the last tremors of pain. She had to disagree with his assessment of the drink, it was useful as a disinfectant, if nothing else. Continuing the painful process over her final and largest injury, the long gash across her thigh, Merona soon returned to the fire, checking her knife's heat before removing it from the edge of the flames.

The blade was tinged with a faint red glow, too hot to use, so Merona watched and waited as it faded just enough to proceed. Once again, she clamped the stick in her teeth. Her thoughts returned to Sasha and Liora, wishing just one of them was at her side, to hold her steady the moment the pain took her, if nothing else.

She brought the blade to her shoulder, feeling the emanating heat as it neared her skin. Blood still leaked from the wound, and Merona could feel the beginnings of faintness taking hold of her.

Finding the deepest part of the wound, Merona tapped the hot blade against her flesh, hearing the harsh sizzle a split second before feeling it.

The branch began to crack under the pressure of her bite, as she tapped the blade against her raw and scorching skin once again. She wanted to scream out, to succumb to the tears of agony her burning flesh brought to her eyes. But those were luxuries this unforgiving wild wouldn't permit without severe repercussions. A scream would be heard, tears would blind against a potential second attack, and she still had two more wounds to seal.

Merona gasped out once again, pulling the stick from her mouth to assess her work. Blood still oozed from portions of the cut, but the main flow had been halted, and so she wrapped the wound in a long bandage, sealing off the remaining cracks.

Next, she peeled back the torn fabric at her leg, its fibers sticky with her still-leaking blood. Merona tilted toward the fire, casting the light upon the long wound that crossed her thigh. It was jagged and deep, and she knew the process of sealing it would be a long and painful one.

Biting down on her new best friend once again, Merona tapped the hot blade against the deepest section of the gash. Familiarity did nothing to temper the pain or streamline the process as the smell of her burning flesh filled the night air.

Gasping out once again in stifled relief, Merona delicately pulled back the folds of her torn pants to assess her work, and as she examined her scorched leg, cracks in the burns began to ooze blood once more. Her blade had begun to cool, and all her efforts had done was leave her skin burned and blistered but unsealed.

Curses flooded her mind as she stared at the wound. Her whole body ached with fatigue, hunger, and the throbbing of her wounds. She had been on this island a mere day and a night, and already she felt pushed to her limit. She had faced the wild many times before, but something about this place had already eaten through her resolve with a voraciousness she had never experienced.

Merona sat slumped, staring at the dancing flames for comfort as she anticipated the weeks of survival ahead: trapped on an island, abandoned, alone, cold, hungry, burnt, and bleeding, with only crude supplies to sustain her. How much easier would it be to just accept defeat? Yet, her body seemed to press on without her, placing the knife near the fire once more to reheat, as a flicker of willpower surged from inside. She would press on. She always pressed on. Giving up was not in her nature.

Her body continued through the motions of resealing her bleeding wound, the well-chewed stick between her teeth her only comfort or release. Soon, her knife was again reheating near the fire, as she warily wrapped the thin strips of makeshift bandages around her tender leg. The soft fabric felt like coarse sandpaper against her raw skin, but the pressure on her wounds and protection against the elements soon began to soothe the throbbing ache, if only slightly.

With her blade now ready, Merona looked to her final injury: her gnarled and bitten wrist. The flesh was jagged and had already begun to scab in places around deep punctures, and Merona hesitated to seal the holes, wondering if the bleeding and douse of vodka had been enough to clean out the kind of filth that such a mouth might have contained. She had experienced the bite of many a wild animal in her colorful past, but never with so few supplies at her disposal to clean it, and even then, some of those injuries had grown infected. Sealing the wound now, if any bacteria remained within the tissue, she would have no means of recovery.

Retrieving her small flask, Merona dribbled the last of the vodka over the wound, pausing to let it bleed and cleanse the wound further, as well as allowing the flammable alcohol time to dry before she risked placing the hot blade to her flesh.

Tap, tap, tap. Pressing the knife against each gouge, each puncture and torn piece of muscle, she applied slow, steady taps that made her body shake from the scorching pain as she struggled not to flinch and cause even more damage.

The process seemed endless, exhausting, but at last the bleeding had stopped, and Merona slumped against the rocks at her back, wrapping her wrist in another bandage before pocketing the remainder.

She was done. Her excruciating efforts had done nothing to ease the pain, adding to it more, if anything. She was hungry and drained. Her limbs throbbed, her head ached, and she was growing dizzy.

Her body was trying to heal, but after such a loss of blood, and little food or water in her stomach, it had limited energy to work with. Retrieving the crushed bag of crackers from her pocket, Merona raised a feeble handful of crumbs to her mouth, crunching the savory bits in her weak jaw as she assessed her next move.

She needed to replenish her body's depleted energy before she could rest, but she had nearly eaten through her scant supplies to make it through even her first day. The few crackers seemed only to whet her appetite, their salty taste leaving her mouth dry and in even greater need of water. But where would she find any means of sustenance that didn't demand even more of her already waning strength?

Looking down at the bodies once again, Merona noticed clusters of small pouches hanging from the cords tied at the natives' waists and wondered at what they might contain. With luck, these men had been scouts, and inside those pouches they might have kept a small ration of food, or even water to sustain them on their treks across the island.

Dragging her tired body forward to investigate, Merona searched each pouch, finding an assortment of dried meats, black roots, and a waterskin pouch of a strange-smelling liquid.

With her thirst taking precedence, she risked the strange liquid first. It seemed unlikely that the men would carry around such a large quantity of undrinkable or even poisoned water, but even still, Merona sipped the contents with caution.

The taste was regrettable. Stifling her reflex to spit it up, Merona swallowed back the much-needed liquid like a child taking unwanted medicine.

Turning to the other supplies, she tentatively sniffed a burnt lump of meat. As she brought it to her lips, she suddenly recalled the gleeful way the gray man had sunk his teeth into her arm, and shuddered to think of what, or *who's* flesh this might have belonged to.

Catching a whiff of the meat brought back an unexpected memory of her time in India and the distinct smell of burning bodies that always accompanied the funeral pyres there, and without hesitation she returned the meat to its pouch.

Next, she attempted one of the black roots, touching it carefully to her tongue. She could taste no hint of burning which might accompany something poisonous, and so decided to risk the scant roots of her dispatched enemies.

"If it kills me, it kills me, I suppose... can't be much worse than my current situation."

The tough, thick skin made the dried vegetable almost inedible in Merona's tired jaw, but slowly and gingerly she managed to consume a few of the roots. Her empty stomach pressed her to finish the rest, but she knew this scant bit of food was all she had left, and that a few handfuls of crackers and roots would be unlikely to last her long. She needed something more substantial. Some kind of protein.

Eyeing the pouch of meat, Merona quickly turned to search for other possibilities. She had only been on the island a day and a night, and refused to resort to cannibalism just yet. But what else was there nearby?

It hurt to move and even think as she wracked her brain for other options, but in the next moment, a hint of movement in the corner of her eye caught her attention. Just within reach of the fire light, a shiny black beetle was making its way up the arm of one of the dead men, and Merona remembered a time when such diminutive game had been her and Liora's only available food source.

Large rocks littered the ground and Merona once again dragged herself up towards the nearest boulder, pushing it loose and rolling it from its settled place. Instantly the light of the fire illuminated Merona's impending feast. Earth worms, grubs, beetles and centipedes, wriggled agitatedly under the sudden flood of light, and Merona quickly began collecting her new meal into the emptied can of beans from the previous night.

With the overturning and scavenging of several more rocks, she had soon nearly half filled the can and nestled it amid the hot coals of the fire to cook. Sounds of sizzling, popping bugs mingled with the crackle of the fire, and Merona allowed herself to rest her eyes as she listened to her surroundings and held tight to a spear in readiness.

Her consciousness drifted in and out as her body grasped at a desperate need for sleep, but her instincts fought against the risk which sleep might leave her open to, and she soon forced herself to waken, as a smell of burning bean residue reminded her of her awaiting "meal".

Plucking the hot tin from the fire, Merona placed it on a rock to cool. The smell of burnt bugs in bean residue was not the most appetizing, but as Merona retrieved her now-cooled meal, she found the smell had been much more appealing than the sight proved to be.

Limp worms and shriveled grubs floated in a beany paste, amid crispy beetles and the burst innards of some of the more over-done insects. Her stomach growled, and with a quick gulp, she slid the stew into her mouth. Odd, misshapen chunks dumped onto her awaiting tongue, and she quickly chewed, eager for it to be over.

But as the unique flavor seeped into her taste buds, Merona found herself gagging less than anticipated, and almost began to appreciate the beany infusion which had been allowed to marinade into the "meat" of her meal. It wasn't remotely the worst thing she had had to eat.

Her meal soon finished, Merona set about assessing the supplies of her fallen foes, collecting any and all useful items or weapons she could scavenge. Cords, leather, pouches, and the remainder of the scanty roots were all collected and pocketed. From the spears her attackers had carried, Merona selected the best two and strapped them to her back, utilizing some of the leather wrappings which adorned the gray men's arms and lower legs, to do so. With the remaining spears, she broke the sharpest head off as a knife, storing it and a hatchet in her belt, then took a final spear as a walking stick for the long trek she knew awaited her.

Collecting whatever she could carry and deemed most useful from her camp, Merona set off once again, her body still throbbing, as the sun rose over the expansive water which surrounded her, piercing through the dense mist of the island for the second time.

CHAPTER VI

SHOTS IN THE DISTANCE

THE rise of the sun brought a hint of warmth to Merona's chilled extremities, as its light struggled to breach the curtain of mist which shrouded the island. But with its welcomed warmth, it also brought the sting and bite of swarming insects, which Merona's endless swatting could not deter.

Hours passed, and though Merona's trek down the mountain took her long into the morning, the light never grew beyond the dull, hazy glow of dawn. Gnawing thirst bit at her throat as her stomach's growling complaints increased in frequency. It had been a solid eight hours since she had allowed herself any food, but far less time since she had tapped into the strange water skin of the gray men, the contents of which was already dwindling to a dangerously low level.

But Merona knew she needed to keep on the move, having no doubt that the small band of gray men she had faced the night before were likely part of a greater tribe. And if such a tribe should catch wind of their slain brothers, a larger hunting party might not be far off. She needed to make it off the mountain and put distance between herself and the camp, but more importantly, she needed to find a fresh source of water, and the game it would attract.

Her limbs seemed to buckle with every step, as her head increasingly throbbed, and at last Merona allowed herself another bite of the gray men's blackened roots. With each bite, the dry root seemed to sap the moisture from her mouth, even as it fought back the fatiguing hunger, but she dared not drain her last drops of fluids before night began to descend.

She trudged on, endlessly pressing through the dense fog and meandering trees. Her thoughts drifted to a description of the mythological underworld of ancient Greece, found at the ends of the earth, an infinite field of gray mist and forgetfulness, and she laughed to herself at the idea that maybe she had wandered into that very place. Perhaps she was in Tartarus, and the natives she had encountered were the forsaken ghosts of the dead, or servants of Hades himself.

"Let's just hope I won't have to battle Cerberus," she said, chuckling to herself to break the mounting tension she felt.

The endless gray slowly dipped into night, and Merona once more set up camp. This time she made sure to take her time in selecting a campsite carefully, choosing a narrow, hollow-like pit that would conceal any light from being spotted by more unfriendly neighbors. With the added aid of the thickening fog, she felt confident in her own concealment enough to risk a fire.

Sparking her blade against the flint rock into a new bundle of shredded wool and twigs, her humble fire was soon alight. Shelter was insufficient that night, and as the wind whipped through the gully, it stung her exposed eyes and cheeks causing her to wrap her thick scarf higher around her increasingly frozen face. The wind now only assailed her back, the fire keeping its chill only slightly at bay as she huddled nearer.

The last of the gray men's drink was consumed along with the roots, and Merona once again resorted to the acquisition of bugs to complete her nighttime meal, this time catching several scorpions which she pierced on a stick to roast over the fire. Their taste and texture were somewhat akin to an over-cooked shrimp, though far more bitter, and Merona found herself actually enjoying the wilderness delicacy, only lamenting her lack of salt or butter to enhance its flavor.

Sleep was prompt in its approach, and though Merona knew relinquishing her faculties would leave her open to another attack, it was a risk her body demanded. More than once she awoke to strange or distant sounds in the darkness around her, and sat, spear at the ready, awaiting her enemy's approach, but always her caution was for nothing. The night passed without incident, and Merona awoke to the unpleasant stings of biting flies.

Gathering up her scant belongings, Merona was swift to get moving, knowing the dry scratching of her throat would only intensify as time went on. She desperately needed water and food, but with that hope to drive her, she also had to put such thoughts out of her mind, knowing the mere notion of water would only serve to heighten her thirst.

Hours wore on much like the previous day and without seeming to notice, Merona soon found herself walking on even terrain. Her first task was complete, she had made it off the mountain, and now needed to tackle her second obstacle; locating fresh water.

Her search was long and arduous, the desolate island offering no sympathy, her only relief found in the gathered dew she was able to funnel off leaves into her parched mouth. And though the relief was desperately needed, it was short lived, and she grew increasingly tempted to stop at every available leaf, an urge which she had to regulate, or lose precious time in finding a proper source of refreshment. Had she not controlled herself, she very well might have gone another full day without a proper drink.

Just as her willpower was beginning to waver, a sound broke through the silent fog, hitting her ears like a train. Rushing water babbled in the distance and with this new promise of relief, Merona found the drive to keep going. The sounds grew louder, and she could almost taste the cooling liquid running down her throat as she sighted the small, snaking stream rushing from the mountain she had descended.

Falling to her knees, Merona cupped her hands into the crystal clean waters, gulping back until her stomach began to swell, all the while, keeping her eyes peeled on her surroundings for danger. With her thirst quenched, Merona immediately seized upon the water skin at her hip, running it through the rushing water first to clean it of its old contents, then filling it to its fullest capacity, drinking and refilling yet more before closing off the precious contents. Assessing her remaining containers, she found and filled the small flask as well, slipping it securely into her coat pocket for future emergencies.

With her water needs addressed for the time being, Merona now assessed her food supplies, of which she still had the sad remains of two small scorpions, and though they were not altogether unappealing, the idea of yet another night subsisting on bugs was not something that overjoyed her. The water offered greater possibilities of game, and Merona was meticulous in her search along the stream for signs of animal life, but as time wore on and no sign of fish or big game tracks presented themselves, Merona had to admit defeat and turn her search elsewhere.

Small rodent tracks skittered off and were lost in the foliage, bird feathers and droppings scattered here and there from hours or days before left little to be followed, and after ascending a tree in the disappointed hope of an egg clutch, Merona sat on a thick limb to decide her next move and tap a little into her fresh new water supply.

Gazing down over the dirt and weeds below, she spotted a rippling line, like the track of a wobbling bike wheel weaving through the dirt, and traced along it from her keen vantage point until an unexpected hint of movement caught her eye. Squinting past the fog, the slick, patterned scales became clear, and Merona instantly recognized the fat body of a python meandering slowly through the grass.

Assessing her weapons, Merona was skeptical if she could hit such a small target as the python's head with a single spear throw. She was far more likely to wound and scare off her meal, or worse, enrage it into attacking. Taking out her hatchet, she swiftly chopped at a limb of the tree, severing its many branches until only a long shaft and forked end remained.

The python hadn't slithered far as Merona leapt from her tree, hatchet and forked staff in hand. With her eyes fixed on her target, she crept carefully through the grass toward it, slowing with each nearing step. She had seen African tribesmen handling snakes with similar tools, and knew that if she could get in close enough to pin its neck, she could easily dispatch it with her hatchet.

Stepping within range to strike, she spotted its body stiffen and in the next instant she stabbed, catching its neck between the forked branches and locking it firmly against the ground. Shifting her hold on the stick, she got in closer as the python's writhing body caught hold of her leg and coiled tightly around it, squeezing in self-defense the only way it could.

With her leg already growing numb from the immense pressure cutting off blood flow, she lined up to take her shot. The python's head pushed back against the branch which held it, beginning to slip free just as Merona delivered a swift strike, severing its head from its body and, all at once, it fell limp to the ground. For the first time since crashing on the island, Merona felt herself smiling from ear to ear. She had caught her dinner, and what a feast it would be.

Returning to the river, she began to skin and gut her meal, her mouth-watering at the idea of actual meat for dinner, but as she slit open the animal's belly, she was faced with a new delight: wriggling within it was an infestation of parasites.

No longer so delighted with her catch, Merona made quick work of cleaning out the snake's guts, having no desire to contract the lively critters herself, she was thankful the infestation seemed to be contained within the animal's intestines and not within its meat. Using her spearhead-knife, the snake was soon skinned and gutted, and all that remained was a long, clean, pink strand of ribs and meat.

To avoid tangling with any predators that might want a drink, Merona set up her new camp a short ways off from the stream. Soon a new campfire was crackling away as Merona held the lean length of meat, pierced with a stick over the flames. With hunger pressing, the wait for her meal to cook seemed agonizing, but when at last she could sink her teeth into her meal, it quite possibly became the most delicious meat she'd ever tasted, as she made very short work of picking the bones clean.

She could see the glow of the sun begin to drift low in the sky behind the fog and she shut her eyes and leaned back against a tree to digest, feeling fully satisfied with her progress that day.

"I've got fresh water, and a solid, filling meal for

once. What more could a girl ask for?" she said aloud to herself.

Breathing in deeply, her body began to relax, but in the next moment her ears were met with a distant, but distinct sound she knew by heart: the sound of gunshots.

Stabbing her half-eaten snake-ca-bob into the dirt, Merona snatched up her weaponry and raced toward the noise, knowing, without a doubt, that the shots were those of her own rifle. Vines clung to her limbs, and branches snapped against her face, as she rushed through the thick forest barring her objective.

More shots rang out, and Merona forced her body to its utmost, charging towards the sounds any rational man or woman would have fled from. But for her, the shots meant more than just looming death; they meant the potential recovery of her gun, her irreplaceable ammunition being wasted, and all the supplies which had been stolen from her luggage after the crash, but most especially, they meant finding the backstabbing pilot who had sifted through her pockets and left her for dead.

~

Deep in the woods, a cluster of gray men surrounded the desperate pilot and his dog. Cornelius Carver held tightly to his rifle, threatening the gray men as they loomed forward, adorned in elaborate snake-like headdresses with spears held high.

"Get back!" Carver shouted, "get back or I'll shoot!"

The gray men looked on with indifference to his incoherent babblings, continuing their measured advance.

Carver had already wasted several rounds of ammunition to dispatch just two of the men. But even

this show of force had failed to strike fear in his enemies' ruthless hearts. With only a few shots left to him, the pilot knew he could never take down the remaining six natives before they closed in around him.

Panic overcame him, as he shouted more nonsensical orders to the gray men to stop. His furry copilot barked franticly at his side, sensing his master's fear and uncertainty. Another shot pierced the air, missing even the dense cluster of men before him as Carver struggled to pull back his rifle's bolt. With his next shot, one of the gray men dropped, but as he fought with the bolt handle once again, his stomach sank as his rifle jammed.

Carver swung the malfunctioning rifle out wildly in desperation as his four-legged companion followed suit, lunging for the nearest man and sinking his teeth into the attacker's gray, dry skin.

Blood covered the ground, as the dog embraced his instincts and tore into the man's neck. Alongside him, Carver swung out with his rifle butt, landing a lucky blow to the temple of one of the gray men.

In the next moment, Carver felt a sharp pain in his forearm, relinquishing the rifle as he recoiled from the spear. Then, as a second spear loomed, a javelin shot from the woods, impaling the attacker and halting his impending death stroke.

Spears in hand, Merona burst from the trees, launching a second spear and dropping another gray man to the ground. Pulling her dagger and hatchet from her belt, she clashed with the remaining natives, as Carver ripped the spear from the body at his feet, rushing in to join the fight.

Carver was not the most skilled of fighters, in fact, he could not recall a time when he had ever had a need for such skills. So, although he was significantly taller and heavier than his starved and sinewy opponents, and their attention was nearly fully occupied with the relentless attacks of the adventuress, Carver still struggled to land a hit of meaningful impact.

Battling alongside each other, Merona took on the brunt of the attacks, as Carver and his dog lent what aid they could, stabbing into the Gray Men's backs whenever an opening presented itself. Bodies dropped to the dirt and, in the wake of the battle, the three castaways emerged miraculously victorious.

For a moment they stood, having fought side by side in a united goal, but now, with their enemy dispatched, the two stranded survivors eyed each other with suspicion and distrust.

"Miss Grant," Carver gasped out. "You're alive."

Merona snarled. "I am. No thanks to my *pilot.*"

CHAPTER VII

A SHAKY ALLIANCE

MERONA gripped her primitive weapons, glaring at Carver with ferocity.

"I can explain," Carver insisted, clutching his spear in readiness. "I was panicked… dizzy from the crash… it was an honest mistake, that's all."

"A mistake?" Merona hissed. "You take the time to rummage through my pockets, and yet, *somehow*, never bothered to check if I was *breathing*?"

"You both looked dead!"

"And with so little food to go around, how much more convenient for you it would be if I was."

"No, no, no! It wasn't like that at all! Mr. O'Hennen was all bloodied up, with his head bashed in, and then you, laying in a heap at the back of the plane! I could hardly believe my dog and *I* had made it out alive! I didn't think to hope anyone else had."

"And why bother checking, right?"

"My head was spinning from the impact. I couldn't see half straight, with the blood running into my eyes! I panicked! The plane was teetering off a cliff so I grabbed what I could carry and got out! I'm relieved you made it out alright. I honestly thought I was going to be stuck out here on my own, and if I had been, I don't imagine I'd still be alive."

Carver indicated toward the bodies of the gray men. "With enemies like *them* to contend with, I don't think it's of any benefit to fight among ourselves or hold grudges, do you?"

He held out his hand, offering Merona the first gesture of civility she had had since crash-landing on the strange and dangerous island.

Only a few moments earlier Merona had been prepared to fight to the death, if needed, to retrieve her stolen supplies, but after the last couple days, Merona was already weary of fighting and welcomed the opportunity of a truce. Even if it was with the very man who'd robbed her unconscious body. At the very least, it showed him to be resourceful.

"No, I don't suppose it is," Merona replied. "In a place like this, we both are going to need all the friends we can get. Besides, I suppose if our situations had been reversed, and I had mistaken you for dead, I would have taken all your corpse had to offer too."

Carver smiled unenthusiastically at the thought. "That's... good to know."

Hands shaken and a truce made, the two allies still eyed the other with residual apprehension. However, on reclaiming her weapons, ammunition, and other supplies with comparable ease to what she had anticipated, Merona allowed herself to entrust her new ally with the transportation of some of the less essential items. More out of a necessity of not being weighed down, than anything else. A fact which she wasn't shy about sharing.

Having returned Merona's rifle and machete to her, in exchange for a spear and hatchet as his only permitted means of self-defense, it was clear to Carver that this Grant woman's trust would need to be earned, and though somewhat irritated at the initial ransacking of his supplies, he assured himself it was worth it, to have such a capable survivalist and fighter on his side.

As they made their way back to Carver's camp, where the rest of the supplies like Merona's bedroll and tent waited, Carver attempted to heal the damage his past actions had created.

"I'm glad you're letting bygones be bygones, Miss Grant. I wouldn't want to think there were any hard feelings."

"I never said I was *quite* there yet."

"Fair enough. But it will be nice to have someone to talk to at least. My pup isn't great conversation."

Merona grumbled. "Neither am I."

Merona had never bothered to cultivate a congenial disposition, even in the best of times. Diplomacy and affability had always been Liora's job, and now, stranded, starving, and being forced to trust a man she had no confidence in, Merona was at her most prickly. By choice or by circumstance, she hadn't quite decided yet.

~

Sasha pulled the grease-soaked rag from his back pocket, running it across his even filthier hands to little effect. It had been four days since Merona had departed with that unreliable, mustache-curling pilot and his scruffy, copilot mutt, and it had been exactly four days since he had last spoken to her.

The flight out to the Azores shouldn't have taken more than a couple of days, and though he knew Merona too well to expect any kind of timely communication upon her safe arrival, he found himself agonizing over the fact that neither he nor Liora had yet to hear even the smallest word of communication from her.

"The least she could do is send telegram," Sasha grumbled aloud. "I not understand her, Katya! She

know how I worry! Would it kill her to at least send word she alive?"

Katya made no reply. Though she was a good listener, she wasn't much for conversation, being a biplane made of numerous bits and bolts. She was a Vickers Viking, an amphibious flying boat with seating for up to six passengers, a wooden hull and retractable undercarriage, which allowed her to operate from both water and land. She was Sasha's pride and joy, and he had spent every free moment, since acquiring her, in making custom alterations and refurbishments to her engine, maneuverability, and fuel capacity until she was a one-of-a-kind marvel of aviation.

Resting his broad shoulder on Katya's sturdy hull, Sasha continued his lamentation to his inanimate companion. "What if something has happened? What if she drown in sea? What if she robbed and *murdered* by that swindler pilot, and there *nothing* I can do?"

Horrific scenarios continued to flood into the burly pilot's mind, as he leaned on Katya for comfort and reassurance. Something the plane was also incapable of providing him, though he didn't seem to notice.

Continuing his ravings aloud to his reliable, though rather unhelpful plane, Sasha soon found his one-sided conversation interrupted by an arrival.

"Hey, pal," called Liora from across the plane hangar. "How's the old bird doing?"

"Katya is model of aerodynamic perfection, like always."

Liora strode closer, catching sight of Sasha's displeased expression.

"Then what's got your eyebrows in a twist?" she asked.

"It Merona. She still not send word of landing safely."

Liora shrugged. "It's only been a few days."

"*Da*, and still nothing!"

"Sasha, we've already discussed my sister's inability to send correspondence in a timely manner."

"But she know how I worry."

Liora reached out and placed a comforting hand on the giant's shoulder. "I don't think she cares. In a week or so, Uncle Quincy will probably write to me to let me know how the job and Merona are faring, and I promise to tell you when I get that letter, but in the meantime, you need to just stop worrying about it all so much, since there is nothing either of us can do."

Sasha stared back in exasperation. "If you know me at all, you know this suggestion be pointless."

"And if you knew Merona at all, you'd know all the reminders in the world will never change her. But if it will make you feel any better, I can write to our uncle and ask if all is well. Just for you."

The tanned features of Sasha's face lit up. "Truly?"

"Of course. What are friends f…"

But her words were suffocated as the pilot's mammoth arms engulfed her in an overpowering hug.

"*Tysyacha blagodarnosti,*" Sasha mumbled in his mother tongue.

Liora smiled against his bulky shoulder, knowing the Russian's words of intense gratitude, and replied graciously. "*Pazhalsta.*"

The touching scene was soon interrupted by the arrival of Sasha's newest clients, who barged into the plane hangar in a flurry of questions, concerns, and dissatisfactions over the small delays to their journey. Sasha did his utmost to abate their apprehensions, but soon found an ally in the diplomatic Liora, who stepped forward to attest to the Russian's impeccable track record of daring flights, impossible landings, and wartime victories.

As Liora worked her magic, all Sasha's apprehensions for the absent Grant sister's wellbeing took a back seat to the more pressing matter of keeping his job. He would have to rely on Liora to discover her sister's fate, and trust in Merona, wherever she was, to fend for herself for the time being. Something he knew her fully capable of doing without him, as much as he preferred to be at her side.

~

The fire crackled between the companions as they crunched their meal of snake, Carver taking more than his share of water to wash down the unique flavor of the meal, until their water supply was fully sapped.

Though Carver had added a small store of food to their supplies, Merona was insistent that her scavenged food should not go to waste, as she grew increasingly indignant at the complete disregard for rationing her new companion had clearly practiced in his short time alone on the island.

Her ammunition was depleted, her water canteen all but empty, along with her lighter's fuel, and her assorted food supplies were more than half gone. Her machete and binoculars were thankfully undamaged, but as Merona assembled the tent, she found that one side of the canvas wall had already developed a sizable tear, a tear which Carver assured her had been the fault of a jagged rock falling from the mountain side, and not his mishandling of her belongings.

With such excuses, Merona's tentative trust of her pilot began to wane even further, and Carver made an effort to shift the conversation away from his sloppy survival practices, hoping to defuse the tension in the air even just a little.

"So," he began, "what's the plan for the night? Finish our food and then try and get what sleep we can?"

"We'll have to take turns," Merona said curtly.

"Take turns?"

"Sleeping. One of us needs to keep watch, in case the natives come back."

"Oh, Buddy Boy can do that," Carver said cheerily. "He's a fine watch dog."

Merona glanced toward the scraggily gray mutt, his large, black eyes looking up at her, oblivious to the true perils of their situation.

"I'd rather not leave my life in the care of a dimwitted animal, thanks."

"Oh, he's smarter than he looks, trust me!"

Merona smiled apathetically. "I think we've established that I don't trust you."

Carver clucked his tongue. "Tut, tut, Miss Grant. I thought we agreed our true enemy was the natives on this island. We can't be staring daggers at each other day and night."

"Agreed, but if you want to turn this precarious alliance of ours into a more stable one, you'll have to do as I say and give me a reason to trust you. So, for now, you are going to keep watch, while I catch up on the sleep I've missed, then in a couple hours, we'll switch off. The dog can be our back up, but we will *not* be relying on him the whole night. Got it?"

"Fine with me. But he really is an exceptionally good…"

"*You* have first watch. Not the dog."

"Fine, fine. Whatever you say, but do I at least get the gun?"

"You mean *my* rifle? The rifle you stole off me and were using as a cudgel because you are too horrendous a shot to hit a few guys at close range? That gun?"

"Y—yes, that gun?"

Merona blinked, waiting for the man to realize the obviousness of her answer. "No," she said finally. "I will not be handing off my rifle and the precious ammo we have left to be fired off at the darkness when you get jumpy."

"But what if more of those men show up? Am I supposed to defend myself with nothing but a spear?"

"No, you're supposed to *wake me up*, and then me and my trusty gun, which belongs to me, can handle the situation, if I decide wasting ammunition is even needed."

Carver sighed. "Alright, alright, the gun is *yours*, I get it."

"Don't forget it."

As Merona slipped inside her tent, Carver began to realize that gaining her trust was going to prove more time consuming than he had anticipated, but he knew it would be worth it in the long run to have such expertise at his side. She wasn't wrong about his wasting of supplies, and though her bluntness stung his ego, he was well aware of his own shortcomings where survival and combat were concerned. The Great War had offered him no training on such subjects, as he had been careful to avoid ever being drafted into combat. Though now, he somewhat regretted his avoidance of involvement in the war... if only for the skills he might have obtained from the experience.

Merona's confidence in her new alliance was far less than her pilot's, after witnessing the state of her supplies, she was resolute that her opinion would only improve upon witnessing his willingness to follow orders. Her sleep was not a deep one that night. When she was not on watch herself, she woke frequently during Carver's shifts, to listen for signs that her partner was not neglecting his duty of keeping watch.

~

Merona awoke the next day to the reassuring sight of her equipment being exactly where she'd left it, as well as her two companions having in no way stabbed her in the back in the night, which forced her overactive imagination to subside a little for the time being.

Chaotic though their beginning had been, Merona tried to reconcile herself to the possibility that her suspicions were nothing more than an overreaction, to a perfect storm of un-ideal circumstances. She tried to trust that this pilot might in fact prove a reliable ally, if still a wholly unreliable survivalist.

Soon the two survivors had assessed their supplies and though their food rations were serviceable, their water had run dry the previous day, before night had fully fallen. The fight with the gray men had left them both inordinately thirsty, and Carver's inability to ration hadn't helped things either. Without hardly a word of instruction to her companion, Merona set off towards the river to address the situation, expecting him to follow, without question.

Conversation proved unsurprisingly scant during the trek down to the river, in one part owing to Merona's concentration being wholly focused on retracing her own footsteps, and the other to the fact that the only individual who held no grudges against his companions, was a four-legged dog.

To the simple mind of the loyal copilot and mutt, his owner had invited a new member, and potential leader, into their rather small pack. A welcome addition, considering their recent scuffle with the strange gray men of the woods. He already rather liked this new pack member, though he hadn't known her long, as she seemed to know things he and his master did not, and she smelled of numerous grubby, fascinating scents; much like a damp dirt hole.

When the companions reached the river's edge, Carver's dog immediately began to lap up the fresh, clear water as Merona topped off her water skin and newly returned canteen, a few feet up stream.

The river babbled on, creating a surprisingly peaceful atmosphere in the dense gray mist, but Carver eyed their surroundings with suspicion.

"I've been here before," he muttered.

"You say something?" Merona asked, half turning her head.

"I recognize this place. I came through here on my trek down the mountain."

"And?" Merona shrugged, waiting for his words to carry some importance.

"And it wasn't like this. It wasn't a peaceful river with clean, drinkable water. It was a swamp."

"A swamp?"

"Yes. The whole place positively reeked, and I just about fell into it, wandering out here in the fog and the dark."

"So, it was night when you passed through?"

"Approaching night, yes."

"And it was foggy?"

"When isn't it foggy on this wretched island?"

"So, in the night, and the fog, you are *positive* that this river was not a river, but a nasty, smelly swamp?" with these last words, Merona's cynicism toward the pilot's story had become fully apparent.

"I'm not making it up! I recognize the trees, and that rock, and the... the bend in the stream near the..."

Carver's words trailed off, along with his conviction.

"I'm sure it looks very similar," Merona halfheartedly reassured. "But you and I both know that water doesn't just clear up overnight."

Carver sighed. "Yes, yes of course. It was a kind of déjà vu I guess. It just... it looked *exactly* like the place I passed through."

"Except there's no swamp."

"Yes, except for that."

Merona slapped Carver's shoulder in solidarity. "Well, at least we can be sure of one thing now."

"What's that?"

"I'm definitely the one who should be in charge of navigation."

CHAPTER VIII

BAD WATER

WITH water procured, Merona's next course of action became blindingly clear: it was time to go hunting, but this new task would mean venturing out into the unexplored landscape and awaiting dangers of the island. Carver at first disliked the idea, saying that the position of their camp was safest for defense in the event of a second attack, and that their food was sufficient for several days at least.

Merona, however, saw their situation in a very different light, and presented him with the facts.

"The little food we do have is all canned, dried, or otherwise preserved, and will be vital to have as long-term backup for the inevitable days we are unable to hunt or trap any game. If we eat through our preserved supplies sooner than necessary, when we hit a dry hunting spell the lack of nourishment will sap our energy in a matter of days, and will not only affect our drive in hunting, but also cripple our chances of defending ourselves against further attacks."

With their situation so harshly laid out before him, Carver was quick to relent, agreeing to serve as temporary pack mule as Merona assumed the role of huntress that afternoon. Merona's instinctual method for tracking down the most likely game, naturally took her back to the nearby river, as any animals in the area must at some time visit the waters to quench their thirst as well.

This logical tactic proved less reliable than anticipated, however, as they proceeded to idle away hours at the river's edge, without one sighting of a single living creature. Confounded and exasperated by the inexplicable absence of wildlife, Merona at last elected to move on to a new hunting ground, but not before selecting several locations at the river's edge where animals were likely to approach, to mount makeshift snares using the thin cords she had salvaged from the gray men.

With the traps in place, they pressed on, moving deeper into the woods in search of their heretofore undiscovered prey. And though Merona and Carver took every step with a mounting concern for their own survival, Carver's dog trotted contentedly alongside them, happy to be venturing away from the waters, and their strange smells.

Carver's jovial demeanor quickly began to grate on the solitary adventuress, or more specifically his insistence on peppering Merona with endless trivial questions in an attempt to further get to know her.

"So, tell me, what was it that took you all the way out to such an isolated spot as the Azores? Or at least would have, if not for our little detour. What's out there that would pique your interest?"

"My uncle, and some good paying work."

"What sort of work is it exactly that you do?"

"Numerous and varied. Mostly on historical excavation sites, doing the more dangerous jobs the academics are... ill-equipped for."

"Oh really? What got you into that line of work?"

"Listen, I know you're just trying to be friendly or what have you, but I'm trying to hunt, and I need *quiet* so I can focus, not to mention so we don't scare off any prey."

"Oh right, of course. Aye, aye captain and all that. I'll defer to your superior knowledge in the hunting department and not say another word."

Merona smiled, returning to her hunt with confidence that her simple instructions would be followed... but she was soon to be disappointed, as Carver once again could not restrain his need to socialize, and began whispering a one-sided conversation with his dog, following a pace or two behind Merona. Rolling her eyes at the man's inability to follow basic instructions, Merona couldn't help overhearing snippets of the odd conversation.

"Well, well boy, if we were going to get stranded in a place like this with anyone, I suppose it's a lucky thing we ended up with a skilled marksman and hunter on our team... though I imagine you wouldn't be so bad at hunting us up some grub if it were just the two of us, eh buddy? But still, it's nice to have the backup, with all these cannibals running around. Even if she isn't all that sociable."

Carver's dog almost seemed to chatter back, muffing and muttering in his incoherent mongrel tongue.

"Oh, you and me both, pal! She's a hard one to figure out. But maybe she'll warm to us in time. You were a little standoffish when I first picked you up, and it wasn't long before you warmed up, so who knows? Maybe she has a soft side lurking underneath that chilly exterior just like you did."

Merona sighed, thinking how hard it would be to warm to a man who refused to follow simple instructions, and as the whispering continued, she at last found herself unable to overlook any more of the endless, and quite frankly pointless chatter going on behind her.

Turning, she called back in a hushed voice, to put an end to the noise once and for all. "Will you stop all that chit chat? I already told you to keep quiet while I am hunting."

"Sorry, I thought it'd be alright if I just whispered… this shaggy boy here was looking anxious, and talking to him usually helps calm his nerves."

"Well, Shaggy Boy will just have to be calmed some other way."

"Ha, ha! Shaggy Boy? I like it! I might just have to name him that."

"Is that not his name?"

"Oh, no."

"Then what do you call him?"

"Oh, all sorts of things! Buddy, buddy boy, pally, shaggy, scruff-ball. I rescued him off the streets a few months ago, and still haven't figured out what name he answers to."

"Why not just pick a name and stick with it?"

"I've tried a few, but he just hasn't really taken to any yet. So, mostly I just call him 'good boy'. He seems to like that."

"Well, maybe he *would* take to one, if you actually *stuck* with one…"

Carver stroked his mustache in thought. "You might be right."

"Probably… so why don't you think on dog names *silently*, while I try to do a little hunting?"

Carver saluted, following with a gesture of buttoning his mouth before they, at last, carried on.

The fog around them pressed in, obliterating their surroundings in a sea of white and gray. Trees surrounded them, stretching up in dark streaks cutting through the distant white, blackening out the sky in a tangle of vines and branches. Thick foliage clung to their feet as they pressed on through the long vines which descended from the trees in crisscrossing webs across their path.

Had Merona's intention been to cover ground in as little time as possible, she would have dispatched the twisted obstruction, machete in hand, with intense vigor. But this was a hunting excursion, and special care needed to be taken to ensure their approach would go unnoticed by the surrounding wildlife, should they ever find any.

Hours passed, and the adventuress and pilot began to wonder if the island did, in fact, possess any life at all, save the gray natives they had already encountered. Presented with the dismal possibility that the only life inhabiting the isolated landmass, other than themselves, was a bloodthirsty tribe of cannibals out to kill them, they wondered if their day had been all but wasted.

Night descended and doubts rose higher, followed by endless questions from Carver, such as, "Should we turn back?" "How much longer before you admit defeat?" "Is it just me, or is the fog getting thicker?" and "Was that a goat?"

This final question, however, brought an end to any further queries, as the three companions abruptly halted, spotting a faint, four-legged shape moving in the heavy mist.

"Finally," Merona whispered, "something to shoot at." And lowering to her knee with measured precision, she readied to take her aim.

"It can't be!" Carver scoffed, his impulsive words echoing amid the trees.

And just like that, their hours and miles of perseverance were rendered unsalvageable, as the small creature's ears pricked up and it bolted off into the mist.

Merona's eyes shot wide. "What is *wrong* with you?" she spat. "You scared it off!"

Carver's hands raised defensively. "I didn't think it

would *hear* me."

"It's a *prey* animal, you halfwit! It's on constant alert for *any* strange noises! And how many times did I repeat, I wanted *silence* when hunting?"

"Well... well, can't you just track it?"

"Track it? *Of course,* why didn't I think of that? We've only been walking for *miles*, it's getting dark and the animal could have run off who knows *how* far, but *sure*, let's spend even more time tracking it in the fog and the growing blackness until we *maybe* find it, and then I'll just shoot it with my incredible, cat-like night vision in the pitch dark and dense fog!"

"We could get the dog to sniff it out?"

"I trust your nameless mutt even less than I trust you!"

"All right, all right, no need to get mean, it was just a suggestion!"

"Stop shouting!"

"You were shouting first!"

"Oh, wonderful comeback... I'm trapped on an island with a school child!"

Carver bit his mustache, fighting the urge to lock verbal horns with the stubborn adventuress.

"Look," he began, "flinging insults and casting blame is pointless. We are both going to go hungry as much as the other if we can't work together. At least we now know there is actually something to hunt out here."

Merona gritted her teeth. She was hungry, tired, infuriated with her companion, and exasperated with the turn of events, but she couldn't argue with her companion's logic, nor could she be exasperated with such a levelheaded response after her own rather childish words. Whether or not they liked or particularly trusted each other, their survival was going to depend on more than just procuring food, but in their ability to work as a team.

With a sigh, Merona relented. "You make a solid point. We aren't going to eat through our food in one night, and we can always try again tomorrow. It's important not to let setbacks knock the confidence out of us."

"Agreed."

"And now that we know there are goats of some sort on this island, there's a real possibility that one of my snares might actually have caught something while we were out hunting."

Carver smiled his trademark jovial smirk. "That's the spirit!"

"But on the bright side, if my snares failed to catch anything, I can always scavenge us up more bugs to help preserve our rations a little better. There are plenty of *those* on this island."

"How is that a bright side?"

"Have you never tried fried scorpion?"

Carver recoiled, shaking his head.

"Buddy, you're missing out."

~

The small campfire crackled at the feet of the two survivors after their long day of unsuccessful hunting. Merona's snares had come up empty, and despite her aversion to the idea, they had been forced to ransack their supplies, having an insufficient meal of tinned tuna and crackers. Merona, of course, supplemented her meal with an addition of scavenged bugs, but her two-legged companion at least declined her grubby addition to his meal.

His dog, however, devoured his bugs and lump

of salty meat on a flat rock in a single gulp before proceeding to beg his master for seconds. As they finished their meal, Merona sat silently assessing a new course of action in her mind, soon deciding it best to include her survival partner in the discussion; to build rapport, if nothing else.

"So," Merona began, "I've been thinking…"

Carver looked up from his food, somewhat surprised by this sudden breaking of the silence by someone other than himself. "Oh? About what?"

"I've been thinking how we might get off this rock."

He perked up even more. "Oh? And what did you come up with?"

"Well, there is the possibility of building a raft. There's a good variety of materials to work with, plenty of vines to bind things together, so if we can gather the right supplies over the next few weeks, we could…"

Carver interrupted. "You aren't seriously considering trying to return to civilization on a makeshift raft out on the open sea, are you?"

"Well, I figure a raft is easier to build than a plane," Merona snarked.

Carver shook his head. "No, I don't like it, it's too risky, I'd rather just hold tight and wait for rescue."

Merona scoffed. "Rescue from whom? We're out in the middle of the sea! Who on earth would come looking for us? And even if they did, how would they know where to look?"

"Because I sent out a distress signal."

Merona sat up. "What? When?"

"Before we crashed, of course. If anyone heard my distress signal, they should have our coordinates and be able to find us in no time."

"*If* they heard you."

"Well, yes, but there is no use making a raft when

there are any number of planes or boats out there that could've received our signal and will come for us, or at the very least relay it to the coast to get help. We should hold tight and give them time to find us before we try anything as crazy as building a raft."

"You might have mentioned this sooner."

"I thought it was obvious. A good pilot always sends out a distress signal when they know they're going down."

"Well, up until now, I wasn't all that sure you were a 'good pilot'. And even now I'm not wholly convinced," Merona casually gestured to their surroundings.

"All right, fair enough. But now you know, so let's just focus on staying alive for the time being."

"I wish it were that simple. If we are banking on being rescued, we can't just sit on our hands. First, we are going to need to find a better campsite with a proper view of the horizon, to spot any ships or planes that might come looking for us."

"Yeah, if this wretched fog ever lifts."

"It can't keep up forever. We need to be ready when it does. We are also going to need to set up a signal fire at our new campsite, to light up in the event of a sighting. We'll need to keep it dry and at-the-ready, at *all* times, with a fresh supply of green wood and foliage to make smoke, as well as scout out the island a lot more, so we can make it quickly and efficiently to shore to be picked up. On top of that, we are still going to have to hunt daily, and stay on guard for another ambush from our gray neighbors."

"You've really thought this out, haven't you?"

"Well, I do have *some* experience living in the wild."

"Glad I've got you and your experience on my side." Carver smiled, raising his tin can of water in toast to his companion.

Merona nodded, and took up her canteen to do the same, but in the next moment their congenial dinner was halted, as Carver spat out a mouthful of green sludge.

"Egad!" he sputtered, "This water tastes ghastly!"

Merona looked to the slippery slime which now coated the patch of dirt at his feet. "That's no water," she puzzled. "Where did you get that?"

"From my water skin, where else?"

"That's not possible, I refreshed our water at the stream when I checked my snares," Merona raised her canteen to her nose, but with a single whiff, abruptly recoiled.

"Agh!" she gasped. "It smells like a swamp! What's *wrong* with this stuff?"

"It's horrific, that's what!"

"But how is that possible, when we just got it from a fresh stream?"

"Don't look at me, you're the survival expert."

Merona got to her feet, emptying the canteen onto the dirt without reluctance. "Well, we've got to go refresh it is all."

"What, right now?"

"I don't know about you, but I need something to drink after all that hiking we did today, and I assume you will want to wash that taste out of your mouth before turning in for the night. It's only a short way off. We'll be there and back in no time."

Though reluctant to move his weary limbs, Carver rose, being indeed eager to wash the lingering, putrid slime from out between his teeth. Making a simple torch from a long stick of firewood, Merona led the trio on, and they soon found themselves nearing the stream, but with their approach, came a familiar and disconcerting smell: the smell of bog.

Exchanging concerned glances with her companion,

Merona pressed on, ignoring the increasing rankness of their environment, since she fully recognized her surroundings and knew them to lead to the river. The dark crack of water in the ground soon came into sight, the glittering liquid catching the light of the torch as they approached, but with their next few steps the light illuminated the waters for what they truly were; a stagnant, patchy bog, jutting through the woods.

With her next step, Merona found her footing snatched out from under her, as her leg sunk into the unstable soil which surrounded the foul waters. Carver grabbed hold of her arm as she scrambled to return to dry land, half toppling backward as he pulled her to safety.

"This... this can't be right!" Merona stammered. "We've gotten lost somehow."

"No, this is it," Carver insisted. "This is the swamp I stumbled into before. Remember? I told you!"

"A crystal clean river can't just turn into a swamp overnight, and then back to clean water come morning. It's insane!"

"Well, that's what's happened. Look!" Carver gestured over Merona's shoulder.

Clearly visible in the torchlight sat her riverside snare, still unsprung, resting near the slimy water just as Merona had placed it along the river's edge.

"That's not possible," Merona gasped. "There is simply no earthly way this could be that same stream. It's just not..."

With a loud snap, Merona's words were stifled, as the adventuress whirled around once again, recognizing the sound for what it was; her second snare being sprung some yards off. Weaving past the pilot, Merona scrambled towards the second snare raising her dying torch towards its contents. But once again, the snare was barren.

"What is it?" Carver called.

"Nothing," Merona called back. "Whatever it was, it got away."

Moving closer, Merona examined the line of cord to find a hint of what might have escaped it, but the cord itself was broken through, cut by some kind of razor-like blade, and on the craggy bank below, long claw marks scraped deep into the muddy soil, trailing down and returning to the still, putrid waters.

~

In the light of day, the stream had returned to the sparkling, clear waters of before, leaving Merona and Carver dumbfounded how such a thing could be possible, because quite simply, it couldn't. And yet, the facts were clear; the river would cease to flow, growing stagnant and filthy overnight, only to rid itself of all traces of grime by morning.

But though these inexplicable facts troubled them, the more troubling fact of all, was that this change in the water seemed to affect their own, separate supply. On that next day, Merona was meticulous in utterly sterilizing their canteen before refilling it. All water was boiled over the camp fire as a precaution, but once again, when night fell, their canteen and waterskin too, fell tainted.

A logical explanation seemed impossible, and the survivors were forced to accept their unnatural predicament and to find a means of working around it. By day, they made sure to drink their fill, as when night fell, all supplies would be turned to sludge. This quickly brought about the habitual emptying of whatever remained in their canteens before nightfall, as the daily re-sanitizing of the container seemed a needless, and repetitive chore if it could be avoided.

Such practices became routine, as they prepared and hoped for rescue to arrive. Branching beyond their former boundaries, the two survivors set out to locate a more suitable campsite with a clear view of the horizon in nearly all directions, and though it would take them several days, and even more long treks in search of such a spot, they were finally able to locate a shallow cave on a defensible cliff near the base of the mountain. Here they could begin to store dry wood and any other supplies safely guarded from the ever-relentless storms that had begun to break out across the sky.

Checking and redressing her wounds regularly each day, Merona was grateful to find they were healing well, with no signs of infection. With all the challenges and setbacks they had faced in such a short time, it was a welcome relief to have something go right for once.

Snare traps were set in any position Merona could find with signs of potential animal activity, as well as a few around the campsite as a defensive measure, and regular hunting trips became a standard necessity. From their first hunting trip, it was clear that Carver was not a natural huntsman, and he quickly became all too eager to "hold the fort" whenever Merona went out on an excursion.

With the gray men about, Merona forced herself to get used to spear hunting, both to save her rifle's precious ammunition for life-threatening dangers, as well as remain stealthy on her hunting trips near gray men territory. And though she never requested assistance, she soon noticed an occasional shadow at her heels, accompanying her more and more frequently as the days passed.

Carver's dog seemed to have grown curious of the adventuresses' daily outings, and soon Merona discovered his natural knack for sniffing out, as well as chasing down, small prey, and began to welcome his company on the off chance that he chose to join her. Unlike his master, the mutt knew to be quiet when stalking a kill.

Carver, finding himself often left to manage the camp alone, was quickly assigned the task of collecting all essentials for assembling their signal fire. And though he attempted to adhere to his companion's meticulous instructions of what to look for, his abysmal ability to recognize basic differences between suitable supplies and unusable scrap was all too clear on Merona's return, when the adventuress would find it necessary to discard, or repurpose the majority of his findings.

Difficulties aside, Merona was eventually able to assemble the basic frame of their signal fire on the flat rock above the cave, storing all necessary dry materials within the confines of the cave itself, preserved at the ready for such a time as they might be needed.

All such preparations, though paramount, were quick to take a back seat as the three survivors soon found themselves the targets of retaliation. The gray men, who had so nearly killed them their first two nights on the island, seemed to have increased their activities within the forest, as regular hunting parties began to cascade closer and closer into the surrounding woods below Carver and Merona's camp.

Every night, the two survivors would take turns keeping watch, remaining at a state of perpetual readiness for the seemingly imminent attack. But as the days and nights dragged on, no attack came, and they began to wonder what barrier was preventing the gray men from staging their assault.

Hunting became all the more difficult as Merona regularly found herself ducking one scouting party, only to very nearly stumble into another. But it was a risk that had to be taken daily, as their small supply of preserved foods was so often on the verge of dwindling.

CHAPTER IX

A TELEGRAM FOR MISS GRANT

SITTING alone, Sasha couldn't help but look at his calendar, counting and recounting from the day he had last seen the adventuress setting off in the reckless hands of an inferior pilot, but every time it was the same result: nearly two weeks, and still no news from her.

He turned from the calendar back to the greasy plane part on his table, trying to force himself to mind his work instead of his worries, but the thought that Liora might have forgotten her promise to contact her uncle, soon crept into his mind.

"These Grant women," Sasha grumbled to himself. "I not know why I put up with them, they so infuriating! One telegram... how hard to send *one* telegram?"

The neglected plane part sat idly in his fingers, as possible explanations for the delay crossed his mind. What if Liora had sent the message after all, he thought, and her uncle was simply as bad at writing back as Merona was? Or perhaps Liora had already received a response and telling him had simply slipped her mind.

"Of course! That it!" he exclaimed. "She too busy working at dig for money to pay off debt. She not have time to come out and reassure my old lady fears."

His nerves were momentarily calmed with this new rationale, but he knew he had only one way to be sure, and with that thought, he deposited his work, unfinished, on the table. If Liora couldn't come out to see him, he would venture out to find her and learn for himself what had become of Merona.

Hours of sand and scorching sun blazed down on the already tanned Russian before he arrived at the ramshackle dig site. Tents, crates, and tables strewn with pottery and ancient findings littered the landscape, clustering near the sandy doorway to a freshly unearthed tomb where Liora and Merona had been hired to assess each newly opened chamber for hidden dangers.

As Sasha approached, voices began echoing from inside the tomb, tumbling out of the shadowy opening as Liora and a bespectacled young man emerged into view.

"I can't possibly be hearing you right, Hubert," Liora snapped. "He's here for two days and he wants to *sack* me? What in the world did I say to the man?"

"It wasn't anything you said, it's just that Mr. Montgomery was led to believe that 'the Grants' were a pair of brothers. He had no idea you were... a lady, until he arrived."

"Well, who told him that nonsense? And why should that make a difference anyway?"

"I did," Hubert admitted, "I knew he would never finance the dig if he knew we had hired women for such a dangerous job, but you two were the best ones for it, that we could afford."

"So, you're telling me that he wants to *sack* me just because I'm a woman?"

"He feels it's grossly unethical, not to mention cowardly, to send a lone woman on ahead of grown men, into a newly unearthed tomb to face its hazards, which might very well maim or kill her."

Liora rolled her eyes. "Well, that's very gentlemanly of Mr. Montgomery to worry, but you should remind him that I took the job *willingly* and have much more experience spotting and disabling these sorts of hazards than any of his academic, 'grown men'."

"He's aware of that."

"I see. So, he thinks it's more *ethical* to let me go jobless and starve on the street, while his inexperienced young scholars, who have hardly set foot outside of a classroom, go get their heads chopped off in a tomb? Sounds perfectly reasonable."

The young man's face took on a sallow tint. "Indeed."

Liora shut her eyes in quiet infuriation. "Well, why don't you ask him if it would be more suitable for me to stay on in an *advisory* capacity? I could instruct the men going in on what to look for and how to avoid any potential dangers. I've seen enough of this tomb to know what to expect, and could at least save a few necks that way."

"I... I hadn't thought of that. Yes, he might actually agree to *that*."

Liora stared back at him in expectant impatience, before waving a hand at the young fellow to run along. Her conversation concluded, Liora's attention at last turned to Sasha, who stood a yard or so off, an uneasy posture in his bearing.

Marching toward him, Liora's hands outstretched in an inquisitive shrug. "Sasha? What are you doing all the way out here?"

Sasha's mind disregarded her query, jumping immediately to the pressing question of his own. "Have you had word?" He asked.

"Had word? Word of what?"

"What you mean, word of what? Word of Merona! Is she alive or dead!" Sasha shouted in rebuke.

Liora bit her lip. "Oh, that. Well, that's the thing."

Sasha's face dropped, preparing himself for the tragic news.

"You see, I sort of forgot to contact my uncle right away, so I haven't actually heard back."

"Forgot? For how long? How can you stand not knowing? How you not hear back yet?"

"Slow your horses, I sent it a couple days ago, so I'm sure I'll hear back soon."

"How soon?"

"*Soon*. She's my sister too, you know? So, you aren't the only one who cares about her here."

Sasha drooped. "*Da*, of course. I sorry, I just have feeling in gut. I worried something happen to her."

"I know, but fretting over it won't help things any. We just have to wait and see."

"Grant!" barked a crusty voice from afar.

Liora gritted her teeth. "Give me a second."

"It's Mr. Montgomery, he wants to see you, now!" he snapped again.

With a voiceless apology and a defeated shrug, Liora turned away to answer her employer's summons before the conversation could reach its conclusion. Sasha stood dejected; he had come all this way for answers, but as Liora strode off to attend to her work, he knew he must do the same, returning to his own job with more questions than he had left with.

Sasha watched the ground, kicking sand and pebbles as he scuffed through the camp before a timid voice caught his attention.

"Telegram? Telegram for a Miss Grant?"

Sasha's head shot to attention, his eyes searching franticly for the speaker of such vital words.

Without thinking, Sasha's voice boomed out across the camp, his words intended to communicate something akin to, "I know Miss Grant. Give that to me and I can take it to her." But English, not being his first language, mingled with the panic of the moment, instead came out more like: "Over here! I Grant!"

A slim, young messenger boy turned with a start before trotting hesitantly toward the massive Russian who waved him down.

"M… *Miss* Grant?" asked the messenger in confusion, hesitating to hand the telegram off to the immense man who had identified himself as the lady in question.

"*Da*! I mean *nyet*, I not Grant," Sasha stammered. "But I *know* Grant, and I just see her over there, near… oh, it not matter, just give me letter!" Sasha spoke these last words in a roar, though to his own ears it was merely a simple demand said with perfectly reasonable impatience.

Snatching the letter from the boy's shaking hand before he could protest, Sasha marched off in search of Liora, leaving the messenger boy to slink away, ashamed and horror-struck at having his very first telegram delivery so viciously intercepted by a "brutish mugger".

Spotting Liora seated on a crate sharpening her knife, Sasha darted to her side and shoved the envelope in her face.

"It here! It letter about Merona!"

Liora shot up off her seat. "Already? That can't be right, let me see."

Ripping into the envelope, Liora's eyes scanned across the words before her, growing wide as she read and reread the slip of paper.

"What it say?" Sasha asked impatiently.

"She… she never arrived," Liora gasped. "Uncle Quincy said he never heard back from us, so he assumed we were uninterested. He's had no word or sight of Merona this whole time! Sasha… you were right. Something's happened! Something went wrong on the flight out!"

Sasha stood silent. All his fears were now confirmed. Merona had never made it to her destination and might very well have drowned in the middle of the sea. He didn't like to think it. He *wouldn't* think it. Merona was resourceful, and if anyone could find a way to survive their plane going down in the middle of the water, it was her.

His clenched fist rose to his mouth. "I knew it not end well," he whispered. "But we fix it now."

"How Sash? She most likely would have been over the ocean when..."

"It Merona! She will find a way to survive until we find her."

"We don't even know where to start looking! Oh, Sasha, this is all my fault! She took that stupid flight because of *my* debts. Because of me! I should have been the one on that plane. I should have..."

"*Nyet*! You not allowed to blame self. It not help find her."

Liora defiantly wiped the tears from her eyes before they could fall. "What do we do?"

"We not stop until we find her."

~

It had been nearly two weeks since the crash, and once again Merona set out on her daily hunt. Often her efforts brought nothing, the majority of their meat coming from whatever small creature Carver's dog could catch, and the scattering of Merona's snares.

The kills rarely had much meat on them, and most always contained some kind of parasite infection when gutted. Often, their meals needed to be supplemented with insects or simply more water, as Merona refused to tap into their preserved food simply to "fill up", which left the three survivors almost always in a state of hunger.

On that day, as the adventuress tracked through the woods, following signs of what she hoped to be a wild pig, a sound of voices drifted through the trees off to her right, and she halted abruptly, dropping to her knee in silent readiness.

Watching from behind thick foliage, Merona could see gray figures plodding through the undergrowth, stomping and nattering loudly to one another in their own tongue. The behavior was odd. Never before had the gray men made their presence so blatantly known, and as Merona spied from her place of concealment, a flicker of movement at the corner of her eye, stirred her attention.

All in an instant, three gray figures leapt from the trees, rushing towards the lone adventuress as they shrieked for their companions to join in the ambush. Returning the call, the mob of warriors rushed in to overtake the adventuress, and Merona leapt to her feet, breaking off into a mad run for safety.

The raucous hunters had been an intentional distraction, and Merona had fallen for it.

The three closest men dashed in, trying to cut off her escape, but Merona charged forward, slamming her rifle butt dead on into the nearest gray face, sending his body plummeting backwards as she wove just out of reach between his remaining two brothers.

Spears sailed over Merona's shoulders, embedding into nearby tree trunks as she raced into the woods, not pausing even a moment to look back.

Merona's heavy, awkward weaponry rattled against her back and limbs where they were strapped, slowing her already inferior movement. Pounding steps thundered behind her, growing louder as their lean, muscled limbs effortlessly gained ground.

She pressed on, willing her body to its limits as she cut through the heavy fog and tangled undergrowth around her. Faster, and faster, she pushed herself, dismissing all pain as her instincts to survive, and outrun her pursuers, took over.

Breaking through the tree line, Merona found herself barreling towards a deep section of the river, her momentum carrying her to its very edge before she could halt herself.

Merona knew the great risk awaiting her in crossing the wildly rushing waters and jagged rocks within, but it was nothing to the enclosing threat of the gray men behind her. But before she could take that first treacherous step, chattering cries erupted out behind her.

Whirling round, Merona came face to face with the thunderous mob who burst from the woods in the next second, shrieking and stamping their spears. With no time to turn and outrun them, she stood firm, clenching her jaw, ready to fight but anticipating death.

The gray men had caught sight of their prey, but in the next moment, their leader uttered a low hiss, screeching and recoiling as he stumbled backward. His men followed suit, letting out hisses and chattering screams of their own as their eyes fell upon Merona. Then, as rapidly as they had appeared, one by one they fled into the woods, a look of vicious terror in their eyes.

Standing in complete bewilderment, Merona scrutinized their retreat as they faded from sight and earshot, leaving her with nothing but the sounds of the wind and river at her back. Looking down, Merona found herself gazing at her distorted reflection in the strange waters, wondering if their only abnormal property was that of shifting from fowl to clear with the rise and fall of the sun, or if there was something more she had yet to uncover. Something that would explain her enemies' fear that day.

~

"Is it really necessary to cover an entire mile with every step?" Carver grumbled, his usual cheerful demeanor was all but extinguished by the long trek of the past day.

Merona continued on ahead of him. "If we want to cover any ground and make it back to camp before nightfall, then yes, yes it is."

"I think we've covered plenty of ground, quite frankly."

"Covered ground, yes, but learned anything? No. And reconnaissance is, after all, why we are out here."

"But why is it so important that we find out where these gray men are located?

Merona let out an exasperated sigh at her need to explain, yet again, the reason for their excursion. "Because, at some point, a big, beautiful plane or boat is going to show up on that horizon, and once we've signaled it, we are going to have to get to that beach in a hurry. And the last thing we are going to want to do, is get lost and run straight into a camp of people who want to kill us. But if we can figure out where they live, we can map out a path to avoid them altogether. Now quit grumbling and pick up the pace, Carver."

Cornelius Carver presented his customary smile. "Yes, ma'am, Miss Grant," he said, before muttering curses under his breath.

The adventuress and pilot had already agreed upon the necessity of a preliminary scouting of the island, but each day Merona had attempted the trek, she had found herself met with increased complaints of tired limbs and sore feet from her companion, and had been forced to return to camp with little knowledge gained.

Today, however, she was determined to succeed, and all the protests and grumblings in the world would have no effect on her resolve. She needed to learn all she could about their gray neighbors, to prevent being caught off guard by future attacks, and though her preliminary reason for the excursion had been the finding of the gray men and their camps, so a clear path to the beach might be carved out, Merona also wished to get to know her neighbors from a safe distance, hoping to find answers to their strange behavior near the river that day. An encounter she had still neglected to tell Carver of.

The woods grew thick and suffocating around them as they pressed forward. The air had begun to thicken from the gathering mist, and Merona thought back on their weeks upon the island, wondering if they had ever seen a single day with truly clear skies. The idea of an unnaturally permanent mist seemed absurd, yet she couldn't recall one instance of clear, blue skies shining through the trees in all that time. And when coupled with the decidedly unnatural nocturnal bog, perhaps it wasn't so strange at all, in a place such as this.

Time passed and Merona began to notice, with increasing frequency, black markings carved into the trunks of scattered trees. The symbols were unlike any she had seen before, with harsh, jagged lines streaking out in an almost claw-like pattern across the bark, and she soon found the markings were occasionally accompanied by long strips of fabric hanging from the branches of the marked trees, each strip baring the image of a vulture and heavily ornamented with small sharp stones and mangled, fluttering feathers catching in the wind.

Trudging through the haphazard dotting of symbols, Merona had no doubt they had been the work of the gray men, and all at once, her supposition was confirmed as the companions found themselves face to face with a dense tree line, each and every tree dotted with the same markings and hanging ornaments as before.

Edging closer, they could see beyond the tightly packed trees to a barren and bleak clearing, dotted with tall, black, domed huts. Each was half encircled by long, sharpened staves that had been staked into the ground, and jutted from the soil at odd angles. Fiery red lights lit up small holes in some of the huts, as smoke wafted from the tops of the black domes.

Amid the huts, situated at their center, sat the smoldering remains of an immense bonfire, and as the two gazed upon it, they thought they could see what looked like blackened human skulls, scattered around its edge, where they had presumably rolled off the heap.

"All right, so we've found them," whispered Carver, a clear tremor in his voice. "Can we get out of here now?"

"Hush," Merona hissed. "We still don't know anything more about them than before. Just be patient."

"Be patient? Waiting around here is going to get us caught and killed!"

"If you're so *worried* about getting caught, then keep *quiet* and watch our backs while I study the camp."

Carver grumbled once again before turning to keep a lookout, and Merona inched among the trees, maneuvering to get a look inside a glowing window of one of the larger huts. Shadows passed by the light in jolting steps, the figures moving this way and that inside the hut, their shadows thrown across the walls from the fire at the center. A small hole at the top of the structure vented some of the fire's smoke, but still the room was filled with a fog, and Merona cautiously peered inside, watching as two of the gray men exchanged words in increasingly angry tones.

She of course could not understand a word of what they said to one another, but could hear the ire growing in their voices, until all at once the larger of the two men snatched a chunk of wood from near the fire and slammed it into the side of the other man's head. Knocking him to the ground, the larger man leapt at him in a fury, landing blow after blow until the man's face was a bloody pulp and he ceased to move.

None of the other occupants of the hut seemed to notice or care about the act of murder which had just occurred before them, as though it were as natural an occurrence as anything else.

The killers' rage abruptly abated with the completion of this violent act, and he then kicked the body of the dead man onto the fire to cook, and Merona turned away from the window in disgust, covering her mouth and nose from the smell to avoid losing her last meal.

Remaining a few moments longer to commit the layout of the small village to memory, Merona was swift and silent as she returned to Carver, and the companions quickly put distance between themselves and the camp.

As the three survivors pressed on, believing themselves to be well out of gray man territory, the strange markings on the trees began to reappear, this time accompanied by a rough depiction of a boar's head, and they found themselves approaching yet another camp, dotted with more black huts. This camp, however, was considerably larger than the last, and substantially more fortified. It sat near the edge of a cliff, looking out towards the misty sea, with sharpened pikes surrounding its perimeter, and watchtowers which made it impossible to get any closer.

From their position, they could still observe that it had a central bonfire just as the last camp, but off center of that stood a towering spire, rising from the earth and adorned with the same scratched markings the trees had borne, while at its top height, rested a glinting gem.

A jewel which caught Carver's eye. "What is that?" he whispered. "Looks like a giant diamond."

"Couldn't be," scoffed Merona. "It's got to be as big as my fist."

"Well, then it's got to be extremely valuable."

"What do you think this is, a backyard treasure hunt?"

"It's just an observation."

"Well, a more important observation is that this is a totally different camp. Which means there are at least two, though probably more, entirely distinct tribes on this island with us. We are going to have to do a lot more reconnaissance to find them all, so we can map out a safe path to the beach for rescue."

"Find them all? Are you joking?"

"Not tonight, don't worry. We can call it a day for now, but little by little, I want to get to know this island. If we are going to survive out here, we need to know more about what's out there, who we are dealing with, and most importantly, how to avoid them."

CHAPTER X

IN SEARCH OF ANSWERS

SASHA eased into a smooth landing on the waters of Lisbon, Portugal. As they glided toward shore, Katya's propellers slowed, slicing through the air in increasingly infrequent intervals until their momentum had all but died away.

Stepping from the plane onto the docks, Sasha slid his bulky goggles from his face as Liora exited the aircraft a step behind him, readjusting her tweed cap and breathing in the fresh, open air for the first time in hours. They had flown all night to reach their destination and even now, exhaustion growing in Sasha's eyes, he would not rest until he had what he had come for; until he had seen Gregory Vance.

"Are you sure this friend of yours can help?" Liora asked.

"If that worthless pilot Merona hire did bare minimum job, then he sent distress signal before crash, and if anyone will have hear it, it Gregory. Gregory hear everything."

"You've said the same thing about the last *Three* friends of yours we've talked to."

"*Nyet*, Gregory different. He has sixth sense about things. If there was distress call, he hear it. Trust me."

"Would I have quit my job and flown all this way if I didn't trust you? This is Merona we're talking about, I'd take the pyramids apart brick by brick to find her, if I had to."

"*Da*, so would I."

The streets of Lisbon were crowded as Sasha and Liora made their way through the throng, the pilot's prominent stature working to their benefit. People scurried this way and that to avoid the towering Russian as he marched forward, his sights set solely on his one purpose. Passing by the local vendors that lined each side of the tight street without notice, Liora struggled to keep up with Sasha's long stride as they pressed on. It felt as though they were climbing a mountain as they wove between houses and in and out of side streets toward their destination, but as they reached a small, stucco house situated near the edge of a cliffside overlooking the water, their quest at last came to a halt as Sasha rapped his knuckles on the dingy door.

"Is this it, already?" Liora asked.

"*Da*. Gregory here for some time. He say it best position to pick up transmissions."

A sound of shuffling steps and irritable mutterings emanated from the other side of the thin door, before a hunched, gray-haired man opened it a crack and peered out from inside.

"Yes?" spat the old man, his left eye crunching up in a suspicious glare.

"It me, Gregory, it Sasha Durov. Open door, I need information."

Old Gregory's crusty demeanor melted instantly away, as his failing eyes recognized the face of his good friend.

"Sasha! Of course, come in, come in! What is it that you need?"

"It very important. I ask everyone I know along the coast and … and they not pick up anything, but then I think of you. If anyone get signal, it will be Gregory. That is why I come."

"You came all the way out here to see little old me? I'm flattered. And who's your fine young lady?"

Sasha glanced back at Liora. "Oh, this Miss Grant, she not... she just a colleague."

Liora chuckled, holding out her hand in introduction. "Pleased to meet any friend of Sasha's."

"Likewise," replied Gregory.

"*Da, da*, no time for chitchat, we need you to remember something important, Gregory. It would have been almost three weeks ago, on Friday or Saturday."

Gregory scoffed, letting out a chuckle. "Me? Remember things? Are you sure you've got the right person?"

"It no time for jokes, Gregory."

"All right, all right, give me that date again, and I'll take a gander at my radio log."

Sasha followed Gregory inside, reiterating the dates as he awkwardly maneuvered his bulky frame through the cramped living quarters, dodging old newspapers strewn across the floor. Shelves of spare radio parts lined the walls and confined the hallway all the more as he passed through, twisting and condensing his shoulders to fit.

Arriving at the back of the apartment, Sasha ducked into the tight room, Liora following behind him. It was furnished with a chair and immense table, occupied by a large radio as its centerpiece. A disarranged, dumpy shelf stood to one side of the table and Gregory immediately began sifting through his records.

"The third or fourth of the month, you say? Let me see here..." he muttered to himself. "It must be in here somewhere."

Gregory's muddled memory gradually kicked into functional gear as he flipped back through the entries, his nobbily finger slapping suddenly on the page before him.

"Found it!" he shouted. "Here it is. Yes indeed. Lilly and I caught lots of chatter that day… very exciting. I got a very interesting call in from a fishing boat that night…"

"I not want ship," Sasha corrected, "I want plane!"

"Hold your horses, I was about to say that the fishing boat radioed in to tell me they had picked up a distress call from a plane, but couldn't find anything when they swept the general area. They relayed all the information they had picked up on to me, but it wasn't much."

"So, they *did* send out a distress call!" Liora cried.

"What did pilot say?" Sasha interrupted, trying to refocus the conversation.

Gregory's eyes returned to his ledger. "It seems they'd hit bad weather… hmm, yes, the pilot was trying to give their heading, and coordinates, but his signal was choppy, and he cut out before he could relay much."

"You have coordinates?" Sasha bellowed. "You write this down, yes? Tell me you write it down?"

"Well, yes. I always keep a proper record of any distress calls that come through on old Lilly, but it cut out you see. There was only partial coordinates given, so there's no telling where exactly they were signaling from. The boat couldn't find anything, so it seemed like it was no use to anybody."

Sasha took hold of the old man by the shoulders, cutting short his ramblings and staring at him with intense desperation filling his eyes.

"It of use to *me!*"

~

The island was far larger than Merona had first realized. To the west, lay the only beach with any kind of accessibility to rescue boats, but Merona had estimated that between that beach and their own camp, sat roughly a solid square mile of dense jungle, which the tribesmen controlled.

This obstacle was made worse, by the simple fact that the gray men did not share a single camp or village. After days of recon, Merona and Carver had discovered a number of villages, dotted throughout the jungle and along the outer cliffs of the island and though, at first, they had seemed to be small, scattered camps of the same tribe, it soon became clear that each was its own unique tribe, that were at war with the other occupants of the island.

Merona quickly began to recognize each tribe by the animal headdresses their warriors would adorn themselves in, to intimidate their enemies in battle. The first gray men Merona had encountered had worn the headdress of a boar and seemed to be one of the larger tribes of the island, as well as their camp the most fortified. The other, smaller tribes wore masks of goats, snakes, or even vultures. These chosen animal effigies would often adorn many of the tribe's cloths and huts around and within their village, and so Merona used them to keep track of each tribe as she scouted the island.

Sometimes one or two of the smaller tribes would form a kind of temporary truce, to team up against another larger village, but these alliances never lasted long, as their hatred for each other was deep-rooted. The sightings of patrols which Merona had initially thought to be scouts or hunting parties, were far more often raiding parties returning from attacks on opposing villages.

Yet even with these continual discoveries, and their growing knowledge of the gray men, their movements, habits, and warrior culture, Merona found her simple hunt to map out and locate the gray men's villages, becoming a seemingly never-ending task. With every camp she located, a new, undiscovered one seemed to crop up, and with the continual raids between tribes, the established villages had a habit of disappearing in flames or perpetually moving shop to new locations.

The island was in a constant state of unrest and upheaval, and Merona found herself at a loss at how best to plot out a clean escape route, which wouldn't become blocked off when the day of rescue finally dawned.

The only option open to them was a regular scouting of the island, that they might keep track of the gray men and their current state of flux on a weekly or even semi daily basis. But as a new day dawned, and the three survivors set about mapping the current whereabouts of their less than friendly neighbors, they found themselves flanked by the shouts and cries of charging warriors.

Another skirmish had broken out, and they had wandered smack-dab into the middle of it.

As they darted to take cover behind the trees, a soaring spear embedded into a trunk, inches from Merona, catching her sleeve and pinning her arm to the tree. Twisting to dislodge it from the solid oak, Merona spotted a charging gray man, just in time to duck beneath his impending hatchet.

The hatchet slammed into the trunk, lodging in place just above Merona's head before she kicked out, hurling her attacker onto his back, gasping for air.

Wrenching the hatchet from its place, Merona severed shaft from spearhead and at last freed her sleeve. Shifting her grip on the throwing axe, she launched it into the skull of a nearing native, pulling her machete from its sheath in the next moment.

A few yards away, Carver and his dog were battling three more of the gray men, two armed with long spears, the other wielding twin hatchets. As the mutt instinctively leapt for the throat of one man, Carver struggled to keep the others at bay.

Rushing forward, Merona snatched up her hatchet from the gray man's skull, in the next moment hurling it forward into the back of one of Carver's attackers.

The gray man choked, dropping his spear as he fell to his knees, contorting to reach the weapon in his spine before collapsing face-first into the dirt.

The hatchet warrior charged in fury, turning his wrath on Merona. A flurry of blows fell upon her, as Merona staggered to deflect the attacks with her machete.

The third gray man rushed in to bring down Merona, forcing her to dodge and deflect both spear and hatchets alike. They cut through her coat and baggy slacks, missing her flesh by a fraction of an inch as she wove and ducked past them. A hatchet sliced inches from Merona's neck as she dodged clear.

His companion in trouble, Carver rushed forward without hesitation, skewering one gray man in his back. Blood gushed rapidly from the wound as the gray man violently screeched out, slumping to the dirt as his companion lunged for Carver, sinking his teeth into the pilot's arm.

The pilot's wails rose above the din of the battle, as the gray man's head jerked back, ripping clean a chunk of flesh. He chewed with delight in his eyes, as blood trickled down his chin and once again lunged back for another bite of human flesh.

With a powerful machete strike Merona ended the gray man's bloodthirsty onslaught before he could take another bite, his headless body dropping at her feet.

The battle continued to rage around them, spears clashing with turtle shell shields as Merona hastily

removed her belt, and cinched it tightly just above Carver's gushing wound to stem the flow.

Snatching up their nearby weapons, the three survivors ducked for cover, making their escape from the midst of the raging chaos of the warring tribes and slipping away unseen.

~

The wait for Katya's depleted tank to refuel seemed the most agonizing delay Sasha or Liora had ever known, but with Gregory's new information at their disposal it meant they could tighten their search for Merona to a significantly narrowed range, and both were determined to set out immediately. Sasha had long since charted their course and would waste no time. They were to depart that night.

Rubbing his hands and tapping his hefty boot, Sasha stood alone on the runway, waiting in agitation as he looked up towards the sky in frustration at his inability to ascend its cloudy steps without the assistance of Katya's wings.

"Come on, old girl," he muttered to the aircraft, "we must get move on. Merona is waiting."

Katya sat steadily drinking back her fuel as Sasha patted her hull like he was comforting an old mare. As he stood reflecting on all he and his trusty aircraft had been through together, a sound of footsteps approached from behind.

"Sasha," called Liora's voice over the sound of the gas pump. "They're telling us to move the plane."

"Move? *Da*, of course. We depart as fast as we can."

A man followed close behind Liora as she approached.

"No, I'm afraid you don't understand, sir," the

runway workmen said. "There will be *no* departures this evening."

"No departure?" Sasha barked. "But that not possible! We need to leave tonight. Merona, she waits for us!"

"I'm afraid not, sir. We've had word that a large storm is headed our way, and it would be highly inadvisable for you to…"

"I not care!" Sasha bellowed. "I fly tonight. It my plane, and you have no right to stop me."

"But, sir!"

"*Nyet.* You hide in shelter like babies, but I taking off. Never mind storm."

"Now look here! I…"

"I said I taking off! Now clear runway!"

"You heard the man!" Liora chimed in. "*We're* taking off tonight."

Tossing his hands up in defeat, the workman retreated. "It's your heads!" he shouted, "Not mine."

Spitting on the asphalt, Sasha ignored the messenger's words of warning, returning to his preparations once more.

"You not need to come Liora, if there is danger, I better to go alone. I sure Gregory will help you find place for the night."

"Don't be absurd! You seem to forget that she's *my* sister. If anyone here has a right to risk their neck in finding her, it's me. Don't think I'm going to sit around waiting for someone else to do all the work."

Sasha knew arguing the point was futile when either Grant sister spoke with such determination in her voice, and soon with the runway cleared, Liora took her seat alongside him as he maneuvered Katya into position, slipping his goggles firmly into place as dark gray clouds loomed overhead.

CHAPTER XI

ONLY A MYTH?

THE small cave was submerged in Carver's screams as Merona struggled to hold back the flow of blood. Pressing the meager scrap of cloth tightly against the gaping hole in his arm, Merona snatched up a nearby stick.

"Here, bite on this," she muttered.

Carver turned his head, his eyes tightly shut and unable to see the stick in front of him as he twisted, and writhed from the pain.

"That hurts!" he screamed.

"Of course it hurts!" Merona bellowed over his cries. "But your screaming is only going to attract attention we *really* don't need. Now bite on this stick, and stop squirming so I can patch you up!"

"He bit me! Did you see that? He ripped the flesh from my arm like it was a leg of chicken!!!"

"Yes, I know! They like to do that around here. Now will you shut up and sit still?"

At last Carver clamped his jaw down on the stick Merona had provided, allowing the adventuress to dedicate her full attention to his injury, but even that did little to help. With such meager supplies, Merona was hard-pressed to produce any clean scrap of cloth to bind the wound, let alone enough material to properly cover it.

Back in the woods, in desperation to stem the flow of

blood and return her companion to camp alive, Merona had cinched her belt tight above Carver's elbow, in a makeshift tourniquet. But the belt had been on his arm for as long as could be allowed just to make it back to camp, and Merona had been forced to remove it or risk permanent damage from lack of circulation.

Rushing to build a fire on their return, Merona had done her best to boil and sterilized what bandages she had, hoping the short bath was enough to cleanse the wrappings. She had no real means of cleaning the wound but did what little she could with what she had, as well as hoped that the free-flowing blood had done its job to rinse the wound clear before she wrapped it.

At last, the crisis seemed averted, and Carver sat shaking, cradling his bandaged arm as Merona submerged any remaining bandages in the turtle shell of boiling water to sanitize, before changing out the blood drenched rags for new, cleaner ones.

"Ow!" Carver spat. "Be *careful*, will you?"

"I'm sorry," Merona protested. "You've lost a good chunk of your arm, here. It's hard not to hurt you whenever I touch it."

"Then *don't* touch it."

"Do you *want* an infection, or better yet, to just bleed out right here? Because those are your options if you don't quit squirming."

"Fine! Just do whatever it is you're doing, but *gentler*."

"If you wanted a gentle touch, you should've gotten stranded with my sister, Liora."

"I'll try and remember that, next time."

Merona sighed. "Honesty, Liora *should* be the one stranded out here with you."

"Why isn't she?"

"Because, like an idiot, I *insisted* on going... I didn't

want to be stuck working a boring old dig in Egypt while she had all the fun."

Carver chuckled at the irony of her statement. "You might not have the best instincts, Miss Grant."

Merona smiled. "You don't have to tell me… And, thanks, by the way."

"For what?"

"You know… for helping me out back there. By all rights I should be the one with half an arm left, or worse, dead."

"Hey, I couldn't just let my survival expert down in her time of need. What kind of friend would I be?"

"Is that what we are now? Friends?"

Carver sighed. "I just keep offering."

"Well, since you've gone and saved my life, I guess it would be pretty stingy of me to refuse now," said Merona, offering a handshake.

Shaking her hand with his only good arm, Carver smiled. "Took you long enough."

~

The gale blasted against Sasha's plane, struggling to drive the man-made aircraft from the sky, or at the very least, rip its wings off.

"Maybe we should have listened when they told us not to fly tonight," Liora shouted over the roaring storm.

"Nonsense!" Sasha bellowed. "This storm nothing compared to German artillery in Great War!"

Bright cracks of lightning split across the sky, narrowly missing the shaky aircraft as it flew on.

"That may be so, but how are we supposed to search for Merona, if we get knocked from the sky before we've scarcely begun?"

"You call yourself a Grant? Where your sense of

daring?"

"Merona was always the more daring sister, and look where it got her."

"So be daring long enough to find her, then you can talk sense into her!"

Liora clenched her jaw. "Okay, just get us through this thing alive, will you?"

"Of course! Who you think you flying with?"

The storm continued to assail them, rocking their plane amid the clouds, but Sasha held steady. His grip on the controls was not tight, nor rigid, and no hint of white showed on his knuckles as he held firmly to his control yoke. He had been flying long enough to know when he was in control, or when he was losing it, and though the storm was strong, his skills were superior.

The winds roared like a beast, furious to break inside, but Katya's strong frame, enhanced by Sasha's countless hours of work on improvements to the craft, kept the gale at bay. Her windows bowed and her frame rattled under the pressure, but never gave way. Her strong wings cut through the unruly wind, resisting all efforts from the storm to knock her off course.

Sasha knew his plane and her capacities instinctively, he had re-engineered and re-built almost every facet of her, so that when they flew, it was as if the controls were an extension of his hands and Katya herself could predict his thoughts.

Just as the storm seemed to be reaching its height, they at last found themselves breaking through the end of it, the hazy, thick clouds slowly dissipating around them as Katya flew on, her wings now steadily gliding through the increasingly calm airs. In the dark sea stretching out ahead, a hint of the Azorean islands dotted the distant water, growing ever closer as they approached.

With the storm at their backs, the companions breathed out the anxious breaths they had been holding in, and sank back into their seats, relieved to be free of the storm's clutches. In what felt like no time, they were approaching the island, circling toward the coast of São Miguel Island to make their landing at Ponta Delgada.

As they dropped low to make their approach, the storm above seemed to finally release them, the ocean below only rippling with a high, breaking wave. Touching down on the water, Sasha and Liora intended to lose no time in locating her uncle, but almost as soon as they came ashore, they spotted him: a barrel-chested man wearing his trademark military coat and slouch hat from his time in the Australian armed forces.

"I leave you two girls alone for a moment and look what happens," Quincy Grant called out as he strode toward them, engulfing Liora in a broad hug.

"Good to see you too, uncle."

"Tell me everything you know: When she took off, where you think she went down... let's get this mess sorted. I've already found several pilots who are willing to do a sweep of the area if I can give them a location."

"Already? That was fast work."

"Well, they didn't exactly come cheap."

"How much?"

"Just about everything I've got, but to find Merona... the cost is irrelevant."

"If we can find her."

"I've known plenty of men who went missing for months to years, and then turned up alive and with most of their limbs and digits intact."

Liora grimaced. "If that's meant to be reassuring, it's not."

Quincy raised an eyebrow inquisitively. "If you think on it, it really is. Besides, you and I both know your sister is a fighter. If there was even a sliver of a chance of surviving, she would have found and utilized it."

"Well, she and I were fortunate to be taught by the best in the business."

Quincy chuckled. "Is that what they're calling me now? And I was just getting used to 'that no-good, lucky thief'."

"I thought for sure you'd been called worse than that."

"Not without a painful injury to remember me by."

"Always the charmer, uncle."

Collecting their luggage from the plane, the three companions made their way to Quincy's quarters, where two small cots had been laid out for their stay that night.

Unfolding a map out onto the table, Sasha checked his notes. All eyes gazed at the expansive blue which marked the Atlantic Ocean, as Sasha's finger dropped onto the paper and circled a point at its center.

"Right here, due west of the Azores... this is where Merona's pilot last sent out signal, roughly."

Liora squinted at the vast nothingness. "But there's nothing out there! No island for her to have washed up on. It's just ocean."

Quincy scratched his stubbly blond chin. "Unless you believe in legends... which I usually do."

"What legends?"

"The legend of the Island of Satanazes."

"What's that?"

"You've never heard of the Island of Devils? Guarded by the Hand of Satan himself?"

"You taught me everything I know, remember? If I haven't heard of it, it's your fault."

"Oh, it's quite the place. Swarming with man-eating

demons, and impossible to escape. The black hand keeps anything from leaving by capsizing their ship as they try to flee. And, of course, there's a supernatural fog that keeps it hidden from the world."

"Naturally."

"Why we talk about legend?" Sasha interrupted. "We trying to find Merona, not buried treasure."

"Well, every myth has a root in reality," said Quincy. "Some speculated that the island was simply the coast of America that some poor 14th century sailors landed on just before its discovery, but others think there might actually be an island out there, with a yet undiscovered culture and people all its own."

"So, you think there might be a chance that island is real? And Merona could be there?" Liora asked.

"Or whichever island started the myths. That's exactly where they were believed to be located, and many 15th century maps even had the island very clearly marked on them."

"Do you have access to one of those maps that we could borrow?"

"You think I just have something like that kicking around in my things?"

Liora raised her eyebrows incredulously. "Do I think world famous explorer, treasure hunter and historian, Quincy Grant, has a very old map? Umm, *yes*."

"Fair enough. I'll take a look in my things and see if I've still got one that might help us."

"In the meantime, Sasha and I will start preparations to set out again."

"Does that include grabbing a bite to eat with your favorite uncle?"

"Of course, us Grants always make time for family. But first we need to track down a friend of Gregory's. A radio man who can listen out for any possible signals

Merona or her pilot might send out."

Being an island, tracking down Gregory's old friend Antonio was an easy task, and upon knocking on the door, they soon found themselves enthusiastically welcomed in, by a convivial old man who clearly enjoyed company far more than he had it.

"Welcome, welcome!" said Antonio as he swung the door wide open to them. "Gregory told me you should be arriving around now!"

Liora, Sasha, and Quincy were perplexedly ushered in with cheerful enthusiasm, seated, and each handed a steaming cup of piping hot cocoa to drink before they had even spoken their names.

Continuing his eager welcome, Antonio began happily announcing their names for them. "You must be Liora, the lady whose sister is missing, and this big fellow of course must be Sasha!"

Sasha and Liora glanced at one another before nodding the affirmative.

"But I didn't expect a third!" Antonio continued. "It's lucky I made extra cocoa. The more the merrier, I always say."

"Glad you think so," Quincey said, amused by the singularly jovial man.

"So, what is it I can do for you all then? Gregory said something about keeping an ear out for distress calls, but wasn't much more specific than that."

"Well, we really don't have much more specifics to go on," Liora explained. "It seems my sister's plane was blown way off course. She went down quite a ways from where she was heading, and we need you to keep an ear open on your radio, on the off chance her plane sends out a distress call."

Antonio saluted. "You have my word! I shall listen at my radio night and day until I hear some good news."

"Thank you. We truly appreciate this. I just hope she's still out there."

"Oh, she's out there," Quincy attested with unwavering certainty. "She's too tenacious to go out *that* easy."

~

Merona and Carver plodded through the jungle, retracing their steps to a small game trap Merona had set earlier. Carver's bitten arm rested in a sling, held tight to his body for protection, as he mused on their increasingly grim situation.

"I don't think I've ever been, or ever will be, in such a surreal situation in my life. It's like we're trapped in one of those dime adventure magazines you read to get a good laugh, because they are too absurd to actually happen… and now here we are, trapped on a supernatural island being slowly gnawed to death by actual, real-life cannibals!"

"You actually read that tripe?"

"Not really tripe now, is it? Seeing as we are living through one."

"Still hilariously unrealistic."

"So, you *have* read them then!"

Merona grimaced in defeat. "There might have been one or two that just looked too ludicrous to pass by without taking a peek inside."

Carver laughed. "Was the adventurer just *too* handsome for you to ignore?"

"I don't recall, I just noticed the seven-foot-tall praying mantis he was fighting and *had* to see how that confrontation played out."

Carver laughed heartily, and they soon arrived at one of Merona's traps, where a large rodent had been snared, its eyes now bulging from strangulation. Clearing the trap, Merona stowed the dead animal in a sack before resetting the snare to await further game.

"How do you know all this stuff, anyway?" asked Carver.

"What stuff? Trapping?"

"All of it, hunting, shooting, patching up wounds, surviving in the wild like some kind of Amazon woman. You must be no more than... what, thirty?"

"Twenty-five, actually."

"How long have you been doing this?"

"My first job was at about eighteen. Just me, my uncle, and my sister going after this impossible treasure in the hopes of getting enough money to save the family ranch, if you can believe that." she said with a laugh.

"Oh, I can believe it."

"I know, rather a cliché story, but let me tell you, the adventures we went on were anything but. Though, I can't say we ever came across a place quite as dangerous or strange as this island... well, that might not be completely true."

"What was the most dangerous thing you faced on your travels?"

Merona laughed aloud. "That's a near impossible question to answer, when nearly every experience seemed just as dangerous as the last."

"Well then, how about this... why do you do it?"

"Do what?"

"Whatever it is that you do... adventuring, treasure hunting, thrill seeking. Why would a young woman want to live a life where she knows how to cauterize wounds, or which leaves won't give you a rash after you've answered the call of nature?"

Merona paused a moment, realizing she'd never really thought too much about why she did what she did until this moment. It just seemed to make sense, traveling the world, living wherever and however she chose, as though this nomadic life was a part of who she was, and required no further thought or explanation than that.

"I don't know really. I've never shied away from a challenge, and after that first venture, it seemed like my sister was always on the lookout for some new myth or treasure to go after... I knew she wasn't going to go without me, and what kind of sister would I be if I held her back? It's been one of the few things my sister and I have in common, treasure hunting. Plus, our respective skills just seem to complement each other."

"So... you go through all this discomfort just to be closer with your sister?"

"I've learned to enjoy it... well, not so much the nearly dying part of it, but you know, the freedom, and new places. Plus, the skills I've learned for situations such as this. So, you might say it has its up sides."

Carver lifted his arm gingerly. "I'm definitely appreciating those skills so far."

"Speaking of which, we forgot to check your wound again today, we need to make sure it's not getting... wait, what is that?"

Merona leaned close to Carver's arm, sniffing at the dark stain forming there.

Carver raised an eyebrow. "Ummm... how's it smell? Good?"

Merona recoiled. "Not good... we should have changed this much, much sooner."

CHAPTER XII

A RELIABLE PILOT

KATYA's propellers whirred through the air, steadily maintaining their course toward the island marked on the old, 15th century map Quincy had dug up for them, as they arced out across the ocean in search of Merona. Sasha scrutinized the waters, soaring low to investigate even the slightest anomaly among the waves. But with every pass, neither his nor Liora's keen eyes could find a single hint of life.

They gazed down into the clear, calm waters, cursing their never-ending expanse of unblemished blue as they each searched in desperation for an irregularity.

"See anything on your side?" asked Liora for the hundredth time that flight.

"*Nyet*. And you?"

"Nothing but clear water. Why do you think I asked?"

"Wait," Sasha gasped. "I see something."

A gray speck had caught Sasha's eye as it bobbed in the distant waves, and without hesitation he altered course, soaring toward the anomaly to investigate. This small hint of movement had been their first sighting in hours, and he refused to let it escape his sights for even a moment.

They both held their breath as they neared the object, studying its elongated form that to their anxious eyes, seemed to resemble a plane's severed wing upon which a tenacious survivor like Merona might have clung. Tears began to rise in Sasha's eyes as he sighted what seemed to be the small shadow of something, or someone perched atop the object, but in the next moment, all illusions of hope disappeared as a spray of water fountained from the creature's blowhole before it descended beneath the waves.

All their hopes abruptly turned to sputtering frustration, and Liora slammed her fist against the cockpit wall.

"Nothing!" she shouted. "We've been searching for days and still, nothing!"

"It take time."

"What if Merona doesn't have time? What if she's clinging to life somewhere waiting for us? Or worse, what if this wretched island doesn't exist and she's already…" Liora hesitated, unwilling to speak that last word with all its finality.

Sasha's throat tightened. "*Nyet*. We not talk like that. We not *think* like that."

Shifting their course back on track, Sasha forced a return to their search without another word. They sat in silence, gazing out the windows of the craft, but their view of the water soon became obscured as an outside mist began to roll in around the aircraft.

With a touch of the controls, Sasha descended out of the mist to escape the void of white which had engulfed them. The clouds rose, scattering around Katya's wings in curling wisps, but Sasha found his efforts wasted, as the same mist seeped beneath his plane across the ocean. Clinging to the waters with an almost disruptive purpose, the fog working without relent to obliterate all sight of the ocean.

Squinting past the pale haze, the aviators struggled to glimpse a clue of their lost sister, or her downed aircraft, knowing her only chance at rescue lay with them and the few other men Quincy had hired. No other search attempts would be made, and they could hardly leave her fate to the outside chance of a fortuitous passing ship.

But, moment by moment, the mist continued to intensify, shrouding their windows in an impenetrable vale, and obliterating their ability to search with any effectiveness. Their fuel began to drift low, and with a muttered curse, Sasha was forced to turn back toward the Azores, abandoning the search until tomorrow. They could only pray that wherever Merona was, she could hold out that long.

~

Clouded pus seeped from the putrid wound.

"It's definitely infected," Merona muttered.

"In... infected?" Carver stammered. "I thought you cleaned it thoroughly! What was all that pain I went through, while you poked and prodded at my arm, even for? Didn't you clean the bandages?"

"Of *course* I cleaned them, Carver. I've been boiling them into oblivion every time I redress that wound for the last three days. But we're out in the middle of nowhere, sanitization isn't exactly a guarantee."

"Great! So, now what? I'm going to lose my arm? You're going to cut my arm off, aren't you?"

Merona tossed her hands up. "I'm *not* cutting your arm off, Carver! Relax!"

"Then how are you fixing it?"

"I'm going to *try* and clean it again. But I'll need fresh water. Go down to the river and..."

"Who me?"

Merona squinted with impatience. "No, the dog...

who else do you think I'm talking to in this cave, on this cannibal infested island?"

"But I'm infected!"

"And I'm only one person! If you want to keep that arm of yours, you'll help me get it cleaned up as quickly as possible."

Shoving the water pouch and canteen towards him, the pilot took them with reluctance and shuffled off toward his objective, muttering cusses to himself as his dog followed closely behind him. Ignoring her companion's complaints, Merona set to work on her task of making a poultice to cure her companion's infection. Something she had picked up from a local tribe in Africa who had saved her from the brink of death.

In the early days of Merona and Liora's career, working alongside their uncle, an encounter with hyenas had left Merona severely wounded. In spite of her attempts to mend her injuries, Merona soon found her wound growing infected, and she quickly became overcome by feverish hallucinations. She never knew how the tribesmen had found them, but simply remembered waking in the hut of a small tribe, Liora at her side, with her infected wound wrapped in a strong-smelling poultice, and all signs of her fever having completely subsided. After her recovery, she and Liora had tried to discover the exact ingredients of the tribal remedy, always on the lookout for remedies that could be procured in the wild, and were able to discover the ingredients were a combination of charcoal, honey, marigold, aloe vera, and wild garlic.

Though Merona knew she had an abundance of charcoal resting in the ashes of her fire and was positive she had run into at least one nasty beehive thus far, she could remember only rarely seeing flowers or herbs of any kind growing in the harsh island's wild landscape, and doubted if she could pull the makeshift poultice together. But even with such limited supplies, she would have to try.

Setting out to try and locate the needed ingredients before the onset of night, Merona wracked her brain to recollect when or where she might have seen plant life suitable for the poultice, as she pressed on through the woods. Distant sounds echoed across the island as Merona hacked her way through vines and overgrown vegetation, and with the fall of a newly severed branch a far-off buzzing caught her attention. At first Merona assumed the source of the noise was a swarm of insects, but the idea quickly vanished as the noise took on a distinctly mechanical element. It was a plane.

The distant whir of a plane engine was unmistakable now, as it grew closer, and without hesitation, Merona sprang back toward camp, barreling through the freshly pruned path behind her as fast as her limbs would permit.

Reaching camp, Merona darted up the rocks, scaling the lean, hidden path up to the cliffside cave opening and dashing to their hoarded supplies. Rummaging through the scant food and blankets, she at last took hold of her objective: The binoculars; then, snatching up a smoldering stick from the fire's remains, she rushed from the cave. Like lightning, Merona ascended the rope ladder she'd hung from the cliff top, to reach the unlit bonfire she and Carver had so painstakingly preassembled above.

The sounds of their long-awaited escape still hummed in the distance, and at last, all their efforts of preparation would pay off. Merona hoped the past days of planning, scouting, and re-scouting a path to the beach would be enough to bring them to safety on the day it finally mattered.

Now out in the open air, Merona could hear the buzz of the plane all the clearer, and franticly eyed the gray sky for a sign of the aircraft. She needed a sighting, she needed to be sure of what she was hearing, and that the aircraft had a clear view through the fog before she lit the signal. Scanning the sky for a hint of movement, she spotted it at last, a distinct shadow flying overhead, engulfed in the haze of gray.

Raising her binoculars, Merona searched for a closer look at the plane which hovered above the horizon. Endless gray filled her tight field of vision within the binoculars as she zeroed in on her target who still maintained a steady course west. Tightening the magnification, Merona could just make out some lettering that adorned the side of the aircraft, and with a second adjustment, the letters became clear. Emblazoned in bright crimson across the plane's body was the name, Katya.

"Sasha!" Merona cried. "Oh, you beautiful man, you found us at last!"

Thrusting the hot torch into the kindling at the base of the towering heap of wood, Merona watched as the flames engulfed the signal fire. Smoke rose high into the air, slowly beginning to mingle in the gray sky above. Spying through her binoculars once more, Merona watched Sasha's plane as it steadily soared along, eager to spot the moment her signal would snag his attention and alter his course. But the plane remained steady.

"Come on Sasha, come on!" Merona muttered to herself. "Just find the signal, Sash."

Still, she could see no sign of acknowledgment.

"What is he doing?" She muttered again. "Why isn't he turning?"

In desperation, she took up more wood, hoisting it onto the fire to strengthen the already blazing signal, but with all her efforts, Sasha's plane still maintained its course.

Smoke now blanketed the misty sky in a thick black curtain, but to no use. Sasha's plane was growing smaller, drifting away toward the western horizon.

"Sasha, come on!" Merona shouted her words now, in full knowledge no one could hear them.

Despair washed over her. It had been twenty-five days since the crash. Twenty-five days of rationed food, questionable water, insufficient shelter, marauding cannibals, and nothing to assist in nature's call, but a handful of leaves. There was nothing that should have taken Sasha out this far over the Atlantic, save news of Merona's disappearance, and his over-inflated sense of loyalty to her and her sister.

Even if he had no knowledge of Carver's distress signal, this meant he must have had some kind of inkling of her fate and whereabouts. Why else could he be out here except in search of her? But if so, how could he miss such a blatant signal? How could he not see the island and rising smoke which he must have been looking for?

Merona paced up and down, staring after the shrinking plane in defeat, as she soon heard a sound of footsteps approaching.

"Where is it?" Carver called from down below. "Where's the ship?"

Merona looked back to find the pilot scrambling up the rope ladder toward her, as his dog took a slightly longer path up to join them, which only his sure-footed agility could manage among the rocky surroundings.

"There's no ship," she muttered in reply.

"No ship? But the signal? You lit the signal fire, I saw it from the woods."

"There's no ship, it's a plane. Sasha's plane, but I

don't think he saw us."

"You don't think he saw us? How could anyone *not* see us, with *that* announcing our presence?"

"He's not turning, Carver."

"You must be mistaken. Here, let me see."

Carver snatched the binoculars from Merona's hand, but before he had raised them to his eyes, a spear shot from the woods, flying straight for Carver.

With a split second to act, Merona dove forward, toppling Carver and herself to the ground and narrowly escaping the spear as it sped by.

At the base of the cliff a mob of gray men, glaring through the black eyeholes of their vulture-like headdresses, rushed into view, launching several more spears toward the survivors as they scurried up the rocks. Merona pushed up from the ground, dashing forward to the cliff edge and snatched up the rope ladder which hung there before the gray men could reach it.

Seizing two large rocks, she lobbed them down, striking one of the climbing gray men in the temple and sending him plummeting to the rocks below, but not before he'd collided with another climber, knocking him from the cliff wall as well. Her second stone pelted another climber's chest, knocking the wind from his lungs and wrenching him from the cliff face.

"Help me!" Merona bellowed to Carver, tossing him another rock, and the pilot swiftly rushed into action.

With Merona utilizing her machete on any gray men who managed to reach the top, the two survivors rained jagged stones down onto their attackers, keeping most of the gray men from ascending the cliff, as spears continued to launch up towards them.

Ducking beneath two more javelins, Merona snatched one from the air, flipping it around and hurling it back towards its owner. With a tangle of charging men

before her, Merona's shot easily hit home, plunging through the torso of one, and the shoulder of another at his back.

Taking up more scattered spears, Merona began giving their attackers a bitter dose of their own medicine. But even as their rocks and spears continued to rain down upon the gray men, the two companions could see their unrelenting attackers quickly beginning to take ground. Already they had reached the mouth of the cave to the survivor's campsite, and it was only a short climb left to reach the signal fire where the three companions stood.

"This isn't working!" Merona shouted. "They're taking too much ground!"

"We've got to make a run for the beach!" bellowed Carver. "The plane! It's our only chance!"

Already the gray men were beginning to reach them, and with her last spear and machete in hand, Merona started stabbing and slashing from above, impaling one man after another in the shoulder, face, or chest as they came within reach.

"There *is no* plane, Carver!" Merona roared. "He didn't see us!"

"You don't know that!"

The gray men climbed on, pushing past their fallen brothers with renewed fervor, and Merona stabbed out once more, but it wasn't going to be enough, and she knew it.

Dropping her spear and sheathing her machete, she swung her rifle off her shoulder, firing her long-conserved ammunition, saved for just such a desperate moment, into the crowd. Gray bodies dropped in tumbling heaps, the warriors so densely packed that each shot took out two or three at a time.

"Merona! We've got to get to the plane!" Carver cried.

"There *is* no plane, Carver! We need to retreat to the river!"

All at once, a gray warrior took hold of Merona's ankle, jerking her down and nearly toppling her over the cliff face. Her head slammed down as she hit the dirt, her rifle sailing from her hands, landing out of reach behind her. Kicking against her snarling attackers as they struggled to force her over the cliff, Merona shouted out to Carver.

"My gun! Get my gun!"

Unsheathing her machete once again, Merona struck out, severing the arm which held her leg and scrambling back from the precipice. More frantic gray arms reached up, grabbing hold of her boots and legs as she fought them back with her blade.

Turning to Carver for help, Merona's eyes locked with her pilot's as he took up her rifle and fired into the swarm. Panic filled his face from the sheer overwhelming nature of their situation, and in the next moment he was darting away along the cliff path, making his escape toward the woods, and from there, to the beach.

He had left Merona to the gray men and their insatiable hunger.

CHAPTER XIII

THE GRAY MEN FEAST

CARVER had abandoned Merona, with his dog following behind him as he ran off, and Merona was overcome with that same desperation she'd felt watching Sasha's plane drifting from sight in the sky moments before.

She knew Sasha's abandonment had been one of error, his honor would never have allowed for anything else, but Carver had made a choice. Be it overwhelming fear that had guided his actions, the fact was, he'd seen a chance of rescue and, with his companion in imminent danger, chosen his own life over hers.

Whatever his reasons, he had left her for dead for the second time, since the crash, and had she been any other woman, the despair of her situation might have overwhelmed her. But despair had long been an emotion Merona despised, and the mere feeling of helplessness had a tendency of bringing out her fury and determination.

Lashing out against her attackers, Merona's blazing rage worked in her favor, as she vigorously kicked free of their grasp. Her boots collided with several gray faces, knocking them from the cliff edge to meet their fate on the rocks below.

Slashing feverishly with her machete, Merona staggered to her feet and retreated down the same narrow cliff path Carver had taken, knowing rescue on

·157·

the beach was a fruitless hope, but still desperate to put any kind of distance between herself and the ascending horde.

Driving her limbs at full vigor, Merona could just make out Carver as he rushed along the path up ahead, his injury slowing his escape just enough for her to gain on him a little. Below, a squad of gray men ran through the trees along the cliff's base, keen on cutting off the survivors in the woods ahead.

Carver was coming on the last stretch of cliff that sloped down towards the woods, and it seemed as though he would outrun his pursuers, but as he and his dog disappeared into the forest, Merona could see the ravenous gray men as they trailed after him, quickly gaining ground on the wounded pilot. If he evaded capture long enough to reach the beach, it would be a miracle.

Inhuman shouts of the men who pursued her persisted at her back and Merona pressed on, knowing her only chance of losing them lay in the thick fog of the woods ahead. Ducking amid the densely packed forest, she weaved among the trees, leaping over fallen trunks and scattered stones.

The gray men pressed down behind her, their lean, sinewy bodies built for exertion, and adept at chasing down and subduing their prey.

If Merona was going to outmaneuver them, she would have to use the one thing they seemed to be weakest in... wits. These men had clearly nurtured their animal instinct, but anything beyond that seemed unnatural to them, and that was the only advantage she knew she possessed. The cliff path having taken her west, she was cut off from doubling back and utilizing the eastern rivers, and the only reliable deterrent she knew the gray men feared. But escape might still be within her grasp, if she could find a new means of outmaneuvering them.

Her eyes glanced from tree to tree, hunting for an opportunity to outsmart her opponents, and in the next moment, she sighted a means of escape. Fluttering from the branches of a distant tree were long strips of fabric, baring a rough image of a goat head, and instantly Merona knew it was the territorial markings of a nearby gray men camp.

Through her time on the island, Merona had begun to know the opposing tribal subsets by the animal headdresses their warriors wore. The men who chased her now were adorned in a feathery headdress of the vulture tribe, but on the distant trees, the fabric which hung from the branches bore the clear image of the goat tribe; a tribe she knew her pursuers to be in conflict with, and she swiftly veered towards it.

Sounds of gray men still clamored behind her, shrieking and chattering in her wake, but the adventuress rushed on, pushing her body to its limit for the crucial sprint ahead. The symbols on the trees began increasing in number around her until all at once, Merona burst amid the unsuspecting tribesmen and their camp, rudely disrupting their day.

Staring faces gaped at Merona in confusion as she stumbled into view and charged through the camp like a wild animal. Gray men of the camp darted for their weapons, rushing to bring down this invader of their peace, but before their hands were scarcely laid on their spears and hatchets, Merona's pursuers made a timely appearance.

Like a tidal wave of spears and snarling faces, they flooded from the mist between the surrounding trees, rushing into the clearing and abruptly clashing with the camp's occupants. The whole of the camp swelled into uproar, and Merona dodged her way through the scattered huts and inhabitants, as violent hands reached out to grab hold of her rapidly running form without success.

As the pursuing war party slaughtered a path behind her, the warriors of the camp were swift to step up to meet them, turning their attention from chasing down the adventuress, and leaving her free to make her escape.

Sounds of battle clashed behind her, slowly dying away as she ran on, her limbs quickly giving out beneath her panting body as the pressing threat began to grow more distant. Skidding to a halt, Merona buckled, hunching over her knees and gasping out for breath. She was safe, for now.

Allowing the moment of respite to wash over her, Merona's thoughts suddenly returned to Carver. Had he fallen to the gray men in the woods? Or had he made it to the beach? If he had, what then? Had she been wrong? Had Sasha truly not seen her signal, or had the weeks of hopelessness upon the island gotten to her head?

What if Carver was right? What if Sasha *was* circling back and returning to find a place to land near the beach, but found only Carver there? No doubt he would insist Merona had fallen to the cannibals; out of ignorance, cowardice, or deliberate deception, it made little difference which. And what then? Sasha would have no choice but to believe him, and Merona would be left behind. Left for dead, to rot on an island, with no hope of rescue.

She knew the likelihood was slim, but if there was even the slightest chance of rescue, she couldn't miss it now. Driven by this sliver of hope, and a desperation for escape, Merona rushed on, hacking through the woods with the rabid intensity of the gray men who had once pursued her.

~

Carver's footsteps marred the untouched sands of the beach, as his dog followed behind in a trail of dotted paw prints.

Whether by blind luck or the use of Merona's rifle, he had managed to take out and eventually lose the gray men in the woods, and as he franticly paced the beach, wholly unable to appreciate the miracle of his escape, he eyed the dreary gray sky for a sign of his airborne liberator from this hell on earth. But just as Merona had attested, the plane was nowhere to be seen.

Carver cursed under his breath at all he held responsible for his miserable situation. First Sasha's plane and its abandonment, then the cannibals and their relentless attacks, and last the storm, which had brought them crashing down onto this doomed island in the first place.

He wanted it to be over, but with no sign of the aircraft to be found, all his hopes of rescue were fading into oblivion. In that moment, his thoughts turned to his companion, Merona, and the horrific fate he had abandoned her to.

Looking down at his dog, and his large, dark eyes, gazing up at his master in confusion, Carver tried hopelessly to justify his actions to himself and his animal.

"Don't look at me like that! There was nothing I could have done... they were pulling her over the cliff!"

But his excuses fell flat, even to him. He had abandoned his only ally for a chance at escape, he had been a coward, and for nothing. He was alone and helpless, wounded, exhausted, and it was all his own fault.

With a rush of regret, Carver turned to go back for Merona, certain his actions would be fruitless, but knowing he'd never forgive himself if he didn't. But as he turned, a piercing cry flooded from the trees. The gray men had found him.

With the sea at his back and the gray men now rushing from the trees ahead, Carver was cut off from all means of escape. Forced across the beach just to put distance between his pursuers, he shot out towards them, as in the same moment his foot caught in the wet sand. Stumbling forward, the rifle flew from his hands as he staggered to regain his footing and race on, abandoning the weapon in his haste.

No matter how fast he ran, they ran faster. The gap between hunters and prey rapidly closing, and in the next moment Carver was struck in the leg, toppling to the ground and shrieking in pain. A long spear jutted from his calf, its gory spearhead protruding from his shin, as blood seeped relentlessly into his tattered slacks.

The dog had run on ahead, darting far out in front of his owner, but with his cry and fall, the loyal animal raced back to defend his prone and helpless master.

Arriving just in time to see Carver's fall, Merona watched from the woods as the gray men descended, swarming around Carver and snatching him up by his hair. Within seconds his attackers had overpowered him, wrenching his arms behind his back as they trussed up his wrists and ankles together like a hog.

Carver's dog snapped and snarled at the men who struck relentlessly out at him with their spears, forcing him back as their allies captured his master. Ducking and dodging, he bit into a spear shaft, wrenching it from the man's hands before dashing out of range, in search of a path to his owner.

Again, they jabbed out as the dog bit back, but with his attention on one spear, another slashed along his side, and the mutt yelped out, retreating along the beach and off into the gray fog of the jungle, the gray men chasing after him.

There was no doubt in Merona's mind that the gray men intended to return Carver to one of their camps to do with him what they would, and though she hated the thought that her life might depend on such a backstabbing turncoat, with no plane on the horizon, the choice of leaving him to die, or making a calculated risk to save him, seemed an obvious one. She could not survive this island alone, and Carver was the only human residing upon it that wasn't actively trying to kill her.

Without enough energy, strength, or weaponry to take them head-on, she would have to follow them to their camp and stage a clandestine rescue, to save the man who had twice left her to die.

With their human prize secured, the remaining gray men retreated into the forest, dragging a gagged and helpless Carver with them. And, from a safe distance, Merona followed. The gray racing figures were growing small amid the distant trees and fog, but Merona maintained her speed, her lungs stinging with every gasping breath. As her muscles burned from exhaustion, red markings of the vulture tribe began to flash by on tattered flags and painted trees, signaling the camp's territory and an end to the miles of ground behind them. But even as they reached camp, Merona knew her difficulties had only begun, as she searched for an opening to extract her companion.

She watched from the trees as the gray men paraded into their camp, chanting incoherent gibberings with

Carver held high above their heads like a trophy, newly won. More gray tribespeople streamed from the huts to join the men amid the chanting throng.

The warriors who carried Carver relinquished their hold, sending the bloodied pilot crashing to the dirt as the thick of the multitude stamped toward the center of the village, abandoning Carver, semi deserted, in a heap on the ground as they made ready their bonfire.

Now was Merona's chance. She would have to risk her life for a man she knew would never return the favor. Would he even be worth the food he consumed? With all she had been through on the island so far, she still hadn't become mercenary enough to just let him die, when she knew she could save him.

Wood and oil were brought from the huts, as the gray people set to work building up a central bonfire, and Merona made her move. Waiting for an opening in the patrolling guards at the perimeter of camp, Merona swiftly and silently crept in among the huts for cover as she approached the motionless pilot. With the gray men still distracted on the fire, Merona took her opening and stepped up, ducking into position nearby behind a small hut a mere yard from Carver.

Eyeing her adversaries, she edged within earshot of him. "Psst!" she whispered. "Hey... backstabber. Over here."

Exhaustion and pain in his eyes, Carver looked up toward her, the bonds on his wrists and ankles restricting his movement.

"Merona? How did...? You're *alive*?"

"Surprisingly, yes. No thanks to you... again."

"I'm sorry! I wasn't thinking! I didn't know what to do, I didn't think you..."

"Save it, Carver, it's not the time *or* place. And lower your voice, would you?"

Pulling a spearhead from her belt, Merona tossed the weapon toward Carver, sending it skidding across the dirt to meet his bound hands. "Cut your bonds and let's get out of here."

"They got me in the leg, I don't know if I can make it."

"We'll worry about that once you cut yourself free. Hurry!"

Snatching up the makeshift dagger, Carver went to work slicing at the bonds of his hands.

"*No*," Merona hissed, "get your feet first, you need to be able to run."

"*Right*, sorry."

Setting to work on the ropes at his ankles, Carver began to whisper out continued apologies. "I'm sorry I left. I wasn't thinking straight, I just didn't think there was anything I could do... I thought you were done for. I thought *I* was done for."

"Okay, okay, I get it, you're not cut out for survival. I've made note of your lacking bravery, but since you're the only other person around that's not trying to eat me, it'd be a waste not to save your miserable life if I can."

"Thank you. I'll make this up to you, I swear."

"Oh, you're going to owe me *big*, for years to come, if we ever get off this island. Now hurry up, can't you cut any faster?"

"I'm trying, but it's duller than it looks..."

In the next moment, several gray warriors were stomping toward the pilot with spears raised.

"They're coming back. Hurry!" Merona whispered, ducking back behind the cover of her hut, as she slipped her machete from her belt, readying for a fight.

The chanting increased as the fire grew and five warriors surrounded Carver, hefting him off the ground as panic filled his face.

"Merona?" Carver sputtered. "Merona, help!"

Merona sucked back a deep breath in preparation for battle, it was time for plan B, but in that same instant a jagged rock slammed into Carver's skull.

Merona halted, gasping back as she saw the pilot's limp body drop to the ground, blood seeping from his fractured skull. Raising the bloody rock, the gray man cratered Carver's head with the second strike, sending blood spattering across his own face.

Just like that, it was all over. Carver, her last and only ally, was dead.

Merona stood in gaping silence in the shadows, watching in a daze as his body was hoisted overhead, and hauled toward the blazing fire, the chanting, shrieking throng of men, women, and even children clawing at his limbs and battered, oozing head for a taste of his blood.

A shaft of wood was passed under his bound wrists and feet, and his body was propped near the blazing flames, situated for a slow, long roast. The gray men were preparing to feast on their catch, and Merona felt a rising sickness stirring in her stomach as she witnessed the outcome of her failure, and the horror she had been helpless to prevent.

CHAPTER XIV

WEIGHING LOSSES

MERONA sat huddled in a shallow cave overlooking the beach, the remains of where she'd been sick slowly being washed out to sea by the waves. All her supplies were still at the old camp, but she couldn't go back. Not yet. There was too much risk the gray men had stayed behind to plunder anything of use after their raid, and Merona had no interest in competing with them for it.

The beach-side cave would give her shelter from the elements for the night and, come morning, she would have to start all over. She would have to begin scavenging for food and the basic necessities she and Carver had taken nearly a month to accumulate. But this time she was on her own.

Rain drizzled outside, funneling down and dribbling off a jutting stone at the cave's mouth. The monotonous trickle might have been soothing, but Merona's mind was engulfed with echoing visions of the moment the rock had struck Carver's head. The crack of bone, the splat of blood, and the limp thud as his body hit the ground. She had been near enough to see every detail, to taste the coppery scent of his blood on the air... near enough she should have stopped it. And she could not wipe the image from her mind.

But could she have even saved him? If she had acted quicker, would she have even been able to overtake the five men who had been surrounding him? Or would her efforts have only brought the whole of the camp down on them, and accomplished nothing more than their simultaneous deaths?

The pragmatist in her insisted it would have been the latter. She had survived, and that was the most she could have expected to gain from the situation, but with Sasha's plane well and truly gone, no supplies, and no one to watch her back, how long was her survival likely to last?

The fury she had felt at Carver for abandoning her at the cliff, had served to fuel her determination to survive, but the guilt she now felt at her own failure to save him, weighed her down like a boulder.

Was she any different than he had been when he abandoned her on the cliff? She had frozen a moment too long, and he had fled for fear of his life. They were both acting on the instinct to survive. Now, she could at last understand his actions, when it was too late for her understanding or forgiveness to do him any good.

Her guilt left her stripped of her will to survive. What was the point in the end, of fighting to live, if all that living entailed was the continuous struggle to avoid starvation, exposure, infection, and her inevitable cannibalization?

She needed to find a purpose... something to hold on to, to push back against the guilt. She needed something to hope for, but her last hope had faded with the departure of Sasha's plane.

"Sasha," Merona muttered to herself, and the thought came to her, that perhaps the fact she had seen him had to be enough. He was out there searching for her, doubtlessly with Liora at his side, and knowing them as she did, she knew they were unlikely to throw in the towel this early in the fight. They would go on searching, and that meant she had to go on fighting and holding on to hope at least as long as they were.

Merona sat, struggling to force her usually dogged predisposition to the surface once more, knowing she would need every one of her most unpleasant character traits to survive even the next few days.

~

The cliffside camp had been left utterly ransacked.

Packs of food lay torn open, with their contents stolen or strewn across the rocky floor. In the corner where Merona's most recent kill of wild boar once hung, only a bloody smear remained. Spears, blankets and gathered food were gone, but as Merona kicked through the jumble of spoiled supplies, she found, to her relief, that the gray men had all but ignored some key items.

The canned food, though scattered and dented, had been left behind, since to the cannibals it would have likely appeared as bulky, useless weight. And though the rest of her packs had been appropriated, likely used to carry off the stolen supplies, one small, torn, waxed canvas pack remained. Gathering the scattered canned goods into the ragged pack, Merona slung her precious findings over her shoulder, and stepped outside to investigate the remains of the bonfire and battle above.

The once carefully arranged twigs and branches sat in a blackened heap, still smoldering from the prior evening. In the dirt lay the broken spear shafts of the battle, and Merona's discarded binoculars, now battered from the tromping warriors who had trodden them in the frenzy.

Plucking them from the dirt, Merona wiped the binoculars clean, releasing grit and pebbles from their scratched lenses. With the next swipe of her sleeve, a front lens popped free, slipping from its dented frame and landing at her feet. Picking the loosed lens from the ground, Merona placed both binocular and lens in a side pocket of her satchel. She would try to repair them later.

Concluding her search of the camp and bonfire, Merona made her way down the mountain with little more than the broken binoculars, salvaged cans of food, and a handful of roots scavenged off the few fallen warriors that were left behind. Both the water pouch and canteen had been in Carver's possession when the gray men had attacked and, for all she knew, had gone into the bonfire with him.

Though the odds were against her, Merona hoped that Carver might have done the stupid thing, and abandoned his water containers at the river when he spotted the smoke signal. And although she would normally have been angered at his incompetence, in this case, she dearly hoped Carver's unreliability might have done her some good.

Reaching the flowing stream, Merona searched its shores with fingers crossed, as she dug through the mud and leaves with one of the discarded spear shafts from the battle. More than once her stick would hit against a lump beneath the leaves, raising her hopes of uncovering one of the water containers, only to dash them against the small stone or branch she unearthed in their place.

Carver, it seemed, had proved dependable the one-time Merona had needed him not to be. She would have to find a means of shelter in the growing dark, abandoning her fruitless search of the river for another day. Left with only her hip flask as water container, Merona filled, drank, and refilled the flask multiple times over before departing.

With no supplies to guard her against the elements

of the night, Merona would need to find a cave or outcropping to block the winds from extinguishing the much-needed fire she was desperate to start. The darkness encroached, and with it, the biting cold, and Merona found herself tempted to return to her abandoned camp on the mountain slope to escape her fruitless search for shelter, but with the gray men having full knowledge of its location, she knew the risk of lighting a fire, let alone resting her eyes, would be far too great.

With every step through the woods, a nagging dread filled Merona's mind. Where could she go that didn't run the risk of being killed and cannibalized in her sleep? With her sole ally gone, a simple hour's rest could be a death sentence, but where was there on the island that would eliminate that risk? Where did the gray men fear to tread?

Almost in an instant, Merona knew the answer to her questions, and without a second thought, turned on her heel to retrace her steps. Night pressed in, and as the last hint of light departed, that distinctive, damp smell of swamp met Merona's nose. She knew the gray men feared the strange shifting waters, and with them lay her only means of defense against nighttime attacks. Why they feared them, she didn't know, but the very real risk of cannibalization far outweighed whatever unseen dangers the gray men believed in. At least for the present.

Guided by the snaking stream, Merona gagged on its oppressive stench as she ventured deeper into the swamp than she had ever previously risked. But her newfound appreciation of the putrid waters, and the protection they offered, only grew, as she spied a shallow cave behind a tangle of vines.

Though her instinct was to draw her machete and

hack through the barrier, the element of concealment it offered had some appeal, and Merona stepped forward, brushing aside the vines to reveal, not one, but several caves and crevices she might make camp in.

Stepping inside the widest of the jagged fissures, Merona ignited her lighter, its orange light pushing back the inky black within and illuminating the craggy walls of the shallow cave. Stones glistened overhead and behind chalky scratches etched into the cave's back wall. Without delay, Merona had assembled a fire, and bed of leafy branches on a flat portion of the cave floor, and was soon warming her frozen extremities near the blaze.

Boggy fumes wafted through the cave opening, filling Merona's new camp with its stifling stench, and though the smell did little to enhance Merona's meager meal of canned soup, the fog gave the solitary adventuress a peculiar peace of mind, as though it were a tangible defense against the gray men and their attacks.

Sleep began to encircle her, and though the uncertainty nagged at Merona's mind of what might lay in the swamp which could so absolutely hold back a force like the gray men, she knew sleep would have to be risked if she hoped to succeed in her much-needed hunt for food the following day.

CHAPTER XV

AN OFFERING OF FRIENDSHIP

ROZEN from a night exposed to the unnaturally clammy air of the cave and surrounding swamp, Merona set out that morning, eager to invigorate her stiff joints and trembling extremities with a day of furtive hunting. She needed a distraction, a purpose to work toward so her mind couldn't drift to thoughts of her hopeless situation, and satisfying such a primal need as hunger was just the thing.

Though the old camp had been raided, Merona's traps had remained in place along the river, and checking them became her first order of business. Merona was disheartened to find not a single prize to be collected among her snares, which still remained empty. The swamp of the night always seemed to dissuade any game from wandering near, and Merona would have to hope for a catch throughout the day.

With nothing left to her but the broken and discarded spears of yesterday's battle, Merona set about fashioning new shafts for the two sharpest spearheads she had found among the carnage, stripping the sturdy saplings of their branches and bark with her machete until each shaft sat straight and clean.

Setting out, Merona found the same fog of the past month shrouded her trail still, and as she pressed on through the woods in watchful caution, she was determined that her movements would make neither

·175·

sound nor disturbance to any nearby animals amid the mists. The fog necessitated a much closer approach than usual to get a clean line of sight, and with this imperfect tactic forced upon her by the thick, overbearing haze, she would have to execute her attack perfectly.

Plodding through the undergrowth for hours on end, Merona's efforts were met with no success, and she was forced to return to camp empty-handed, and pilfer her measly supply of canned rations, blackened roots, and scavenged insects. Day after day she ventured into the woods, hoping to track some kind of edible prey but, more often than not, nearly stumbling head-long into another patrol of gray men.

The fifth day of her solitude dawned and once again Merona set out, restless for a sight or sound of movement which didn't belong to her man-eating neighbors. Hours passed and once again she believed her day a wasted one, until at last a distant rustling of trees caught her ear. Shrouded in fog, she was forced to trust in her ears alone, pausing to listen with every few steps and altering her course to slowly hone in on her prey.

With each step the sounds grew louder and soon hints of scraping wood began to intermingle with the rustling leaves. Through the thick fog a faint gray shadow began to take shape ahead, and Merona finally sighted the wild goat who was the culprit of the noise. There it stood, vigorously rubbing its head and horns against a slim tree, causing the branches above to sway and rattle against each other.

Raising her spear, Merona crept closer, still cautious not to make a sound in spite of the scraping and snorts of her prey helping to mask her approach. The animal was clearly old, its fur patchy and its frame emaciated like most beasts of the island. But in spite of its unideal condition, Merona wasn't about to abandon her target. This animal could be her breakfast, lunch, and dinner, with meat to spare if she rationed her meal portions. It was a prize she didn't have the luxury to pass up.

Taking aim, she made her shot, plunging her spear sidelong into the creature's flank. A sharp cry filled the forest as the animal's back legs dropped to the dirt. It kicked and scrambled wildly for escape, fighting against its unavoidable fate.

Raising her second spear, Merona took aim to put an end to the shrieking beast's misery, but in the next moment, something else leapt into view, locking onto the flailing goat's throat, struggling franticly to pin it to the ground as it clamped down on its windpipe.

Merona froze, unsure what new beast she had now encountered, but as the dust settled, a familiar shaggy, gray muzzle and black eyes looked up toward her. It was Carver's dog, who Merona had all but forgotten in the chaos and wake of his master's death.

The lifeless goat's now broken neck rested in the mutt's jaws, limp and dripping with blood as the two survivors stared off. Eying the mutt's posture, Merona still held her spear in readiness, poised to strike the animal if it attempted to run off with her precious food, but as his large dark eyes gazed up at her, Merona's survival instinct slipped back, as she took in the dog's wholly pitiful appearance.

From head to paw, his scraggled coat was dotted with burrs and brambles which clung to his damp and matted fur, while along his side she could see several streaks of crusted blood, where the gray men's spears had grazed him in his attempts to save his master on the beach that day. His frame was thin and weak, and Merona speculated he had scavenged little to no food since the attack; much like her.

With a timid first step, the mutt moved forward, dragging the goat's carcass towards the adventuress with reticent caution before placing it at her boots as though in offering of friendship.

Lowering her spear, Merona stared down toward the pathetic creature, his dark eyes still pleading up toward her.

"That's a good boy," she said at last, "good dog."

With a gentle scratch beneath his matted chin, she took up the deceased goat and turned, tapping her leg for the dog to follow. With eager speed, he fell in step at her side, happily looking up at her as they plodded back toward camp. The trek was short, and Merona found the tapping footsteps of the happy animal strangely comforting to have at her side.

Back at camp, Merona cut free yet another clump of burr-ridden fur from the mutt's side as he sat patiently waiting for her to finish her strange grooming practices. The two companions' small fire blazed near the mouth of the cave, smoke drifting from the opening as the slaughtered goat roasted on a spit of Merona's own fashioning.

With another slice of her pocket knife the final clump of brambles was cut clean, and Merona flicked the furry wad from her glove with difficulty as it clung furiously to the leather.

"There," she huffed. "That's finally over."

With a wag of his tail, the mutt turned towards the adventuress and began licking her hands in gratitude that the tugging of his fur was at last concluded.

Merona smiled as she patted his now patchy head. "You're welcome. Though I hope you realize you look like crap now."

Carver's dog cocked his head at the sound of her unfamiliar words, his tail still wagging.

"Yeah, you probably don't care, huh?"

The dog let out a huff, as though her incomprehensible words offended him.

Merona raised her hands playfully. "All right, I'm sorry. I'm sure it will grow back soon. In the meantime, though, why don't we have a bite to eat? I think we've both earned it."

Moving up towards her crispy roast, Merona sliced off a chunk of well-cooked flesh and tossed it to her companion who dove in and nearly swallowed it whole.

"I'm glad you like it," she said, chuckling as she hacked and twisted off one of the goat's back legs for herself.

Comfortably situated in the warmth of their cave and nearby fire, the two survivors sat side by side, feasting on their small lunch in companionable silence, with Carver's dog only breaking the quiet every so often to remind his new pack member for his share of the meal.

Though Merona's instincts told her to conserve the first bit of food she had been able to procure in the last five days, she knew the benefits her animal companion could offer in hunting and especially vigilance in the nights, far outweighed the amount of food he might consume, and as she tended the long, scabbing gouges along his side, acquired in the defense of his late master, she hoped his instinct to defend might finally give her the reliable ally she had been lacking these past miserable weeks.

CHAPTER XVI

VITAL DISCOVERIES

SASHA scrutinized the array of maps and charts before him. Over the last fourteen days, since their departure from Morocco, they had systematically explored the North Atlantic in a 460 mile radius out from the Azores, but to no success. Not one unexplored island, undiscovered rock, or even a hint of wreckage could be found in all that time, and they were beginning to doubt if their efforts would ever bear fruit.

Pacing up and down Antonio's lodgings, Liora glanced repeatedly over Sasha's shoulder as he hunched over the squat table plastered with maps. The old radio buzzed in the other room, awaiting the faint hope of snagging a new signal.

Sasha sighed. "What we do wrong? How it possible we search for this long and *still* find nothing?"

"We just have to keep looking," said Liora firmly.

"But where? We not have time to search across whole ocean."

"We only have partial coordinates, what else can we do but keep searching that general area?"

"Merona not be able to hold out that long."

"We are talking about the same Merona, right?"

"This not time to joke."

"I just mean, she can handle herself."

"Against what? We not even know what she facing out there."

·181·

"I know, I know…" Liora sank back in a nearby chair, feeling the weight of the hopeless situation begin to settle on her. "This is my fault," she muttered.

"Talk like that not help us."

"It was my *stupid* debt that forced her out there, Sasha. Just to find a job to pay it off."

"It not help anyone to talk like that. Merona chose to get on plane, and maybe she already gone, we not know for sure, but maybe she *not* gone. Would it not be worse to let despair make us give up too soon?"

Liora rose and sat down silently next to Sasha as Antonio emerged from the kitchen, handing out two large mugs of coffee to the weary search party, Sasha's immense hands making his look more akin to a teacup, than any mug.

"Now," Sasha continued, "we just need to correct course to cover wider range."

Antonio tentatively placed a comforting hand on Sasha's shoulder. "Dear boy, your loyalty is admirable, but haven't you two already run through your funds? How long can you keep chasing after this phantom island? It pains me to say it, but I understand the pilot sent out a signal *before* they crashed. The likelihood that they survived the impact, is, well…"

Antonio halted, seeing the anguish in Sasha and Liora's faces as his words hit home.

Liora's hands trembled, releasing her mug onto the table with a clunk before her head slumped into her hands.

"This is all my fault," she whimpered.

Sasha's bulky arms engulfed Liora, fully obscuring her slim frame behind his mammoth one.

In the other room, the radio continued to hum and buzz, awaiting a signal from afar. But as Liora's despairing sobs grew louder, a faint, disjointed voice came crackling over the speaker, catching their ears and arresting their focus.

"Hello? ...Hello, is anyone reading this? We have an urgent message from a plane crash survivor by the name of Merona Grant... Hello?"

~

Merona secured the muskrat's plump corpse inside the pouch at her hip before resetting the cord which had snared it near the stream's edge. At her side, Carver's dog trotted along, eager to accompany his new leader on her hunting trip that day.

The previous day's meal of goat had been nearly completely consumed by the two companions the night before, and one muskrat, though an excellent catch, wasn't enough to eliminate the need for hunting that day.

Merona's sleep that night had been made far more comfortable by her new furry colleague's presence, who insisted on sidling next to her and contributing his body heat and scraggly fur coat against which she gladly huddled. By morning her hands and face were surprisingly warm, and Merona found she had renewed fervor for the day's work ahead.

Having reset her traps, Merona soon set off into the misty woods, wondering the best path to take to avoid any contact with her neighbors, but as she ventured down what seemed the best route, Carver's dog quickly halted, growling toward the untrodden trail before turning back to find a new path. Hesitant to follow the animal and his skittishness, Merona slapped her leg, calling to the retreating mutt to follow on, but he refused to attend her command.

Halted in the midst of the path, Merona grumbled

to herself under her breath. "Come on boy! Let's go!" Merona called.

But he remained in place, kicking up dirt as he danced in agitation.

After yesterday's events, she'd hoped to have found a useful hunting partner. Someone to watch her back and chase down the more uncooperative prey, but with this new hitch already interrupting their first day out, Merona wondered if the mutt was more hindrance than help.

"What is the *matter* with you?" Merona muttered.

The words had scarcely left her lips when a mutter of voices echoed at her back, and she knew at once the dog's instincts had been to her benefit, for who else was on this island that could speak, save the one threat she wished to avoid: The gray men.

Hints of spears and faded figures approached through the fog from seemingly all sides, and Merona knew that in moments they would be right on top of her. Retreating back to her four-legged companion, she hastened to follow the astute animal and his keen senses, hoping his instinct to avoid their adversaries might help her do the same.

Darting through the undergrowth and increasing fog, Carver's dog led the way, his acute ears and nose guiding his every step away from their gray enemies as he darted in one direction and then the next, knowing what lay out of sight in the mists around them.

Moving at a rapid pace, it wasn't long before they had once again reached the river, outrunning the gray men to a place they dared not venture. Looking down toward him affectionately, Merona patted the mutt on his scraggly head.

"Thanks for getting us out of that one boy."

With a cheerful wag of his tail, he nuzzled his head

against her hand, lapping up his moment of glory with glee.

Catching her breath, Merona gazed into the clear waters of the river before her, her thoughts shifting from their enemies and on to the strange waters around them. She had been on this island over a month, and still she had barely ventured beyond the stream where she gathered her daily water, and which the gray men dared not touch.

Though she had told herself that the gray men's unfounded fear of the water made for a useful survival opportunity, the waters and their nightly corruption still unnerved her. Nothing in her mind could explain the phenomenon, and though she had witnessed no strange activity in the streams, day or night, their very unnatural nature gave her pause.

Beyond the river, she could make out a tangle of streams which seemed to intertwine amid the fog, but still she hesitated to explore further.

"This is stupid," she muttered to herself. "It's just water."

Carver's dog cocked his head at her words, and she looked down toward her companion for validation.

"Right, boy? I mean, why not give it a look? I don't know about you, but I'm getting tired of dodging cannibals all day on our hunting trips."

The mongrel dog merely cocked his head further.

"Right," Merona affirmed. "We'll give it a try. What's the worst that could happen?"

Spotting a shallow point of the stream, Merona stepped into the rushing liquid, pushing all trepidation from her mind as she resolved to follow logic, on an island which seemed determined to disregard it.

~

The fog was extreme, and more than once Merona almost lost track of her four-legged companion in its depths. Wide rivers and trickling streams snaked through the whole of the tangled jungle, cutting up the ground in interconnected crisscrosses and Merona slowly made her way across the growing wetlands.

Endless fog and rivers seemed to be all that surrounded her now, and she wondered if the gray men's fear had sprung from the eeriness of the place more than anything else. Normal sounds of life seemed all but absent from her surroundings, hardly a twitter of birds or even a chirp of insects was audible in the vast expanse of mist, and Merona began to understand the gray men's fear of the increasingly eerie place.

What was the use of it? With hardly a sign of life, what were they hunting for? But with this thought, a sign of life appeared, though not in the form they had hoped for. In the next moment, Merona felt a strange crunch beneath her boot unlike the usual dead twigs or scattered rocks she had been treading upon. Kneeling, Merona felt through the fog which shrouded the ground, and grasping the strange object, pulled it from the haze.

In her gloved hand she held the skull of a small animal, bits of fur and flesh still hanging from the bone like scraps of moss on a log. The meat was fresh, tightly clinging to the skull in bright red patches. Along the bone, Merona could make out long gouges where the animal's executer had torn at and devoured its flesh.

Measuring the distance of each tooth mark between her fingers, the sheer size of the carnivorous creature's maw became clearly apparent, and Merona felt a growing dread at what kind of animal could have made them. Gingerly, Carver's dog sniffed his companion's findings, at first intrigued by the smell of a fresh kill, but quickly recoiling with the new scent of what had slain it.

With her brave companion's tail tucking tightly behind him, Merona felt that making tracks back toward their camp was well overdue, but as she rose to make her departure, a loud clanging sounded behind her.

Whirling to face the noise, Merona gripped her spear at the ready, exasperated with the loss of her rifle more than ever. Holding her ground, she waited, but as the clanging continued in an almost rhythmic pattern, Merona noted the unnatural, metallic ring to the noise, something which seemed to remove it from all the other sounds she had become used to on the island. This was not a sound of nature, but of man.

Stepping forward with caution, the dense fog for a moment began to recede, and a glint of something moving up ahead sparkled through the haze. The noise grew louder, and Merona kept her eyes fixed on the object, squinting through the mist to make it out.

Clang... clang... clang. It rang out still, continually bobbing and glinting up ahead, and with her next few steps the strange, but no longer threatening object became clear: It was a piece of wreckage caught in a tangle of weeds in a shallow stream, the current of water continually cracking it against the rocks.

What part of the plane it belonged to, Merona wasn't sure, but whatever it was, it must have meant the rest of the aircraft was nearby, further upstream perhaps, and in it, the possibility of additional supplies. Merona had made a quick search of the plane before its untimely descent off the cliff, but had been nowhere near thorough, and with her limited options, any kind of supplies that could be salvaged could very well be lifesaving.

Though Carver's dog was reluctant to follow as Merona made her way up along the riverside, deeper

into the misty wetlands, he was even more unwilling to stay behind alone, and so trotted hesitantly behind her in protesting whimpers for the first few yards.

The mist grew heavier as the river grew wider and Merona trudged on, ignoring her companion's whimpers in the knowledge that whatever creature had so recently killed and eaten the carcass, was far less imperative a concern than the supplies they might uncover should they locate the crashed plane. Soon, Merona began to spot more signs of wreckage caught along the stream and her suspicions were proven correct when the shadowy form of a large, crumpled heap came into view ahead.

One wing of the plane jutted straight up, towering overhead as the aircraft rested on one side, the other wing completely severed from the body and laying a short distance away. Bits of wreckage littered the ground in every direction and Merona sized up each piece for its usefulness as she approached the aircraft, collecting a few lightweight metal struts for possible use later.

Taking hold of the crumpled landing gear, Merona ascended the body of the aircraft and swung her feet into the still open side-door. Leaning on the sides of the opening, she carefully lowered herself inside as the dog's barks echoed out behind her. Though the aircraft had sustained less damage on its interior, the tornado of scattered debris, blood, and supplies still gave the impression of carnage.

Broken wicker chairs littered the windows and wall of the overturned cabin, along with several empty and spilling bags of luggage, but one familiar bag caught Merona's eye; it was the backpack she had loaded with leftover supplies before the plane had made its unexpected tumble down the cliff.

Checking its contents, she found nearly all her

gathered goods still inside. Spare slacks and shirts to replace her old torn ones, several clean undershirts, that she might cut up into bandages, torn baggage netting, that would be useful in laying traps, and so on.

Slinging the pack of supplies over her shoulder, Merona looked around and couldn't help remembering the once tidy cabin on their flight out, starkly contrasting its disheveled state now. Even after the crash, the cabin had been more or less intact, besides the scattered luggage and the caved-in side that had killed her fellow passenger in his chair. Suddenly, a jolting realization came over Merona: there was no body.

Casting her gaze around the aircraft, Merona could find no sign of her fellow passenger's corpse. Could it have somehow fallen from the plane during its descent down the cliff? Or been buried beneath wreckage in the fall? Moving forward to the front of the plane where she had left him, she spotted dried blood trailing up along the floor toward the door of the plane, and it seemed clear something had dragged the body from the craft after it had fallen. Stepping back from the disturbing evidence, Merona felt the strong need to finish her search and make a hasty exit, before whatever it was that had taken the body, decided to return.

Carver's dog continued to bark outside, but had no increased sounds of panic in his protests, and so Merona set about picking through the bits of broken wicker chairs, collecting some parts that might work as kindling. Next, she cut down the tattered curtains that adorned the tiny windows, since large squares of fabric like them were a rare find in a place such as this.

Giving a final glance around for any last supplies worth scavenging, her gaze drifted toward the cockpit and the radio therein. The chance seemed a long shot, but with nothing to lose in simply trying, Merona climbed up into the catawampus cockpit, tilting her head to evaluate the sideways controls and flipping on a few switches before something suddenly hummed to life. A sound of static crackled through the lopsided plane as several lights flickered on, and hope rose in Merona's gut at the possibility of what the sound could mean. The radio was working.

CHAPTER XVII

A DEBILITATING DROP

MERONA struggled to remember what basic Morse code her uncle Quincy had taught her, as she relayed only the most important information over the radio.

"SOS. Name Merona Grant. Plane crashed. Between Morocco and Azores. Stranded on unknown island."

She kicked herself for not getting the exact coordinates from Carver before his untimely death, but continued sending what little information she did have. But the radio transmitter only answered her with static.

With a deep sigh, Merona continued on. "Anyone receiving? Plane went down between Morocco and Azores. Stranded on island. Pilot dead. One survivor..." but she quickly corrected herself, "and dog... SOS."

Again, more static answered.

Merona pressed on, repeating all pertinent information for what felt like the hundredth time, and once more she was answered with the same grating fuzz.

"SOS, SOS, SOS," she repeated over and over, growing tired and hopeless at the endless silence in response.

Clenching her fist, she wanted to kick the useless transmitter, but held her restraint, knowing its value outweighed anything else she could hope to salvage from the wreck. But still, nothing had come of her hours of effort, and already the light outside was growing dim.

A timid yelp sounded from outside and Merona remembered her abandoned companion. The day was spent, and she knew the wreckage would be exactly where she left it by morning. She could try again tomorrow. Her day seemed wasted, and as she trudged back along the river toward her camp, her growling stomach reminded her of the dwindling food supply which awaited her there.

She cursed under her breath at the spent hours of precious hunting time she couldn't afford to have idled away as Carver's dog looked up at her with a timid eye, hoping the harsh words weren't directed at him. Oblivious to his glance, Merona walked on, preoccupied with her predicament of dwindling supplies.

She couldn't turn back time, and the chance of sending out a signal that someone, somewhere might hear had been too vitally important to ignore, but she couldn't fall back on her long-term canned supplies forever. She needed food more desperately than ever now, and not just a meal for that night, but enough meat to actually begin cold smoking and storing up for a future emergency. Though the light was already waning, Merona was determined to catch something, *anything* before calling it a day, even if it meant hunting in the dark.

With the find of the baggage netting from the crash she could set a snare and net trap, and knew just the place; an old, lesser used game trail the natives tended to ignore, where she had seen some luck in the past. Though her past snares had often broken when larger game, such as goats and boars, had wandered through them, the new netting offered the hope of being able to keep hold of these meatier catches, and might finally allow her the option of storing up.

Stopping at camp, Merona was quick to exchange her month-old shirt and slacks for the newly procured ones, securing the rest of her findings in the cave before starting off. The glow of twilight hung in the mist as she trekked through the increasingly familiar landmarks of the island. An old, rotted stump, a moss-encrusted boulder, a pike adorned by an increasingly putrefied head atop it, which one gray tribe had left as warning to another, all markers to guide her around the island, all far more familiar to her than she hoped they would ever have become.

A cluster of trees came into view on Merona's left and she knew the game trail was close. Light was dwindling, but if she could get this new trap set, she could have food by morning. The ground began to slope at an abrupt angle, and Merona took hold of available branches or saplings for stability in maneuvering the uneven terrain.

Reaching for the nearest branch Merona felt her boot slipping in the wet leaves. Her hand grabbed hold of the branch in haste, but in the next moment the limb gave way, and her imperfect footing sent her tumbling down the hill, her head meeting with something hard, before plunging her into blackness.

~

Merona's skull pounded as her eyes flickered slowly open. Her limbs refused to move, weighed down under a crushing weariness. Something brushed repeatedly against the skin of her shin, accompanied by steady exhales of hot breath against her cold, exposed leg. It was a tongue. The tongue of some animal was vigorously licking her lower leg.

She struggled to force her eyes open, the licking

animal aggravating her stinging, torn flesh. Pushing up, she forced herself to her elbows and barked out a feeble warning toward the carnivorous scavenger. The shadowy creature shrank back momentarily in the dusky light before returning to the bloody wound.

Merona kicked out to shake the animal off, but pain shot up her leg with the sudden motion and she yelped out. The animal stepped closer to Merona's face before beginning to lick her cheek like a wolf licking its cub.

"Is... is that you boy?" Merona mumbled, as the mutt's large tongue lapped against her chin, lips, and nose.

Her weak hand rose to push him from her face, but already he had returned to her leg, carefully cleaning the raw, open wound he had found there. Merona groaned, willing her body to find the strength to push him away, for fear his efforts might infect the wound all the worse, but her body rebelled, expelling her stomach's contents into the dirt beside her.

Her throat burned as she spat out the remaining acidic taste from her mouth. At last, she began to feel strength returning to her limbs as Carver's dog moved to sniff the new mess his wounded "pup" had left for him and promptly began lapping up Merona's regurgitated leavings. Feeling a rise in her throat at the sight of it, Merona turned away, looking to address the seeping wound on her leg.

The light was all but faded from the sky, and Merona knew she would have to make it back to her cave and campfire before any assessment or cleaning of her injury could be attempted. Pushing up with her arms and good leg, Merona struggled to stand without jostling her injury, but with the first inevitable stabilizing hop, pain shot through her limb, silencing her urge to scream as she toppled to the ground again.

A smell of vomit assailed Merona's senses as the dog nosed up to her face to check her wellbeing with a lick on the cheek. She paid him little mind, her thoughts focused on how to begin her long trek back without endless, crippling pain. A thick branch lay nearby and with slow, methodical adjustments, Merona inched toward it, painfully crawling on her side to keep her injured leg out of use.

Nearing her objective, she reached out for the stick, her fingers just brushing against the rough bark which sat annoyingly out of reach.

"Blasted thing!" Merona spat, propping up on her elbow to inch just a little closer, but before she had scarcely moved a centimeter, her objective was snatched from her.

Taking up the hefty stick in his jaw, the mutt tilted his head at his companion in bewilderment as she waived her hand at him to leave it be. Then, showing an unexpected attunement to her thoughts, he stepped forward and dropped the stick conveniently at her side.

Merona gazed up, surprised and unaccustomed to the animal's instinctive, helpful nature, but delighted with the idea of getting used to it.

"Thanks... good dog," she said, scratching appreciatively under his chin before taking a deep breath and slowly rising on her new crutch.

It was time to start her trek back to camp, and she knew every step would be anguish.

~

Merona's bleeding shin throbbed. Each step, each momentary jostling, no matter how small, seemed to make her limb scream, to scrape at her nerves and demand she halt and allow her body to rest. Scarcely a third of the way back and already her body was relenting to the constant, repetitive pain of walking.

Gingerly resting against a tree, Merona took out her flask to quench her mounting thirst, but moments before the fresh water hit her lips, a realization of the paramount importance of the liquid hit her.

She had learned to manage her drinking water throughout her stay, satiating her thirst during the day, before sundown could putrefy her water sources, but the sun had all but set, and in moments the small flask would be undrinkable. But more than that, its clear waters were the only means of cleansing her injury she had to hand, and if she did not address it now, the risk of infection would grow.

Without hesitation she pulled back her pantleg, spilling the water out across her shin in the darkness before the last hints of light had vanished away. A final trickle of water ran down her skin, washing clean the blood and dirt before Merona pulled the flask back in haste. A few moments later, as she lifted it to her nose, she could smell a hint of that boggy scent at the rim. She had used the water just in time and now would have no drinkable liquids until morning.

Leaning against her sturdy stick, Merona trudged on, wincing with every step as the dog followed along wondering what he might do to ease his companion's endless whimpers.

Darkness closed in and Merona's steps were disrupted all the more by the uneven terrain. Her leg was crippled, her sight now blinded by the night, and every painful stride was made all the more difficult by the unseen vines and stones which caught hold of her boot or smashed against her toes. Ordinary annoyances for a nighttime excursion, but now, each became an agonizing torment which swiftly ate away at her endurance.

Hours passed and her resolve waned. Leaning against a tree, Merona halted for what seemed like the hundredth time to overcome the blinding pain that assailed her. At her back, a small nose nudged against her leg, her four-legged companion doing the little he could to encourage her on. Merona marveled at his loyalty. It had only been a few days since they had become one another's only companions, and though he had likely clung to her for protection in the beginning, he seemed now to show full dedication in watching her back.

Leaning on her crutch, she walked on, pain once more shooting through her leg, but the discomfort was getting worse. She could feel her knee beginning to swell and stiffen and she knew that in a few hours' time, it would be all but unusable. Her teeth gritted, clenching back the pain as she pushed on, demanding the unbearable from her battered body.

Carver's dog danced in front of her, a guiding beacon of reassurance to follow along the road, as he silently steered her onto softer, winding paths. Tighter, and tighter, her muscles resisted every stride, punishing her for every pigheaded step, every dogged show of grit to keep going.

She could smell the swamp now, the welcoming stench of safety, but as the fumes hit her a wave of nausea overtook her and she fell to the dirt as all went black for the second time that evening.

Merona awoke to a tugging at her coat collar. Hot breath puffed against her neck as the ground beneath her slid out from under her legs, bumping against her boots as she went. Her eyes fought to stay open, fluttering groggily as her body bumped along.

The nauseous smell of swamp grew stronger around her as dampness seeped in at her back, but still her limbs and mind would not wake. Time and consciousness drifted in and out and when Merona's eyes at last chose to open, a small red ember flickered weakly before her. She was inside the cave.

A heavy panting echoed in her ears and Merona turned over to find the mutt's glinting black eyes staring down at her. Strength slowly flowed back into her weak limbs and she pushed up onto one of her elbows, crawling toward the fire to reignite the embers.

In the blackness, she felt for more wood, slowly rebuilding the fire back into life until the small, damp cave glittered with light. Next, she pealed her tattered pant leg back from the wound, the fabric sticking and tugging free from the crusted blood which coated her shin. The wound was ragged, partially scabbed over from the long return trek, and Merona gingerly examined the deeper gouges before crawling toward her newly acquired pack and rummaging for a clean shirt.

She slit the fabric into long bandages, wrapping one after another around her leg until the exposed, raw flesh was fully covered. Every movement sent stifling waves of pain through her swollen, stiff leg, and when at last her bandages were secured, she sank back on the stony ground, gulping in deep breaths of air as her only means to ease the pain.

Sleep seemed the only thing Merona's mind could think on, and as her eyes fell heavy once again, she felt a warm, furry body shift in and huddle up beside her as she drifted off.

~

Light flickered through Merona's eyelashes as she slowly awoke. Shifting on the rough rock floor, her stiff leg throbbed, the pain stabbing at her with even the slightest twitch of movement. She gasped out. It hurt much worse than before, and for a moment Merona sat still, fearful to move even an inch for the risk of more pain.

Foggy light filled the cave, illuminating the small stash of food in the corner just out of reach, and with the sight of it Merona's hunger assailed her. She eased up onto one arm, careful not to jar her leg, but with the single jolt of settling onto her elbow, pain shot through her limb, nearly sending her dropping back to the ground.

Catching her breath from the moment of blinding pain, Merona readjusted, trying to find a position where she could begin to crawl toward her supplies, but with every attempt to adjust, the pain intensified, gouging at her ability to even move.

Again and again, she tried to shift into a position that would serve any kind of use, but with each attempt, the pain came close to bringing tears to her eyes. It was no use. She had lost all mobility and her scant food supplies, which lay only a few yards from her, were wholly unreachable.

Her stomach growled, gnawing at her ribs with every moment that passed. Feeling through her pockets for a solution her hand hit upon the flask, and without thinking she flung it to her mouth, but the old dribbling remains of swamp assailed her senses, and she dropped the container with a ringing clank. The putrid taste still lingered on her lips, increasing the nausea the past hours of pain had brought on.

Something churned in her stomach, rising up her throat until it forced its way to the surface. She retched, her mind thinking only on the precious fluids spilling to the floor that her body could not afford to lose.

The jolting of her body jarred her leg still more, but the sickness would have its way. Spitting out the last remains of stomach acid, she tried and failed to clear the taste from her teeth and lips, gazing down at the wasted liquid as she remembered the dog and his instinctive solution the night before, of re-ingesting it.

She turned away, pushing the thought from her head to avoid reigniting the churning in her stomach, which growled all the more vigorously from being emptied. Her head rested on the rough stone floor, as she stared at the pack of food still sitting in its corner. Weak, hungry, dehydrated and immobile, a sudden dazed smile crossed her lips, and Merona found herself emitting a feeble chuckle.

"So, this is it?" she said aloud to herself. "I'm going to starve to death, stuck in a cave, in my own vomit, with food laying just out of reach?"

The satchel sat in its corner, almost mocking her to reach it, but her leg still throbbed, even in its unmoving state. Slowly she tried again, to push herself up onto her elbows as she turned toward the lifeless fire. On its edge, a large stick rested mostly unburned, and Merona took in a deep breath and reached for it. Her hand fell upon the wood, and with measured restraint, pulled it from the fire. Her leg remained still, coddled in its semi-bent posture as Merona worked to move her upper body wholly independent of her lower limbs. She would reach the food, no matter how long it took... no matter how painful it would be.

Placing the stick on the floor, Merona slid one end slowly toward the pack, extending her reach as far as possible, but as she came to her limit, the stick fell a few feet out of reach of the food. She cursed. She would have to move closer. But pain was preferable to starvation.

Turning her back toward the pack, she placed her

palms on the ground at her sides, pushing out with her good leg in a tripodal crawl. Her swollen knee flexed, the stiffness screaming at her to halt, but she pressed on. Each agonizing inch stabbed at her injury; the stomp of her boot on the stone, the jostling as she shuffled along the ground, the thud of her body as she shifted her hips backward across the cave, crawling, inching, the pain mounting with every awkward movement.

Tears fogged her vision, but she clenched her teeth in defiance of the pain, shifting closer to her target. Halting, she turned to find the pack and reached out toward it with the stick once again. The end of it just touched the bag, and Merona strained to flick open the top flap. The pack stood stubbornly against her efforts and she hit toward it with frustration, jarring her leg with the attempt.

She cried out, turning and clutching her knee as a small thump and metallic clink sounded behind her. Looking back, she spotted a small can rolling from the satchel across the jagged stone, halting on a lip of rock not far from the pack. "Red Salmon" was scrawled across the tin in bold red lettering and the word alone made her parched mouth water.

Stick in hand, she reached for the canned fish, tapping, and nudging it in the hopes it might roll closer toward her, but with each prodding attempt it seemed to roll further from her reach. She struggled, resolute in her persistence to attain the can, but as her next attempt sent a jarring shock of pain through her leg once again, she released her hold of the stick, sending it tumbling across the floor out of reach.

Merona cussed repeatedly. "This is ridiculous, woman!" She snapped at herself. "Here you are, sitting on your *rear*, poking at a tin from a distance because going over there and getting it might *hurt* too much.

Grow a backbone, you worthless waif!"

With her personal pep-talk concluded, Merona rallied herself to press forward, teeth clenching without relent. At last, reaching the tin, she sank against the back wall of the cave, un-pocketing her pocketknife and prying into her well-earned breakfast with keen fervor.

Within moments the can had been emptied and Merona sat still, her nausea abating for the moment as she stared towards the cavern opening in empty thought. But her exhausted mind soon raised a nagging question: where was the dog?

Since waking up that day she had not seen one scraggly hair of his head, and she wondered what might have taken him from the cave. Where had he gotten to, and what was keeping him? Was he hunting for his own meal or had something frightened him off? Or worse, had something taken him by force?

Watching out the mouth of the cave, she waited; hoping he would return as she sat, imagining all the dangers he might be facing out there alone. She knew there was nothing she could do to find him or the answers to her many questions. The dog had left, either of his own accord or by force, and she was powerless to discover why. For all she knew, he had abandoned her in her weakened state, with no intention of returning. If he was able to return and chose to do so, she would have her answer, but until then she needed to focus her worries on her own survival.

Still hungry after her meal, Merona inched painfully toward the satchel, eager to assess her remaining food rations in the hopes that they might see her through the days of healing that her injury would require, but those hopes fell with the few small remaining tins of food that tumbled from the bag.

She would barely be able to ration her scant supplies

through the next couple days, let alone the weeks it might take to fully heal. She would have no chance of hunting to replenish her supplies with such an injury, nor be able to make it out to the river for water to stave off her increasing dehydration.

Her unavoidable starvation flooded her mind, along with the knowledge that she could do nothing to prevent it, but knowing the mere act of allowing her mind to wander into such despairing thoughts was detrimental to her survival in and of itself, Merona searched the small cave for a means of distraction.

The cave had little to offer. The space was small, dank, and dimly lit in spite of the glow of day which fell inside, and Merona's gaze drifted across the trail of light, which softly landed on the wall opposite her, illuminating the jagged rocks. Within the shadows of the stone, a slight hint of shapes caught Merona's attention, and she gingerly shifted herself closer to the images.

Across the wall danced painted figures, faded into near oblivion by time, but still barely visible in the daylight. Human figures were scattered across the jagged rock, half painted in white, the other half painted in red, bearing the boar head which was all too familiar to Merona. The two tribes clashed in battle across the wall, with the boar head tribe clearly overwhelming the other in each successive and violent depiction. Some paintings were too worn to be seen, but the final drawing showed a small family of white figures huddled around a fire, a great green-eyed creature standing over them.

Merona found herself fascinated by the images and the history of the island they depicted. Had the natives painted them in years past? Had they once lived within the caves of the swamp she now occupied? Had they fled here for refuge from their enemies just as she had? And if so, where were they now? What had become of those who had left behind the paintings on the wall?

She gazed at the images, wondering if they might present some kind of answer to it all, but the light outside the cave began to fade, and the faint figures with it. Her stomach growled, turning her thoughts from cave paintings to more pressing concerns. The small tin of food had been insufficient, and she found herself eyeing one of her last remaining tins with parched lips.

Phillips Delicious Condensed Chicken Noodle Soup. The words ran through her mind again and again, the word "delicious" catching her eye far more than the rest. But she knew she must ignore her stomach's complaints and ration the meal for as long as she could stand. She had to hope her knee was healing fast enough, and if she could hold out until she could walk again, one rationed meal might be the difference between life and death.

She pushed the food out of sight, waiting in silence as the day wore on. Hours passed with still no sign of the mutt and Merona found her thoughts drifting to any and all subjects she was presently powerless to do a solitary thing about. What had happened to her dog? What was in the swamp that the natives feared so much? Was she going to heal fast enough to go out hunting? Or was this how she was going to die?

She struggled to think on questions she might actually find a means of addressing, but little came to mind. Her leg was immobilized, and any attempt to utilize her other working limbs, only exacerbated the pain. She needed to be strategic in her movements, only pushing herself when absolutely needed, and so the day wore on. Hunger grew, light faded, and night approached, forcing Merona to make the choice between holding off the growing cold, or sparing her dwindling pile of wood.

Huddling near the feeble embers, she tried to

convince herself that this night was milder than the others had been, but the sharp winds attested otherwise, and she had soon wrapped herself in the thin curtains from the plane salvage the day before. Events which now felt ages past.

Her consciousness drifted, and for a moment of wakefulness, she thought she felt that familiar warm gray hide, as he huddled beside her in the night.

CHAPTER XVIII

IMMOBILIZED

HELLO? We read you. This is Liora Grant. Are you telling me you have news of my sister's whereabouts?"

"Affirmative," returned the gravelly voice of the ship captain over the radio. "We have received a distress call from a Merona Grant, saying she is stranded on an island."

"What island? Where?"

"No coordinates were received, but given our location at the time we received the call, she is likely in the Macaronesia region of the North Atlantic."

"Were you able to communicate with her to ascertain if she was injured or in immediate distress?"

"Negative. We sent back a message, but had no acknowledgment that she received our reply. Only a repeat of her original distress call. We suspect her receiver is broken, but we will continue to try and make contact."

"Of course," muttered Sasha to himself. "Crash would have broken radio. It miracle she can send out signal at all."

"So, she can't receive any message to tell her we're on our way?" asked Liora.

"It seems not," replied Antonio. "But what's that matter? What's important is she's alive! And stranded on some island, just as you hoped. Let's count our blessings that she could transmit *at all*."

"All right, thank you, Captain," replied Liora into the radio. "If you receive any further information on her whereabouts or condition, send them on to us."

The captain responded in the affirmative before signing out.

"*Da*, that it," said Sasha. "Merona is alive out there, so we must not waste time. We head out tonight."

"As much as I want to," began Liora, "we haven't any money left, Sasha. And we aren't going to get very far in our search on *fumes*. Not to mention those repairs on Katya that you've been postponing."

"Katya fly just fine until Merona is home."

"A nice sentiment, but we can't borrow money off my uncle forever. He's already had to dismiss several pilots he had out searching for Merona just to keep us up in the air, and the captain listening for further signals. No, he can't fund this search forever, we need to do our part to replenish our funds."

"We not just *leave* Merona out there."

"Well, of course not! This is a momentary delay, that's all."

"But…"

"Sasha, she's *alive*. We aren't just searching on hope now. And besides, this is Merona we're talking about; if *anyone* can survive on an island for over a month, it's her. We'll find her once we've got the funds."

"But where we get money?"

Liora smiled. "I know exactly where we can get some."

Sasha squinted. "If this is another money lender…"

Liora blinked innocently. "Sasha, I'm hurt. I know how to get money in other ways than borrowing it from shady lenders."

"We *not* stealing it."

"Okay, if you insist. Money lender it is."

"That not what I mean..."

Before Sasha could argue, Liora snatched up his bomber jacket off the back of his chair and tossed it in his lap. "Let's go get some money and find my sister."

Soon after, Katya was humming to life on the runway, preparing a return trip to Cairo. Sasha slipped his goggles into place as Liora took her seat beside him, renewed determination running through their blood. Merona's message had given them the ray of hope their fruitless search had needed. She was alive, and on solid ground, and they both knew she would fight with every last ounce of willpower to stay that way. They could hardly show less fervor in finding her.

~

A sharp gouging in Merona's leg stirred her from sleep. The pain was getting worse.

Outside, the darkness of night still clouded the sky, an imperceivable hint of morning just beginning to creep into the shadows. Merona shifted beneath her insufficient coverings, wincing with every move.

Hours passed and pale light began to grow outside, though the stifling smell of the swamp still hung in the air. Merona's eyes drifted open and shut with each passing moment, struggling between her need for sleep and the shooting pain which held sleep at bay.

The cave was devoid of all life but her own, with still no sign of Carver's dog to be found. She remembered the feeling of fur and warmth as she had drifted off before, but had she only imagined his return in the night? She suspected so.

On the floor nearby still sat her last cans of food and Merona forced her eyes to turn away, keen to ignore the tempting labels and the persistent gnawing of her stomach which the mere sight of them exacerbated. As the thought of food filled her mind, an unearthly chattering jarred her attention. It had been nearby, only a few yards from the mouth of the cave, and Merona sat upright, still and silent as she waited for a repetition of the noise.

The chattering sounded once again, its resonance deep and bubbling. Merona slid her machete from its sheath, careful to make no noise as she drew her weapon. A shadow fell across the rocky floor outside her cave in the form of an upright, misshapen, humanoid figure.

Was it a gray man scout? Merona struggled to ready herself, but with still no ability to stand, her foot awkwardly kicked out as she shifted, spilling a few shards of burnt wood across the stony floor. The soft tumble of firewood rang out like thunder in the hushed stillness of the moment, and Merona cursed her carelessness as she gripped tightly to her machete, her only means of defense.

She waited, watching the shadow as it wandered closer to the mouth of the cave. The vines which partially concealed its opening trembled in the breeze, and a sound of hoarse breathing approached. The sounds grew nearer, a faint gurgle bubbling up between wheezes. Merona readied herself, despising her weakened state as much as she feared it.

She was trapped, not only in the cave, but on the small patch of ground at its center. Nothing stood between her and her approaching foe, save the small pile of ash and wood from the night's campfire. In the next second Merona grabbed hold of a handful of ash from her fire, arming herself with a means of temporarily blinding her foe, in the hopes of gaining some kind of upper hand in the desperate situation.

Plodding footsteps neared, sloshing amid the swampy grounds beyond her cave, and with each step, the stench of bog increased. Merona threw her elbow across her mouth and nose to keep the suffocating smell at bay, stifling her urge to cough it from her lungs, but as she struggled not to make another sound, a hand reached out to part the vines at the opening.

Merona squinted in disbelief. The hand was not human, though complete with five fingers, each ended in a long, razor-like claw, connected by fibrous webs which grew between them. It glistened with slime, dripping film and boggy sludge as it reached out to part the vines which barred its path.

The growing light of day cast a glistening halo over the slimy arm and webbed claws, but as Merona raised her weapons in readiness, the strange hand halted, trembling in the light as the slow breathing grew rapid and tremulous. Without warning it jerked back, vanishing from sight, the slap, slap, slap of its rapid footsteps the only sounds which followed, but with its departure, so too departed the gagging smell of bog.

Merona sat, breathing deep and tentatively as she did the only thing she could, waited and watched the cave's entrance for the creature to return. The light grew brighter and day fully dawned, and soon Merona loosened her hold of her weapon, grateful she had been spared the necessity of using it. What had it been? Why had it vanished? And what would she do if it chose to visit a second time? These questions nagged at her mind, along with many others, and she cursed her inability to do anything about it all.

Many a time in her past, Merona had been forced to face a formidable challenge head-on, but here she was trapped, trapped with her thoughts, her fears, her restless need to *do* something about her increasingly hopeless situation, and no way of doing it. She had felt less helpless facing a wild lion, or the teaming armies of gray men than she did now. She could barely stand, and it made her defenseless against attack. She couldn't move but a few feet around her isolated cave without severe pain, so that even venturing out for water seemed impossible. She was penned in like a caged animal forgotten by its owner, and as the hours passed, her hunger and thirst steadily mounted.

Merona struggled to ignore her last remaining tins of food, focusing on anything and everything else she could find, but in the cramped, dingy cave, her lack of mobility left her with limited options. The day wore on as Merona shifted her attention from stirring the fire's embers and trying in vain to soothe the growing pain in her knee and stomach.

Her stomach growled, its gnawing pain almost overpowering the stabbing in her leg. The tins sat out of sight behind her, almost seeming to call out to her as the dampness of the cave drip, drip, dripped against the metal of the cans, like the pounding of a hammer on an anvil, but she knew the longer she waited the better the chance of waiting out her injury became. She had eaten the night before, she could force herself to wait until night fell and leave herself the hope that her leg might recover in the next day or so.

Her head began to pound with every drip that rang out against the tins, the hours without water taking its toll. But as the sound rang through her ears, Merona realized her own stupidity.

"Dripping!" she spat. "Water dripping in the cave!"

Turning toward the tinned food, Merona painfully crawled toward it, and the gathered water which dripped from above onto her supplies. Pulling her flask from her pocket, she held it beneath the precious liquid,

waiting as the painful moments dragged by before it was at last filled.

Throwing the flask back in nearly one gulp, she returned for seconds, drinking back as much as she could gather to quench her debilitating thirst. The food nearby grew ever more tempting as the natural next course, but she persisted in her resistance.

Hours felt like days, but at last the light outside began to dim, and Merona tapped into one of her last remaining tins. As she wolfed down its contents in only a few heaping bites, her trepidation for the coming days and how she could possibly survive, consumed her every thought.

~

Merona awoke to a crushing headache and ashen dryness in her mouth. It had been three days since her injury and though she had a small supply of water dripping within her cave, it was hardly enough to hold back the effects of dehydration.

Every stiff joint and tired limb resisted her efforts to sit up and move toward the trickling, life sustaining liquid for a much-needed drink. The swelling of her knee remained, and the violent, stabbing pain along with it, dismantling her leg's mobility, and forcing her still to crawl. She could feel the cool water as it cascaded down her throat and into her hollow stomach, her last can of food having been long since consumed the day before.

Laying back against the wall of the cave, Merona's willpower to move fully abandoned her. The light had been streaming in at the mouth of the cave for some time now, she didn't know how long, as her mind was scarcely able to process the change of night to day. Her weak eyes gazed sluggishly around the cavern, finding still no sign of her dog's return. Hours passed and she began to drift off, her starving body fighting to conserve its last remaining traces of energy.

Her mind wandered to dreams of the figures on the cavern wall as they began to come alive and run across the ragged rocks, one group slaughtering the other, burning their homes until the few remaining survivors were forced to retreat into the swamp for protection, just as Merona had done.

Then, creeping from its place on the rock wall, the strange inhuman figure began to grow within Merona's dream, morphing from the scratched art of the rocks into a fully formed creature, growing until it towered over her, its webbed hands dripping with slime and bog water... until a thunderous bark shook her into consciousness.

Merona's eyes flickered open to find the familiar, happy, shaggy gray face sitting before her, puffing continuous waves of hot, stagnant breath down across her face. His wagging tail thumped against the stone floor, and as Merona's eyes creeped fully open, they fell upon the sight of a ragged, bloody kill resting across his paws.

Merona stared in disbelief, laying prone on her back and blinking toward the happy animal and his dumbfounding presence. She could not believe the sight before her, wholly astounded that after so long the mutt had returned at all, let alone bearing the very thing she vitally needed: food.

But as the mutt remained, his foul breath continually washing over her, Merona forced her weak limbs to stagger upright, reaching for the kill with a desperate, shaking hand. Fur and blood seeped between her fingers as she grasped the dead animal. Her hunger clawed at her, urging her to bite into the raw meat of the kill, but her rational mind still held out, forcing her to skin and clean the kill, before reigniting her fire with her last remaining bits of wood. But even with these tasks complete, the agonizing delay as the rodent roasted over the fire, filling the cave with its mouthwatering smell, was more painful than any hunger she previously experienced.

Well-cooked or not, Merona hastened to sink her teeth into the seared flesh, feverishly ripping chunks of meat from it. Grease dribbled down her chin, but the well in her stomach seemed incapable of being filled, and as she turned it over in her hands to begin on the other half, her eyes turned toward her savior who sat patiently watching her, his large, black eyes gazing up at her in complete trust. With a small moment of hesitation, Merona tossed the rest of the carcass toward him, watching as the still hungry animal tugged every last bit of flesh from its bones.

She reached out and patted his scraggly head. "Hope that's enough buddy. Got to keep your strength up too."

His tail wagged in reply.

"And thank you," Merona whispered. "Thanks for coming back to look after me. I think you just saved my life, boy... you're a good boy."

CHAPTER XIX

LOYALTY ON FOUR LEGS

WITH the backpack Merona had salvaged from the plane now safely holding all her supplies, her small, torn waxed canvas bag could now serve a new, more pertinent purpose. Merona had spent a good many hours cutting up and restringing the fabric into a good sized water pouch, and now sat securing it to her dog's neck.

"There," Merona muttered, feeling quite satisfied with her hours of tinkering to complete the simple task. "This actually might work."

The mutt looked at her with simple confusion, oblivious to the task he was being set as the open pouch hung low from his neck.

"Okay boy, can you go to the river? Yeah? That's right, go run through the river and get me some water."

His head tilted in bewilderment.

"Come on boy, go get it! Go get the water!" Clapping her hands with enthusiasm, she gestured emphatically toward the river.

He stood still, glancing at her hand itself, instead of what it was indicating toward.

"Come on boy, go get it!" Merona repeated, doing her utmost to manufacture a voice of cheerfulness, but the result remained the same.

Repetition after repetition, the mutt seemed incapable of comprehending the request of his human, but as Merona's frustration mounted she reached out for a twig, hurling it across the cave in exasperation. Like lightning, he dove for the stick, snatching it from the ground and returning it to her with delight.

Merona's weary eyes fell on the stick, now lying at her feet, and for the first time in days, a smile spread across her face. "Hey, boy," she said with true enthusiasm, "you want to play?"

His tail wagged wildly and without hesitation Merona took up the stick and began to crawl toward the cave's mouth, eager and desperate to find any means of retrieving drinkable water. If the dog couldn't understand her words, she would speak to him in a way he would understand: a game of fetch.

Her hope was that the water pouch might gather up some water from the river as he ran through to retrieve the stick, if she could manage to throw it that far. Halting at the entrance, Merona made one last check on the secureness of the pouch at her loyal companion's neck, then with a powerful heave, she lobbed the twig toward the river.

The eager dog leapt forward, diving for the stick which had landed on a patch of soggy moss, dragging his water pouch through the grime of the forest floor as he snatched up the stick and rushed back toward the awaiting adventuress.

Her throw had fallen short that time, but Merona was still determined. Shaking the pouch clean, she then hurled the stick out once more, this time hitting the river with ease. He dashed out, gulping up his prize along with a mouthful of water, and Merona watched in anticipation as his body submerged cleanly into the running stream.

The mutt returned, his soggy tail wagging as Merona patted his head, hastily unhooking the water pouch hanging around his neck.

Taking up the pouch, she gulped back its refreshing contents as her companion shook his dripping fur out across her legs and face. She couldn't be bothered to care, as she enjoyed a second and third drink of cool water. Breathing a sigh as the fresh gulp of water seeped into her dried-out mouth, throat, and stomach, Merona resecured the water pouch around her mutt companion's neck for another trip outside.

The stick flew from her hand once again and he rushed from the cave, dunking the hanging pouch into the water as he snatched up his twiggy prize for a second time. Throw after throw, and drink after drink, Merona began to regain her strength, the throbbing in her head and stiffness in her joints slowly subsiding.

Once again, the happy mutt had been her savior, and as the day came to a close, Merona enjoyed the last sip from her pouch, stroking behind her dog's ear as he lay panting at her side.

"You're a good dog, you know that? I won't forget this, not in a hundred years. You're sticking with me buddy."

With a flopping wag of his tail, he plopped his chin on her swollen knee.

Merona bit her lip against the jolt of pain and breathed a halting sigh. "Thanks boy... that was *just* what I needed."

As Merona sat looking at the animal who had now saved her from both starvation and dehydration all in a matter of hours, she couldn't help thinking how wrong it felt to go on calling him "boy" or "dog" or any of the other impersonal words his former master had used to address him. In the short time she had known him, this animal had shown incredible loyalty, instinct, and smarts, and deserved to at last have a proper name to capture such qualities.

"What should we call you then?" Merona said allowed. "All the dog names that come to mind seem too mundane for an exceptional animal like yourself. Toto is too small a namesake... Bull's Eye might do... or maybe Buck?"

But the dog lay still, not responding even the slightest to any of the names listed.

"Hmmm... yeah, I don't think any of those are right for you either," Merona went on, thinking aloud. "What you need is a legendary name, like Haracles!"

The mutt looked vaguely concerned at the suggestion.

"Only something less predictable than that... and preferably a figure not so inclined towards insanity or murder... Perseus perhaps? Or *Cerberus!* Hmmm... no, too much of a mouthful. It needs to be short and simple, but strong... wait a minute, I know who you remind me of... I saw a picture in one of Liora's books once and I swear the dog looked just like you! We'll name you after Argos, Odysseus's loyal dog! If there is one ancient hero I'm feeling a lot like just now, it's *him*. What do you say old boy? I'll be your Odysseus, if you be my Argos?"

The mutt raised his head, perking up to her words for the first time.

"Argos..." Merona repeated. "Yeah, I think it suits you. You think you could warm to it? Argos."

His tail wagged slightly at the word.

"There you go! You're warming to it already! That a boy, Argos! I think we found your name at last."

~

A week passed and Merona's leg saw little improvement, but day after day she was increasingly grateful for her four-legged companion and his continued, though not always consistent, kills. Each day she would awake to an empty cave and idle away the hours as she eagerly anticipated Argos' return with food.

Some days his hunt would garner nothing, and Merona would be forced to face an agonizing crawl to the edge of the cave to scavenge for what bugs and grubs she might find in the nearby mud for both of them. Other days, however, Argos made his return with a muskrat, gofer, or snake, and the two would feast on fatty meat, but on the chance day that he returned with a kill of baby boar or goat, Merona was conscientious enough to set it aside, carefully cold smoking the extra meat over the fire for extended preservation for any unlucky days to come.

In her idle hours throughout the day, Merona found any task to occupy herself with. Spare shirts were torn into bandages, the holes in her clothing from past wounds were re-stitched with a makeshift needle whittled from a sliver of wood, threads being scavenged from any fraying piece of fabric available.

Gathering any available leather cords, she also began stringing together her collection of curtains into a crude blanket, and though it still contained many holes which the cold night air might find its way through, the guard against the elements proved a welcome change, and well worth the hours of effort.

The nights soon became a time of uncertainty for the two companions, as the shadow of the strange figure made yet more appearances outside the cave. One night, Merona awoke to Argos' rigid silhouette standing next to her, his gaze fixed on the mouth of the cave as something moved outside. The stagnant water sloshed as the menacing shadow loomed closer, before halting just outside the cave entrance, its shuddering breaths trembling through the camp as it sniffed near the mouth of the cave, scenting out, she knew not what.

Merona awaited its invasion into her unprotected camp, wondering if all her good luck (not that she had had a startling amount of it) was about to turn south. But once again, the figure moved off, leaving behind nothing more than strange, webbed footprints in the mud outside the cave for Merona to discover, come morning.

The nights that followed became a waiting game to see if the web-footed creature might return, the uncertainty eating away at Merona's sleep each night it didn't reappear, and completely disrupting it, when it did. But with every return, something would always send it off before Merona could get a proper glimpse of it.

Days and nights passed on, and at last the swelling in Merona's knee began to subside, leaving the stir-crazy adventuress almost too eager to get moving. Taking up a stick as a crutch, she began making daily trips to the river for much-needed water, as well as to, once again, begin a routine of setting and checking her traps. Soon her storage of smoked meat began to grow, but with it, her knee's healing started to regress.

Every step began once again to stab at her, urging her to return to her sedentary life within the cave for further healing as much as possible, but with each new day that dawned, Merona found yet more imperative tasks required for her mere survival, and pushed her injury to its limits each day. At last, her body could take her abuse no longer, and with a single misstep Merona's knee suddenly buckled beneath her, the days of warning bringing about an abrupt relapse to her hobbled condition. She tried in vain to stand until at last she was forced to admit defeat, crawling back to her cave to sit out the remaining day.

Another week passed with agonizingly slow improvement, but as she found her mobility once again beginning to return to her, she was determined to take it easy, allowing her leg its chance to heal as she lived off the remaining stores of smoked provisions and Argos' occasional kill.

Merona was convinced, as she lay down for the night, that she had idled too long and, no matter how much her leg still hurt, she would need to venture outside to reset her traps once more, come morning. Sleep was taking hold of Merona, but a strange scratching pricked her ears awake. Something besides Argos and herself moved within the cave, and it was not the web-fingered creature, as the sounds seemed too low to the ground.

Before Merona could ready herself for whatever invader had entered her camp in the blackness of the night, she felt a thick pressure on her injured leg, crying out in pain as she suddenly saw what creature had taken hold of her: an immense boa constrictor was squeezing tight around her knee.

In the next moment she was wrestling the writhing serpent, as it slithered up her body, twisting rapidly to enclose around Merona's throat and head. She fought to force it back, her tired limbs collapsing against the strength of its gigantic body, but Argos leapt into action, biting and ripping the animal from her in a desperate, snarling panic.

Switching targets, the snake coiled around Argos, who whimpered and yelped in reply. Snatching up her machete, Merona scrambled to grab hold of the python's head, slamming her blade down into its neck.

With what she felt must have been her luckiest break yet, or perhaps only her tenth luckiest break, all things considered, the python soon lay dead on the ground.

"Well, boy," Merona said, panting. "Looks like our dinner came to us for once."

Argos snarled at the snake, now laying limp on the ground, still not quite over the trauma of having it grasped around his head. But the danger had passed, and all the companions need do next was feast on their meaty spoils, smoking and saving what remained for the days to come.

It would be nearly a month before Merona could walk without the aid of her crutch, but for the spirited, and impatient adventuress, it felt more like a year.

CHAPTER XX

THE SHADOW OF THE SWAMP

MERONA limped through the tangled underbrush. Her knee had finally had a proper chance to heal, and only slight residual pain persisted as she set out that day for a long overdue hunt. Argos was delighted to have his hunting companion returned to him at last and trotted joyfully at her side as they trudged on.

The scant remains of smoked python were running low, and the traps she had set up near the river had garnered little, leaving Merona determined to bag a goat or boar that day. Nothing less would do. Her body was rapidly becoming a lean mass of muscle and sinew after more than two months on a diet of predominantly grubs and lean meat, and she hoped to finally procure enough fatty meat for a proper full meal that night.

"You've been hunting out here on your own for a while, Argos. Care to show me some of your favorite spots?"

Argos's tail waggled, stepping out in front as though he understood exactly what she was asking, and Merona followed along, eager for him to somehow lead her to a game trail of value, but in the next moment, as he snatched up a stick from the brush and shoved it against her leg, her hopes quickly dwindled.

"It's not time to play, boy. Drop it."

The stick remained in his jaws.

Argos's eyes gazed up at her in pleading, and finally she relented to hurl the object as requested for just a moment or two. Throw after throw and his eagerness for the game was still not sated, so Merona decided to continue on regardless. She had no interest in trying to argue with the languageless animal, nor was there any point in trying to convince him to put the game to rest, and so as they walked along, the slobbery stick continued to be nudged against her leg with every step, Argos eager to renew his companion's former interest in the exhilarating game.

His incessant efforts eventually fading, Argos still trotted along, stick in mouth, as Merona was at last left to focus on her misty surroundings. It seemed her months on the foggy island had honed her senses to function beyond sight alone, as she listened for creaks and skitterings in the distance, or breathed in the scents on the air. The fog restricted her view, but she had learned other means of tracking her prey.

As she pressed on, a thick aroma of sour musk drifted through the wind, and though not long ago her mind might have dismissed the smell as yet another unpleasant odor of the island, Merona knew now that she was nearing an illustrious prize.

She had found the trail of a goat.

Moments before the scent had hit her nose, the stick had fallen from Argos's jaws, his nose soon twitching and exploring the air with renewed excitement for the hunt ahead. All at once he hastened out in front, and Merona was glad to follow behind his much keener senses, to lead them all the quicker down upon their prey.

The soft tapping of Argos' paws and Merona's boots became the only sounds to be heard, as the two moved swiftly along the forest floor, Merona trailing quietly behind with her spear at the ready. An echoing bleat drifted toward them and in the next moment Merona could see the goat's pale, gray shadow ahead.

Raising her spear for the killing shot, she heard Argos snort out at her side, and before she could reach down to hush him, he had bolted free, beelining straight for their prey. Merona's hand stretched out in vain as Argos was engulfed by the fog, charging into the pale void after the franticly fleeing goat.

Merona stamped her foot. He had scared off their prey, and if he failed to catch it, she would have to return empty-handed from her first hunting trip in over a month. But before her bitter frustration could begin to dissipate, a loud clattering of hooves hastened toward her from the mist. The goat was now rushing in her direction from out of the fog.

Argos had herded it back toward her. Back toward his pack. Only a few yards from colliding with her, the goat sighted Merona and skidded to a halt, tumbling to the dirt before veering off to her right in a frantic scramble to escape its pursuers.

With the goat darting by at point-blank range, Merona took her shot without hesitation, finding her target with an expert eye. Her spear hit home, plunging into the animal's heart, and with a rolling thud, it lay on the ground in a lifeless heap. Her hunting for the day was more than done, and with a spring in her gimped step, Merona slung the animal over her shoulder and headed back to camp, tossing Argos' chosen stick down the path as a "thank you" game, for his assistance in bagging the hefty prize.

~

The rushing waters carried the blood and bits of

flesh from Merona's hands as she dipped them into the river. Her work skinning the hefty goat was finished, and next she began cleaning and preparing the carcass to be cooked.

Argos flopped his stick near her leg for the hundredth time that day, eager to chase down the unruly wood yet again. Merona obliged, hooking the gnawed branch with her boot and kicking it across the river without a second glance.

Argos splashed out of earshot and Merona's knife went to work, extracting the many parasites from the animal's digestive system, but with her focus completely engrossed in the meticulous and rather foul process, she failed to notice Argos's long absence. She had all but finished extracting the last worm when the complete silence of her surroundings hit her.

Argos was nowhere to be seen.

Calling out, she scanned the trees for a sign of his scraggled, gray face or wagging tail, but no hint of him appeared. She struggled to recall if he had even once returned since she'd thrown his stick and wondered what new distraction could have taken him from their game of fetch. Repeating her calls, she heard no return bark of her companion, and at last took up the gutted goat, hefting it back to the cave in the hopes that the smell of cooking meat might tempt his interest if her call could not.

Hacking off both back legs, Merona skewered them on her wooden spit, suspended over the flames to cook as she cut up and hung some of the remaining meat to begin smoking in her newly assembled smoking tent. But as her meal slowly cooked, she found herself missing the companionship of her dog, and more importantly, fearing for his well-being.

Merona stepped outside once more. "Argos!" she

shouted, walking a short way from the cave. "Argos, dinner time! Here boy!"

Still there was no sign of him. It had already begun to grow dark, and rapidly that familiar smell of bog began to ooze into the air around her. Lifting her boot, Merona could feel a dampness seeping into the soil, rising up in a bubbling green sludge beneath her. The woods were transforming from streams to swamp around her, and though she had seen the transformation from the safety of her cave for some time now, to stand in the midst of it sent a shiver through her.

She stood still and silent, unwilling to move while the swamp grew around her, but as the transformation seemed to settle, she found her body anxious to return to her cave. Letting out a final sharp, long whistle towards the woods beyond, Merona listened as it echoed forward, dancing amid the trees ahead before fading away, but before the last reverberation died out, a piercing yelp shot back toward her.

A rhythmic tramping sounded ahead, growing louder and closer before all at once Argos burst into view, racing toward her, a bright red gash across his side trailing blood in his wake. Merona had no doubt who had caused her animal's wound.

Seconds after Argos had appeared, a rush of gray men emerged from the trees, hissing at the animal as he fled their hurtling javelins. Abruptly, they halted at the edge of the boggy waters, their torches lighting the darkness as they searched for their prey.

From their ornate headdresses, Merona recognized the men before her as belonging to the goat tribe, the tribe she had rushed headlong into and used as a decoy to escape her cannibal pursuers the day of Carver's death, the tribe she had left to be slaughtered in her wake. Their teeth clenched as the light of their torches illuminated

Merona's figure and she saw the recognition in their eyes at her distinctive, and memorable appearance. Several men made gestures toward her, and she could see in their faces the full remembrance of that day as they began to chatter, stamping their feet and slamming their fists against their chests with hostile rage.

The men shrieked out, several lobbing spears toward her as Merona ducked behind a tree for cover. She could hear their shouts, as they stood at the edge of the water as though it were the edge of a chasm. They would not approach. They would not risk the water; she was sure of it.

Standing out of range of the spears, Argos barked for her to follow him, blood dripping from his side as he stamped agitatedly in place. The gray men's chattering grew into chanting before shrieks of vengeance filled the air, and as Merona peered out from behind the tree, preparing to make a run for the cave, she spotted six men surging forward, venturing through the water they once feared.

Merona rushed from her cover before it could be overtaken. Spears sped past, grazing her sleeves and cheek before disappearing into the swampy mire ahead as she raced on, the sounds and shrieks of the gray men close on her heels. This was it, their fear of the water had not outweighed their hatred for her, and the slaughter she had brought upon their camp. The gray men had ventured into the swamp for the first time since Merona's arrival, and she felt sure that her easy life of hiding behind its mysterious wall had come to an end. But as she limped on, ducking behind trees to avoid more javelins, a piercing cry rang out, sending the frenzied chase to a grinding halt as Merona spun around, her gaze locking on one of the six men's thrashing arms as he sank beneath the boggy sludge.

The remaining warriors spun in all directions, searching for the danger which had taken their brother, but without a moment to recover, a second gray warrior was swallowed into the swamp, his gurgling face wrought with terror before it vanished from sight.

Spears plunged into the water, stabbing down into the murky depths as two more men fell. Standing in the same knee-deep water, Merona searched franticly around her own feet for a sign of the danger below, but as she searched, a form began to bubble up beneath her, rising from the depths in a gurgling, flood of bog and blood.

The figure rose before her, bobbing limply to the surface, its limbs spread out awry at its sides, gnawed and stripped of all but a few scraps of flesh, as its one remaining eye stared blankly up in lifeless dread. It was not the creature of the swamp, but rather its leftovers; the mangled remains of a gray man she had just seen taken into the waters only moments before, now drifting down stream like a discarded carcass after a lengthy feast. How could any living thing have devoured him so rapidly?

The remaining warriors rushed to escape the swamp, and Merona stood frozen as an immense black figure rose from the depth directly behind the fleeing gray men, tearing into their backs with rapid, relentless, slashing claws. Towering above its prey, the creature smashed one warrior's head between its hands, before smothering its next victim into the boggy swamp.

In seconds, nearly every warrior was devoured, their limp bodies bobbing to the surface around the figure. The distant gray men fled for their lives as the creature turned towards Merona, its bright, green eyes blazing out from the blackness of its form. A rush of panic surged through Merona's body and, in the next

moment, the creature sank back into the water as Merona took hold of her wits and darted from the trees, limping toward her cave in a mad dash to get free of the water and clear of the creature's hunting ground.

Distant screams of the last fleeing gray men echoed through the swamp, as Merona scrambled into the cave alongside Argos, grabbing hold of her machete and spear to ready for the horrific swamp creature's arrival. Merona's gaze flicked up to the mouth of the cave, then back to Argos' bleeding side, and as they waited for a sound of the creature that never came, she made a choice to prioritize her bleeding friend over her fears of the beast's return.

The gushing blood had done its job to clean the wound, and with only scant supplies available, Merona dropped her weapons and rapidly set to work closing the wound with what clean strips of cloth she had at hand. Gingerly, she wrapped and rewrapped her precious companion's side, doing all in her power to stem the flow of blood, and keep her dear friend alive.

Her eyes still glanced repeatedly toward the cave opening, anxious over what lay beyond. For whatever reason, it seemed as though the creature had chosen to feast upon the gray men only, and leave Merona and her animal untouched, at least for the time being.

But still the image of the dead warrior's fleshless face, as he floated through the water, haunted Merona's thoughts, and she hastened to distract herself from the memory.

"So, Argos," she began, making small talk with herself more than the animal. "Do me a favor next time. If you're going to wander off, try to avoid upsetting the neighbors, will ya?"

Argos looked to her with large black eyes, and opening his mouth in the start of a yawn, let out a lengthy series of whimpering yowls, as though he were refuting the accusation that he would do something so foolish as intentionally set about attracting trouble.

Merona smirked. "Well, I'm sure you didn't mean to, but all I'm asking is you try a little harder *not* to draw so much attention our way."

Argos muttered a growly harrumph.

"All right, all right, I'm sure it wasn't on purpose boy. Forget I said anything. And anyway, after that… whatever it was, that attacked them, I doubt we'll be seeing much more of them for a while yet."

Argos looked up toward the cave entrance at the mention of the creature, and the two sat listening in momentary silence to the creaks and groans of the trees and the night.

"Yeah," Merona whispered. "I don't much like the idea of sharing our swamp with whatever is out there either, Argos."

With her work on his wound finished, Merona began cooking the kill of that day with tentative restraint, hoping the strong smell of the meat wouldn't attract further attention. But as the night wore on, and no further sounds or shadows approached their cave, Merona reassured herself with the unsettling knowledge that the creature's hunger must have been satiated by its feast upon the natives, and she began to wonder if there was something particular about them that had invoked the creature's ire, and what exactly she could do to avoid their fate.

CHAPTER XXI

A MATTER OF MONEY

IN a bar in Sicily, Sasha sat on a shrunken bar stool, his massive form dwarfing the seat and counter before him as Liora stood at his side, leaning back against the bar and surveying the surrounding patrons.

"I not like this idea," said Sasha, hunching further into his posture of protest.

"Of course you don't," replied Liora, "it's a shady deal, with a shady character, but we've got to get some funding somehow."

"I still have… *some* money."

"Pocket change," Liora scoffed. "We need enough to fully fund this search for a while to come, Sasha, and Mr. Baker is as reliable a lender as they come. It takes him a good long while before he starts sending his muscle to rearrange anyone's face."

"Oh, good. That very comforting. And what about other man?"

"What other man?"

"Other man you owe money?"

"Oh, *that* other man. I'll cross that bridge when it tries to kill me again."

Sasha shook his head in disapproval as a lean, bespectacled man in a dark suit stepped into sight.

Liora nudged the pilot's arm. "There he is," she said, nodding toward her target as he took a seat in the most shadowy corner available. "Now, just let me do all the talking, you're too much like Merona when it comes to negotiations, you two have absolutely *no* tact."

"Well, it lucky you so tactful then," Sasha muttered.

Liora strode forward, approaching the man with elegant confidence as she took a seat at Baker's table.

"Good evening Mr. Baker, mind if I sit for a moment?"

He looked her up and down with visible indifference. "Yes."

Liora's confidence dropped, but her expression remained undeterred. "Trust me, you'll want to hear what I have to say."

"You're clearly a very confident and determined dame, but I'm here for my dinner, and I don't like talking business with my food... it makes the taste go off."

"Then I'll get to the point. You like money..."

"Is that a question or a statement?"

"An observation. Based on the bold stripes and pristine cut of your suit, I'd say that's a Hart Schaffner Marx you're wearing. Then add to that those black pearl cuff links, plus the high-quality silk band of your fedora... well, I'd have to be blind not to see that you're clearly a man of means, who doesn't shy away from flaunting the fact."

Mr. Baker looked Liora over with a distinct eye of interest now. "A woman of taste, I see."

"I like to think so, though sadly not someone of quite the same affluence as yourself."

"I'm sure an attractive dame like you could always find a way around that."

Sasha's teeth gritted. "She not interested in *that* kind of offer."

Two burly men at Mr. Baker's back stepped forward.

Liora's eyes shot wide toward the Russian. "*Sasha*, I can handle this."

Mr. Baker glanced up at the towering pilot. "Who's the muscle?"

"Just an associate, pay him no mind. English is his second language, so he can sound a little... dumb."

Sasha bristled.

"Evidently," Mr. Baker snarled.

"As to your comment," Liora continued, "I prefer to use my *brains* over anything else, and think I might have... let's call it an *investment* you'd be interested in."

"What sort of investment?"

"Are you familiar with the Grant Sisters?"

Mr. Baker laughed. "Those two Jews that run around digging up treasure? Who hasn't? They're nuts!"

Liora smiled. "Only when we have to be."

"You? You're one of the Grant girls?"

"The pretty one."

"Ha! And what's a treasure-hunting broad like you got for me to invest in?"

"Me, of course."

"You?"

"Yes. You see my sister and I have been working on a project."

"What kind of project?"

"One involving diamonds. There's this island, you see, known as the island of diamonds, a goldmine of riches for anyone who chooses to go after it. Thing is, no one knows where it is, it's said to be shrouded in a mist, completely concealed to the outside world, but my sister and I found... clues. Clues to its location and the potential for unimaginable wealth. About two months ago my sister found it *and* the diamonds. Problem is, her plane got a little wrecked in the landing, and her radio's been sketchy, so we only have partial coordinates. But if you were willing to fund Sasha's and my search, we would be more than willing to split the findings with you, once we've traced the island."

Mr. Baker scoffed, "An island of diamonds, huh? Sounds like a myth."

Liora smiled. "Myths are our specialty. And like I said, she's already found them. This is a sure thing."

Mr. Baker smiled back. "You know what, I like you, and for that I might be willing to go in on this *investment*."

"Let me guess, but only under one condition?"

"Nah, I'm feeling generous today. No conditions, just half of all you find, not including repayment in full."

Liora held out her hand. "Deal."

The bargain was struck, and plans were made for when and where Liora could soon collect her money. As Liora and Sasha walked away from the table, the pilot leaned in to Liora's ear.

"Liora, why you say all that?"

"Say what?"

"Garbage about the island being full of diamonds?"

"I didn't make it up... just tweaked the truth a little to gain his interest."

"You lied."

"The island we think Merona landed on was actually rumored to be rich in various gems, but it was a myth on top of the myth, so the likelihood is... slim, yes."

"Why you not learn from mistakes? It this kind of recklessness that get you into last mess."

"In any other circumstance I wouldn't have gone that far, but this is for Merona."

Sasha nodded in solidarity. "You right. It for good cause."

From across the bar, a voice called out, "Oy! Grant! Where's my money?"

Liora halted, catching her breath for a moment before letting out a disgruntled sigh.

"Great. Just my luck."

Turning around with a sweet smile gracing her face, Liora walked toward her snarling debt collector. "Mr. La Roche, how's business?"

"How's business? You *take* a thousand from me, then you pulverize my man when he comes to collect your debt, and you have the nerve to ask, how's business?"

"In my defense, most of the pulverizing was already done by my sister before I came in the room, and in my sister's defense, your man was trying to kill her in a toilet."

"Shut up and give me my money!"

Sasha snarled, stepping protectively in front of Liora. "She not have it, and you not speak to her like that *again*."

Mr. La Roche looked up, unimpressed by the towering Russian before him as his five lackeys began to surround the pair.

"Your hired muscle doesn't intimidate me, Grant."

"Why everyone think I hired muscle?" Sasha muttered. "Do I look like nothing but brainless sledgehammer?"

The five men now formed a tight circle around them, drawing glinting knives from their pockets.

Liora shrugged. "Maybe a little. But don't take it personally, Sash. It just means people underestimate you, and in my experience, that's usually beneficial." With that, her fist shot up, slamming into the nearest man's chin and knocking him out cold.

The dazed thug hit the floor with a bang, and Sasha blinked back in surprise. "What?" he stammered, before dodging a telegraphed right hook. "We fighting already?"

"Yup," Liora chirped, and ducked beneath a knife.

Sasha's hefty elbow slammed down on his opponent's head. "Well, that happen quick."

~

Merona shoved the last of her supplies into her backpack. The previous night's slaughter had shaken her more than she cared to admit, and any reason to remain within the swamp couldn't outweigh the growing dread she felt at another chance of encountering whatever that creature was who lived within it.

It seemed only a matter of time before the swamp beast decided to invade her camp again, and though the idea of leaving the safety of the swamp and once again potentially contending with the hordes of gray men which surrounded her, filled her with unease, the memory of the unseen beast as it swallowed them into the bog only to spit back up their corpses when it had finished, was far more disquieting to her mind. Her choice was made, and with a quick glance around the now empty cave, she made her exit, Argos trotting loyally at her side.

Argos' injury was recovering well after the few days Merona had given him to heal, but lingering within the cave any longer was not an option, and as the companions meandered through the braided river system, Merona wondered if another cave to make camp in would be so easily found again.

Her past months on the West side of the island had made it clear that the gray men had strongholds dotted all over the landscape, and now, knowing that there was a tribe who knew her by appearance and craved her blood so fiercely they were willing to brave the swamp beast, Merona knew she couldn't travel west if she wanted to stay alive, but instead would have to venture through the swamp and beyond toward the eastern half of the island in the hope of finding a new, less treacherous wilderness. Passing through the creature's territory was a risky act, but in this game of survival, every moment of the day was one kind of risk or another. There were no exceptions on this island.

Slogging forward through the winding streams, Merona munched on her smoked-goat-jerky, tossing Argos the occasional piece to keep him going on the long trek. The wetlands seemed endless, slowing Merona's progress even more by the uneven, muddy ground, and Merona knew she had a long trek ahead of her before she would even catch sight of the plane wreckage, and from there onward, who knew how much more ground she would have to cover before she came to the end of the wetlands themselves. If she ever made it that far. With every approach of a new river or stream, Merona was careful to plunge her spear shaft into the water ahead, to check the depth before crossing, and as a means of steadying herself when the current was strong enough.

Stopping regularly to refill her water skin in the surrounding rivers, Merona made sure to quench her thirst during the daylight hours while the fresh water lasted, but with each pause to kneel beside the river, the slightest of noises would send Merona shooting to her feet and scrambling from the water's edge. She hated the skittishness that had taken hold of her. Though she told herself again and again that she had only ever seen the creature come out at night, her anxiety still got the better of her, gnawing at her nerves with every out of place creak or mutter the habitually silent surroundings emitted.

Merona grew to take note more and more of Argos's reactions, knowing his keen senses were a far better guide than her own paranoia. When he stopped to listen, she stopped to listen, when he hesitated to continue on, she found a new route, and when an unnerving noise sounded amid the trees, yet Argos persisted in sniffing his newest discovered scent, Merona would allow herself to breathe and continue on her way.

Night seemed slow in its descent, and before it had fallen, Merona once again came upon the river which led to the plane crash. She had seen no camp-worthy spots through the whole of her trek, and though the plane wasn't ideal, the alternative option of camping out in the open of the swamp come nightfall, was not on the table.

The crumpled plane soon came into sight, and a small part of the adventuress felt a pang, almost like returning home. Not that the aircraft had ever been a home for her, quite the opposite in fact, as it had been the means of her stranding and nearly caused her death when it had fallen from the mountain face. No, the feeling stemmed from the sight of technology itself, though utterly crumpled and unusable, it was still a reminder of the world beyond and left an ache in Merona's gut as she hefted Argos up, and crawled inside the plane after him to wait out the night, pondering for the hundredth time if she would ever see civilization again.

CHAPTER XXII

BAD INVESTMENT

LIORA ducked beneath her attacker's fist, snatching up a nearby chair before a previously uninvolved patron could occupy it.

The chair's former owner thudded to the floor as Liora smashed the stool across her opponent's back. A furious roar rang out as the once disinterested patron staggered up off his rear, his seven comrades shooting up from their seats, snatching bottles off the table as their leader whirled around to find his chair's thief.

Stout arms grappled Liora from behind as her eyes locked with the enraged patron and his impending beer bottle. She ducked, leaning her head as far forward as the stranglehold would allow, and in the next moment the bottle hit behind her with a crack, shattering against Liora's opponent's skull like confetti.

The hold loosened around Liora as the man dropped unconscious behind her, and she smiled up toward the menacing patron and his now broken bottle.

"Thank you."

Liora slammed her fist into the bridge of his bulbus, red nose as the bar erupted into chaos, patrons clashing with thugs, as Sasha and Liora fought back-to-back at the heart of it all.

Two men clung to Sasha's massive arms, struggling to bring the giant down, but with a swift pound of his fists, he brought their faces smashing together.

At his back, Liora snatched up a tray of empty shot glasses, flinging one after another at the heads of each of her attackers as they rushed toward her. The thick glasses cracked against their skulls, clattering to the floor as unconscious bodies joined them in a heap.

Sasha spun round just as Liora's tray ran clean of projectiles and she smacked the last man across the face with the round, metal tray, sending him staggering only for a moment before turning back with even more rage in his eyes.

In the next instant, Sasha's bulky skull rammed against the man's temple, sending him crumpling limp to the ground.

"We need to get out of here!" Sasha bellowed above the din.

"I like the sound of that. Which way?"

Sasha grabbed hold of Liora's hand. "Follow me!"

Barging through the fray, Sasha's free fist pounded each head that stood in his way as Liora shoved and dodged past the raging crowd. Catching sight of the back door, Sasha felt Liora jerk from his grasp, wrestled to the floor by a wiry attacker. The crowd thickened around Sasha and he pounded and shoved his way back toward her.

The thug tightened his grip around Liora's throat as she reached out, grabbing a stray ashtray off the ground and slamming it into his temple. He buckled, slumping on top of her before she shoved him aside. A bulky arm reached down toward her and she grabbed hold of it, flying to her feet with Sasha's strong pull.

"You alright?" Sasha gasped.

"Well enough."

Another goon charged at Sasha abruptly from behind, piledriving his boots into his spine. The Russian scarcely stumbled with the hit, turning to deliver his own blow to the man's face. His fist hit like a sledgehammer, sending teeth clattering to the ground as the man teetered and finally toppled like a tree, smacking face-first onto the floor.

Sasha turned back to Liora. "Good," he replied, as though the interruption had never occurred. "Let's go."

The pair rushed on, shouldering their way past every obstacle, but just as they were about to reach the door, the three largest of Mr. La Roche's thugs stepped up to bar their path.

"You're not going anywhere until Mr. La Roche gets his money."

Liora's hand fell on her hip. "I thought we explained about this already? I haven't got it!"

"Wrong answer!"

A blade rushed toward Liora's face as two thugs tackled Sasha.

Reeling back, the blade flew over Liora's head as she took up a stool, blocking and parrying each stab and thrust of the knife that came her way.

Arms wrapped around Sasha's throat, as one thug leapt on him from behind, his feet dangling as he struggled to secure a strangle hold on the Russian. Sasha grabbed at the arms around his neck as the second man delivered blow after blow to Sasha's ribs and gut.

Reaching back, Sasha gripped his attacker's hair and wrenched him to the side, before slamming the blubbering thug into his companion, toppling both men to the ground in a heap.

Searching franticly, Sasha spotted Liora backed into a corner, stool in hand, as the thug's glinting knife plunged toward her. Rushing forward, Sasha's fist rose high into the air, his powerful blow as imminent as the knife's, when all at once the bar quaked with a booming gunshot.

Fists halted, bottles dropped, arms were released from jaws, and all eyes turned toward the smoking double-barrel of the barkeep's shotgun.

"Alright!" the barkeep bellowed, clicking the new rounds into her weapon. "Anyone who wants to keep fighting, take it *outside*. Anyone who wants to keep drinking… clean this mess up."

Like scolded children, the patrons began to collect their broken bottles and toppled chairs, those of them who could walk, at least, while most of the rest began to shuffle out the door, and Mr. La Roche signaled to his men to stand down, knowing the bar owner's reputation for having no hesitation where it came to using her gun.

"All right, Grant," said La Roche as she approached. "We'll let the matter rest… for the time being. But just make sure I don't find you out of pocket on our next meeting."

"If you can find me at all," Liora said with a smile.

La Roche snarled, turning abruptly and stomping off toward the door, his men limping after him in defeat.

Returning her shield to its prior life as a stool, Liora and Sasha began to assist in the bar's clean up, but as they replaced chairs and swept up bottles, a booming voice shouted to them from behind the bar.

"What are you two still doing here?" the bar owner bellowed.

"We help to clean up," Sasha explained timidly.

"I don't want your help!" she barked. "Do you think I'm blind? I saw *who* started this fight!"

"We're terribly sorry for all this ma'am," Liora attempted. "but the explanation is really very simple…"

"Simple? I'll tell you what's *simple*, you two ever come in here again and I'll shoot you! So, you can just take your apologies out of my bar, because I don't want them! You hear me?"

Seeing the chance for diplomacy had passed, Liora chose to graciously slip out the door and for a moment, she and Sasha slumped on a curb, exhausted from the preceding fight.

"Well," gasped Sasha, "at least we still alive, and got funding to continue search for Merona."

"That's true," said Liora. "All in all, I'd say tonight went pretty well."

"*Da*, I not see how it could have gone better, really."

"Well… I mean, I could have done without quite so many people trying to pulverize and gut me. But still."

"*Da*… It still kind of fun though."

A slow grin spread across Liora's face. "Maybe a little."

Both sat smiling to themselves for a moment, until the squeak of the bar door sounded behind them, followed by the clear, severe voice of Mr. Baker.

"The deals off."

"What do you mean, the deals off?" said Liora rising to her feet as she spun round to face him.

"You're clearly in the hole for a hefty sum to Mr. La Roche. Which tells me you have a bad habit of not paying your debts. Why should I lend you a penny for this foolhardy scheme, if you still haven't paid off your previous dues?"

"Because I like you more than Mr. La Roche, so you can be sure I'll be paying you back first."

"And when he learns I was repaid with *his* money, just how long do you think it will take before he comes knocking at my door to collect it?"

Liora scoffed. "I'm sure a powerful man like you can handle a little worm like him."

"Oh, I most certainly could, but I'm not in the business of cleaning up other people's messes for them. Sorry, Miss Grant, you and your sister are looking more and more like a bad investment."

"But she's *stranded* out there!" Liora spat, letting her cool exterior slip.

Baker looked her dead in the eyes, and said with ice cold indifference, "Then I guess she'll *rot* out there."

~

Merona awoke to the smell of bog. The sun had yet to rise, but a hint of the approaching day still crept in through the airplane windows and Merona began to roll up her blanket in preparation for travel. The smoked goat meat was still in decent supply, and the adventuress chewed through several pieces as she gathered up her other small supplies, tossing the half-asleep Argos a bite of meat to stir him awake.

By now, the sun was beginning to rise, and as Merona slipped from the aircraft and landed in the swamp, the foul sludge transfigured around her boots into the clean, clear water of day. Stooping down, Merona rinsed and refilled her flask and water pouch, downing a much-needed drink before topping off for the trek ahead. Though she was still no closer to explaining it, the swamp's impossible transformation had grown commonplace to her, and even Argos began lapping up the water in Merona's wake as she rounded the plane to leave.

As the wreckage sank into the fog behind her, Merona knew she shouldn't miss the chance that the plane presented. Her attempts to signal for help over a month ago had seemed fruitless, but what if someone had been able to hear them? What if she passed up this chance to send out a second message that someone, somewhere might actually hear, even though Merona herself could receive no response?

Looking at Argos, Merona sighed. "I guess there's no harm in trying one more time before we leave this place for good, right boy?"

Argos wagged his tail.

"And anyway, I remember Sasha telling me once about plane transmitters, and how the thingy that sends out the signal is independent of the thingy that receives it. I think… he was talking a lot, for a long time. But hey, maybe whatever sends the message is still working?"

Argos tilted his head, looking toward her with dubious puzzlement.

"All right, all right, so I'm probably reaching, but what's the worst that could happen? No one hears us… and we are no worse off than before."

And with that, she strode back toward the plane, muttering to herself as she climbed inside once again. "Who am I kidding, the worst thing that could happen is that swamp monstrosity showing up and killing us both."

Her attempts went much as they had before, message after message going out, as nothing answered back in return. Merona grew increasingly tired with each seemingly failed attempt, and finally she chose to move on. She had done what she could, giving herself and Argos the best chance at rescue, but now she needed to focus on survival. After all, what use was a rescue plane if they were too dead to get on it?

The gray expanse ahead was vast, with trees and winding rivers fading off into the void of fog beyond. Where did they end? This question assailed Merona's thoughts again and again with every mile crossed. Would it ever end, or would this latest gamble for survival prove her last? She refused to think on it for the time being. It was still early in the day, or so the warm glow of the dense fog seemed to suggest, and there was still plenty of time to reach the other side of the wetlands before nightfall.

"There's still time," she muttered to herself. "There's still time."

But the rivers wove on. Bending and crossing this way and that as Merona struggled to press east, following along the riverbanks and their guiding water flow. Looking ahead, she continually thought she could make out an end to the boundless trees and wetlands only to be proved wrong as yet more trees came into view through the mists before her.

Up ahead, a wide river cut through the landscape, rushing rapidly across Merona's path. As she neared, the raging water looked increasingly treacherous to cross, and Merona began following the river downstream in hopes of finding a means of crossing. But the river wove on with no signs of a shallower path until she spotted a fallen tree, suspended just over the rushing water.

"Looks like we're in luck, Argos."

Approaching the bridge, Merona pushed against it with her boot, testing its stability before risking to venture across, but Argos showed even more hesitation to follow as she took her first steps out onto it.

"Come on, it's perfectly stable, boy."

But the mutt only looked at her suspiciously.

Stepping out even further onto the tree, Merona patted her leg for him to follow, but as she glanced back over her shoulder at him, her boot slipped on the damp log, slick with the river's spray, and all at once she was falling headlong toward the water and rocks below.

Argos barked frantically as she tumbled from the tree, but before she could meet her fate, her body jerked to a halt, catching and dangling just above the wild, rushing waters. Looking up, Merona realized the strap of her backpack had caught on the thick stub of a broken branch of the log, just saving her from the fall. But as she twisted to try and reach back and reascend onto the tree, the old, rotted branch she dangled from began to crack.

"Oh, brilliant!" she spat, straining to reach for another limb of the tree, to catch hold of anything other than the ever-destabilizing branch she hung from.

Slipping loose, she felt the force of the water start to slap against her boots, before a sudden jolt tugged her back up, and she looked up to find Argos gripping tightly to her pack with his teeth. Pulled up just enough, Merona grabbed hold of a sturdy limb now within reach, and hefted herself back to safety atop the log, thanking the animal for his assistance before the two scrambled across to the opposite bank.

"Well," gasped Merona, "that was cutting it closer than I would have liked. What do you say to no more near-death encounters from here on out?"

Argos panted happily in agreement, and they pressed on. On and on they plodded, eating through their smoked jerky supplies as they went, and soon night had fallen, with little visible advancement to show for their arduous efforts, besides the sore limbs and aching feet both companions shared.

The day seemed wasted, but Merona refused to give up. She had learned to tolerate the boggy smell during her nights within her small cave camp, but the deeper she went, the thicker the smell became, until Merona relented to hooking her scarf over her nose for a little relief.

Up ahead, it seemed yet again that she was reaching the end of the swamp, but as she squinted to see past the fog, she found her path blocked by a familiar, but unwelcome form. Concealed within the shadows of the trees, the swamp creature stood a short distance off, dripping with sludge, its rasping breathing echoing across the swamp.

Merona froze. She knew she stood no chance against the monstrosity, but neither could she outrun it. At her side, Argos shook, too terrified to even snarl. Before Merona could gather her wits, the creature's glowing eyes locked on her, and in the next moment it dove, disappearing beneath the boggy waves.

Moving back, Merona began her retreat of the swamp with slow, cautious steps. Her eyes still fixed on the place where the creature had vanished beneath the water, Merona hastened her escape before the creature could reemerge, but as she turned to run, thick clouds fell across the moon, bathing the swamp in darkness in mere seconds.

In a surge of bubbling sludge, the blackened figure rose from the mire directly in front of her, every inch dripping with bog as it stood towering. Hot breath washed over her face and arms as its glowing green eyes pierced through the darkness. A wave of nausea flooded over her as she staggered in place, Argos' snarls and barks sounded miles away before blackness overtook her vision.

Collapsing, Merona's unconscious body was snatched up by the figure, her feet and arms hanging limply as she was carried through the swamp to her awaiting fate.

CHAPTER XXIII

DEN OF THE BEAST

GREGORY'S door opened to the exhausted, battered and disheveled duo.

"You're back!" Gregory beamed. "That's excellent! Because I have good news."

Sasha blinked his hazy eyes. "Good news?"

"Yes! We received another signal from your Miss Grant! She's *still* alive and well! Er… still alive anyway."

Liora let out a curse.

Gregory was taken aback. "I'm sorry. I thought that was a good thing."

"Oh sure," Liora snapped. "My sister is still alive, rotting on an island for two and a half months now and we can't do a *blasted* thing to find her!"

Sasha sighed. "It be all right Liora, we find a way."

"How? We're broke! The pilots my uncle hired have all given up the search, and the last lender I knew of who didn't know me and my *glorious* reputation for outstanding debts, just turned us down."

"We figure it out because we *have* to," Sasha barked, his booming voice shaking the walls of the cramped room. "Because I not ready to give up on Merona when she out there fighting so hard to live."

"Well, neither am I! She is *my* sister, after all."

"Good!"

The two companions stared each other down for a moment, unsure of what exactly they were still fighting about.

"All right, then," continued Liora, "but we still need money. So, what's the new plan?"

"I have offer for work. I take that, be finished in few weeks, and then we keep looking."

"Weeks! Merona is alive *now*, she might not make it another few weeks, we need money now, Sasha, not soon."

"What you want me to do? I have one plane; I can't do job *and* continue search at same time."

"Then *I'll* get work."

"What work? You can't even pay off debt, what work you get that make enough?"

"Max Copperhead. He's been begging Merona and I to take work with him for ages, and the pay is obscenely high."

Sasha squinted. "Then, why you not?"

"Because Merona didn't like him. Thought he was overzealous about his grand schemes. 'He's the sort of scab that would throw you under the collapsing door just to keep it from shutting him out of the tomb' to use her words."

"I not like the sound of *that* at all!"

"I'll be fine, this latest job offer of his is just outside of Cairo on some old dig site. Perfectly safe."

"*Nyet*, I not let you go work for such men."

"Well, it's a good thing it's not up to you then, isn't it?"

"Liora."

"Sasha, Merona is stranded out there because of *me*, because of this stupid debt I couldn't pay off, and I'm going to take any job I can to help find her, you hear me?"

"There must be other option."

"If there were, we never would have gotten into

this stupid situation in the first place. I'm going, no arguments."

Sasha looked down toward Liora, and her lean frame, a fear welling up in him that he was about to lose yet another dear friend to this dangerous lifestyle. He bent down, his immense arms engulfing her slender figure in a hug.

"Good luck."

Liora coughed, trying to breathe within the vise-grip of affection, her small hand reaching out around the pilot and patting him on the back.

"Don't worry Sasha, I'll come back safe and sound. Promise."

"You better."

"I will. I'll make sure I get paid in advance and send you everything I can, and you make sure to keep me posted on your search, all right? I want regular updates."

Sasha leaned back out of his embrace, a look of affront on his face. "Of course, I write! I the only one here who any good at keeping in touch!"

Liora shrugged. "You know us Grants, too busy nearly dying to pick up a pen."

Sasha's lower lip quivered, and once again his arms engulfed her. "You not take any risk, you listening? I not spend all this time finding Merona just to lose you too."

Liora smiled. "Oh, come on, you'd be happy to be rid of us both, admit it."

Sasha scowled. "Sometimes I think I just might. It would make life simpler. Like back when I was fighting in Great War."

~

Rising vomit jolted Merona from unconsciousness.

A mouthful of stomach acid churned her onto her side as she retched out the foul taste. Her eyes hung half open as she spit the last of the bile from her mouth, blinking to see past the blackness which still clouded her eyes, struggling to discover her surroundings. A dank smell of bog suffocated Merona in her struggle to regulate her breathing, dampness soaking her back and side as she worked to regain her equilibrium.

Mud oozed between Merona's fingers and she pushed her shaky body off the ground, an incessant dripping echoing in her ears as she stood. Her vision finally adjusting to the blackness around her, Merona scanned her surroundings and found little to raise her hopes. Green sludge shimmered off the walls which enclosed her on all sides, oozing endlessly down and puddling into a reflective pool at her feet. Within the pool was mirrored a green tinged reflection of the misty moon overhead.

The fog in her head drifted back as she slowly recalled her last sight of the beast blocking her escape, and Argos snarling defensively at her side, before his absence was registered.

"Argos?" Merona sputtered, but the mutt was nowhere to be found.

Stumbling from the putrid green puddle at the pit's center, Merona felt along the walls, searching for a root or any means by which to ascend the pit, but as she clawed through the dripping mud, she found nothing but slippery ooze that offered no chance of escape from the hole.

The cavity must have been no more than four meters across, containing nothing but a muddy puddle at the center and the filthy adventuress herself. She was alone. A captive of whatever horror called the swamp home. And she wondered what purpose it had for her within

the pit, besides some kind of living food storage.

Perhaps this was it. This was where she would meet her end. It seemed likely, but every new encounter on this island seemed yet another promise of imminent doom.

"Get a hold of yourself, woman," she muttered aloud. "You're starting to fear it's the end every few days now. It's getting tired. How long has it been... about three months? And here you still are, alive and kicking, more or less. You've faced cannibals, infection, starvation, dehydration, and in all likelihood, some growing madness, but you keep pulling through somehow, so let's not give up altogether, just yet."

The speech was hardly inspirational, but it was all she could muster to motivate herself, before she quickly occupied her mind with assessing her resources. Her backpack was gone, as was the machete which had hung at her waist, along with the spear she had strapped to her back. Within her coat she found none of the rags or bandages she'd pocketed, nor the pocketknife that had seen her through the many months of horrors. There was nothing left.

Whatever the creature was that had slung her unconscious body into this dank hole, it had picked her clean of supplies as well, and the memory of its glowing eyes, its dripping form, and bitter breath brought acid to her throat. She pushed down the memories to prevent a second upheaval and set her mind a new task.

Slipping off her belt, Merona began to assess its length. Her boot laces too were extracted and measured, as Merona eyed the deep pit and evaluated its height. Measuring and calculating all cordage available to her, it seemed that no amount of knotting and stringing such items together would bring her any closer to reaching the opening nearly two stories above.

But Merona refused to give in to the insurmountable hurdle staring her in the face, and set to knotting her bootlaces, scarf, belt, and straps together. Feeling through the mud at her feet, she retrieved and secured two rocks to the end of the line to act as weight and grapple.

Swinging the stones out in a circular arc to build momentum, Merona pitched them up toward the opening, where a jagged stone jutted out at the top as a potential grapple point. The line sailed high, stopping short halfway up the pit before plummeting back in a defeated splatter amid the mud. Again, Merona heaved her line up, snarling at the futility of her efforts, but still determined in her course of action, which seemed her only option.

Again and again the grapple ended its flight in the boggy puddle at Merona's feet, and with a defeated sigh, she sank back against the muddy wall. With a final effort, she struggled to reconfigure the line to stretch to its full capacity, but no matter how she restrung it, the line inevitably fell short.

Raging at the failed grapple, Merona hurled it to the ground, clawing at the walls in a desperate attempt to scale them, but more and more her struggles met with exhaustion and defeat, until at last the harsh truth of her situation fell over her.

She was absolutely trapped.

This dank pit of mud and swamp was where she would stay, and though her mind still fought to think up new means of escape, with little more than the clothing on her back and the slick walls which encircled her, what other tools or options were open to her?

Huddling beneath her coat, Merona lay in the mud to regain her strength, her thoughts drifting to Argos and the sickening fear of what could have happened to him in the jungle after she blacked out.

~

The next day dawned, and Merona was relieved to find that the dank, boggy puddle of the previous night, had been affected by the island's magic, and transformed into clear, drinkable water. Rushing to quench her gnawing thirst, she gulped back on the cool liquid, smiling for a moment at her incredible good fortune. The moment did not last long.

The hole above her looked all the more distant in the cool light of day, and Merona half laughed at her actions the night before, seeing clearly how far escape stood out of reach. She was trapped there, a mere eight or nine yards of muddy wall separating her from freedom.

And so, the day dragged on, Merona quenching her thirst at regular intervals as her stomach grew more ornery with each passing hour. Now and then she dug through the earth for worms or grubs, or any bite of protein to assuage her growing hunger, but even these were scarce.

Merona soon found herself pacing up and down the cramped space, looking and feeling very much like a caged animal. She had no means of escape, and felt a rising tension at the helplessness of her situation as her mind imagined all the ways her captor might choose to kill and eat her.

More than once that day she attempted the climb up the slick, muddy walls, trying each section for potential hand and foot holds, but of course, in spite of her determination, her efforts only served to sap her already waning strength. It felt as though days had passed before the light above began to dim, and once again Merona lay down to sleep for the night, having exhausted all options of escape that day. The next day passed as eventlessly as the one before, with only the puddle and muddy worms to address her thirst and hunger.

Creeping steps woke Merona from her restless sleep, and she staggered to her feet, grabbing hold of the only weapon available to her, the leather cord and rocks knotted at its end. The clouds above still carried a dark green tint, dawn having not yet made its approach into the sky, and Merona knew the creature who had brought her to this putrid dungeon might have finally decided to pay her a visit.

As the footfalls grew closer, Merona held fast to her improvised bola, readying herself to face the coming danger, but as the soft steps grew quicker, a glossy black nose crept into sight at the edge of the hole, bobbing rapidly as it sniffed the air.

"Argos?" Merona muttered in disbelief. "Argos, is that you?"

The mutt's scraggly face popped into view, his lopsided ears dangling forward over his face as he gazed down at her.

"Argos!" Merona cried. "You're alive!"

The spastic wriggling of Argos' upper body made it clear that the mutt's tail was overcome with excitement at the sight of his companion, and in the next moment he began to bark into the black pit toward her, agitatedly digging at the edge to reach her.

"Quiet! It's all right, boy," Merona soothed. "I'm okay. Even better, now that you're here. I can't believe you got away from that... thing! Well... I mean, I can. You're fast as a whippet. But how did you find me?"

Argos stared down in silence, his head drifting to one side as he awaited his companion's realization of the absurdity of asking him questions.

"Right…" Merona said. "You can tell me about it later. Right now, we need to find a way to get me *out* of here."

Hearing the excitement in her voice, Argos barked back at her with matched enthusiasm.

"Yes! That's a good boy! Now, I need you to find a rope or something to lower down to me. Can you do that Argos?"

Again, Argos responded in a blank stare, his head tilting at the strange instructions coming from his companion.

"Right… of course. You're a dog, and here I am talking to you like you're a person." Merona sank back against the wall. "I'm going insane, aren't I?"

Argos slumped down, his paws hanging over the muddy edge of the hole as he let out a whimper.

"It's not your fault boy," Merona said with a sigh, her head drooping into her hands. "You're just a dumb animal, but you're the only one I've got. I am glad you're alive though, even if there is nothing you can do to help. It's nice to have a little company, you know?"

Up above, Argos and his nose began to investigate his surroundings, wandering off unnoticed as Merona continued her lamentations.

"I mean, even if you bring me a kill, once in a while, like you did back in the cave, I would still have no way of cooking it, and in the end, what would be the point in it all? I'd still be trapped down here."

The absent dog gave no reply, but Merona continued. "I don't know, Argos, I can't seem to muster the energy to keep going. Not in a place like this. Nothing ever goes right."

Merona's gaze turned up to find the empty hole above, devoid of her smiling companion's face.

"Argos?" she called. "Argos, where are you?"

The silence dragged on, no sound of reply tumbling down the hole in answer to her call, but just as Merona's hope was fading, the scraggly shadow of Argos' head, popped back into view.

"Argos! Don't scare me like that!"

Argos cocked his head in that familiar way, a stifled bark sputtering from his mouth, which now carried something.

"What... what on earth have you got in your mouth Argos?"

The strange, flopping object dangled out either side of his jaws, like an immensely long snake of some kind, but as Merona squinted up in confusion, she at last recognized the object for what it was.

"Argos you *genius* animal you! You found a vine!"

Argos's body once again began to squirm with excitement, as he trotted in place, unsure of his next move.

"Drop it, Argos!" Merona called out. "Drop it down here for me, boy!"

But in spite of his seeming brilliance in retrieving the essential item, he seemed incapable of grasping the simple command.

"Argos, don't mess around. This is *not* the time. Just drop it!"

But still he held tight to his prize.

Again and again Merona coaxed, pleading for him to drop the precious line that could mean her escape, but just as it seemed he was ready to release his hold, a scratching hiss startled his focus, and with acute fear in his large eyes, he darted from sight, taking the vine with him.

"No!" Merona screamed, her fear for her companion's safety overwhelming any despair in her stolen hope of escape.

Argos's scampering footfalls had vanished away, and only a rumbling breathing remained, echoing down the hole. Though she could see nothing through the narrow opening, Merona knew what waited above, and with slow, cautious steps, reached for the bola at her feet to arm herself again.

A large shadow fell against the wall of the pit, as sounds of scratching and snarls shuffled overhead, followed by an abrupt and unforeseen object descending from above. Merona fell back against the wall of her cell to avoid being struck, but as it thumped to the mud, she saw that it wasn't an object at all, but a bound and bloody gray man, limp and lifeless.

For a moment, she froze in place, watching to see if the man would move, or if perhaps he was already dead. Her conjecture that the swamp creature had thrown her down here as food storage seemed all the more probable with this new arrival of fresh meat, a thought which unsettled her.

Up above, the shadowy creature moved off, its footsteps fading away out of earshot as Merona remained still, hesitating to go any nearer to the unconscious or dead stranger, waiting for him to move. Scrutinizing his figure, Merona's eyes quickly zeroed in on the long length of rope binding his wrists and ankles, which looked strikingly like her missing lasso, but with the uncertainty of her new cell-mate's mortality status, she was reluctant to approach.

"What are you being such a coward about," Merona hissed to herself. "Dead or unconscious, it doesn't matter, he is trussed up like a pig and can't touch you. Just go over there and check his breathing to see if you can take those ropes without risk."

Swallowing back her fears, Merona approached the limp body lying half submerged in a puddle, listening keenly for sounds of breathing. Leaning down, she peered over his shoulder to see his eyes, hoping to find a vacant, dead stare looking past her, but instead the eyes were tightly shut, suggesting what she had first feared. He was alive but unconscious.

The cannibal's eyes shot open as his head whipped toward her, his black teeth snarling and gnashing at Merona's face as she fell backward out of reach. The gray man thrashed out in a furious frenzy, unable to break free of his restraints to reach her, and Merona scrambled backward, halting with her back against the wall to keep as far out of reach as her tight confines would allow.

"Idiot!" Merona spat. "Of course, he's alive... why else would he be *tied up*, you dolt!"

Reaching out instinctively, Merona grabbed hold of the first weapon nearby, a hefty, jagged rock. For the next moments it seemed the cannibal's fury was unending as he struggled and writhed to reach her, but Merona only stood still, rock in hand, as she watched and waited for her enemy to break free. At last, he fought against his bonds no more and lay still on the other side of the pit, his pale, unblinking, yellow eyes locked on Merona's every move.

Hours seemed to drag by as they watched each other, neither one speaking nor allowing themselves the privilege of taking their eyes from the other. Merona still watched his bindings with jealousy, infuriated that the long line of rope, which could mean her freedom, was also the only thing keeping her bloodthirsty attacker at bay. Thoughts of stealing the rope once he'd fallen asleep, or helping him along with a solid thwack from her stone, ran through her mind, and even the possibility of cold-blooded murder presented itself to Merona in her desperation, but as she gritted her teeth at her own steadily decreasing humanity, some unexpected words left her lips.

"Well, this is quite the fix we've got ourselves in, isn't it?"

The gray man silently glared at her in response.

"You see, I want that rope you're tied up with to use to escape, but you seem to want to kill me... which, when you think about it, really shouldn't be your top priority right now. It honestly makes things on my end rather difficult. I mean, we both want the same thing, right? To get out of here. I don't suppose you could hold off on that whole cannibalizing my entrails thing until after we've reached the top of this bog hole?"

The gray man continued to stare, his lip quivering with suppressed rage.

"Yeah... I didn't think so," Merona said with a sigh. "You know, you might try appreciating the fact I'm trying to find a way out of here that doesn't involve bashing your head in. I mean, I understand it's hard for you, given that you don't understand a solitary word I'm saying... but the least you could do is recognize that if I wanted to kill you, I could have easily done it already."

The gray man only glared in answer.

Merona let out a long sigh. "This... this is going well."

For several dragging minutes the two sat in silence once more, eyes fixed on the other, waiting for... they didn't know what. Merona knew she had the upper hand, but the idea of killing someone so defenseless, even if he wouldn't blink to do the same, if their positions were reversed, still didn't sit right. But on top of that, she had a sneaking feeling that was what was wanted of her, as though the creature had thrown him down there for that exact purpose. And the idea of being backed into a corner, with only one option open to her, had always pushed Merona to search for an alternative of her own making.

The idea of talking the cannibal round seemed an improbable solution, particularly given the language barrier, but Merona was not yet ready to embrace the cold-blooded killer within just yet, especially since she had no way of knowing if this particular man before her was, himself, even a cannibal. There were many fractured tribes on the island, and though all she had encountered had shown violent hostility toward her and the other tribes, only two or three were confirmed cannibals.

Again, and again Merona attempted to break through to her cell-mate, using every means of communication she could think of, from drawing pictures in the dirt, to something resembling charades, but the gray man's dead glare refused to shift.

"Come on, buddy, give me something, here!" Merona spat. "I know you aren't just some dumb animal, you must see that I'm trying to communicate with you here, even if you can't understand me. I don't expect we'll be friends after this, but even *you* have got to have a word for truce, haven't you?"

And in that moment, she thought she saw a flicker of understanding in his yellow eyes. His head began to rise, looking toward her with renewed interest in her indiscernible words.

"You understand me... don't you?" Merona whispered. "At least, you understand that I don't mean you harm... that this doesn't have to get bloody."

The gray man shifted up, looking eagerly toward her, and then did the seemingly impossible, and raised his bound hands toward her in an almost pleading manner. Merona stood silent for a moment, shocked that all her efforts had made any kind of a dent. Slowly, she moved forward with cautious steps, her empty hands raised in a clear sign of peace.

The gray man raised his wrists all the higher, with eager glee in his eyes as she reached for the ropes and began to untie them. But as his bonds began to loosen, a strange gleam in his eyes caused Merona to hesitate for only a moment.

But it was a moment too late.

His bonds were now loose, and with bloodlust already returning to his eyes, he scrambled to free himself, tugging the rope from his legs as Merona staggered back, clawing in the dirt for any means of defending herself.

She had been so desperate for a human ally, she'd let down her guard and reason in favor of hope... a hope which had not been rewarded.

Chapter XXIV

ESCAPING THE PIT

The hot air of Cairo swept across Liora's face as she stepped from the plane. In the distance, her new employer, Max Copperhead, stood awaiting her arrival, his keen anticipation to finally work with one of the Grant sisters showing as his arm shot out to wildly wave her down.

"Miss Grant!" Max called, "At last, you're here!"

"Wouldn't miss it," Liora called back, striding briskly toward him.

"You have no idea how long I've looked forward to finally working with you. I'm *so* pleased this latest venture of mine could pique your interest."

"You've only been pestering my sister and me for the last two years, but with the amount you were offering, I'd be a fool to say no. Speaking of which, have you got my advance?"

Max smiled, reaching into his pocket and retrieving a hefty roll of bills. "You Grant's cut right to the chase, don't you?"

"Oh, trust me, you got the least blunt Grant sister of us all."

Copperhead handed off the cash. "I don't mind a little candor in the least. Now, may I help you with your luggage?"

"Be my guest."

After Liora's few shabby bags were loaded into

Copperhead's car, the drive out soon became an impromptu consultation on the quest ahead.

"So," Liora began, "speaking candidly, what exactly is this new discovery of yours? You weren't terribly clear before as to what the job would be."

"Oh, with your reputation, I'm sure it's nothing you won't be able to handle. But I promise you, if my findings are correct, this expedition could lead to the discovery of the century. Or quite possibly the greatest discovery of all time, and *all time* to come."

Liora let out a hearty chuckle. "All time to come, huh? And just what myth are we chasing here?"

"Oh, Miss Grant, I'm afraid I can't possibly tell you that."

"You've hired me for a job, but you can't tell me what it is?"

"I'm afraid not. This expedition must be done in the utmost secrecy. I can't risk my findings getting out. I'm sure you understand?"

"I see, you're hoping to avoid catching any competition for the prize."

"Exactly."

A smile grew on Liora's lips as the clear opportunity before her became unmistakable. Copperhead wasn't only eager for expertise, he was very nearly desperate for a professional who was willing to work in the dark as they risked life and limb. And it was just this kind of desperation she knew how to cash in on.

"Well," Liora began, "I've always found a little healthy competition adds to the fun, but I can appreciate your position Mr. Copperhead. Though, in light of this new information, I'm afraid it's going to cost you extra."

"Extra?"

"I only work for a regular fee on regular jobs. Going in blind makes this, irregular. I hope you can appreciate *my* position?"

"I see, and how much extra are we talking?"

A congenial smile washed across Liora's face. "Oh, under such conditions my rates always increase by at least thirty percent. It's standard practice, you understand."

"Thirty percent?"

"Afraid so."

"That's absurd."

"What's absurd is asking a lady to risk life and limb on a job you refuse to give her any information on."

"And *if* I relent, and tell you more, would your price return to what we had agreed upon?"

"You've made it clear you have no intention of sharing such details, and I don't suspect you'll suddenly cave on that point over a little extra money. So, if I'm honest, I'd be rather unconvinced that anything you say next would be the truth... No, I genuinely don't wish to pry into your secrets, because if I'm honest, the extra money is far more appealing to me. In fact, I think things are working out perfectly, you will have enough experts willing to go in blind, to finally get this world-changing-expedition of yours underway, and I will have more than enough cash to fund my own ventures. Really, we both come out winners in this if you think about it."

"It's difficult to argue with you, Miss Grant."

"I'm glad to hear it. Are we in agreement then?"

Copperhead sighed, extending a hand. "It seems so."

The two shook hands in accord, and the car soon reached the small hotel they would stay at for a few days before the expedition set off. Liora was situated more or less comfortably in her room, and immediately sent a letter containing the money to fund Sasha in his search.

Liora knew her mind should have been focused on the impending mission, but found her thoughts always turning to Merona, knowing that whatever danger lay ahead for herself, it would be nothing compared to the perils Merona still faced. Whatever the risk, it would be worth it.

~

The gray man pushed up to his feet, now fully free of his bonds as he locked eyes on Merona. Scrambling back through the muddy pit, her hands clawed for a weapon as her fingers landed on her old line of leather cord.

Teeth gnashing, the gray man lunged for her and Merona spun her grapple line out, the stones at its end colliding with his jaw in a shatter of blood and teeth.

Her strike's effect was short-lived, as the gray man turned toward her with increased rage in his eyes. Swinging for him again, her line sailed overhead before he snatched hold of the cords, ripping the weapon from her grasp in one sharp pull.

Dropping it to the mud, he now lunged for her as Merona scrambled to escape in the tight confines of the pit. Clambering out of reach, her escape was halted as her foot caught on something in the mud. All at once, Merona toppled forward, before the all-too-familiar feeling of fingers gripping her hair, pulled her back.

She clawed at the muddy ground as he dragged her up, her fingers grasping onto the same object which had tripped her. Next, she felt his sinewy arms wrapping around her neck from behind, cinching off her breathing in an instant.

Scratching at his arms, Merona knew a battle of strength was hopeless, but in the next moment, she recognized the object she had pulled from the mud in her desperation... a femur bone, broken, sharp and jagged on one end.

Without hesitation, her hand shot back over her shoulder, stabbing the bone into any part of his face she could reach.

A hideous squelching sounded before his screams ripped into her ear. Relinquishing his hold, he clutched at his gouged eye socket, blood oozing between his fingers as he shrieked out in mounting rage.

Merona held tight to her new weapon, bits of fleshy matter still sticking to its sharp end.

"Fine," Merona hissed, "you don't want to play nice, we won't play nice."

The gray man released his hold on his bloody, hollow eye socket and clawed out toward Merona, snarling, and frothing in a tornado of fury. Dodging backward out of reach, Merona stabbed for him, piercing his hands and forearms more than once before he suddenly grabbed hold of her wrist.

Wrenching back her arm, he forced her hold of the bone and it dropped to the dirt. In a blink he leapt upon her, sending her body thudding back hard into the mud. His bloody hands locked on her neck, gripping like a vice around her windpipe.

Merona clawed at his fingers, blackness just beginning to fog her eyes, before her uncle's years of training took hold of her instincts, and she hooked her free leg around the gray man's neck, locking her thighs around his arms as she shoved him sideways to the ground. In the next moment she arched back, shoving up his elbow with a snap.

His screams echoed up the pit as Merona snatched a stone jutting from the earth and slammed it across his temple. His body at last fell limp as she smashed the rock into his face yet again. She didn't stop to look at the results of her work, or check his breathing... was he dead or just unconscious? She didn't care... instead she rushed for the long-discarded rope to knot her lasso.

Her hands still shaking with adrenalin, Merona knotted and re-knotted the line before at last it held, and she eyed the same jagged rock that had been her target in her past attempts at escape. Circling the lasso rhythmically overhead, she soon launched it up. Sailing high above, the loop brushed the edge of the rock before slipping free and falling in a coil near her boots.

Again, Merona flicked the lasso into motion, tossing it up toward the rock, and once again the lasso failed to take hold of her target. Cracking her neck to each side, Merona took in a long deep breath to steady her nerves, and with a third and final throw of the rope, it caught hold.

Tugging down, she felt the line holding true and secure on the rock above, and looking around the dank pit for one last time, snatched up the discarded cord and broken femur as her only means of defense against whatever awaited above before she ascended.

Leaping up, Merona gripped the rope as she planted her boots against the slick wall, her feet slipping out from under her as she struggled to make the climb. Foggy sounds drifted into clarity above as Merona recognized a familiar bark.

"Argos! Over here boy!"

Up above, Argos's shaggy paws dug at the opening, his enthusiasm growing as he peered over to watch her ascend from the hole.

"Nice of you to stop by again."

His tongue flopped out in joyful recognition of his dear friend.

Just then, strange sloshing sounds began echoing down into the pit, and Argos turned away from Merona, growling a stern, low growl toward the darkness.

Whatever the nearing threat might be, Merona at once knew she must give up on the slimy walls of her prison. Hooking her leg and boot around the line, Merona began to scale quickly up the rope, struggling to reach her lone and vulnerable companion above, before the looming creature could find them.

All at once, the line began to slip from the rock, and Merona sprang up, rocketing up the rope before leaping for the edge of the pit. Grabbing hold of the muddy rim, her grip almost instantly began to fail, as the slick edge gave way. But like lightning, Argos was there, biting hold of her sleeve and tugging at her to climb up.

With a little help, Merona found the strength to scramble free from the infernal pit, mud and slime coating nearly every part of her.

Catching hold of her slipping lasso, she began coiling it as she looked around, finding herself in some kind of immense cave, a hole to the early morning sky broken in the ceiling and tunnels running off in all directions, while in the corner, laying in a heap, she instantly spotted her stolen belongings.

Nearby, Argos began to bark, dancing agitatedly at one of the tunnels as though he were eager to be followed. Without hesitation, Merona snatched up her supplies before the two rushed down the cavern, the approaching, sloshing steps fading quickly out of earshot behind them.

Merona followed close at Argos' heels, trusting in her companion to lead her out of the beast's lair. The path was dark, but soon a small light began to grow up ahead, and all at once they burst out into the open air, rushing from the lair without stopping or looking back, trusting to luck that they were headed in the right direction.

~

"Well," Merona muttered. "I've decided that traveling through this blasted swamp was a terrible idea."

Argos seemed to bark in protest of his companion's lack of faith.

"Oh, come on! We've been out here for *days*, I was captured as living food storage by a swamp beast, and nearly killed in a pit! Plus, since our escape, we've seen no sign of this boggy wilderness ever ending! Add to all that, that we're almost out of food... again, and there hasn't been a single sign of edible game this whole time. Sure, we have all the water we could want, at least in daylight hours, but that's not enough to last on."

Argos harrumphed in understanding of her defeated tone.

The situation was indeed grave, but what else had the duo to do but press on, hoping this new part of the island would take them out of the reach of both the gray men, and the mysterious creature of the swamp. But now Merona began to wonder if the swamp merely engulfed this whole half of the island, and their choices were either the gray men's jungle territory, or the beast's endless swamp. Neither of which seemed very appealing.

Not a sound rustled in the trees above or ahead, offering little optimism for a chance at food that day, as the last of the jerky was consumed. Merona gulped back plentiful water to fill the empty feeling in her stomach, and stopped, more often than she would have liked, to answer the call of nature because of it. She craved the taste and crunch of solid food, but as she forged ahead in the desperate need to kill the next living thing she clapped eyes on, Argos halted her steps as he began barking toward the water of a nearby river.

Though the swamp beast only ever seemed active when the swamp itself had taken hold in the hours after sunset, Merona still feared its reappearance and another abduction to its slimy pit, that this time she might not escape from. Even in daylight, any hint of a danger lurking beneath the water was something she understandably wished to avoid.

"Leave it alone, Argos!" Merona snapped, prepared to run should whatever he had spotted appear.

But the mutt persisted.

Panic rose in her voice. "Argos! Leave it alone and get over here!"

Argos growled, irritated at her inability to understand him. And so, rather than continuing in his attempts to signal his companion of what he knew, and she did not, he chose to simply show her, yet again, why it was always best to just listen to him.

Diving into the rushing river, Argos splashed along the chest-high waters for a moment before emerging with soppy limbs and head held high, a fish held proudly in his jaws.

Merona beamed. "Argos! Where in the… how'd you find that?"

Never before had she seen a single creature living amid the waters of the ever-changing rivers, besides the one unnatural beast come night, and now, standing before her, sat the puddling mutt, a flapping fish between his teeth.

Patting his matted head, Merona took the fish from his mouth. "Good boy, Argos!"

For that moment, escaping the swamp fell lower on the duo's list of priorities as they found a small, dry-ish patch of dirt to skin and cook their meal while it was still fresh. Sizzling above the flames, the fish's white,

parasite-free flesh soon turned a golden brown, and the companions readily sank their teeth into the crispy meat, Merona still marveling at the impossible sight of the river trout in her hands.

The taste was delicate in comparison to the smoked jerky of the past two days, and the change was a welcome one. Spear in hand, fishing became the standard means of sustenance along the trek, and both companions' moods were greatly increased for it.

Night soon fell and still they had not reached the end of the braided river system. Fog closed in tight around them and Merona waited for the stench of bog to follow but to her complete disbelief, the water remained unchanged.

Merona stood stunned. The abnormal waters she had come to trust for their consistent inconsistency had done the unexpected, continuing to rush on as fresh that night as the proceeding days. She had had no explanation for the bizarre change of the water in the months before, but had grown used to it. But this? What normally wouldn't even take her notice, as most water was not inclined to change its very matter with the fall and rise of the sun, now baffled her.

Perhaps the swamp truly did have an end to it, a thought which gave Merona a great deal of hope as she turned in for the night. She was discovering new and strange parts of the island, parts that seemed far more hospitable to her survival, and she greatly hoped it lasted.

When the light of day crept through the island fog, Merona stretched out each limb before rising in readiness for the long trek ahead. She had spent days within the strange swamp, and could only guess how much more ground she had yet to cover. But as her eyes slowly blinked back the night of sleep, the unusually sparse fog around her revealed an unexpected sight; the trailing rivers of the woods snaking out onto a rocky beach, and the clear ocean beyond.

For the first time since crashing, Merona could just make out the blue of the sky and waters. The fog seemed thinner here, letting a warm glow of sun fall on the sandy beach ahead, and as Merona strode out toward the horizon, closing her eyes and feeling the warmth on her skin, she had soon removed her mud and slime-encrusted scarf, boots and jacket, and dove into the water.

Dunking back her head beneath the waves, she felt the water washing away a great deal more than just the long weeks of grime, sweat, and blood. Her fears and memories of past horrors seemed to disappear, even if only just for that moment, as she felt the refreshing waters rush around her aching limbs.

Argos watched for a moment as his normally sullen companion began to smile, letting out unfamiliar sounds of laughter and enjoyment, and soon he dove in alongside her, splashing in the blue as she tossed water toward him in playful companionship.

Once back on shore, Merona collected her supplies and returned to the water, spear in hand. Fish of all kinds and colors darted around beneath the water, and after a couple failed attempts, Merona at last impaled her meal. Raising the spear high above the water, she looked to Argos in triumph only to find a scaly catch, of far greater size, flapping within his maw.

Merona laughed. "Trying to one-up me, eh? I see how it is."

Argos happily trotted through the sand, his dripping gray head held high as he sat near a log and began ripping into his kill.

"Well, I guess you deserve the bigger kill, this time.

You caught it, after all."

With chewing mutters between bites, Argos seemed to whole-heartedly agree, and had finished his meal long before Merona had even started a fire to cook her own.

Burying her spear butt in the sand, the gutted meat of the fish was soon hanging limply from the spearhead over the fire as Merona leaned back against the log, looking out toward this new horizon. She couldn't tell what the next few days would bring, or if this seemingly safe spot of land only offered a false hope of peace, but for now, she breathed back with contented ease. She was out of the swamp, and free of the cannibals at last.

CHAPTER XXV

A SECOND SIGNAL

MERONA'S days seemed surreally calm when compared to the past months of chaos, blood, death and abduction. Since crashing, she had been robbed, stabbed, bitten, starved, betrayed, and hunted like an animal, and the idea that somehow, she could now live out her days out of reach of it all, awaiting rescue in peace and relaxation, worrying only about catching enough fish and keeping protected from the elements, began to unnerve her. After all she had been up against, it couldn't be that simple. Not on this island.

In the days that followed, every sound and every shadow that passed among the trees around her set Merona on edge. Each and every time something stirred, her bed would be abandoned, or her food dropped to the dirt, as she made ready for an attack by the creature or her cannibal neighbors, but each and every time, no threat would emerge.

Day after day her heightened nerves would rouse her panic, only to dwindle out into false alarm after false alarm. She felt unsure about accepting the seeming safety of her new situation, but with every uneventful day, it seemed foolish to remain on edge. In all this time since escaping the swamp, she had seen no sign of the creature that lived within being willing to venture outside of its domain, and she felt confidant the gray men were too fearful to venture through it as she had done. And so, the swamp would act as a barrier between herself and her bloodthirsty neighbors, at last fully dividing her from the dangers of the island.

Yet another day dawned, and Merona awoke to spear breakfast once again, and once again a shadow moved among the trees. Ignoring her own instincts, Merona kept her sights on the water and fish. Argos lay nearby, calm and unfazed, and she remembered to mind his attuned instincts for danger more than her own surroundings.

As the evening sun broke through the thin mist of the island, Merona floated out into the sea, scrubbing her arms and legs in the cleansing saltwater just offshore before dinner. Argos flopped and splashed nearby, chasing an unruly stick which continually fell from his gnawing mouth to be temporarily lost in the waves.

Merona lifted her head from the water, popping a finger from her ear canal to clear the salt water. As sound returned to her, a low humming sounded in her ear, and she grumbled, again attempting to clear the water and ringing from her ears, but as the hum grew closer, she recognized it for what it was.

"Sasha!" Merona spat, splashing from her relaxed posture and diving through the waves toward the beach.

This was it. This time Sasha would find her. The sun was setting, the fog was thin, and the light of her fire would show through it. It had to.

With desperate vigor, her arms chopped through the waves, rushing toward the shore and her dim campfire flickering ahead. She fought and struggled to reach the beach in time, and at last, her feet hit the sand.

The plane still buzzed within earshot, closer and louder than before. Her eyes shot up, scanning the sky before zeroing in on the distinct, bi-winged silhouette.

"Hold on, Sasha! Just stay where I can see you, pal."

Reaching her fire, Merona fell to her knees, tossing a heap of dry, leafy branches she had collected for just such an occasion, onto the pile. The bright flames of the fire grew, shooting embers into the sky in a cyclone of smoke.

Merona stood motionless, watching the distant plane as it drifted through the clouds. The mist was scarce as the bonfire blazed beside her and she knew there would be no missing it this time. This time he would find her, and all her struggles would at last come to an end.

But the plane flew on.

"Sasha, look at me," she muttered to herself. "Sasha! Turn the plane! I said turn your stupid plane, you big, dumb, blasted lug!"

But the plane only flew on.

Falling to her knees, Merona clenched the sand in her fists and let out a scream she'd been holding back for months. A scream she could not have dared utter on any other part of the island.

Looking up toward the aircraft as it drifted away once again, she shouted at it. "No... No, no, no, *no*! Sasha, just turn around. Please, just come back here. It's been months... just *please*, come back."

But the hum of Katya's propellers was gone, and Merona sat slumped in the sand, gasping out breaths of rage to hold back her tears as Argos licked her cheek to soothe the unknown stress that plagued her.

"I just want off... I want off this miserable, cannibal-infested island..."

Merona's hopelessness grew. Was there any escape?

Twice, the impossible had happened; Sasha's plane had flown within sight of the minuscule island. A tiny spec of land in the middle of nothing, and yet somehow, he had found it, not once, but twice. But even with this impossibly good luck, both times he'd failed to spot her signal. The bright glow of the fire in the dark void of water standing out like a beacon, and yet still he'd missed it?

She knew he must be looking for her, he had no other reason to be this far out over the Atlantic. How could he not have seen the light her signal had created, when his eyes must be peeled for it? How could he have missed something so noticeable in the unblemished blue of the ocean?

The questions plagued her. There must have been a reason why he hadn't seen her. There was something strange at work on this island, she had seen daily proof of that already within the swamp, but something about it was keeping her from rescue, something was keeping her hidden.

Sitting in the sand, Merona gazed out toward the island that held her captive and wondered what could possibly be keeping her signals masked, and how, if at all, that might be changed. She had had two fruitless opportunities at rescue, and if by some miracle there came a third chance, she needed to be sure she would be seen. She needed to find answers to the many riddles of the island, and that meant she needed to explore.

On this new side of the island, there seemed little life but her own, though she would still proceed with caution, she hoped to at last be free to move about unimpeded. With her firewood sufficiently stockpiled, her belly full of freshly cooked fish, and her weaponry newly sharpened, Merona set out the following day across the sand with a determination to push aside her despair and hold a little longer to hope as she followed along the beach in search of answers and solutions in this new wilderness.

Argos followed eagerly beside her, happy to be

adventuring with his fearless leader as he took in the smells of each and every new rock along the beach. This side of the island seemed to have a strange stillness to it, though not the kind that left a feeling of uneasiness like the eerie silence of the swamp, but rather a stillness that begged to be filled, either by whistling a tune or with light conversation. But, since Merona had never been the whimsically whistling sort, she soon found herself voicing her many thoughts and questions about the island that had been plaguing her mind.

"What kind of curse do you suppose this island is under, Argos?" she said, "I've read many a myth of cursed islands, plague-ridden islands, sunken islands, but I never thought I'd land on a real one. Guess I should have paid more attention to my studies like Liora was always pestering me to do, perhaps I would remember the one about an invisible island full of bloodthirsty cannibals, and how exactly I'm supposed to lift the curse that's keeping Sasha from seeing my signals."

Argos trekked on just ahead of her, fully listening to everything she said, and awaiting just one word or command he actually recognized as Merona went on.

"That's assuming the fog can actually be lifted at all..." Merona paused, trying to envision the rest of her life on the secluded island, with no other living thing for company save the shaggy mutt. "Well, if we are to be trapped here forever, you're going to have to learn to be a much better conversationalist. I mean, I like my quiet solitude better than most, but I can't be expected to carry this whole relationship. You're going to have to participate too, sometimes."

Argos glanced back, responding with a simple harrumph.

"Don't talk back to me like that! I'm not saying I don't appreciate all that you've done. You've had my back more than most humans I've worked with... I'm just saying it would be nice, if we end up stuck here for much longer, to not always be having one-sided conversations."

Argos made no reply.

"I mean, I understand you have your verbal limitations, but a nod or some more regular grunts and barks could go a long way. At least some kind of indication that you're listening to me."

Argos continued to walk on in silence.

"See, this is what I mean, half the time it seems like you can almost read my mind, with how well you seem to understand me, and then you act like *this*, and it's like you're deliberately ignoring me. I need someone to talk things over with, you know? Bounce ideas around until we think up a solution to get off this rock... I mean, I can't be the only one coming up with ideas around here. You have just as much reason to want off this island as I do, so we've got to work as a team."

At last Argos looked at her and responded with a clear, protesting bark.

"All right! Fine, I get it, you're not an ideas guy. I'll just be grateful you pull your weight with hunting and the night watch far better than your deceased master did. I've just never had to call all the shots before. Usually, my uncle or Liora liked to take the lead on things. Not that I mind it... I'd honestly prefer it to being bossed around. Just got to hope that this side of the island has answers for us, instead of more trouble."

And with those final words, she drew her weapons, trekking on in silence as she readied herself to face just about anything this island chose to throw at her. Merona hadn't the slightest idea what she might find that could aid in their escape, but with all the strange occurrences she had witnessed while on the island, she could no longer ignore the blatantly supernatural elements that were at play, and hoped to find some means of utilizing them to her advantage. She held onto the hope that a solution, any solution, no matter how abnormal it turned out to be, might be within her reach now, if she could only find it.

The beach stretched on, curving and bending out ahead of them before a jutting cliff barred their progress. As Merona was forced to follow along the cliff, she began to spot familiar signs of civilization. Tattered strips of threadbare fabric hung from the trees, signaling the territory of a nearby gray men camp, and in a blink, Merona's machete and spear were drawn and at the ready as she crept cautiously forward.

Uneasy to venture further, Merona was nevertheless determined to discover exactly what she was up against on this new side of the island. If she was going to have to fight for her life again against bloodthirsty locals, she'd rather not be taken by surprise this time. The thickly packed trees and dense mist closed around her in a familiar choking, and not remotely comforting way, and soon the tops of scattered huts came into sight between the trees and Merona slowed her pace all the more, but with her next few steps it became visibly evident that this camp was nothing like the others she had encountered.

This village had long since been abandoned. Huts were caved in or dotted with holes and other signs of decay, while broken weaponry littered the ground alongside the scattered bones and skulls of fallen tribespeople. It had been a massacre that was long since passed and forgotten. All tension in the air eased, and Merona soon found herself ambling through the uninhibited site, searching among the ransacked huts for further answers as Argos trotted to and fro nearby, sniffing every inch of dirt his nose deemed most fascinating.

The scattered skulls and decay made it clear this camp had been from a time long past when the gray men had occupied this side of the island, but to Merona's wonder, the huts and spears seemed of a distinctly superior make than those she had previously encountered beyond the swamp. It seemed the people of the island had regressed in more ways than one.

A grand hut of fine workmanship stood at the center of the camp, with half its roofing caved in on one side, where signs of scorching still remained. At the front of the hut an elaborately woven door now hung limp and burnt from the open doorway, framed by two tall windows to either side.

With two long strides, Merona cleared the fallen door and stepped inside the lofty hut, now illuminated by the streams of light that fell through its half-collapsed roof. The ground was littered with fallen debris, skulls, and bones, as though the villagers had been forced inside by their attackers to burn alive or suffocate. To the left, sitting apart from the others who had crowded at the doors and windows to escape, a lone corpse caught Merona's attention. At least, it had once been a corpse, now reduced to a scattering of bones and a jawless skull which rested atop a large leather wrapping.

Moving closer to the singular remains, Merona carefully removed the skull and bones from off the precious bundle. Folding back the scorched animal hide, her gaze fell on a stack of broken, gray slates, each slate covered with precise grooves and divots across the surface of the clay.

"Well, would you look at what I just found, Argos," said Merona.

Trotting over at the sound of his name, Argos tapped

his wet nose against her findings.

"It's some form of writing," she continued, taking out the delicate pieces to puzzle them back together. "This might hold the answers we're looking for, if we can figure out how to decipher it."

With care, Merona extracted the first layer of slate, placing the largest chunk in the dirt as she gradually shifted the smaller pieces around it. As the bits locked unevenly together, Merona's experienced eye began to see a familiarity to the writings, noticing a strong resemblance to ancient Persian or Sumerian cuneiform. There were few individuals who could actually read such writings, and Merona had only ever personally met one who had a moderate grasp of the language.

"Liora, where are you when I need you?" Merona muttered under her breath, looking over the carefully guarded records, in a desperate attempt to remember anything her sister had taught her of the ancient writing method, but as the words before her read out, "Illuminated grandfather, childbirth fruit fish," it was clear the similarities with anything she knew about cuneiform, were superficial at best.

Translating her findings clearly wouldn't be as easy as anticipated, but with nothing else to do besides sleep, collect water, wood, and fish, a little light reading material of a dead language seemed a welcome change to her recently humdrum days.

CHAPTER XXVI

A LOST CIVILIZATION

Liora gritted her teeth, shifting her books amongst her other supplies within the inadequate pack. "This is ridiculous," she muttered, "I don't even know what I'm packing for."

Copperhead's refusal to divulge even the slightest hint of information regarding their expedition, or even to explain why their departure was to be delayed yet again, was beginning to wear on even Liora's unflappable patience.

Liora had incessantly utilized her powers of diplomacy to try and explain that even the slightest piece of information to go on would greatly assist her in packing efficiently for the expedition, and that she had no intention of repeating what she was told to even the other members of the team. But even her tactful reassurances had no effect on her immovable employer. He had paid her extra to ask no questions, and he would hold her to that.

She would be setting off blind, and though she had tried to accept the idea at the start, Copperhead's repetitive reply of, "That's information for select ears only." to every question she put forward, was no longer amusing.

"Maybe Merona's been right this whole time about diplomacy," Liora thought aloud, her sister's wise words coming quickly to mind. "You might catch flies with honey, but you only get answers by pulling off wings."

A scrawny boy popped his head around the door, interrupting Liora's growing thoughts of violence to inform her that Copperhead required her presence immediately.

Liora returned her standard reply to the bespectacled assistant that she had every day before. "Tell him I'm on my way."

With a nod, the boy ducked out of sight as Liora returned to the heap of books refusing to fit within her small pack and huffed in defeat before turning to follow after the courier.

Frothy water dripped from Copperhead's chin into the sink below, as he scraped his blade across the last remains of stubble on his jaw.

"You wanted to see me?" said Liora.

A jovial smile spread across his face. "I did! I have excellent news, Miss Grant, I hope you have all your things in order, because we depart for the dig site *tomorrow.*"

"Tomorrow? You said we weren't leaving for several more days!"

"Things changed."

"What things?"

"Nothing to worry your pretty little head about. Just make sure your things are ready by tomorrow morning."

"I could have been ready days ago if I had a little more information on what exactly I'll be doing on this expedition. Ancient Egyptian cultural and mythical expertise is a pretty broad job description. Hard to fit every book, tool, or resource I might need into one or two packs, light enough for travel. What exactly is the specific mythical expertise you hired me for?"

"Like I said before, that's information for only a select few."

"Understood, but as much as I relish the idea of carrying an entire library on my back, it really isn't practical."

"I've already told you, you don't need to worry about what books to bring. I'll have all you'll need when we get there."

"But if you could just tell me…"

"I've told you *all* you need to know!" Seething rage filled his bloodshot eyes with an intensity his once smiling exterior had seemed incapable of harboring. "I've been patient with your endless questions, Miss Grant, but if you can't comprehend the simple idea that they *will not* be answered, then you can easily return the generous advance I gave you, and be on your way."

"Return the advance?"

"Yes. Or have you already sent it on to your friend in Morocco?"

Liora had no words.

"Yes, I do know about your correspondence."

"Well, it wasn't exactly a secret."

"No, but you see, when I hire someone for a highly sensitive expedition, I don't much like discovering they are sharing all they know with their friends. No matter how trusted they think they are."

"I didn't tell him anything…"

"You corresponded when on a highly secret job! That's plenty. And it will *not* be continuing."

"Excuse me?"

"I said it ends now. There will be no more outgoing letters."

"You don't have the right to tell me I can't send letters or—"

"While you work for me, I *own* you, understand?"

Liora clenched her jaw. "I beg your pardon, but no one *owns* me."

"Then return my money if you can't hold up your end."

Fuming at the corner he had backed her into, Liora stood silent. She wanted to call Merona into the room to help her give him a thrashing, or to throw his money back in his face and tell him she would rather chew glass than work with a dog like him. But she could do none of those things, because Merona *wasn't* there, and all that money was with Sasha, funding his search for her.

Liora forced a polite smile. She had to show restraint; her sister's very survival depended on it.

"My apologies... you're absolutely right. I agreed to work in the dark and maintain your confidentiality in exchange for more money, and I will hold to that arrangement. No more letters, no more questions, I'll get my things packed and be ready to set off by tomorrow."

"Good. And Miss Grant, now that you understand your role in all this, I do hope we can work together more cordially from now on."

"Of course."

Bottling back her contempt, Liora returned to her quarters, pulling books from her pack without consideration to the intellectual loss on her supplies. She would do her job, but if he insisted on tying her hands, she wouldn't upset herself if his expedition suffered for it.

As she buckled up her pack and satchel, Liora had the sudden realization that after tomorrow, Sasha would have no means of contacting her with news of his search for Merona. But with outgoing letters now forbidden, how would she inform him of her new location? Perhaps Copperhead was worried about exactly that... the location of his precious find becoming known to the public and his competition. It seemed a likely reason for all the secrecy, but Liora bristled at the idea of leaving Sasha in the dark, and sat down to write a final, hasty letter, to inform him of her planned departure the following morning.

Dear Sasha,

My departure has been moved up to tomorrow, so I will not be sending or receiving any longer from this address. I hope the money I sent you is enough to make all the necessary repairs to Katya, and continue your hunt for our sister.

I've enclosed a little more money, and will try to send you more as soon as I'm next paid, as well as my new address as soon as I know it. Though, with how insistent Copperhead is being on maintaining secrecy on his expedition, it might be difficult to slip past his watchful eye to send any further letters for some time. He's decided there are to be no more outgoing letters, at least for the time being. You'd think the man had the government watching his every move with how paranoid he is. Oh well, I should be accustomed to working with eccentric characters by now.

Try not to worry about me though, I'm more than capable of handling myself, and you need to focus on your hunt. If you need any further assistance, you still have my uncle's address to apply for help, and I know he will want you to keep him updated as well about how your search fairs.

Your faithful friend as always,
Liora.

Sealing up her letter, Liora licked shut the envelope and strode for her door to make her way down to the hotel front desk. Yet, as she reached the lobby, a foreboding dread fell over her, that Copperhead was not a man to be challenged lightly. Surely, he would have eyes watching to see if she, or any of his team, sent letters from the hotel, so without halting a step, she slipped casually outside, careful to go unnoticed as she went. If she was fast, she was sure she could slip out to the post office and be back again before anyone noticed her absence.

Liora made her way down the street and to the nearest post office with urgent haste, sending off her letter in a frenzy and rushing back to the hotel where Copperhead's team had set up temporary base. She was sure she couldn't have been gone more than a few minutes, but as she entered the lobby, there was Dr. Strenburg, a middle-aged archaeologist, standing near the stairs as though he had been waiting for her. If there was anyone out of the expedition's team members who seemed thickest with Copperhead, it was him.

"Miss Grant, and where have you been?" asked Strenburg, "Copperhead has been looking for you."

"I was… just stretching my legs," replied Liora.

"Oh, no need for that. I suspect you will get plenty of exercise once we set off tomorrow."

"I suppose so. You all packed?"

"Oh yes… long since."

"Then you knew we'd be leaving soon? Unlike the rest of us…"

He flashed an unconvincing smile. "Hmmm, yes, well, some of us know how to keep on our boss's good side. So, might I suggest you save that inquisitive mind of yours for the job ahead, and refrain from asking too many *prying* questions. Someone might get it into their head that you are some kind of spy."

"Spy? And who would I be spying for?"

"You tell me."

"I would, but there's nothing to tell. I just needed

the money, it's that simple."

"Informant can be a very lucrative job, I hear."

"Well, I wish someone had told me sooner, at least I would've been paid extra for all the suspicions and coded accusations I'm dealing with."

"Well, perhaps if you didn't slip out to send letters, there would be a little less suspicion cast in your direction."

Liora stared fixedly at him without blinking. "I told you, I was stretching my legs."

"Yes, of course you were. I won't bother to mention it to anyone then... wouldn't want to get our fearless leader paranoid, now, would we?"

And with that, Dr. Strenburg walked off, leaving Liora to puzzle out what exactly he hoped to gain with this vailed threat of his, and how exactly she was going to handle this new snag in her increasingly complicated job.

"Liora, Liora," she muttered to herself, "what *have* you gotten yourself into? I swear, there's got to be an easier way for me to earn a little dough."

~

The campfire flames danced at her side, as Merona scrutinized her clay tablet discovery. Some tablets had been almost wholly unharmed, remaining unbroken in the bundle, and from these complete writing samples Merona was able to match and puzzle together the others. On the beach before her, the bits of clay lay strewn out in the sand, slowly taking shape in the fire light, but still the words were lost on her.

Amid the writing of many of the tablets, she had noticed occasional small images, not unlike the paintings on the cave walls, though greatly simplified, scattered between the other symbols. Each seemed its own symbol for a word, such as the image of a fish or boat, and Merona quickly hoped to utilize these clear, more universal images to better understand the unreadable texts before her.

At her side, Argos' snout nudged against her leg, a twisted stick in his mouth. At first, Merona dismissed his continual prodding for play, keeping her focus on the puzzle before her, but as the hours wore on, she found that his incessant appeals for her to join him in a little leisure time became harder to refuse.

It had been a long day, and the simple act of throwing a stick out across the beach and watching her furry companion, who had more than once saved her life, scamper back in a state of overjoyed exuberance again and again, helped to bring a smile to her weary face. Allowing for small moments of amusement during her months on the island had been sorely lacking.

Watching Argos dance across the sand, leaping and spinning far more than necessary to retrieve the stick after every throw, Merona breathed a contented sigh that she at least had such inexplicably joyous company to pass her time with. To the dog, they were on an adventure, exploring a glorious wilderness full of new sights and endless smells, and though it had its dangers, Argos only ever concerned himself with them in those moments of immediate threat, never dwelling on the past, fully enjoying and living in these peaceful moments of play whenever they came along.

Merona watched him as he ran and leapt across the beach, marveling at his unflappable resilience, and determined to embrace his moment-by-moment mindset as best she could from this point on. What good did it do to worry over things she could not control? She would work each day to survive, to uncover the islands secrets, and face each new problem as it came, but most of all, she would make time to enjoy the small moments of peace as they arose, for who could say how long they might last, or how far off the next one might be?

As the game went on, drool transferred from mouth, to stick, to hand with every throw, until the contented mutt lay down at his companion's side, exhausted by the rigors of play.

Merona scratched his belly, relieving his itches while simultaneously cleansing her hand of its accumulated slobber in his fur. "Have a good run, boy? It's nice to stretch your legs without cannibals in pursuit, isn't it?"

Argos let out a short huff in seeming agreement, and Merona carried on, the scraggled mutt providing a welcomed, though completely inattentive listening ear to her ramblings.

"I got to say, though, this is the closest to a vacation I've had in years. I mean, not the past few months where we've almost been killed about a hundred times. But this... this beach is actually quite relaxing."

Leaning against the log at her back, arms crossing behind her head, Merona gazed out across the sparkling waters, and twinkling stars that peeked through the cloudy sky, realizing she no longer felt a chill in the night air since reaching this side of the island.

She let out a comfortable sigh. "Nope, not bad at all."

As if to punctuate her words, the row of fish began sizzling on their spear over the fire, and Merona sat up, pulling her spear from its place in the sand to begin picking clean her meal, tossing Argos his share between bites. In the beginning, Merona had often felt a twinge of hesitation in sharing her limited food supplies with her backstabbing pilot's animal, but as the two rested on the beach, such past unfamiliarity between them was long forgotten.

Merona no longer thought of Argos as Carver's dog, but rather her only ally, and friend, who understood her plight more than anyone alive could, or ever would. He had saved her from starvation, pulled her from certain death within a slimy pit, been her guardian in the night, and her watchdog by day. Few men had earned her trust in so short a time as this animal had, and every chunk of meat she tossed his way was relinquished with an air of gratitude and true camaraderie.

~

The following days were spent hunched over clay tablets, laboring to decipher their meanings, and in additional treks out to the abandoned camp in a continued hunt for new clues. At times the need for answers seemed a fruitless one, but the strange island had left innumerable questions in Merona's mind, and to sit, day after day without answers, went against her very nature. If she could understand the island, she felt certain she could escape it, or at the very least, find a better means of surviving it.

Within the desolate village, Merona picked through the scattered and broken relics of the forgotten lives which had once inhabited it: clay pots, woven baskets, and other tasks left unfinished and abandoned by their makers, most likely during the attack which had decimated them.

As she searched on, small tokens seemed to tell a story of a far more peaceful and intellectual people than seemed possible in such a place. Though now broken from battle and worn away by time, care had been shown with everything that they did. Their clothing and dress, though now faded, had been of a fine make, adorned

with many details of shells and crystalline pebbles. The huts were of careful craftsmanship, with woven doors, and expertly assembled framework.

As Merona passed through, a doll of twigs caught her eye, carefully and lovingly clad in a blue fabric wrap dress, lying not far off from the bones of a small child, and Merona paused her search a moment to return it to the small hand. It was as though these people had never known war until this day... they had been so wholly unprepared for it.

At one end of the village a snaking path led through the trees, stretching a short hike from the main huts of the village before it reached a low, wide cave opening. More fabric hung from trees and dried, faded adornments dotted the ground around the cavern. Inside, the walls were lined from floor to ceiling with intricate crafted clay pots, placed in hollowed out cavities within the walls. Written into the sides of each pot were clean symbols, identical to the writing on the clay slates, and several pots lay broken, their contents spilling out across the floor, clearly revealing the cave's purpose.

"It's a mausoleum," Merona whispered.

The bones of the dead had been scattered across the floor, from the many broken pots which the years of neglect had cracked and weakened, and Merona carefully examined them, surprised to find no signs of knife or teeth marks upon the remains. These people had not consumed their dead like the gray men she had encountered before, instead they carefully gathered and stowed their burnt remains in beautiful pottery, marked, presumably with their names in remembrance.

These had been families and neighbors who took pride in every part of life, and full respect in death. Nowhere could Merona see a hint of the bloodlust or ritual violence that she'd witnessed beyond the swamp.

But what had happened? What had changed? Had the other, more violent tribes simply wiped these people out? In her search for answers, she seemed to collect a thousand more questions, and her days became consumed in knowing these people, and what had become of them.

At the grave site, Merona had seen a set of abstract, carved, wooden statues bordering the cave entrance, and soon began to discover identical figurines and carvings scattered around the village. Their appearance was humanoid, but an emphasis was always given to the long clawed and webbed fingers, and the fins which framed the head. Merona's memory could not be turned from the hands which so closely resembled the creature of the swamp, and though this reminder sent a chill over her, the affection in which they had been carved spoke through the artistry. This was not something the extinct islanders had feared, for it bore a regal posture, and could be found guarding the doors of sacred places, or hanging around the necks of women, children, or soldiers like a token of good fortune, protection, or perhaps even worship, like the Christian crucifix.

These revelations, though insightful, still left Merona with numerous questions remaining unanswered, and she hoped to find more answers within one of her very first discoveries: the clay tablets. Though the clearer images of a canoe, a spear, a man, a hut and so on, offered an insight into the subject matter of each tablet, such as the building of a prominent structure or a raid on a camp, the dots and dents, which made up the other symbols that covered the rest of the tablet's surface, were a complete mystery to her.

Going back to the basics she recalled of deciphering unknown text, Merona decided to set about her translation as systematically as possible. Her first task in decoding the texts was to identify and number each individual and unique symbol present in the writing, but with no paper on which to transcribe her findings, Merona took to scratching her discoveries onto scraps of bark peelings with a burnt charcoal stick as her makeshift pencil. The quantity of unique symbols only seemed to number in the hundreds, which was considerably less than she had at first anticipated.

Though they had clearly valued the importance of their own history and record keeping, their language was clearly a very young one, only in the fledgling stages of creation, and Merona hoped this fact might make the decoding of its meaning relatively painless. It did not. Hour after hour and day after day she pored over the clay inscriptions, becoming no more the wiser to their meaning than the week before.

With the meaningless symbols refusing to speak to her, Merona once again set out towards the village for answers.

"Perhaps we'll find a Rosetta Stone," she quipped to Argos, who looked up toward her with incredulity in his eyes.

"Hey, a girl can dream, can't she?"

Argos gave no reply, trotting along toward their destination with indifference to her ludicrous words.

Arriving at the growingly familiar village, Merona walked among the toppled huts and structures, unsure of where next to explore. She had systematically searched through nearly every hut and down every winding path, and doubted if there was anything further to discover, but as she traipsed down the main road, she found herself standing before a familiar structure; the burnt-out building in which the clay records had been found. On this approach, however, her gaze became transfixed on a symbol etched into the wood framing above the door. A symbol she knew well.

The meaningless symbols from the clay tablets had become imprinted on Merona's memory, and she began to see them in places she had not noticed before. Above doors, stitched into clothing, or carved into clay pendants which lay among crumpled heaps of bones. Astounded with her own blindness, Merona at once stripped a piece of bark from a nearby tree and began recording her findings upon it. What kinds of structures bore what kinds of marks, the colors and make of their garments, or the apparent status of the individuals who had once worn these pendants.

The light dimming, Merona once again returned to her camp, and as she worked to piece together her new findings within the village, with the writings on the clay, far more concrete concepts soon began to emerge. The symbol above the burnt structure appeared most on a tablet she had once assumed to be about the construction of the village, but with this new information, it seemed to speak exclusively of this apparent house of records, she began to realize it was a tablet detailing the construction of their first library of sorts.

Next came the symbols on the garments. Many were at first indistinct, but finding some alongside images of fish, or huts, she soon realized they were indications of the individual's profession; fishermen, hunters, scholars, warriors, woodworkers, and holy men. Perhaps they were a kind of guild emblem given to individuals learning, or those who had completed their trade. She could only speculate.

One mark which was often pared alongside the other symbols, always on an intricately carved pendant, had been worn by adult individuals in far more opulent attire than most, and Merona guessed this to be their symbol for leaders of the various guilds.

As she searched through the writings once again, though a majority of the words remained indecipherable, she found herself beginning to understand the meaning behind each story written upon them. At last, she could begin to better understand the beliefs of this village and its people. From her earlier findings, she'd seen signs that they trusted, rather than feared, the swamp, but it soon became clear that whatever it was that lived there, had not only been trusted, but sacred. Its image was pared with holy symbols as well as their symbol for guardian or warrior in almost every iteration. Had the creature been seen to protect them in some way?

As she lay down for the night, Merona's thoughts and dreams were once again consumed with the many symbols and the stories they told, and the following day her return to the village was made with renewed resolve. Searching into every corner and through every knickknack, Merona grew ever more absorbed in her thoughts on the wholly opposed natures of the east and west peoples of the island. One was peaceful, cultured, and yet had seemingly worshiped a monster, and the other violent, bloodthirsty, but feared that same creature. But as her mind shifted through these musings, the distant sound of engines fell silent on her ears.

This, however, was not the case for Argos.

With a thunderous bark, Argos snapped Merona from her silent contemplations, her heart sent pounding as she whirled around toward him, and the danger she assumed he was alerting her to. But Argos stood still and quiet, his head cocked up toward the sky.

No longer occupied with her thoughts, Merona at last detected the anomaly, the sound of an ever-nearing plane came rocketing to her ears, and within seconds, both dog and adventuress were hurtling through vines and bush, racing toward the beach and their signal fire.

In her gut, Merona feared this third attempt would again prove fruitless, but her instinct for survival refused to let the chance slip away once again. It had to work this time. Her luck couldn't be *that* bad.

Slender branches whipped against her face and shoulders, lashing her skin as she pressed on. The beach came rapidly into view and soon Merona's worn boots were plunging through the sand with ever rapid steps. Falling near the coals of her dead campfire, Merona ignited the flames anew into a bright blaze, tossing dried leaves and fresh greenery upon the heap to build up a smoking signal.

The plane was still in sight as thick black billows rose from the sand, blanketing the sky as Merona held her breath, watching and waiting for the plane to change course toward them... waiting for Sasha at last to find her.

Chapter XXVII

YET TO BE UNVEILED

SASHA's sharp eyes scrutinized the waters below once again, renewed determination to find his missing "sister" consuming his every waking thought. Liora had taken work with an unscrupulous rat in order to fund this final chance at tracing Merona, and this time, Sasha would not fail. He could not, or else Liora's selfless efforts would be in vain.

With the last radio signal reigniting his hope, Sasha flew with the confidence that Merona was still alive and fighting to survive until rescue could reach her, and he would not let her down. She was out there, and he was her last hope at liberation.

The fog hung thick over the water, but Sasha was resolute in making a comprehensive search of the area, even if he had to retrace his path a dozen times over. He would find this island that did not exist and rescue her from its clutches before another month passed.

"Come on, come on, give me signal, Merona. If you out there, you would have signal fire... where is signal?"

Then, as though in answer to his plea, a hint of smoke began to rise in the distance, but as he approached, he could find no signs of where it originated from. No ship or wreckage in the water, and most certainly no island on which to land. Sasha looked on in puzzled confusion, unsure what to make of the sourceless smoke rising from the nothingness of the open sea. But as he flew closer, all

·315·

at once the smoke seemed to vanish away, as though it had been a trick of light, or his own hopeful delusion.

Sasha circled the area again and again, hoping the signal might return, but with no further signs to follow, he turned back toward the Azorean islands in defeat, to replenish his already dwindling fuel. But as he turned, he made note of his present coordinates, where the smoke had appeared, feeling that somehow, in that moment, he had found Merona's location, yet through some unfathomable force had been prevented from seeing the mysterious island which had entrapped her.

Sasha liked to think himself a rational man, but could never help falling into the possibility of the supernatural being at play, especially when he was witness to the seemingly impossible, when out searching for a mythical, invisible island. However unlikely the idea might be, he would not dismiss any possibilities until Merona was found.

Yet, with still no further word or funds from Liora since her first letter, the likelihood of being able to continue his search was dwindling by the day. A sinking feeling that both his Grant sisters were slipping ever further away from him knotted his stomach, but he was a good twelve months away from giving up just yet.

He could not know if the smoke meant anything, but being one to trust his gut over anything else, Sasha was determined to return again, and again to this same location, until whatever had been the source of the strange smoke signal, at last revealed itself.

As he flew on, back toward Ponta Delgada and Uncle Quincy to report his findings, a strong wind began to blow in, and Sasha soon found himself struggling to maintain control of his aircraft. Though he prided himself on his long-held record of never crashing, he feared he might be in for a rough landing ahead.

~

In the distance, Sasha's plane seemed to circle back, turning toward Merona and the island for the first time, and as his circles grew tighter and nearer, Merona held her breath, feeling at last that she had a hope of rescue. But as her hope rose, the fog in the sky rapidly thickened, rushing in from all sides like tentacled arms to all but obscure the familiar plane as it searched above, Sasha's circles growing looser with every pass until all at once he turned away, giving up his search once more in defeat.

He had not stopped, he had not landed, and Merona watched for the third time as Sasha's plane dwindled out of sight, leaving her to lament her useless efforts and wasted wood supplies once again. She was sure this time he had seen something... her signal perhaps? But if he had seen her, why had he not landed? There was no reason she could think of that made any sense, unless...

"...He couldn't see the island," Merona said aloud.

Staring up at the now thickly fogged sky, Merona began to truly believe in the island and its supernatural powers to remain hidden from the world. With all she had seen, it would be madness to hold onto doubt for what was plainly before her. The swamp and the creature within it, the unceasing fog that had grown unnaturally thick in the very moment the island needed to be obscured from view... and even the memory of the strange black wave that had dragged their plane to the island in the first place... none of it seemed of this earth from the very beginning, and all of it was bent on one thing... holding her captive here forever.

But this only filled Merona with a determination to fight against all that prevented her, to take back her freedom and find a means of escape. Supernatural powers or no supernatural powers. Yet, unbeknownst to Merona as she thought on all these things, someone had sighted her distant smoke signal rising from the eastern side of the island for the second time, the side of the island which had long since been uninhabited. Someone who Merona had gone to great lengths to escape.

With no knowledge of her observer, Merona once again returned to hunt among the huts for further answers, with renewed stamina in her determination to explore. After a small discovery of more markings on pottery shards and even some fully intact pots, Merona could now add the words for various food items to her vocabulary. Old fish bones littered the bottom of one partially intact container, while shriveled signs of grain could still be identified within another.

However, her discovery at the cave of the dead became the most groundbreaking find of all. First, the countless symbols marking the burial pottery were written in a distinctly unique, more curving style, to designate the names of people from all other writing. But second, and perhaps more vital to Merona's deciphering, were the many personal items inside the pots, which painted distinct pictures of the life and death of each man or woman laid to rest within: An insignia of occupation, jewelry showing an individual's status, other personal items of various milestones reached throughout their life, a tree of names, perhaps listing genealogy? And so on.

Carefully, Merona cataloged the names, matching them with each name mentioned in the historical texts. For the first time since she had begun, she could start to follow the appearances of individual natives within the stories on the clay. The names began to take on personalities in her mind, formed from the various items buried with them, and she began ascribing nicknames to her long-dead neighbors to help keep them straight.

But an even greater find still lay within the burial site, undiscovered for some days as Merona cataloged her latest findings, until at last she unearthed a pot unlike all the rest. Within it lay bones like any others, but the items that accompanied them were a startling find, for within this clay container she found artifacts of another world... a world she was once a part of. First was a silver pocket watch, next a wooden pipe, then a pair of scratched spectacles, a box of matches all but empty, a deck of cards, a small pencil worn to a stub, and lastly, but by far the most important, a leather journal. Within its pages was the account of another castaway, like herself, by the name of Lord Westwick, who had been stranded upon the island many years before, in 1912. Clearly an academic sort, he had been welcomed into the tribe with openness, adapting and acclimating to their ways and customs over time, and had slowly begun to try and understand their language, cataloging in detail all he had learned within his journal.

Much of his writing was on trying to understand their spoken language, which appeared much more complex than their writings, but that too he had begun to decipher, cataloging symbols and their meanings in scattered lists throughout his journal. Much of his findings happily backed up Merona's own speculations, with some helpful corrections to be gained as well. But most importantly, he had uncovered the meanings to many of the symbols she had, thus far, found no means of understanding. And though his work was by no means complete, for it seemed a lung complaint began plaguing him near the end of his entries, this substantial finding soon meant that Merona could now begin to understand the rudimentary meanings behind most of the texts.

As she read over the ancient stories aloud, Argos filled the role of unwilling listener.

"It seems this tribe, at least, abhorred cannibalism," said Merona. "Apparently their ancestors practiced it for a time, but luckily for old Westwick, it was done away with well before he was marooned. They don't have a unique word for it, but 'hunter' or 'eater of brother flesh' comes up a lot and seems to be strongly disliked as a shameful part of their people's history."

Merona grimaced. "I have to agree with them on that point. But it seems clear that several tribesmen turned back to cannibalism, believing it gave them the strength of those they devoured. This name," she pointed to a claw-like symbol. "Blood-maw, let's call him, seems to have been the instigator of returning to the old ways, and he and his followers were outcast because of it. Somehow, Blood-maw gathered more and more people to his side, showing displays of his and his followers growing power from those they had eaten, with regular raids on the once peaceful village. After a village leader, or holy man, gave an offering of some kind to their deity for protection, the island was split by the swamp and a guardian summoned to keep the eastern village safe from attacks, trapping Blood-maw and his followers on the west half of the island. You don't think the guardian is... the creature?"

Merona looked instinctively to her sole companion, Argos, who gazed back at her, offering even fewer answers to her questions than she herself had. The idea that the creature could have once been a force for good seemed unfathomable.

"But what else could it be? They seem to have his icon scattered all over their village. Like a gargoyle to ward off evil. Well, whatever it was, the writing continues on, and it looks like things seem to return to normal in the village for some time, with the guardian patrolling the swamp, only allowing deserting members of the outcast tribe to return once they had passed some kind of test within the swamp. It also seemed to have a protective power source of some sort, which granted the swamp guardian control over the fog to conceal the village, and a hand of the water, to prevent boat raids."

Merona's mind drifted back to the black wave that had risen out of the water the night of the crash, and the unnatural shape it had taken. "The hand! The black hand that forced our plane to crash! It was controlled by the guardian... or at least it was... it says here that some warrior cannibals defied the swamp to try and raid the village, and some even broke through the barrier, which emboldened them to make more attacks on the swamp, and it seems they took some of his power for themselves somehow."

"Because of this, it's clear that the holy man and his followers hoped to find a means of escape, but even though they had canoes of some sort, they were unable to leave the island. Most likely because the boats weren't fit for a long ocean crossing, only fishing around the island, I think."

Leaning back in her sandy bed, Merona closed her tired eyes as a yawn momentarily overwhelmed her voice. "But I might be reading that wrong. Heck, I might be reading all of it wrong, for all I know."

Merona let out a long, forlorn sigh. "Oh, Liora, how I wish I had your encyclopedia brain with me right about now. With all that other castaway's notes, we'd have this deciphered by now, if you were here."

Argos circled repeatedly in the sand, dropping down in a compact, shaggy ball at Merona's side as both settled in for the night, the fire dwindling to crackling embers nearby. Her eyes drifting shut, Merona listened to the waves sloshing against the shoreline as sleep washed over her, still in disbelief at the uninterrupted peace of the last several weeks.

Food had been plentiful, given the situation, with fish in ready supply in select pockets along the coastline. The freshwater rivers flowed day and night, out from the woods, into the ocean, not far from her camp. And with no more need to take daily trips to refresh her supplies, she had instead been able to accumulate several water skins full of storage at her camp.

With the cursed swamp, and cannibal threat, well behind her, Merona's primary focus had been on the village, its history, and finding answers. And she marveled at the stark contrast of her life a month prior. She longed to be rescued, but if her situation persisted as it presently stood, she knew she had resources enough to survive until then.

At least, she thought she had.

The sound of the water had been lulling Merona toward sleep, but before it could take her, the rhythmic undulation of the waves was interrupted by an encroaching murmur of voices. For a moment, Merona dismissed the sounds, trusting that her anxieties were playing tricks on her, but as the voices grew louder, their abrupt silence stirred Merona awake.

With sudden fear in her stomach, she searched out through the surrounding darkness for the source of the voices, but the night and mist barred her gaze, her cold foggy breath catching in the dimming firelight and obliterating her view all the more with every exhale. She breathed in a deep gulp of air, holding her breath as she tried once again to see through the blackness.

A once-faint splashing and rhythmic thump of hollow wood grew ever-closer, and the memory of the clay tablets and their mention of "boat raids" flew into

Merona's mind. They had canoes; and at one time the gray men had used them to circle the island in raiding parties.

"It's them," she whispered, reaching for her machete in the dim glow of the fire's embers.

Argos sat upright at her words, instinctively recognizing the warning in her voice as she took up a spear in her free hand. He rose to his feet, following alongside her as she skirted from her bed to a large, distant boulder for cover on the rocky beach.

Again, Merona looked out toward the vast black ocean, squinting to catch a glimpse of the approaching raiders in the darkness. The night sky shifted in her favor, as a strong wind, sweeping high through the air, tossed the fog from the sky just enough to allow the moon's light to catch on the water.

All at once, two clear silhouettes appeared on the waves, their oars cutting into the water with clean, unified strokes. The canoes sat low in the water, weighed down by the gray warriors huddled in each.

Merona swallowed back a rising lump, her limbs and muscles feeling weak and ill-prepared for the battle ahead. Her machete and spearhead were dull and poorly maintained, their care having taken a backseat to the translation of the clay tablets. Merona cursed her complacency, knowing this negligence in her defenses might very well cost her her life.

The thud of canoes hitting sand met her ears, and Merona shook the nerves of her arms, cracking her neck from side to side, to little effect. Her gaze fell momentarily down toward Argos' large black eyes, and both let out a sigh.

"It's official, Argos," she whispered, almost inaudibly. "I hate this island."

CHAPTER XXVIII

BLOOD IN THE SAND

MERONA held still, her body tightly pressed against the rock at her back. Sloshing footfalls rushed forward from the water, growing louder with every warrior that leapt from their canoes.

The impending attack loomed, and Merona stood still and silent in her place of concealment. Resting a calming hand on Argos's shoulders, the mutt took her lead, standing motionless next to her as the gray men neared. Shadowy figures rushed by on either side of her, ignoring the rock Merona and Argos crouched behind as they moved up the beach, drawn to the faint firelight of her camp. Four... six... ten men had sped by, falling upon her campsite ahead and halting their companions with raised spears and hatchets.

A final figure passed Merona's rock, his back toward her as he looked up and down the beach only a few feet from her. Raising her spear, Merona plunged her weapon straight through the side of the oblivious warrior's neck. A strangled gurgling spat from his mouth, unheard by his companions as Merona caught hold of his limp body and slipped back into the shadows of the rock.

Another gray man split from the others in search of footprints leading away from the camp, and Merona crept toward him, keeping hidden in the black shadows of the boulders as she made her approach.

Backed up against the boulder, Merona waited for

the stray warrior to round it, and just as his spear came fully into view, she lashed out with her machete, slitting across his throat before pulling his writhing body out of sight. A swift spear through the heart and he lay still in the blood-soaked sand, as Merona crept forward once again to dispatch her next assailant.

The men were scattered amid the rocks, searching for the tracks of the occupants of the camp, which they had unknowingly trodden over and obscured on their way up the beach. Her course of action was clear; take them out, one by one, before her presence was discovered. Slipping among the shadows of the rocky shore, Merona silently dispatched a third, then fourth warrior, but as she inched closer to her fifth isolated target, the warrior turned, their eyes locking as they stood mere feet apart. Spear in hand, Merona lunged for his heart, but the gray man leapt back, shrieking out for his fellow warriors.

Six shadows raced across the sand toward the two grappling assailants, and as the gray warrior twisted to plunge a stone dagger through Merona's gut, Argos leapt in, teeth and claws tearing at the man's arm until the weapon was relinquished.

With a chop of her machete, Merona separated his head from his body, just in time to duck a club aimed for her skull. A second strike followed, but Merona leapt back, dropping her spear and grabbing the dull club from her attacker's grasp. In that moment, the weapon felt strikingly familiar, and Merona's eyes suddenly locked on her lost rifle, now resting in her hand.

The gray man held the rifle backward, using its forestock and barrel as a grip to wield its butt as a battering club.

"You're kidding me," Merona muttered, shifting her grip on the stock and reaching for the trigger.

The air erupted, sending the gray man hurtling back

as a slug tore through his abdomen. Tossing the weapon up onto its accustomed place against her shoulder and sliding the bolt swiftly into place, Merona smiled at her absurd luck that the weapon even still worked.

The air cracked as she discharged another shot, rapidly worked the bolt, and fired again. With each shot she dropped her foes with expert ease before a fourth and final pull of the trigger ended in an unsatisfactory click. She was empty.

"Well, it was nice while it lasted."

Dropping the useless gun to the sand, Merona snatched up her machete once again as the final three gray men charged forward, enraged. The display of their opponent's power had only halted their resolve for a moment.

In a split second, they were upon her, spears and hatchets launching toward her face and torso, but as she ducked and weaved clear of their attacks, Argos dove in once again, clamping onto the neck of the largest warrior and toppling him to the sand.

Another warrior rushed in, raising his spear to impale the mutt who tore into his brother's throat. With a sweep of her machete, Merona intercepted him, slicing across his thigh.

A third warrior forced her back before she could strike again, slashing out with hatchet and dagger as Merona stumbled to dodge and retreat.

In the next moment, Argos was lunging for his new target, the wounded gray man clutching his leg, as a hatchet fell toward Merona's face. In a blink, her machete intercepted the weapon, hooking its blade and wrenching it from her assailant's grip.

Flipping through the air, the hatchet flew out into the darkness as the gray man snarled, plunging his dagger up into Merona's side. The jagged stone blade caught in the fabric of her jacket before piercing her flesh, as he caught and held back her machete hand.

Merona snarled at the pain, teeth clenched, her attacker's face almost touching her own. Then, with a swift jerk of her free hand, she drew and plunged her own stone dagger deep into his neck.

Blood spat out across Merona's face as the gray man gurgled and fell, his dagger twisting slightly in her side before his hand fell limp and released. Merona winced, the pain stifling her scream as she clutched at the weapon embedded in her side.

In the sand ahead, Argos ripped into the neck of the last warrior, his blood swirling and mingling into the water as the waves washed over his corpse. Leaning on a spear, Merona staggered toward her camp, her legs buckling with each step as blood seeped down her side. Reaching a small pile of wood, she fell to her knees, struggling to rebuild her fire as she stoked the small embers to grow into a flame. Next, she rummaged through her supplies, seizing upon a couple clay pots she had salvaged from the village.

Limping back toward the water line, Merona dunked one of the vessels into the waves, submerging and filling it with the salty liquid. Careful that her faltering steps would not spill her cargo, she soon returned to the camp and rested the pot near the flames as she continued to build her fire.

As the flames flickered, slowly beginning to boil and cleanse the saltwater, Merona retrieved her pocketknife, carefully cutting at the hole in her jacket until it was large enough to peel back her coat from off the dagger's handle, leaving the dagger still protruding from her side. She knew she needed to extract the weapon, but until all her supplies were ready to hold back the blood flow, it would only serve to increase the bleeding.

Gritting her teeth against the pain, Merona began to delicately cut away the fabric of her shirt, opening a clean hole and exposing the wound. She could see the jagged knife still protruding from her flesh, and though continual deep breaths would have been her instinct to remain calm, the dagger prevented any comfortable rise and fall of her chest. Even short, shallow breaths were scarcely bearable, and Merona struggled to clear her dizzying head from the loss of blood.

Looking between the weapon in her side and her own spear which lay on the ground, it was clear only a third or less of the knife had pierced into her flesh. She had gotten lucky it hadn't pierced deeper. These rudimentary weapons were thankfully poorly made for piercing the layers of thick fabric of her jacket, which had miraculously safeguarded her from the brunt of the blow. Placing her hand on her side, she pressed down around the wound and protruding knife to keep back the blood flow as best she could, while she readied her supplies.

Spotting her pain, Argos eagerly trotted closer, trying to lick and clean his distressed partner's injury, but Merona pushed him back, hoping to add no further filth to the wound if she could possibly help it. Blood seeped out around the knife slowly, but steadily as Merona reached for her satchel. Her supply of bandages was predominantly untouched since her arrival on the eastern beach, and she took care in her preparation of the bandages not to dirty them.

Near the fire, she could hear the saltwater coming to a boil in the small pot, and after giving it a moment or two longer, pulled it from its spot by the flames and placed it in the cold night sand to cool. Her bandages prepared and her wound exposed, she waited for the cleansed saltwater to cool enough to handle as she pulled a spare, clean shirt from her things. Placing this cloth covering over the mouth of her other pot, she slowly poured the sea water into the new container, watching as all the bits of debris were strained out and gathered into the cloth. Tossing away the extracted filth, her saltwater cleanse was now ready, and it was finally time to draw out the blade.

She held her breath. The sharpened stone scraped against her ribs as she gripped the leather wrapped handle, easing the knife from her flesh. Her hand began to shake and Merona halted, still breathing in short, constrained breaths as she struggled to steady herself.

"Just a little further," she gasped, placing her hand on the dagger once again.

Blood oozed from the wound as the blade at last slipped free. Taking up the clay pot with shaking hands she gently rinsed the cleansing salt water across her wound. Merona's cries flooded the beach as the stinging salt met her open wound, cleansing her gouged flesh with a blistering touch.

She gasped out, the dagger no longer inhibiting the expansion of her lungs, and reached hastily for her bandages, mopping dry the water from her skin before clutching her gushing side with the dressing to stem the flow of blood. Her body throbbed, as she wrapped the bandage across her ribs and waist, cinching and securing the fabric in place with a final knot.

Merona lay near the fire, feeling the soggy comfort of Argos' tongue brushing her face as exhaustion took hold of her.

CHAPTER XXIX

A TURN OF LUCK

SASHA paced up and down his cramped room. In fact, it was of average size, but to his bulky frame and long stride, it was more akin to a closet. Fears and worries consumed him, as he awaited not one, but two letters.

It had been far too long in his mind since he had last heard from Liora, and he hoped only that her letter had been delayed in the mail, going first to her uncle Quincy in Ponta Delgada, and then forwarded on to him. If only the storm hadn't knocked him off course, he could be there awaiting her letter right now, but he had instead been forced to land in Vila do Porto, an island just South of Ponta Delgada, and to add to his misfortune, had crumpled Katya's landing gear beyond use on his emergency landing.

And so, he was stranded there until he could get enough money to cover her repairs, but with little means of easy communication with Quincy, and no new money coming in from Liora, he had been forced to apply to several local jobs, none of which he felt altogether qualified for, just to try and rebuild his funds.

Meanwhile, his remaining funds were slowly dwindling on the cost of his room at the inn, and rental fees for the use of an old farmer's barn, just to keep the broken Katya comfortably stowed away.

"This waiting is unbearable!" Sasha spat. "Why no

one can write letter on time but me?"

Watching the clock tick by, he awaited the next postal delivery with extreme agitation, rushing from his room several minutes early, to wait at the front desk for any new letters to arrive. At last, the postman appeared, exchanging pleasantries with the lady at the front desk before taking his leave and allowing Sasha to rush up.

"Any letters for me?" His voice boomed, making the little woman jump as she turned to face him.

"I... umm... let me check. What name please?"

Sasha answered and held his breath as he watched her hastily rifling through the stack of new letters again and again, at last looking up in fear to relay the bad news.

"I'm very sorry... but there are no letters for you, Sir."

Sasha slumped against the wall. He had sent a letter to Quincy to tell him where to forward all Liora's letters as soon as he'd landed, but had still heard nothing from him. Getting a phone call to go through in this place would cost far more than he cared to think about, but rather than return to his cramped room at the inn to think over his next course of action, Sasha marched outside, to begin the long walk towards the farm where Katya was being kept.

Even outside, in the open air, he felt trapped. He hadn't enough money to get passage on a ship off the island, at least not enough to bring Katya with him, and with the expense of even a three-minute phone call, he had no direct means of communicating with anyone outside the island. But how much worse must Merona feel? Truly trapped on an invisible island with no hope of escape or chance of calling for rescue. He chastised himself for bemoaning his own circumstances in the first place, determined to find a way of continuing his search, by any means necessary.

Arriving at the farm, he greeted one of the young farm hands as he strode into the barn to find comfort alongside his plane, but somehow, seeing her sitting lopsided on her crumpled and damaged landing gear, only served to lower his spirits rather than raising them.

"Back again so soon?" said the farmer's voice from the corner of the barn.

"*Da*, I thought maybe she help me clear my head."

"She? Oh, you mean the plane! Yes, yes, she is a beauty. Or at least, she will be once you get her all ship shape again."

"*If* I ever can."

"Oh, don't say that, I'm sure that friend of yours will send you more money soon."

"*Nyet*, I don't think so, I already start looking for work here, but have no luck so far."

"A big strong man like you? I shouldn't think you'd have any trouble finding work."

"It because I too big that is problem! They tell me I will scare away customers or that my accent too thick to be understood."

"Well, if you don't mind hard labor, I could find some work for you on the farm. I'm always in need of extra muscle here."

Sasha looked up as though the crusty old farmer were some kind of angel sent down to answer his prayers. "Really? You truly mean that?"

"Of course! It would be at a reduced wage, so as to account for what I'm charging you for the use of my barn, but it'd still be a reasonable pay."

Sasha engulfed the man in a bear-like embrace, thanking him over and over for coming to his rescue, and after all details were finalized, he set to work almost immediately, packing his things and checking out of the inn that same day to bunk in the farmer's barn and limit his expenses as much as possible as he saved up for Katya's costly repairs.

~

The sun filtered through the fog, streaming across the sandy beach where Argos and Merona slept. Light crept through Merona's eyelashes, stirring her awake to the pain still gouging her side. Though she had been able to get a lengthy night's sleep, the hole in her side remained as painful as before, if not more so as she struggled to sit up. At her side, Argos bolted up at the first sign of movement from his companion, immediately circling and sniffing her every motion.

The sun had not risen high, remaining mostly obscured by the ever-present fog, but Merona still squinted from the glare, rubbing the sleep from her heavy eyes as she lifted her shirt to recheck her injury. Old blood had seeped into every part of the fabric, staining her surrounding skin and shirt, but thankfully no hints of infection were apparent yet. With a relieved sigh, she set off to gather some supplies of honey and any other natural local plant-life that could be used to ward off infection in the long run, before carefully cleaning and redressing her bandage that morning.

With her wound addressed for the present, and her old bandages rinsed and left to boil in water near the fire, Merona hobbled out across the sand. The scattered bodies of the fallen gray men had already attracted the interest of scavenging gulls, yet the grizzly sight left Merona unfazed, her thoughts on her own hunger and satiating it. Her mind still moved in a slow sluggish rhythm, unable to process or focus on anything beyond the rote monotony of catching breakfast for the day.

This lethargic trance remained well into the cooking and eating of her catch, and only began to lift when the rattle of clashing canoes in the water met her ears. For a moment, she sat chewing, her head rising to watch the two long canoes sitting partially beached on the sand, rising and falling as the water sloshed them against one another with each mild wave. Swallowing her last bite, the miraculous objects before her at last sank in, and Merona suddenly felt herself choking on that final bite.

Bits of fish sputtered from her mouth as Merona looked toward Argos, who still lay gnawing clean the carcass of his own fishy breakfast.

"Boats, Argos. We have boats!"

The mutt looked up with a tilt of confusion, his ear flopping lopsidedly over his head.

"Boats!"

Shooting to her feet with too much exhilaration to acknowledge the pain in her side, Merona clapped her hands together. "It's a miracle, Argos! I mean, I nearly died to get this miracle, but do you see what this means? We could sail out of here! Our escape is finally in *our* hands."

A wave of nausea finally caught up with her, and Merona bent forward, leaning on her knees and gripping her side.

"Okay, maybe not tomorrow, but soon. Well, maybe not even soon. We'll need to get supplies together first, and make sure the boats are seaworthy. Plus, I'm thinking a sail would be a good idea. You know, so I don't have to kill myself paddling the whole way."

Argos snorted in acknowledgment, his attention still transfixed on her every incomprehensible word.

"But that shouldn't be too hard, right? I mean, I should probably take a day or two to let this hole in my side close up. But I mean, I can start collecting the stuff.

I can still walk... sort of."

A jut of pain gouged her side, and once again she keeled forward.

"Okay, yeah... I'll take it slow."

In the days that followed, Merona did very poorly at keeping to her word. More than once, her slowly healing side was exacerbated, and even once or twice, early on, began bleeding again, and though with every setback to her healing, she promised herself again to slow down, she would find a necessary reason to break that promise.

Supplies to improve the canoes needed to be collected, food needed to be caught and smoked for storage on the journey, fresh water from the uncursed rivers needed to be gathered. But perhaps the most challenging of all, Argos needed to learn not to fear the canoes they would be making their escape in.

Argos had been accustomed to flying alongside Carver in his plane, so riding in a boat seemed an easy next step to acclimatize him to, or so she had thought. Again and again Merona attempted to coax the mutt to step inside the wooden vessel, but its unstable teetering within the water inevitably sent Argos leaping from the canoe at the first opportunity.

Knowing his ease within the water was a necessity, Merona soon began tempting her companion within the perfectly stable, beached canoe, utilizing smoked fish as a lure to entice him. Though beginnings were shaky, Merona soon had her companion licking from her palm and resting his head happily in her lap as she sat comfortably in their beached boat, weaving rope and stitching sails for their impending expedition.

The abandoned village had been a useful source for supplies such as leathers, baskets, hefty ropes, and fabrics in need of only small refurbishments to make each item sufficiently usable. These smaller tasks completed over the early weeks, Merona's wound had finally had time to heal, and she set out with new vigor to tackle the more daunting task of making the small canoes seaworthy. The boats were of a simple make, clearly crafted for trips around the island, or short jaunts off the coast for fishing. But floating in the water, and being capable of withstanding the storms she would no doubt face out on the sea, were two whole different things.

Each canoe was narrow and easily flipped in rougher waters, and finding a means of addressing this deadly flaw would prove an undertaking. For days, Merona examined and prodded the vessels, pondering the most effective means of improvement, and with each examination, the idea of transforming them into something resembling the double-hulled Waka Hourua of the Māori seemed the best answer. She knew the task of securing two canoes together would be a daunting one, but if she hoped to escape the island and survive out on the open sea, the work would be an absolute necessity.

Merona had gathered and reinforced rope enough to execute the job, but the more daunting task would be finding, cutting, and assembling the material to construct a flat, raft-like centerpiece to secure between the two selected canoes. Remembering the Maori sailing canoes, she thought a small, covered hut in the center for protection during storms was also a sound idea, and so, already built materials were gathered from the huts of the village for use on her own humble dwelling. The structure would be large enough to house herself and Argos, as well as essential food and supplies. Other necessary supplies would be kept equally split among both canoes, distributing the weight as evenly as possible.

The sails would be another tricky task, though perhaps requiring more finesse than backbreaking labor. They would need to be lashed to the vessel so securely that any violent winds they might face would have no chance of ripping them free. But to make all this; the sail, the huts, the central platform, secured together and capable of withstanding the kind of storms they might face, seemed a task beyond the materials at Merona's disposal, no matter how much rope she might manufacture or collect. She cursed her lack of hammers, nails, or indeed tools of most any make, resorting to assembling a kind of crude cudgel, made of a hefty rock and sturdy stick by which she might pound or wedge parts of her craft together.

The work was slow and laborious, taking its toll on the adventuress's muscles, but with this chance at escape, the pain seemed trivial, and she worked as feverishly as ever to complete her many tasks.

CHAPTER XXX

SETTING SAIL

MERONA kicked dirt over her recently dug hole in the ground.

"I can't wait to get off this island and have access to plumbing again," she muttered.

Nearby, Argos stood watching intently, his head tilting in curiosity at his companion as Merona shot him a disgruntled glance,

"Not to mention a little privacy."

Re-tucking her shirt and buckling her belt, Merona continued absentmindedly talking to her dog. "Mind you, one of the last times I had access to a bathroom, someone was trying to drown me in my own bathwater… which was the main reason I ended up taking the job that got me into this mess… I'm not sure if that's ironic or just a perfect example of the insanity that is my life."

A slow unfurling of her life decisions played out in her mind, and a long-held sigh escaped her lips. "My mother was right… I don't know why I live like this."

Argos looked up at her with wide, black eyes, a hint of sadness in his face for their predicament.

Merona patted him soothingly on the head. "Well, at least I got to meet you out here. You're not a bad dog at all, really. And you have a nice instinct for saving my life, which I definitely could not have survived without."

His matted tail wagged as they strode toward the beach.

"Though, in a way, I saved your life too by being on your plane in the first place… that pilot of yours would have never been able to keep you both alive here without me, and even if it hadn't been this island, I suspect he would have inevitably crashed you *both* into the sea one of these days. So, you're welcome for that, I guess."

Argos grumbled, perhaps because he didn't quite see the situation in exactly the same light as his companion.

Sand squashed beneath their boots and paws as the two castaways approached their grand escape project on the beach. The double-hulled canoe was well underway, its deck mostly assembled and fastened between the two vessels, with the main mast almost completely erected and secured at the center.

Materials for the small hut that would go at the center of the vessel were scattered across the sand nearby, ready to be sorted and assembled after the rest of the wood for the decking had been gathered and added to complete the full base. Merona had taken a short break from her work to spear and cook lunch that day, growing tired of the bland taste of fish, but reminded herself and her companion, that at least it wasn't grubs or snake anymore.

Taking up her machete, Merona set to work once again, hacking down more small saplings to add to her resources. With each chop, the muscles of her arm would begin to grow weary, and she would soon switch hands to give one limb a rest while the other took its turn.

Though she gave her appearance little notice, anyone who had seen Merona before her fateful flight, would have had difficulty recognizing her as she now stood. Her arms and legs were lean bundles of sinew, every vein and tendon bulging amongst the rolling muscles beneath her tanned skin. Her ragged clothing hung from her ever-thinning frame, only resting slightly snugger where her muscles now bulged. Clothes, hair, and skin seemed all perpetually caked with dirt, and though she had had her fair share of scars before, the months of grueling survival had left her arms, legs, and face forever marked with thick, ragged scar tissue. Her matted and tangled hair, though a little longer, looked more or less the same, since Merona rarely took the time to brush it even when on civilized land.

The days of labor slogged by, with Merona's attention fully engrossed in her endless tasks. The wound in her side was at last mostly healed, and Argos trotted around her, eager to help in his way, though incapable of much more than getting under foot. Eventually, his boundless energy proved useful, when Merona found a means of strapping timber and other objects along his sides with a makeshift harness, to lessen the number of trips to and from the jungle and her work site on the beach. His keenness in fetching things even came in handy in retrieving nearby tools when Merona didn't feel like walking any more than needed to complete her many tasks.

Looking out to sea in her moments of rest, Merona pondered the important matters she would tend to on her return. Teeth would come first. She had done all she could to scrape clean the buildup each night, but a proper brushing and fresh mouth would be a welcome change on her return. After that, would come an uninterrupted bath, with no debt collectors trying to drown her, and a full bar of soap at hand... or maybe even three. Last, or perhaps first when it really came to it, she would feast. Pastries, brisket, a hearty side of fried potatoes. Her cravings seemed to shift from day to day, but always she envisioned a bountiful meal laid out before her when she returned, even if she had to go into a little more debt to get it.

Though the idea of all the food she would never stop eating was a key driving motivation for her, the idea of sharing her findings of the lost civilization with Liora was also something Merona eagerly looked forward to just as much. She had meticulously packed away the journal of Lord Westwick's writings, as well as added her own numerous notes to the back of all she had learned on her own from the village remains, and wrapped it carefully in leather with some of the more intact slates of the people's original writings and a few other artifacts that she had found, determined to return with her findings.

Merona had never been the brains of the Grant adventuring team, but to be able to show all that she had discovered, decoded, and learned about this lost people and their way of life, would be something she knew would fascinate Liora, as well as be rather impressive for the "muscle" of their family to present her with. They would have so much to talk over on Merona's return, and talking with her sister was something she was dearly beginning to miss.

Her return… what a glorious prospect that was. It seemed so inevitable, yet the sea was unlikely to be kind. But still, escape had become the only thing that drove her now as she gazed out toward the misty horizon. Merona wasn't ready to let go of that hope.

"It's not long now, Argos. There's only a little more to do, really, and then we set off. Pack up all we can carry and set to sea."

Her hand rested comfortably on Argos' neck, working the knots from his fur in a slow, absentminded rhythm.

"It won't be without risk, of course, but so is staying put. So, we'll have to brave it, you and I. You're up for the challenge though, aren't you boy? Of course, you are. You've never complained this whole time. You just get to work and do what needs to be done. Probably why we get along so well."

Argos slapped his tail against the sand, his head resting comfortably in Merona's lap.

"Plus, you're a good listener. Liora was never great at that. She was always the one who did the talking out of the two of us. But I think you'll like her all the same. She'll spoil you rotten."

Uttering her sister's name left a lump in Merona's throat. Since their childhood the two had been inseparable, and remembering a time they had been apart for anywhere near as long was impossible. As much as they chided one another, there was an aching in Merona's core to see her again. Taking the plane out here had been her own choice, and she held no blame for Liora over the debt which had brought about her decision. No, she only longed to see her sister again. To feel the comfort of having her at her side and watching her back.

"Soon," she sighed. "Soon the daring sisters Grant will reunite, and all this madness will be a thing of the past."

~

The sail flapped in the wind. It had taken some doing, but the mast was now erected, with stitched together sheets of fabric stolen from the village, now serving as a Frankensteinian sail. Woven baskets and other containers from the old village had also been utilized to gather and store all the supplies the two companions would need on their journey.

Fish, snake, muskrat, and even goat meat had been

thoroughly smoked for storage, and fresh river water gathered in as many water skins as could be found. Over the weeks of work, Merona had made sure to accustom Argos with the rocking of the boat, taking him on short canoeing excursions near the beach until he began to trust both her and the vessel enough that he no longer felt the need to leap into the water and swim back to shore.

Though it dented her hope not to have seen a hint of Sasha in weeks, she made use of it as an added resolve to her approaching escape. He'd given up the search, at least in this part of the ocean, and she had to accept that she was truly on her own. This expedition was now her only chance at rescue, and she had to make it work.

Wind swept around the island as Merona loaded the last of her supplies, checking and rechecking her camp to be sure she'd left nothing of use behind. There would be no going back. No stopping to resupply, no changing her mind once she was out on the open water. She would be at the mercy of the sea and its unforgiving waves. In all likelihood, she would die out there, but these had become her options; sit and wait for another attack from her neighbors, or set out onto the water before more gray soldiers were mustered.

Every day of preparation, she'd felt a winding spring in her stomach. Watching the horizon for more boats, waiting for a second attack that never came, but now the day of departure had arrived and she allowed herself permission to breathe just a little easier as she set sail. Argos had been more hesitant than usual to enter the ship, somehow sensing Merona's own apprehensions toward the expedition ahead, but with a small offering of meat in hand, she at last coaxed him aboard.

Pushing off from shore, Merona guided her craft with a rear oar acting as rudder, using a line of cord

to angle her sail and catch the winds as she rode it out toward the open water. The waves remained calm, gently rolled by the wind that tumbled over them, filling her billowing sail as she shifted her craft back and forth to ride upwind away from shore, but as Merona let out a long-held breath of relief at having escaped the island and its dangers, a broad headed spear launched over her shoulder, impaling the mast.

Three canoes rushed forward in pursuit, propelled by four strong rowers in each, another spear sped past as a second canoe came in range. Merona's eyes darted between the bundled spears in the raft to her right, and the paddles to her left. Though the last attack had left her with an abundance of weaponry, she hadn't enough spears to dispatch the dozens of pursuing gray men, and would need at least a few spears for fishing in the days and weeks to come. If she survived long enough to make it out to sea.

Argos barked and snarled wildly toward the approaching danger. He seemed to recognize his own helplessness against the gray men and their weapons, ducking into the safety of the small shelter at the base of the mast.

The gray men neared. Spears thudded into the wood around Merona as she worked her sail, each shaft embedding nearer its mark with every shot. With her back to the horizon, Merona stared down her pursuers as she shifted again to catch the wind and gain more speed, waiting for the next spear to hit home as she stood trapped in position, gripping tightly to her line to hold her sail and rudder steady, hoping the wind might pull her out of reach of her enemies.

Waves began to swell around her as another spear lodged in the wood of her ship, its wide blade slicing across her calf before impact. Wincing, Merona sailed on, pushing her body to its limits to harness the wind to her advantage as more spears sped past. The ship groaned, water crashing against Merona's makeshift bindings and rigging, the weaker points of her work quaking and creaking in the rising currents.

The distant gray men surged forward, their narrow ships tossing violently in the rising waves before one canoe crashed against a sudden surging wave, capsizing in an instant with the impact. Frantic men spilled into the black water, yet Merona's raft still held firm, her long days of work and preparation at last paying off.

Another swell of water raised the vessels high, and a second canoe was lost to the waves. Distance began to grow between Merona and her pursuers as she expertly caught the growing winds, riding them out to sea. The third canoe began to drift back, relinquishing the chase in an attempt to salvage its remaining men as Merona sailed on.

Waves crashed around her as the canoe drifted from sight, returning to its home or lost to the water, she could not tell, nor did she care.

"We've done it, Argos," Merona gasped. "We're free of it."

At last, she'd escaped the island and its bloodthirsty inhabitants, and that thought alone was all that filled Merona's mind as she watched the island shrink and fade behind its endless gray mists, and unanswered secrets. It could keep them. She had the sea and all its horrors to face now.

CHAPTER XXXI

SOMETHING IN THE MIST

MERONA re-lashed a crossbeam which had separated in the chaos of their escape. It had been a solid hour since the island had vanished from sight, and she occupied herself with repairs on her vessel while the calm waters held.

The sky still hid behind a blanket of fog, which encircled Merona and her raft, having grown denser to the point that it now blotted out the distant sea in all directions. Argos still hid within the small shelter that stored the most vital supplies, while other necessities, such as oars, spears and extra rope, were safely secured within the canoes.

Merona's calf still throbbed beneath its fresh bandaging from the spear gash she had sustained in their escape. Slumping down on the raft, Merona coaxed Argos out of hiding with a small piece of smoked trout. Wind ballooned the sail out to sea as Argos licked the fish from Merona's palm, soon settling down beside her, his head resting on her good leg.

The two companions enjoyed a meal from their supplies of smoked meats as they looked out to sea, their confidence rising with every passing moment.

"Well, Argos," said Merona, "I think we might finally have a chance out here. I'm mostly unwounded, for once, we've got a good supply of food to last us a good while, and fishing over the side shouldn't be too hard. Even if I have to go for a swim now and then to do it."

Argos muttered, his chin still resting on her leg, licking his nose and snout in reply.

Merona chuckled. "Don't worry, pal. There isn't anything out here more dangerous than what we faced back there. Exposure, infection, dehydration, starvation... you know, the normal stuff. We really aren't any worse off than before, except for our limited water supply. Anyway, the important thing is, no more *cannibals*. Anything has to be better than the risk of having our limbs bitten off in our sleep, right?"

Argos eyed her from his place on her knee, offering not even a snort of agreement.

"Well, *fine*, be a pessimist then. Personally, I'm thrilled to be free of that miserable island, and neither you, nor anyone else out here is going to talk me out of it."

Endless fog rolled on ahead of the two castaways, still refusing to break as they drifted ever farther from the island of the gray men. Behind the mist the sun began to drift low, and with a grumble Merona rose, stretching the stiffness from her legs and taking up a spear to hunt dinner.

Now adrift on the sea, Merona had limited means of cooking her meals. She had a good supply of sea salt to cure her meat for long-term storage, and a very limited supply of firewood for emergencies. But being out on an unstable, wooden raft, she didn't like to risk an open flame unless the need was dire. Raw fish would have to do for the majority of meals, and though Merona didn't much care for the taste, she imagined Argos would quite enjoy it.

Feet planted wide, she gazed over the side of the raft with a spear clutched tightly in her grasp, awaiting a flutter of motion beneath the water that would never come. At least, when it eventually did, she had been too distracted to notice.

The sight which took Merona's attention from her hunt emerged slowly, almost imperceptibly out of the fog ahead, and Merona herself might not have noticed it, had Argos not abruptly begun to snarl.

Her attention snapped up, following the mutt's eye line to what had unnerved him out across the water; an immense, rocky, dark shape jutting from the water ahead, looming ever closer as they drifted toward it. Merona could not believe what she was seeing. A second island.

Was this part of a small island chain, and the island of the gray men had only been one of many? Was this where the occupants of the abandoned village had fled to? Or would she find yet more hostile inhabitants to contend with? She had no way of knowing, but with the opportunity of fire and a cooked meal before her, she began steering toward the new island.

The raft soon slid ashore on a rocky beach and immediately Argos leapt from the shaky platform, eager to plant his paws on solid land. Hulling the raft a little further up the sand, Merona then strode out across the beach, eyeing the tree line and distant, foggy mountain range silhouetted by the setting sun. Something about the island gave her a feeling of foreboding, but with night falling, she needed to secure dinner.

Stripping free of her heavy jacket and slacks, Merona waded out into the shallows. It seemed the best course of action to catch as much as she could that night, and let it smoke while Argos and she feasted off their supplies. The smoked fish from before could only last so long, and cooking a new catch fresh would prolong their supplies a little.

Spear in hand, Merona fought against the fading light to spot a catch before nightfall fully descended, and before the last hints of light had crept behind the mountains, a tentacle moved beneath the water. Remaining still, Merona edged closer to the unaware creature, raising her spear to her shoulder. Another hint of movement flicked near her leg, and she instantly spotted a second tentacle reaching for her ankle.

Launching her spear into the water, thick, dark pigment swirled out around her legs, and she knew she had hit her mark. The impaled octopus thrashed beneath the water, its tentacles wrapping around both Merona's legs and spear in a frantic effort to defend itself. Feeling her spear firmly planted in the animal and sand below, Merona held tight to her weapon, pinning the creature in place as it feverishly writhed out its last surge of life.

The waters calmed, and with a jerk she hoisted spear and beast from the water. And beast it indeed was: its mantle seemed as large as her own head, while its tentacles hung longer then the length of her legs. They would feast well tonight.

With Argos' help, a small hole was dug in the sand for a fire pit, and gathered sticks were soon ablaze, roasting the chopped and squared chunks of octopus shish kabob as the two companions gnawed on their supply of smoked fish. With the immense size of their new catch, Merona was liberal with her distribution of food supplies, knowing the beast would more than restock all they could eat that night.

The fire was beginning to dwindle as Merona licked the last bits of greasy fat from her fingers, and she soon trudged out across the beach in search of more wood to renew it. A distance behind her, Argos barked out, still laying by the fire's warmth and growing upset at being left alone.

Ignoring his complaints, Merona continued in her hunt. As she picked through the abundant driftwood which lay all over, she spotted a distant black mound, silhouetted on the beach. Her curiosity to investigate this new island and the strange shape ahead piqued her explorer instincts.

Approaching slowly, Merona drew her machete and nudged the pile. Shifting the black mound with her blade, a thick, ragged log rolled out toward her feet, and Merona recognized the pile for what it was, or had once been.

"A bonfire," she muttered aloud. "Someone else was trying to signal for help here?"

But as she turned back toward the tree line and distant mountain range beyond, a second realization fell upon her. No other survivors had built this burnt-out signal fire, no other survivors had occupied this island.

"This is *my* signal fire. The fire Carver lit before he was… we're back on the island."

Driftwood clattered to Merona's feet as she raced back to camp. The glow of the fire alone could have signaled the gray men to attack, and with the wasted hours of eating and setting up for the night, they might already be upon them. She and Argos needed to get off the beach, fast.

Charging into camp, Merona scrambled to repack the supplies she had so carelessly scattered across the sand amid her new camp. The distance to the beach from the gray men camps was dangerously short, and she knew it would only be a matter of moments before they might arrive. At least she wished it might be that long, until Argos' hackles rose and the still trees rustled behind her.

CHAPTER XXXII

ESCAPING THE ISLAND'S GRASP

MERONA cursed under her breath. Gripping her machete, she turned to face the noise. By the dim firelight alone, she could detect no hint of movement among the trees, but Argos continued to glare toward the jungle, hackles raised, clearly hearing and seeing what she could not.

Reaching for a spear, Merona readied herself for the onslaught she knew was coming, but as her fingers brushed the spear shaft, the gray men charged forth.

Dozens of shrieking, vicious faces burst from the trees, and in an instant, Merona knew the fight was lost. Like lightning, she darted across the sand, rushing for the beached raft as her only hope of escape as Argos bolted out in front of her.

Spears peppered the sand all around as she closed the few yards that lay between her and escape. Skidding to a halt, Merona raced to push the raft from the beach as Argos leapt aboard and several more spears embedded nearby. Merona struggled to free her vessel from the wet sand, but it refused to shift, and Argos barked out from the raft, snarling toward their pursuers as two swift warriors caught up with Merona.

Spinning round, she slashed out across the forward

warrior's stomach, dropping him to the ground in a heap of gore. The second attacker sprang out, but before he could reach her, Argos was upon him, ripping into his neck as both toppled to the ground.

Merona's instincts told her to help her animal, but with the gray army nearly upon them, there was no time. She had to deploy the ship, or neither of them would survive.

Pushing with all her strength she could hear the struggle behind her, and with every yelp from Argos, her resolve slipped, but at last the raft started to move. Water rushed around her legs and she felt the tide pulling the raft forward. Leaping aboard, Merona grabbed hold of the oars, rushing to push through the water as she called out to Argos.

"Argos! Come boy! Come on!"

Turning from his kill in the sand, Argos sprang out into the water after her, a look of panicked abandonment in his large, black eyes. More spears peppered the surrounding water and raft, and Merona knew she could not stop, as much as she yearned to go back for her animal, she had to put as much distance between the island and her ship as possible, for both their survival.

Argos's paws slapped against the water as he paddled after her, and she ached to reach out for him, to row toward him and pluck him from the waves. But they were still within reach of the gray men's weapons, a fact which hit home as a spear slammed into the mast just behind Merona's head. If she stopped rowing now, they would become easy, stationary targets, but with Argos out in the water on his own, he was small and unnoticeable, and her large raft presented a much more enticing target for the gray men. Or so she told herself. She struggled to resist the pleading of Argos's wide eyes, paddling feverishly against the waves as she called out to him with reassuring words.

"Good boy Argos! That's right, keep going, keep swimming, boy! I'm here, I'm right here, you can make it."

Fear remained in his eyes, but she could see him getting closer. He was only feet from her now. In the next moment a spear pierced the water, hitting near where Argos swam, and with a gut rending yelp, he began to sink.

Without a thought, Merona dove into the water, spears still plunging into the waves around her, but she was resolute in saving her loyal Argos, who had leapt from the safety of the raft to save her moments earlier.

Rushing beneath the waves, she kicked vigorously forward, reaching out in the blackness for her dear friend's furry paw. Pitch black water stretched out in front of her, a stinging spearhead slicing across her forearm, but she clawed forward through the darkened void.

A flailing shape appeared before her, and she snatched hold of the desperate animal, clasping him against her chest. Spinning in the water, she kicked wildly for the surface, breaking from the black waves with a limp Argos still clutched to her body.

The raft had drifted away from them, and Merona scrambled to reach it, kicking and paddling out with her one free arm. All was silent as her hand slapped against one of the canoes and she heaved their dripping bodies aboard.

For a moment, she lay there, trembling as she clutched to Argos' limp body, but his stillness roused her to action. Pressing against his ribs, water at last came sputtering from his drenched snout, and he shot up from his lifeless stupor. A dazed whimper choking out, Argos struggled to stand before slumping down again and turning to lick the long gash running down his thigh.

Argos now safely stowed aboard, Merona unfurled her sail, allowing the wind to pull them out of harm's way before another spear could hit.

"I'm so sorry, boy," she muttered, hacking up water before she could choke out the words. "Never again... I'll never leave you again, I promise."

The island soon drifted away, and the gray men threat with it, and Merona scrambled for her supplies, searching for bandages to tend her companion's injury. Gingerly wrapping the bandage around his leg, she paused to stroke his sopping wet ears as he gazed up toward her panting with hesitant relief. The island had drifted nearly out of sight now, the wind having carried them out to sea once again, and Merona looked back with a sinking fear, knowing the blankets, her freshly caught octopus, and a portion of their supplies still lay on the beach, lost forever.

~

Merona awoke in a huddled heap next to Argos in their shelter. The sun was just starting to crawl over the horizon and Merona blinked against the growing light outside. Her tired, stiffened joints fought against every effort to move them as she rested her hand over her sleeping companion's chest. Calm, steady breaths swelled his ribs, and she sighed a stifled breath. He had made it through the night.

Checking his leg, she tenderly redressed the wound without a care for her supplies. This dog's life had grown as vital to her as her own, if not more so, and she would treat it with the same concern. Only once as she worked did his head raise to inspect what she was doing, licking his exposed wound for a moment before calmly flopping his tired head back down, and trusting his companion with his care.

With her work on his wound and then her own finally done, Merona crawled from the shelter, leaving Argos to rest inside. Still waters stretched out in all directions, that same endless gray fog still clinging to the sky. In all the time she'd been stranded, five months now, not one day could she recall the gray mist ever fully lifting.

Embedded spears dotted the back of the raft from the previous night's attack, and Merona forced the slimmest, most streamline looking spear free from the planks as she eyed the water. Their food supplies were limited from the night's run of bad luck, and catching something fresh for breakfast was an absolute necessity. Small darting shapes flashed by beneath the surface, never showing themselves for longer than a momentary glimpse, and Merona knew she would need to dive to catch anything.

Securing her lasso to the mast, she dropped the free end into the water before slipping free of her heavy slacks and jacket and diving over the side with spear in hand. Water engulfed her body as bubbles pushed from her nose, the salty water stinging her eyes for a moment as they blinked open, searching through the clouded blue world beneath the raft.

Kicking deeper into the void, distant schools of fish fluttered below in glittering waves as Merona altered course toward them, careful not to scare the fish away as she swam in slow, stealthy movements. Nearing her targets, several came within reach of Merona's spear and with lightning speed she struck out, grazing a darting fish to no effect. Turning back, she kicked toward the surface, rushing up for another breath of air. Breaking the surface, she gasped out, breathing a few deep easy breaths before swallowing back a great gulp of air and plunging back in.

Kicking into a rapid dive, Merona plummeted toward another school of plump fish. Deeper and deeper she dove, rushing to reach her prey before the air held in her lungs could escape. A target came within reach, and her spear launched forward, piercing cleanly through its side as the surrounding school dashed clear. Rushing for the surface, water began to tickle her nose moments before she broke into the air.

Sputtering, Merona paddled forward, snatching her lasso from the water where it trailed behind the drifting raft. Climbing up the rope, she soon reached the craft, tossing her spear aboard before she scrambled up after it. Flapping on the end of the spear against the hull of the canoe, the small fish gasped out its last liquidy breaths.

Argos soon came patting out of the shelter, hopping into the canoe alongside Merona, and leaning his shaggy snout in close to lick at her tired face. Merona chuckled at his awkward affection before pushing him back to retrieve her machete and the fish from her spearhead. The blade had grown dull and jagged from the months of excessive use, but still it served its purpose for gutting and skinning the duo's breakfast.

Slitting the fish down the middle, Merona picked the thin bones from one half before handing Argos his portion of raw flesh, and both hungry survivors tore into their meals without hesitation. Fluids trickled down Merona's chin without notice as she ripped into the meat, cleaning and spitting the bones over the side as she ate. Licking the last bits off her fingers, Merona picked at her teeth with a thin bone, gazing out at the new horizon obscured by the lingering, endless gray. Low winds pushed them along as Merona redressed herself and squeezed the last remaining drops of water from her damp hair, their raft drifting through misty shrouds above and below.

Distant and unseen, a dark shape began to form in the fog ahead, and Merona found herself vacantly gazing toward it as it gradually revealed its form. Just as before, the silhouette of that all-too-familiar island lay at their bow, drawing the raft toward it on steady winds. Merona gritted her teeth at the sight, climbing to the mast and drawing up the sail with speed before taking up her position at the oars. She pushed vigorously against the winds, retreating from the looming shape which refused to release her.

Merona's oars sliced through the water in a monotonous slog, every moment lingering like an hour before the island's shadow began to recede. Still, she persisted in her efforts, determined to build distance from the island as much as her energy would allow. Hours passed, and her muscles screamed for relief before at last she relaxed her efforts. Crawling to her small supply of food and water, she gulped back as little fluids as her dehydrated body could stand, aching to consume every available drop, but knowing her survival depended on restraint.

Catching the few precious drops that fell down her chin before they could be lost, a familiar shrouded shape grew in the fog ahead. The water had drawn them back to the island once again.

It had all been for nothing, the hours of rowing,

of pushing beyond her limits, and within moments of halting her efforts, there it was, this looming island that refused to free her from its hold. Gritting her teeth, Merona snatched up the oars once again. Her arms throbbed from exhaustion, but dogged tenacity took hold and she slammed the paddles into the water, fighting against the pull of the island.

Growing clouds crept in overhead, slowly reaching across the sky as the light beyond began to dim. Pressing on, the waves around began to swell, slamming against the raft in rising intervals. Springing up with the next wave, Argos scrambled from the canoe where he was resting, limping for the refuge of the shelter where the other supplies lay safely stored.

More water began to surge around them, waves rising up and crashing across the raft over and over. Water blasted against Merona's face and body as she rowed on, struggling against the violent turmoil around her.

Dark clouds had consumed the sky, blotting out all hints of the sun as blasting winds railed against them, and stinging rain began to fall. The waves had grown higher now, smashing down upon the raft in tumbling walls of water. Struggling to keep her pace, Merona looked to Argos, still huddled beneath the shelter, the baskets and packs of supplies all but shattered and torn from the raft, and she knew the storm would take them both.

Leaping from her seat, she grabbed her lasso, still lashed to the mast, and knotted it around her waist, and with the remaining end, she lashed the rope around Argos' underarms, securing a hurried harness to her companion. Gripping the animal close with one arm, she grabbed hold of one of the packs in her other hand, clinging to all she could as the storm raged in full.

Blinking against the endless cascade of waves, she squinted out toward the storm, and watched in breathless horror as a familiar sight grew in the raging waters. She had convinced herself it had been a dream, or delusion, but once again, the great, black hand rose up from the waves, rushing down upon them with long clawed fingers, just as it had the day their plane first crashed on the island.

Chapter XXXIII

UNTANGLING THE MIST

SALTWATER choked Merona to consciousness, rolling over and sputtering water out across her face and chest as her eyes flicked open. Sand stretched out in front of her, throbbing waves pushing up from below, as a faint whimper reached her foggy ears.

All at once, she felt an emptiness in her hands; Argos was gone and she turned over, feeling for the rope which was no longer at her waist. The yelps grew louder, and Merona pushed up from the sand. Every muscle shuddered, failing her as her legs buckled. Coarse sand met her face as she fell, but once again she pushed up, refusing to succumb to the weakness in her limbs.

Stumbling along the beach, Merona called out, following the sound of Argos' yelps and barks before spotting a scruffy, gray snout sticking out from under a hefty chunk of broken raft. Rushing forward, Merona tore back the slab of wreckage where Argos was pinned, exposing his soppy, huddled form, rope and seaweed tangled around his limbs and neck.

She gently stroked his head, rubbing each ear and whispering words of comfort as she pulled the tangle of lasso from his trembling body.

"It's all right, boy. I'm right here. I've got you."

Argos stared up with wide, black eyes, licking her wrists and hands as she worked to free him, before scrambling from the sandy pit where the wreckage and rope had trapped him, still favoring his back leg.

Merona checked his other limbs meticulously for further injuries but found no signs of any. They had both pulled through their trials with miraculous good luck.

Now reunited, Argos limped along at Merona's side as she set out across the beach, wrapping her lasso over her shoulder as she picked through the debris to assess what supplies had survived the wreck. Little more than shattered wood seemed to have made it through the storm, but through her efforts, she had soon gathered a small assortment of supplies. A spear, a few strands of extra rope, tattered fabric from her former sail, an empty pack, the machete which still hung from her belt, and lastly, her battered, rusty rifle, which in all this time, she still had managed to save a little ammunition for in her coat pockets.

Searching her pockets, she found the small flask and pocketknife still within, and allowed herself to breathe a little easier, knowing her past months of survival had been possible with as little as the small assortment of supplies she had managed to collect.

With a stormy sky still swirling above, and daylight all but vanishing on the horizon, Merona set out to gather up the small, shattered wood which lined the beach, knowing a fire was next on her priorities. But as she worked her way up the beach, a familiar, yet unsurprising sight met her eyes. The camp she and Argos had abandoned only days before, setting off with so much hope, still sat untouched, the fire pit black and crumbled in the center.

They were back on the east side of the island, and she breathed a sigh of gratitude for small miracles, dropping her wood nearby and slumping in her old spot against her log in the sand, she gazed out to sea.

Her plans of escape had failed, the raging waters which had thwarted her seemed to have already calmed, as though the storm had done its job and need no longer remain.

"Well, Argos, I guess that's it. We did all we could, spent weeks building up that raft, and... and here we are again. Just as stranded as before... except now with even less resources."

For a moment, Merona let the despair wash over her, for the wasted weeks and effort at such a foolhardy attempt at escape.

"What was I thinking, believing for a second we could get off this rock by mortal means? I must have been delusional."

Argos' head took its accustomed place on her leg, his large black eyes staring up into hers.

"I'm starting to think we might be stranded here for good, Argos. Whatever it is on this island that's keeping us here... It's like nothing I've ever been up against before..."

Memories flooded back of the immense black hand growing out of the waves to dreg their raft from the sea, as though it were the very embodiment of the island's grasp on them, refusing to let them leave.

"I'm not sure I know how to fight it... I'm not even sure I can."

~

As a necessity of survival, Merona's days returned to their routine of fishing, gathering water, and collecting firewood, but her growing dread, for the island that held her captive, haunted her thoughts and left a pit in her gut.

Had she been stranded anywhere else, she might

have drifted out on the open sea for days before being rescued or spotting land, or simply been capsized and drowned in the storm. Either way, she would have at last been free of the months of danger and isolation, but instead something had pulled her back over and over with its unnatural power.

It was the kind of power that made you feel hopeless: hopeless to get free of it, and hopeless to fight it. But as Merona's thoughts churned over the months of phenomena and survival, over all she had done in the seemingly endless fight against her own demise, the encroaching feeling to give up was replaced with the realization of all she had already overcome.

The cold, hunger, and thirst. The endless wounds, and risk of infection. The loss of Carver, the bloodlust of the cannibals and their never-ending hunt for her head, the shifting swamp and the creature that dwelt there. The fog which hid the island from sight, and the immense black hand in the water which had dragged her here in the first place.

She had faced it all, and yet continued to fight on. She had fought these long months against foes far greater than herself with little to no hope at all, why should she despair now, when she was so close to finding answers?

Yes, her weeks of labor on the boat had been for nothing, but even before she had that hope of escape, she had been close to uncovering the secrets of this strange island, and though her notes had been lost to the sea, she could still read the writings that had been left behind in the village. She felt grateful now that she hadn't made room for them within her boat.

"We are no worse off than when we started out on this island," she said aloud to her companion. "If anything, we're miles ahead."

Understanding the legends and myths had always

been Liora's specialty, in fact, the more she thought on it, the more she realized she had often left the mental heavy lifting to her older sister, a fact she was regretting more and more. But was she not still an adventuress? An unearther of legends? It was her job to find answers, to venture into the wild and toward danger to uncover mysteries of the past. What made this any different? All this time she had focused on survival, on escaping back to civilization, but hadn't she and Liora chosen this line of work for the very purpose of avoiding a quiet, civilized life? Who better to find the answers than herself?

The writings on the clay had spoken of a powerful spell which had been placed upon the island, to divide and conceal the village from their cannibal enemy, and Merona had read of it as only superstitious beliefs of a long lost society, but now, retrieving the written history from the village, Merona began to read the writings once again, no longer trying to rationalize what it said, as was her natural instinct, but rather she tried to open herself up to the possibility that all of it, not just the unnatural things she had seen for herself, might be true. If she hoped to escape whatever powerful force held her there, she would have to fully understand, and believe in it.

Poring over the scratchy symbols each night, Merona found herself once again missing Liora and her expertise in ancient languages more than ever. The writing she had been able to decipher so far had given her much to work with, but still it was littered with gaps.

Though he offered her little collaboration, Argos became her ever-listening ear once again, as Merona rambled aloud to solidify her thoughts. Argos's head rested on his paws, his eyes and shaggy eyebrows shifting from side to side as he listened to her mutterings.

"What do you think? Am I crazy? I always thought the myths I read about were so fantastical, they couldn't possibly be real, but... with all we've seen here, isn't it madder *not* to believe all this? If all that's written here is true... how do we fight the supernatural with nothing but a few spears and our wits? Especially something as powerful as this seems to be..."

Merona's eyes stung from the endless symbols before her. She had read them again and again, searching for mentions of the hand, the foggy veil, the swamp guardian and the elder who had summoned it, anything that would give her answers to what this power was, or how to lift it. She knew the elder had somehow been in control of it, before he had passed at least some of that power to the swamp guardian, but short of seeking out the creature in his swampy lair and kindly requesting he lift the fog, what use was this knowledge to her?

Was this power source even tangible in some way? Even if she could uncover the origin, would it even be something she could utilize? Poring over the writings, she noticed a distinct symbol pared with the elder, but couldn't recall what its meaning was. Then, shuffling through the writings to find another passage where she was sure she had seen it before, she found it at last, in part of a passage detailing the swamp guardian's creation, and in that very passage it stated the elder had given this unknown word to the heart of the beast... but what did it mean? What did the symbol represent?

It wasn't the symbol for power, she knew that symbol on sight, but what else had the elder given to the guardian on his creation? Soon, Merona felt she began to see the new symbol everywhere, not as common as so many others she could read, but not uncommon either, and she started to write down each line it appeared in, to try and find the context behind the symbol's meaning.

Elder gifted blank to guardian... Blank rested in guardian's heart... Elder carried blank upon him... Elder channeled his power through blank... Blank was stolen from guardian's heart... and on and on.

As she wrote down these passages, it became clear that this was it... whatever this symbol referred to, it was the source of the power she needed to attain to escape the island, but she still could not decipher what the symbol meant.

Argos waited to the side, anxious with how much attention his companion was giving to a pile of slates instead of the much more fascinating twisty stick he had discovered on the beach. Yet Merona still pored over the writings, and in his frustration, Argos slapped his paw down over them, to get her attention.

"Not now, Argos," Merona muttered, pushing his paw away, but once again he dropped it down on the writing, this time his shaggy fur pointing directly at two symbols which caught Merona's attention. Sitting directly one on top of the other in two separate lines, were the symbols for stone or rock, and sun or light, words Lord Westwick's writings had helped her decipher, but which she now recognized as her elusive symbol split in two.

"How did I never see it before? This could be a compound word! I didn't expect that... But what does it mean? Light rock? Nah... Sun rock? Or fire rock, like an ember? Or fire stone, Like some kind of flintstone? Or maybe sun stone, like the gem..."

But as the image of a sun stone came into her mind, she remembered a place on the island where she had seen a stone, glittering with sunlight caught within it and held in high honor... the diamond Carver had spotted atop a spire in the cliff side village of the boar tribe.

"That's … that's it! A rock that catches the light of the sun… it's a diamond! Argos, you genius, you!" Merona shouted, grabbing his face with both hands and kissing him directly on the head. "The diamond is the power source we've been looking for! The diamond is the key!"

Argos reeled back, startled by his companion's excitement as the joy of her discovery was completely lost on him. But as Merona continued to look over the writings, checking and rechecking to be sure her guess at the word's meaning was correct, Argos began to embrace the excitement of the moment along with her.

"I can't be one hundred percent sure, but everything points toward that diamond being the key… I don't know, does it sound insane to you? It seems to make sense… why else would they have it on display that way, unless it were valuable to them… like an outward show of their superiority over the island? To show they were the ones daring enough to venture into the swamp to retrieve it…"

Merona had no way of knowing if she could even use the power, once she attained it, but if she was willing to risk her life out on the open sea at a scant hope of escape, how was this risk, or scant chance of hope, any different?

Sitting back against her log, Merona looked toward Argos. "You know what this means, though, don't you, boy? We are going to have to infiltrate that camp and steal that diamond."

CHAPTER XXXIV

ONE LAST HOPE

MERONA'S dull machete got a much-needed sharpening, as well as her spear a new, sturdy shaft. The swamp was vast, and Merona made sure to spear and cook a supply of fish for the journey back through it, as well as several small skin pouches to gather fresh water each day through their trek.

She wished there was a way to leave Argos behind, knowing that venturing back to the western side of the island might very well mean death for both of them, but she had no command he would heed to remain behind, short of tethering him to a tree. But that would only be leaving him alone to face a slow death if she failed to return. He would not leave her side willingly, and as much as Merona wished to spare him the danger ahead, she knew their fates were long since entwined.

Tossing another stick onto what would soon be their last fire on the beach, Merona looked at Argos as he leapt this way and that, tossing about his most recently discovered twiggy toy, which was already almost chewed to oblivion.

"Well, someone's feeling better," said Merona, eyeing the steadily healing gash on his back leg.

Argos halted in his play, the stick hanging from his jowls as he stared into her eyes. Huffing out an abrupt snort, he flung back his head and continued in his game, kicking up sand as he went.

"You have no idea at all, do you? No idea that this time tomorrow we'll be knee deep in bog. I wish you did. I wish you could tell me I'm crazy to try it. That this whole plan is ludicrous and we're better off just living out our lives on this beach."

Pausing his game at the sound of her words, Argos stared toward her, his head tilted as she went on.

"Well? Do you think it's a crazy plan? We will be risking our lives just going back there to track this diamond down, and then on top of that, we'll have to infiltrate the camp, and steal the rock out from under them. And if we survive all that, who's to say we won't just end up with a useless great big lump of carbon. I mean, I don't know about you, but I don't know how to summon forth ancient magic to lift fog or control gigantic, tidal wave hands. What if we go through all this, and it doesn't even make a difference in our chance of being rescued?"

The stick fell from Argos's mouth as he sat silent in the sand, still trying to understand her.

"Yeah, I don't know either. I'm just... I'm running out of options. If we were willing to risk our lives out on the open sea, this can't be any more dangerous. And if what these people believed was true, and that stone is somehow the key to controlling the fog, it will be worth any risk to get us out of here."

Argos padded closer, his nose nuzzled into her hand, stealing a scratch against her palm before she complied, rubbing his eyes, ears, and face with both hands.

"I wish I could talk you out of coming with me. If this is all going to go up in smoke, at least *you* could be spared it, and live out your life eating fish on this beach."

But with her words, his shaggy paw rose up to swat and silence her mouth, smearing a streak of sand across her lips and chin as it fell.

Merona blinked. "Okay... point taken."

Argos's pink tongue fell out in contented panting as he leaned in to lick her cheek, adding drool to the sandy paste now coating her face.

Whatever came next, they would face it side by side.

~

Boggy marsh water seeped in beneath the trudging duo's boots and paws. Night had only just encroached, and the swamp had already taken hold of the water around them. Merona recalled the past months discovering the island and all the otherworldly properties it possessed and marveled at how innocuous she found the swamp's nightly shift. She'd learned to anticipate and even accept it in a way, but the idea that she would venture into such a place so glibly, fearing what awaited her on the other side more than she did the creature within... that she had embraced the supernatural of the island so much, she even planned to use its magic for her own escape, seemed madness.

Had she gone mad? This question had been slowly plaguing Merona's thoughts more and more with every passing day, and she hoped the mere fact that she recognized it as a possibility, meant she must be holding on to some semblance of sanity. If there was one rule Merona and Liora had always held to, it was to follow their gut instincts, and out in a place like this, intuition was the only reliable resource she had.

With night upon them, Merona removed the tattered sail from her pack, suspending it between the trees as a hammock for herself and Argos. Squeezing out his soppy paws, she hefted the squirming animal up to the relative dryness of their new sleeping quarters, before slipping off her boots to join him.

Wrapped tightly within, the two companions soon shifted into a comfortable tangle, Argos' warmth cascading around a shivering Merona as she stroked his matted, muddy fur. For some time, they lay comfortably, until a distant scratching echoed outside, growing louder, nearer, before halting into silence.

Merona peered through a crack in the fabric and scanned their surroundings for movement. There was no sign of life, and Merona knew that allowing every distant creak and sound to interrupt her night of sleep was useless. At her side, Argos seemed calm and restful, and so Merona let his instincts be her guide, rather than her own paranoia.

Creaks and groans continued to sound in the distant night, the once still swamp now alive with sounds that had gone previously unnoticed by day, and though Merona forced herself to dismiss what noises she knew to be far off, the habitual skittering, scratching, and sloshing was enough to torment even the soundest of minds. She would find little sleep that night, and soon her thoughts had turned to the insane plan she was committing to.

"Well, Argos," she whispered, "this is it. For better or worse, we're going to track that stone down. I have no idea if we can even find a way to use it, if we live long enough to get our hands on it, but at least one way or another, this insanity will come to an end."

When day dawned, the babbling of fresh water proved a soothing relief, and both companions allowed themselves a few peaceful moments of rest amid the tranquil streams before rising to drink their fill. The idea of spending another night within the swamp was the last thing Merona wished to think on, but with the miles of ground that lay ahead, it seemed impossible to avoid.

The day would be spent covering as much ground as their strength allowed, and of course drinking all the fresh water they could stomach before night fell.

But always when the sun went down she could feel the presence of the creature plaguing her, even sometimes spotting its glowing green eyes watching from the darkness, and yet, it never approached, never again tried to recapture her back to its slimy pit... as though whatever purpose it had for placing her there was finished, and Merona couldn't be sure if this idea was comforting or added to her unease. The creature being simply a carnivorous beast made its actions predictable, but the idea that it might have motives and goals beyond the instinctive animal filled Merona with uncertainty of what to expect from it next.

The trek was long, but at last she and Argos reached the end of the swamp unharmed, and made their way up to the old camp within the cave at the base of the mountain. Not willing to risk a fire that night, Merona and Argos huddled together for warmth, as Merona looked out toward the cave opening and the distant fog rolling above the tops of the jungle trees, dreading the task before her.

The trek out the next day to find the camp where she last knew the diamond to reside was a slow and cautious one. It had been some time since she had been back in the jungle on this side of the island, and she had no idea where the new gray men camps might be scattered now, as well as being a little rusty in her tactics of dodging hunting parties.

Voices and chatter grew in the mist of the densely packed jungle ahead, and Merona redirected to avoid colliding with them in the fog, yet still she could hear the gray men approaching her, and she was forced to rush on to outrun their ever-looming footfalls. But as she pressed forward, trying to avoid an encounter of the violent variety, she began to feel herself losing her way in the fog.

Hints of a gray man camp came into view among the trees, and Merona was cautious to scoot around its edge, knowing the camp she was on the hunt for would be at the coast of the island, not at its center. Nearly running into a gray warrior who patrolled the camp's border, Merona once again moved to expertly avoid his notice, and felt as though the jungle was crawling with cannibals even more thickly than before, weaving through the never-ending dangers that cropped up around her.

Unsure exactly where she was headed now, Merona pressed on, hoping to soon recognize a landmark of any kind, but with her next few steps, she found her boot plunging into a snaking stream. They had wandered back into the swamp and she harrumphed a sigh of frustration, knowing the camp she was searching for lay far up the coast, and how off track she was now.

For a moment, she thought to try and turn back, but a better thought came to mind and she began following the river out as it rushed toward the coast. A twinge of uncertainty came over her as she walked on, a longing to return to the safety of her isolated beach. But she had long since imagined the eventual end that path would lead to, and knew it would be better to risk all now for the chance of escape, than idle in perceived safety awaiting a slow, inevitable death.

Chapter XXXV

DIAMOND HEIST

THE muted sun filtered through misty clouds as Merona and Argos moved along the rocky island shore. River water still rushed out into the sea beside them as they jumped from rock to rock, Argos's face wearing a slobbery grin, clearly thrilled to be free of the tight jungle and out in the open air. Merona's outlook, however, could not reach such cheeriness, as her thoughts buzzed with all the catastrophic possibilities that might be ahead of them.

How could she be sure it would work? She would be risking her life and limb to steal from the heart of a gray men camp, but without that risk, she might be trapped on the island forever... or far more likely, she would reach the cliff-side to find the diamond had already been stolen by another camp, but it was the only hope she had.

As they plodded along, the shoreline gradually began to rise into a sheer cliffside, wild waves crashing against jagged rocks below. Merona kept as close to the edge as the cover of sparse trees would allow, before the top of a watchtower came into view. She ducked low, the shadows of the trees concealing her as the lookout moved within the tower, shifting to survey a new section of forest.

Taking the opening, Merona moved in closer, peering from a thick cluster of foliage as she surveyed the camp. Spindly watchtowers dotted the perimeter of the village, and running between each tower were sharp, wood shafts jutting from the dirt at intersecting angles, creating a jagged spiked wall encircling the huts.

The fortifications were far better than any of the other tribes of the island, and it seemed doubtful that the diamond would have been stolen back after this tribe had taken it. And sure enough, at the top of a thin spire resting at the center of it all, she spotted the glint of the immense stone. An object they clearly still revered. But this knowledge left Merona with little reassurance, as it only made the task of stealing it even more impossible with such impenetrable fortifications. She was, after all, only one woman with a dog. What chance did they possibly stand?

Scanning the perimeter with a meticulous eye and determination against the odds, Merona searched and searched again for any kind of opening in the camp's defenses, but found none. Watchtowers would spot her approach from every angle and even if she could slip past them, warrior tribesmen would halt her entry at any opening she could presently see.

Infiltration seemed hopeless from where Merona stood, but as she slipped higher among the hefty branches of a tree to gain a better view, a clear opening caught her eye. The village sat near a cliff, she had seen this on her approach, but with her new vantage point, she could see that the defenses utilized around the village were wholly absent on the cliff side. With only rustic technology available to them or their enemies, the gray men clearly had no reason to fear an attack from the cliffs, and so saw them as a natural defense of their position, not a weakness.

But if there was one thing Merona was good at, it was climbing. Trees, fences and barn roofs had all been a staple of her childhood, and she had only grown with experience through her and Liora's years of adventuring. It wouldn't be easy, but it was the one and only possible vulnerability in their defenses that she had found to exploit.

Merona took great pains that day to not be seen as she analyzed the camp and its comings and goings. She could not risk being discovered to be observing them, or their watchmen would doubtlessly become extra vigilant and stifle all her chances at reaching the diamond at all.

With a clear layout of the village captured in her mind, Merona retreated into the woods for cover and to map out the village in the dirt to assess her best strategy. She knew she must wait until nightfall, as the darkness would offer the best concealment. There would be fire light to contend with, but more crucially, there would be heavy shadows to utilize to her benefit.

She hardly needed to assess her gear to know she had little of use to assist in her treacherous climb along the cliff face. No pitons, carabiners, hammer, or swami belt to prevent her from plummeting into the waves and jagged rocks below... nothing save a single rope and her own muscle and grit was at her disposal.

"Well," Merona whispered, looking at Argos with exhausted eyes. "This is going to be fun."

The sun was already making its way toward the edge of the sky, and Merona set about her next task: planning her escape. After all, getting into the gray men village and retrieving the diamond would be rather useless if she couldn't get out again.

She knew a return climb would be risky, as she would be weary from the first, and should she be spotted, such a slow escape would make her an easy target for spears. But the situation was not completely hopeless either, since the defenses of the village were all built with the aim of keeping invaders out, not in.

If she could sneak up on one of the guards at a less fortified opening, she could dispatch him quietly and slip out undetected. By the time she could be spotted by one of the watchmen in their towers, she would have almost reached the tree line where she would have a chance at outrunning them to the swamp. Tracing all possible routes of escape in her scribbled map in the dirt, Merona nodded to herself in satisfaction. It wasn't foolproof, but it was the best plan she could pull off on her own.

Argos whimpered softly at Merona's side, seeming to know instinctively that she was formulating yet another foolish plan he had no say in. He snorted in protest as she measured out her available rope to begin her descent over the cliff, and even began pawing at her leg as she tied one end to a sturdy tree near the edge.

"I have to do this, Argos," Merona whispered, pausing her work to rub his ears. "Right now, we've got no other option for getting off this island, and last time I checked, you can't climb a cliff, so as much as I want to keep my promise not to leave you behind again, I've got to do this alone."

Argos grumbled in reply, and Merona offered one last scratch of his head before securing her rope and disappearing over the cliff side. The coarse fibers scraped against Merona's shredded old gloves as she held tightly to the line, cautiously finding her footing as she rappelled down the cliff. The sun was well into its descent, and soon she would have little light to see by, but if she could reach the camp before the light was gone, the darkness would be key in aiding her infiltration.

Descending only a few feet down the length of the rope, Merona reached for the rocky cliff wall and found it slick with moisture from the still-overwhelming mists around her. Her grip began to slip as she shifted her weight from the rope to the stones, and she grabbed for the rope before she could be plunged into the rocky waves below.

She had scarcely begun and already the climb was more treacherous than anticipated, and she had already anticipated a high chance of death. Reaching for a new rock, Merona tested the stone's slickness carefully before shifting her weight. Her grip was firm, and she was cautious in her selection of footholds before fully relinquishing her grasp of the rope.

Though survival instinct might have urged a normal person to turn back, or better yet, never attempt the climb at all, Merona's instincts told her to ignore the jagged rocks and water below, and force her mind to focus on her breathing, weight distribution, and grip. Nothing below was in her control, nor should any of it matter, if all her efforts kept her aloft and out of the deadly fall's clutches. Such thoughts could only serve to unbalance her.

Perched high above the crashing waves, Merona kept her focus on each new hand and foothold as she worked her way horizontally along the cliff side, inching toward the gray men's camp, and her objective. Planting her toe into a rocky crevasse, Merona checked the stone's stability and, feeling it solid beneath her boot, began to shift her weight, but as she moved over, the wet stone began to crumble, disintegrating beneath her foot as she clung to her remaining three holds. Scrambling to plant her foot back on a sturdy crack in the rocks, Merona took a moment to catch her breath and calm her racing heart, before attempting the climb again. She could not afford to make mistakes like that, the rope which had saved her the last time was far out of reach now. If she

fell, she fell for good.

Moving quickly along the rock face, she struggled to find reliable footholds, feeling each stone begin to give way as she released to take hold of the next. Her heart thumped beneath her chest as the next handhold crumbled within her fingers mere seconds before her hold was relinquished.

Regaining herself, Merona pressed on, refusing to allow a little near-death mistake to interrupt her momentum. The light of the sky had all but faded from sight, and Merona now found herself reaching out in closing darkness. She had to reach the camp before the light was fully gone, or finding proper handholds would be impossible.

The tops of the camp's lookout towers peeked up past the cliff's edge, guiding her to the exact spot she would make her infiltration. Though she could see her objective wasn't far off, each yard of progress along the cliff tore at her cramping fingers and aching arms, making the distance feel like miles.

At last, she reached it, the blind spot directly between the two rear towers, where she could ascend out of sight of both. With a last agonizing push, Merona scaled up the cliff, peering over the rocky edge to assess what obstacles lay before her. To her right, three warriors milled about outside a hut, speaking to each other in their own, indistinguishable tongue. To her left, a large stack of firewood sat beneath a rickety shelter of branches and palm leaves, an ideal spot to take cover when an opening presented itself.

But no opening came.

Clinging to the cliff edge, Merona waited for the three gray men to leave, but still they stood in place, muttering and chattering to one another. The rocks dug into her fingers as Merona gripped the cliff's edge.

With three men in eyesight, any dash for cover would certainly be spotted by one of them, but with the growing pain in her arms, she knew her grip would not last long. Adjusting her hold, she felt stone crumble beneath her boot, tumbling down the rocky precipice beside her.

Flinching from the echoing noise, Merona ducked back behind the ledge, listening for a change in the three chattering voices as they approached to investigate the sound, but with no audible change to their mutterings, she slowly peered up again, finding them fully oblivious to the ruckus. The cliff clearly offered no threat to the camp's safety, acting as such a reliable barrier that attentions grew lax the further back into camp you went. Being a foolhardy choice for an invasion of force to ever take, no one was on the lookout for invaders from the cliff, of this she could rest easy.

Just as her grip began to fail her again, someone ushered the three men inside the hut, and like a bolt from a crossbow, Merona leapt up, scaling the cliff edge and darting for the wood pile. Ducking down, Merona peered through the cracks of the clustered timber, looking out across the camp for threats to her impending theft. A scattering of figures passed through distant, foggy parts of the camp, but no one seemed to stand near the central spire. Though the watch towers would have a clear line of sight to the spire itself, the watchmen's attention seemed to be distinctly focused on the outer perimeter, not the interior camp.

Settling her nerves, Merona crept forward, keeping to the shadows of the huts and scattered structures as she slipped unnoticed amongst her enemy. With her target in sight, Merona readied for the final approach, mapping out in her mind the best route open to her. Heart racing, Merona crept forward, mud clinging to her boots with each cautious step she took. Spotting a pair of gray men turning her way, she ducked behind a muddy hut once again, edging around the small structure to keep out of sight as the warriors passed by.

The spire and diamond lay only a few yards out of reach now, situated near a long-extinguished bonfire. But before Merona could step any closer, figures from all sides began to gather around the spire. Fresh wood was tossed upon the bonfire as it was swiftly set ablaze. Tribesmen and women circled around the growing flames in the beginnings of a ritual as their voices rose, rushing through the camp in chattering, screeching chants.

Merona remained still, crouched out of sight within the shadows of a small empty hut's open doorway as the tribe assembled around the bonfire and spire. Had she missed her chance? With all this sudden activity at the center of camp, would she be discovered and captured? Her heart pounded in her ribs, as she feared her only option now was to abandon her scheme of thievery, and attempt escaping alive and unseen.

As she searched for a path away from the growing numbers of tribesmen, she noticed that each and every one of them had fallen to the dirt, their outstretched arms and bowed heads pointed toward the spire as they lay a few yards off around the bonfire, their voices still raised in chanting choir. Looking around, Merona began to see that every individual in sight was doing the same, including the watchmen in the towers, and she knew this might actually be her only chance at retrieving the artifact unseen.

The ritualistic, bowed worship might last only a few moments, but she had to take the chance; and she could not hesitate. Slipping in on tiptoe, Merona inched silently toward the spire, her footfalls drowned out by the natives' voices, and with a deep breath, she began to climb. Her eyes continually flicked toward the prostrate natives, as she scaled the towering pillar right before their tightly shut eyes, gripping to the nubs of hacked off branches that once covered the uprooted sapling, now used to display the diamond.

Arriving at the top, Merona reached for the immense diamond, and felt its weight as it fell into her grasp at last. Dropping from the spire unheard amid the chanting, she halted for a moment, gazing in awe of the diamond's sheer size. It was raw and uncut, but its surface still glinted with a nearly unparalleled brilliance. Its draw was more than beauty, more than the call of a valuable treasure, something else seemed to grip Merona to never let it out of her possession... something unnatural.

Merona shook her head, her attention snapping up from the diamond, and her eyes locking on a nearby gray child. Though everyone still lay bowed toward the spire, this one child had looked up, its bright, pale eyes staring right toward Merona as she crouched within the shadow of the spire.

For a moment, she was sure the child would call out, alerting the whole of the camp down upon her, but as the seconds dragged by, she saw that the boy stared not at her, but at the top of the spire where the diamond should have rested. A hiss of reprimand came from a native woman next to him, and instantly he shut his eyes, returning to the same prostrate position as all the others.

Dropping the hefty diamond in her coat pocket and buttoning down the flap, Merona crept from the shadow, ducking behind huts to keep hidden from the watchtowers as the chanting echoed on. Creeping past the bowed villagers, she soon reached the edge of the village, but as she looked for an escape, bowed gray men seemed to bar her every path. Her plan had suffered its first casualty, as the option to slip out undetected by one of the openings in the outer wall was cut off from her.

The chanting began to wane into an eerie silence, and she knew she had little time left to make a decision, and in an instant, she moved swift and silently toward the cliffside, now her only means of escape. Only a moment after she'd reached the cliff's edge, a chattering roar echoed across the camp behind her. The people had awoken, and the diamond's absence had been discovered.

CHAPTER XXXVI

THE FOG THICKENS

SCRAMBLING over the edge of the cliff, Merona could hear the pounding footfalls of rushing gray men just above her. Clinging tightly to the rock, she pressed her body to the cliff face, hidden from sight.

As Merona edged along, the diamond weighed heavy at her side, thumping against her hip within her bulging pocket, and making her climb all the more difficult with the new imbalance it created. Shouts and chattering cries echoed overhead as the gray men searched frantically for their missing treasure, oblivious to the thief which climbed just out of sight behind the cliff wall.

Merona knew that if just one of them chose to peer over the edge, her clandestine escape would be brought to a bloody end, for a single spear could send her toppling from the cliff side, down into the jagged rocks and waves beneath her. Yet the idea that anyone would attempt to infiltrate the camp via the cliff face seemed an impossibility in the gray peoples' minds, and Merona clung to that hope as tightly as the rocks.

The sounds of voices and footfalls seemed to drift back, as they expanded their search out from the camp, and Merona's thoughts raced to Argos' safety out in the woods. If they found him as he waited for her to return, he would stand little chance against their hunters.

Hurrying her climb, she utilized parts of the path

she had already taken, but more than once, the sturdy rocks she had used before crumbled from her weight, and the distant rocks threatened below. Fighting to find her rhythm, Merona raced along the cliff side, sighting her rope dangling in the distant mist.

Stone by stone, she moved sideways along the cliff face, already growing weary from the previous climb, the strain to her muscles began to mount, and the growing fatigue of the long climb quickly began sapping her strength. If she didn't pick up speed, her weakening limbs would prove a greater risk of failing her than the wet stones she climbed along. Grabbing into the next divot, Merona swung forward, taking hold of rock after rock, without giving herself the luxury of time to double check its stability.

Reaching the last stretch, her muscles throbbing from the arduous climb, she at last came within reach of the dangling rope. In the next moment, she felt the rocks at her hands begin to crack, and without thinking, Merona leapt from the cliff.

Her fingers brushed the rough cord, and in the next instant she grasped the rope. Her body slammed into the cliff wall, swinging from the momentum of the jump as she clutched tight to the lifeline, planting her feet against the stones and beginning her ascent. Light rain began to fall as she reached the top, and Argos barked as she came into view.

Rushing up, he vigorously licked her face, very nearly pushing her back over the edge before she had fully clambered onto solid ground. For a moment she sat, leaning against the tree gasping out in relief, but her peace was not long lived.

The sounds of the gray men's search expanding beyond their camp flooded toward her, they had heard the eager barks of her companion, and Merona had no choice but to pick herself up and press on, rushing through the trees toward the swamp and her only hope of escape. Leaping to her feet, Merona raced forward only to barrel near headlong into a pair of gray scouts searching far out in the jungle.

Drawing her machete, Merona ducked a scout's incoming hatchet, slicing her blade across his stomach and leaping over the toppling body before it hit the earth, only to land a hit across the second scout's throat.

Other gray men spotted the fight, and familiar shrieks and calls to battle sounded behind Merona and Argos as they rushed on, barreling into the dark jungle at breakneck speed. Vines and branches struck against her face and arms as she sprinted forward, the sounds of her incensed pursuers growing closer in spite of all efforts to push herself, her energy was finally running dry.

Her weak limbs faltered beneath her as she ran on, tripping as her feet began to drag and the sounds of the gray men grew nearer. She had pushed her body too far and knew she could not outrun them as far as the swamp, and in the next moment, her foot caught against a root, sending her plummeting toward the dirt. The glinting diamond burst from her pocket, rolling out across the ground in front of her as her body slammed down.

Argos had bolted out ahead, but raced back to Merona's side with the sound of her fall. Pawing agitatedly at her to get up, Merona felt a twinge in her ankle and knew the fight was lost. The gray men would be on her in minutes, and she had no hope of outrunning them now.

"Run Argos, go!" Merona hissed, trying at least to save him, if she could not save herself. But of course, the loyal mutt refused to leave her side.

Scrambling to find cover in a nearby thicket, she pulled Argos in alongside her, knowing the attempt to hide would be fruitless, but having no other options. But as she huddled within the insufficient cover, she spotted the glinting diamond laying in the dirt, and in a moment of desperation, reached out and snatched it up.

Clutching the stone to her chest, Merona began to mutter a prayer of sorts. She could not speak whatever language the gray men might have used to control their enchantments, and so she was left to hope that whatever magic was at work here, it might be controlled on faith alone.

The gray men closed in, and Merona's eyes shut tight as she muttered her incantation with increasing fervor. Footfalls began to pound around her before, all at once, they slowed to a halt. Cracking an eye open, Merona peered out at her surroundings to find that she had none, for the gray fog had fully consumed the jungle which she had once sat in. Not even Argos was fully visible as she reached out for him, and pulled him to her side. The footsteps of the gray men were all around her now, groping and muttering through the blinding void as they pressed on, their voices growing fearful in the oppressive fog.

Merona held still, not daring to breathe as they passed by all around her, fully oblivious to her location. Waiting, the crunch of their footsteps and the thumping of her own heart were the only sounds she heard, until at last the footfalls began to grow distant, fading fully out of earshot as the gray men searched on in vain through the dense fog.

Allowing herself at last to fully breathe, Merona looked to Argos, and then to the diamond still clutched in her hand, and whispered in disbelief, "It worked... I can't believe it worked. Argos, I think we might actually make it off this rock."

~

Summoning the fog a second time proved far more difficult than Merona had anticipated after the night of the diamond theft, but even more elusive was finding the power to expel the mists from the island completely. The writings about the diamond and its powers had been vague at best, but now, faced with trying to tap into such an inexplicable power source made her fully feel her lack of knowledge, and her own insignificance against such supernatural forces.

How could she, a weak and meager castaway, hope to understand or control the grand powers around her? She had summoned the fog once, it was true, but the exact words that had made it work had become muddled in her head, if they had even mattered in the first place. More and more, she felt the power had been summoned by an emotion or a desperate need, but what need could be greater, or more earnestly desired than her need to escape the island?

In an attempt at not becoming overcome with desperation, Merona returned to the basics, first she tried by reciting the exact words she had used before, then attempted to tap into its power at the same time each night, as the night she had summoned the fog. With no success, she next tried returning to the exact spot where she had summoned it, but only succeeded in nearly getting herself captured by a group of patrolling gray men.

With little else to try, Merona resorted to searching the island for spots where the fog was already sparse, but only raised her hopes when she mistakenly thought her efforts were finally beginning to have an effect, the moment the fog began to fade even a little. Merona was reaching the end of her rope, her hopes having risen with the belief that all she need do was this last, dangerous thing of stealing the diamond, and then she would be home free, that her escape would be imminent. She rebuked herself at her own stupidity in believing that tapping into an unexplainable power source would somehow be the easy part.

Sitting in her cave near a low fire, Merona stared between the gem and the cloudy sky, muttering made up incantations with little hope of success as Argos lay at her hip picking clean a bone from that night's dinner.

"I know I can make it work... at least, I know I did once. Or maybe I just thought I did. If only the villagers hadn't all been killed... if only I had someone who'd used its power, and didn't want to *kill* me, that could show me how to..."

And just then, a crazy thought sprung into her desperate mind, that there was someone on the island who the records had spoken of using the diamond's power, who had shown no overt desire in killing her in all this time. If it could be called "someone". The swamp guardian had been given the stone the day of his summoning, and had used it for what seemed years, keeping the gray men at bay.

Before Merona allowed herself to even consider the idea, she had already dismissed it as insane. "What am I thinking? I'm going to just march into that swamp and strike up a conversation with that thing? Just because the villagers trusted the thing to protect them, doesn't mean I should. I mean, look where they ended up."

Looking out toward the sky, Merona thought on how the final attack on the village must have played out, had the gray men circled the island by boat as they had done to Merona that day on the beach? Or stormed through the swamp with their new power source in hand? However they had done it, the scattered dead had seemed fully off guard when Merona had explored the remains of their civilization. They had, no doubt, fully trusted in their guardian to protect them, but it was a trust which had been unfounded, it seemed.

As these thoughts wove through her mind, Merona could almost hear the march of approaching gray men, just as the villagers might have on that fateful day, and shuddered at the looming rumble that had announced their doom. Yet as the sounds began to grow rather than fade as she came out of her deep thoughts, she realized the sound of marching men was very much in the here and now. The gray men had tracked her down, and come for their diamond.

Snatching up her weapons and satchel, Merona pocketed the sacred gem and rushed from the cave. She could try to lose them in the woods as she had done before, but where would she have left to go if they pursued her all the way to the beach? No, her only option became blindingly clear as the lights of their torches began to flicker through the trees… she would make for the safety of the swamp and hope, as the villagers had, for the guardian's protection.

CHAPTER XXXVII

A TREMOR OF CHANGE

ERONA'S boots sunk deep into the steadily softening ground as she raced for the swamp, Argos following closely at her side. The shouts and flashing torches of the gray men pursued doggedly behind her, seeming to know exactly where she was fleeing, and determined to catch up before she was out of their reach.

Thudding steps neared from her left, as a gray warrior leapt from the trees in front of her, cutting off her path in a flurry of spear thrusts. Merona staggered to a halt, dodging backward out of reach as she parried his spear with her own. Argos flew suddenly at the gray man's leg, biting violently into his flesh as he raised his spear to strike the animal.

But Merona's reflexes were faster, plunging her spear through his neck before his blow could fall on her companion. Abandoning her weapon in his body, Merona and Argos raced on, the gray men now closing in swiftly behind them.

Time rushed by like the surrounding trees, and suddenly Merona was wading into the boggy waters of the swamp. Mist swirled around her, defusing and reflecting the cascading moonlight into an eerie green glow. The unnerving stench seeped into her lungs and thoughts, as the putrid swamp sloshed around her knees with a monotonous gurgling. The lifeless silence of her surroundings clawed at her nerves as she pressed on, her pulse still racing from the miles of jungle behind her.

She couldn't tell how far she'd waded through the sludge, her focus consumed in putting as much distance between her and her gray pursuers as possible, but as she pressed on, their footfalls grew nearer, and she knew not even the swamp would deter them from recovering their prized diamond. All chance of escape seemed lost before the unexpected happened... the fog began to thicken.

Ducking behind a hefty tree trunk, Merona held Argos close at her side as the gray men neared, daring not to venture too swiftly into the blinding fog ahead. The voices of the gray men muttered all around, and though the words were unintelligible to her, their voices bore a distinct tone of dread. Their leader hissed and chattered orders at them, but their voices began to rise in protest, and all at once, just within sight in the mist, several of the men surrounded their leader, silencing him and his orders with a swift dagger thrust. The remaining men fell back, abandoning their quest and the body of their slain captain as he floated in the water, drifting closer toward the concealed adventuress and her dog.

Merona held her breath, waiting for the murmuring voices to fully fade out of earshot before allowing herself to breathe. Had she at last succeeded? Had her great need in that moment allowed her to control the fog in her favor? Her hope in the diamond's powers began once again to rise, but as they rose, so too did the unseen figure from the water.

Concealed within the mist and shadows of the trees, the creature stood a short distance off across the swamp, dripping with sludge. At Merona's side, Argos' hackles rose, his gaze fixed on the creature behind her, obscured in the mist. Merona froze, slowly turning toward the rasping breathing that now reached her ears. Hidden in the shadows, two flashing green eyes met Merona's own, as the water at her ankles began to rise up to her knees.

The clouds grew thick in the black sky, blotting out all light from the moon and plunging the swamp into darkness, but still the green eyes flashed clear and bright, the only remaining light in the blackness which surrounded her. Yet, in the next moment, they had vanished from sight.

Machete in hand, Merona spun in all directions, searching desperately to locate her foe. Then, at her back, she felt the ripple of water against her leg, and hot breath on the back of her neck, and all at once she turned, Argos barking franticly toward the creature now standing behind her. The night was dark and the fog thick, but still she could clearly see it, mouth agape and unearthly eyes blazing green before her.

Instinctively, she struck out with her machete, aiming just below the glowing pupils for its neck. The green eyes flashed bright before dropping at Merona's boots, vanishing beneath the water with a heavy splash.

Merona waited in the blackness, feeling the ripple of water thrum against her legs as it slowly settled. Had she just killed the beast so easily? She stood in place, waiting for a definitive sign of life or death, but nothing came. No sound, no ripple of water to suggest it had moved elsewhere, nothing, until, beneath the surface of the water, she felt the distinct touch of clawed fingers brushing past her leg.

It hadn't fallen into the water, it had dived, and now she felt it a second time, a slick, scaly form brushing past her other leg as it circled around her, the glow of its eyes

·407·

fully hidden beneath the murky waters. Staggering back, she struggled to spot the faint glow of green beneath the sludge, before, in desperation, she began striking out blindly with her blade into the water, hitting nothing but slime.

A short ways off, she heard Argos barking for her. Even the dog had recognized the futility in fighting in pitch blackness against such a foe in its own territory. Retreat was her only chance now, but as she waded forward toward the call of her companion, a rush of motion beneath the water rippled against her legs, and with a bubbling surge, it rose up before her, blocking her path. Its green eyes burning in the black void nearly three heads above her own.

In desperation, Merona struck out again, slashing as high as her weapon could reach, but the blade cut through nothing but air. Again, and again her strikes missed by a mile until the faint green eyes dropped, sinking out of sight beneath the water before its slick scaly body brushed past Merona's legs once more.

Sounds of the sloshing creature circling her beneath the water echoed off the trees, and Merona knew it was only toying with her now. With its size and strength, it could overpower her in seconds, if it had wanted, but instead it circled. It's clawed hands increasingly grabbing and tugging at her coat and slacks with every pass.

Water sloshed around her legs as she waded forward. She could hear every thump of her heart as though it were echoing off the surrounding trees, as the ripples of the circling creature continued to brush against her legs. She had to get out, had to escape the swamp and the creature's grasp. It didn't matter how much the tribespeople had trusted it, she was not one of them, and had no way of knowing if it looked on her as friend or foe.

Then, on its next pass, she felt it; its long claws groping at her coat once again. This time it took hold of the large lump of the diamond which lay within her pocket, and in the next moment the creature flew into a frenzy, clawing and pulling at the diamond as though it knew exactly what power Merona held.

In moments, its clawing grasp had overpowered her, and she felt her footing slip as she fell back in a splash of mud and slime, her tailbone thudded against the swampy floor as water flooded in around her. Water choked up her nose as she fought to keep her head above the water. Pushing up, she struggled to rise to her feet, grasping for the precious stone to keep it from slipping out the new hole now torn in her coat.

Just managing to stagger to her feet, the water now reached up around her hips as she stood, feeling an abrupt and painful force slam into her thigh. Knocked off balance by the hit, the diamond within her hand was sent sailing through the air, hitting the water with a slap before slipping out of sight beneath the gurgling mire.

In the next moment, the shadowy figure rose from the water, diving forward after the sinking gem and disappearing beneath the boggy surface. As it dove, the water began to clear, rippling out from the very spot the creature had submerged and with it, the heavy fog began all at once to lift.

For a moment, the clear silver moonlight shone peacefully down on Merona and Argos. All was quiet around them, save the gentle sloshing of the water at their legs, until a hint of movement caught Merona's eye in the distance amid the trees.

Rising from the water once more, the creature stood tall, now twice the size it had been when it had vanished into the swampy depths, and in its sternum was set the diamond, pulsing with green light as bright as the creature's own eyes.

For a moment, Merona stood frozen, her eyes locked upon the creature in its new form, but this moment of stillness was not to last. The ground beneath their feet began to tremble, growing in violence until Merona struggled to stand.

The roaring quaking of the earth echoed around her, and Merona hastened to escape the swamp, shouting out for Argos to follow her as she staggered forward. Fighting to keep her footing, she felt the cold waterline rising around her legs, choking her movements and slowing her progress.

Merona surged forward, the quaking roar of the island growing intensely violent around her. Staggering to stay upright, she fell to her knees and into the sludge of the rapidly expanding rivers. She already regretted her actions of venturing into the swamp for safety, for all her efforts seemed only to have hastened the end of all things, bringing her no closer to rescue than she was before. But it was too late, the damage was done.

A sharp yelp echoed out behind her as she rushed on, and Merona whirled round, spotting Argos falling behind, his legs having become tangled in some kind of vines beneath the water. Rushing back to aid him, she found him holding his head high now, desperate to avoid drinking in the putrid water which had risen up to his chest. Drawing her machete, Merona reached beneath the water and drew up every vine she could lay her hands on, hacking at the tendrils until at last their hold was severed and Argos sprang free, ducking near her legs for safety as the earthquake raged on.

It seemed as though the island itself was sinking into the depths, but the struggle to survive surpassed Merona's fears that her actions might have hastened

their own deaths. With the water line still rising around them, Merona rushed forward, intuitively making her way to higher ground to escape the flood.

The ground beneath them rocked back and forth, jolting out from under their feet with every step, as deep fissures began to shoot through the earth all around. Leaping over the growing chasms, Merona hardly knew what direction she was headed. Groping in the darkness, her only instinct was to make for higher ground, and she pressed forward up any incline before her.

The ground began to grow steep as she reached the mountain, and Merona and Argos continued on, struggling to climb the rocks and outrun the rising water. As the island shook and quaked, a hefty rock shot loose from the side of the mountain, rocketing straight toward the two survivors.

Grabbing hold around Argos' belly, Merona dove to the side, narrowly escaping the boulder's path as the two rolled clear. Catching her breath, she pressed on up the mountain, loose rocks flying past or slamming into Argos' paws and Merona's shins and shoulders, as they struggled to keep going.

More large stones came loose, and they scrambled to dodge them in the chaos of the uproar, but as they clawed their way up the mountain side, an immense boulder dislodged directly above them, its shadow blotting out the still bright moon as it hurtled down toward them.

Chapter XXXVIII

THE FINAL DAY DAWNS

I T had taken some time to save his funds, and yet more to hunt through every scrap yard, factory, mechanic, and aviation enthusiast he could locate on the small island, to barter and buy any and all suitable parts they were willing to sell to complete his repairs on Katya's landing gear. But though the necessary parts had proven elusive, Sasha had finished his repairs in a month and said his goodbyes to the farmer who had done so much to save his seemingly unsalvageable search.

At last, the whir of Katya's propellers glided over the ocean once again, as Sasha peered out his cockpit window, searching for this mystery island which his dear friend had found herself stranded upon for so many months. Thin clouds whipped around the wings of his aircraft, only partially obscuring his view of the water below.

Sasha had been sure to contact Merona's uncle before departing on his search, hoping for news of Liora and her expedition, but even Quincy had received no word from her in all that time since Sasha had been stranded, and as he flew out across the water, Sasha couldn't help fearing that the worst might have happened.

"You always fear the worst, Sasha," he could hear Merona's voice saying in his head. And he couldn't truly argue with it. Liora might be in trouble, or her assignment might simply have taken her out into the wild where no letter could reach her. He could only speculate over her situation, but Merona was most certainly in need of help. It was going on six months since her plane had gone missing and she was stranded and struggling, but hopefully still alive on an island somewhere. She had to come first.

The sprawling blue waves rushed out before Sasha as he looked on, feeling the hopelessness of his never-ending search. He had not seen a hint of land in countless hours, and with the long miles he had already covered, his fuel was threatening to run too low for the return trip. But still he pressed on, his gut telling him to hold his course, if only for just a mile more.

His fuel gauge jittered, edging lower as he flew on. His hope began to wane, and with a deep sigh he was beginning to accept his failure, but a strange pull inside urged him to continue on. And if there was one thing Sasha never ignored when in the air, it was his gut.

Ignoring his fuel gauge as it jittered even lower, Sasha flew on, his eyes scrutinizing the glittering waters ahead for the island. In the sinking sunlight, it would be hard to miss: a long, dark shadow cast across the waters from an unmoving rock, jutting up from the waves. His eyes had searched so long for it, it was as though he could almost see it up ahead, black and clearly floating amid the blue waves. But as he blinked to wipe away the hallucination from his exhausted eyes, the distant island still remained.

A rush of excitement caught in his throat, and he pushed forward, rushing toward the target with bolstered hope. Rocky cliffs and shores enclosed green jungles and jagged mountains clustered in the center of the island as Sasha approached, turning to circle around and search the angular landmass for signs of life.

This was it. This had to be it. Even the rectangular

shape was the same as the depictions he had seen on Uncle Quincy's old maps. As he rounded the island for the third time, a hint of smoke began to drift up from behind the mountain, and Sasha sped to circle around to the other side, praying his dogged efforts would at last be rewarded.

~

It had been weeks since the great earthquake had rocked the island to its core, and the diamond had been reclaimed by the swamp. The mist had lifted, and the guardian of the swamp had stretched its power beyond the confines of its former limited territory, striking out at the ruthless gray men who refused to relinquish their cannibalistic practices, or attacks on one another's tribes, swiftly forcing them to retreat to the edges of the island.

But one key, new development in all this time that made Merona wish she had stolen the diamond and handed it over on day one after crashing, was the guardian's relentless determination to keep any and all native threats fully at bay from her and her camp. Never could she have expected such devotion from a creature she had so eagerly avoided and even tried to kill, but she was grateful for it. Even if she still had no desire to make friends with the beast.

The cannibals had become one less worry for Merona in her daily struggles for survival. They no longer dared to venture within the swamp creature's territory, which now eclipsed nearly all of the central island, and Merona and Argos could safely take up residence in their old cave on the side of the mountain, rebuilding the old signal fire to keep at the ready should Sasha's plane ever reappear.

Only a very few of the smaller tribes still occupied

their camps in the center of the jungle and the guardian's expanded territory, seemingly the only ones willing to hunt for animal meat now, rather than the flesh of their brother tribes. But even though they had passed the test of the swamp creature's scrutiny, Merona chose to keep out of their way, all the same.

The weeks which followed the earthquake had been surprisingly calm in comparison to the prior months, save for the distant screams of the cannibal tribes if they ever dare to raid one another and face the swamp creature's retribution. This had allowed Merona to give her full attention to preparing for Sasha's return, setting her signal fire near her camp, just as before, so it might always be near at hand. But with the gray men still occupying the edges of the island, slipping past them to reach the beach for rescue had become her primary obstacle. The swamp creature had shown itself a reliable guardian, should the tribes attack Merona's camp, but she had no idea if that protection would extend if she ventured outside the creature's territory.

It was true their numbers had dwindled with the return and renewal of the guardian's powers, and they seemed no longer to dare fight amongst each other for fear of the guardian's retribution if they returned to their violent ways. For Merona however, their bloodlust had not abated.

It seemed to be known among all tribes that she had been responsible for the diamond's retrieval and return to the swamp, and if ever she ventured near their camps, it was not uncommon to see nightly rituals of her twiggy effigy, with its distinct green scarf, being burnt amid chanting and screams. All their hatred had turned toward her, for she had been the one to release the swamp guardian, and so she hid within the safety of the creature's territory. But when the day finally dawned that the sound of Sasha's plane buzzed in the distance, Merona readied to face the gauntlet which awaited her.

With her signal fire lit, Merona snatched up her weaponry and satchel, which contained her few meager belongings, and watched the sky as Sasha's plane circled to find the source of the smoke, waiting to see which part of the beach he would make his approach to land. As she had hoped, his plane began to turn toward the nearest beach to the west, dropping closer to land in the water just offshore.

With a deep breath, Merona called to Argos to follow, and the mutt turned from an abandoned rodent hole which had caught his attention, and raced after her. Surging through the brush, Merona hurried to reach the beach in time, knowing that the moment Sasha had landed, the gray men would be drawn to him and his aircraft, no doubt to pillage its contents. And if he landed within range of their spears or boats, she might not have much time before he was under a full-on attack.

Branches and vines beat against Merona as she sprinted forward, rifle in hand. It had been clogged and rusty when Merona had retrieved it from the gray warrior in her fight on the beach, but over the weeks since, she'd made time to clean and refurbish it back into serviceable working order. The built-up rust had been scrubbed clean with citrus juice and a rag, then the rifle was cleaned thoroughly before lubricating it with tallow she rendered from the animal fat off her kills. It wasn't perfect, but it was working again, at last.

Surprisingly, through all her time on the island, Merona had been able to save a small supply of ammunition for a rainy day, which looking back, had probably come and gone about twenty times over. But with escape now fully in sight, she was ready to let loose the firepower she'd been holding back.

Nearing the beach, the shouts and cries of the gray warriors rose in ferocity, and soon Merona could hear the clear sound of Sasha's revolver cracking in the distance as he fought them off. Merona knew it wouldn't be long before he would run out of ammunition… Sasha never brought enough ammunition.

The beach was scattered with gray men as Merona broke through the tree line. Boats had already been launched into the water, rushing toward Sasha's plane as he scrambled to dodge their flying spears, picking them off in their canoes with his revolver.

One gray warrior leapt from his canoe, grabbing hold of the aircraft's landing gear and scrambling up toward Sasha, who stood in the doorway of his plane. Turning to his attacker, Sasha raised his gun to fire, moments behind the shot that slammed into the side of his attacker's head.

Out on the beach, Sasha spotted Merona as she fired again, dropping two more warriors as they scrambled from their boat toward Sasha's plane. In the next moment, she was slamming the butt of her rifle into the face and gut of two charging gray men, before drawing her machete to permanently dispatch them.

Sasha choked back tears of joy which pricked his eyes at the sight of his dear friend, not only alive, but alive and kicking.

Reloading his weapon, Sasha bellowed out to Merona, "Get to boat! I hold them back!"

Raising her rifle, Merona sidestepped and fired into three gray warriors lined up in front of her, her point-blank shot sailing through their bodies before they toppled right and left into the sand. Jumping over their bodies, Merona and Argos raced for an unlaunched canoe in the sand, dropping to her knee for a moment to take quick aim down her rifle and dispatch two more charging warriors before they could reach her.

Rising and rushing on, she drew her machete and sliced through the throats, chests, and guts of the warriors who barred her path, as Argos ran alongside her, going for the throats of those she'd missed.

Skidding to a halt in the sand, Merona flung her satchel and rifle into the empty canoe and pushed it off the shore before leaping inside, taking up the oars as Argos scrambled in behind her. Slicing through the water, Merona drove the boat rapidly forward, hostile canoes racing toward her as Sasha fired into them to drop as many gray men as he could hit.

Spears sailed overhead before one pierced through the wood just between Merona's feet, and all at once water bubbled up into the canoe's hull, swiftly puddling around Merona's ankles as she paddled on. Only a few yards from Sasha's plane, the weight of the flooding water dragged down her vessel, and Merona snatched up and slung her gear crisscrossed on her chest and shoulders, before diving from her boat, Argos following immediately behind her.

Kicking forward with rapid arm strokes, Merona's hand soon reached the hefty landing gear of the sea plane, and she looked up in relief at the Russian's friendly face.

"Hey, Sash," Merona called up from the water between gasps. "Good timing."

"Really?" Sasha called back, firing several more rounds at the still swarming enemies on the beach, before extending his immense arm towards her. "I thought I was little bit late."

Reaching up, Merona grabbed his hefty paw and hoisted herself onto the landing gear.

"No, you're good," she panted. "This... this is good."

Sasha nodded towards the water. "Is that pilot's

dog?"

Glancing back, Merona spotted Argos, his frantic paws slapping the water as he paddled close after her.

"No... he's *my* dog now," said Merona. "The pilot got... dead."

"Dead?"

"Yeah... eaten."

"*Eaten?*"

"It's been a long... long six months, Sash. I'll tell you all about it sometime... later."

Reaching out, Merona scooped the drenched gray mutt from the waters, lifting him into the plane with some assistance from Sasha.

Merona fired a final few shots into the gray men to deter them in their pursuit as Sasha leapt into the pilot seat, pushing the plane forward into a speedy take off. Merona slumped to the floor of the aircraft, breathing in a stifled sigh as the cannibal threat rapidly fell out of range.

Scratching behind Argos' soppy ears, Merona called over the noise of the engine, "Hey, Sasha?"

"*Da?*"

"Thank you... thank you for coming for me."

Looking back over his broad shoulders, Sasha simply nodded, smiling softly behind his thick mustache in silent understanding.

"And remind me never to fly with any other pilot but you, *ever* again."

"You see!" Sasha jumped in, breaking his stoic silence. "Didn't I tell you he not be trusted? Why you not listen to me when I say these thing? Always you think you know better about planes, and pilots. But who is pilot here? Me! So why you not listen when I tell you?!"

Sasha's words trailed off behind the engine noise, and Merona's gaze drifted out the window, looking back toward the doom she had just escaped. Pulling the scarf from her neck, she began wiping across Argos' exhausted, drooping face, sopping up his dripping fur as the strange island and its mysteries slowly shrank away.

The obscuring mists began to return, and Merona watched as the island faded swiftly out of sight, not knowing that in that moment, her memories had begun to fade too. In the weeks that followed her rescue, her recollection of the unexplainable, supernatural events she had witnessed felt more and more like strange nightmares she had only dreamed. The black hand within the water, the shifting swamp, the scaly creature that lived within, and the diamond and its powers, all of it drifted away the further from the island she went, until they were nothing more than incomplete memories she no longer believed.

CHAPTER XXXIX

EPILOGUE: THE SEARCH BEGINS

THE thud of their hefty boots echoed through the room as Merona, Sasha, and Uncle Quincy strode into a dingy bar in Cairo, searching for their expensive, and reluctantly procured contact. It had been months since Liora's last letter to Sasha had arrived, with no word since, and now this man, a former employee of Copperhead, was their only lead.

"Are you sure he'll be here, uncle?" inquired Merona.

"I'm sure," replied Quincy. "I get the feeling he's desperate for money."

"Aren't we all."

"But how you know he have any information?" asked Sasha. "Liora seem clear in letters that boss tell no one of plans for expedition."

"He's the only lead we've got... I don't think we have much choice."

Searching around the bar, a small, weasel-faced man eyed them from the shadows, at last waving them over in a failed attempt at inconspicuousness.

"Mr. Quincy Grant? Yes? I recognized your hat."

"Mr. Wringer is it?"

"Shhh! Not so loud!" The man hissed. "Did you bring the money?"

"Of course."

"Then let's see it."

Merona and her uncle slid into the booth, while Sasha remained standing guard, recognizing that the cramped space was unlikely to hold his bulk. Sliding their envelope of cash across the table, they waited for Wringer to count it out silently before pressing their inquiries.

"Now you have your money," Quincy began, "what can you tell us about this expedition of Copperhead's? Where were they going?"

"No one knows. Copperhead was extremely tight lipped with all of us about the expedition, and I was let go before it was getting underway."

"I thought you said you were a part of it?" insisted Merona.

"No, no. Copperhead had a habit of switching out people on-the-regular, just to make sure no one person knew too much. I was dropped as soon as he had a new lead for his next step."

"A new lead? What next step?" Merona hissed. "Stop talking in riddles and tell us what you know already!"

"All I know is he was obsessed with immortality. When I was working for him, it was the fountain of youth he was after, but then he found something new… some obscure Egyptian myths that he became obsessed with. One in specific about a sphinx, I think. He was convinced they held the answers to everything he'd spent his life looking for… and the next thing I know, I was given the sack."

"What myths? What was he going after?"

"How should I know? I was fired, remember?"

Merona slammed her hand over the envelope which still lay on the table. "Then what are we paying you for?"

Wringer tried in vain to extract the money out from under her grasp. "Hey, a deal is a deal! Money for all I know."

"Which just so happens to be *nothing*."

"I need this money!"

"You think we don't? You get the money when you give us something useful!"

"I don't know anything else!"

"Then, we'll take our money and be on our way."

"No! I need this to get out of town!"

"Not our problem."

"You don't understand, Copperhead has sent someone after me, to shut me up, and I have a plane I *need* to be on tonight!"

"Then talk faster."

"Okay, okay! I did overhear Copperhead talking to Dr. Strenburg once. He's one of the men in his close circle, men he trusts above anyone else, not that he *truly* trusts *anyone*..."

"Get to the point, what did you hear them talking about?"

"Well, it was about the legend, see, Copperhead was saying that he had found the key, the key to opening it!"

"Open what?"

"To open a hidden chamber beneath —"

But before he could speak those final key words, a shot rang out through the crowded bar, sending Wringer slumping over in his seat, and the crowd of patrons into a frantic rush to escape harm.

Looking on in horror at her severed lead, now lying dead on the table, Merona turned toward the mayhem of the bar. "What happened?!" she bellowed over the din of noise.

"There!" Sasha snarled, ducking near the table and gripping his bloody shoulder as he pointed vaguely with his other hand. "Shot come from over there!"

Merona searched through the crowd for the gunman, and in a moment, her keen eyes had locked on a figure, moving calmly against the flow of the panicked patrons. Springing into action, Merona raced through the throng, pushing past everyone to reach the swiftly vanishing assassin, but as she reached the edge of the crowd, she had lost sight of him.

"Where did he go?" came her uncle's voice at her shoulder as he caught up with her.

"I don't know! He was *right* here!"

"Wait... there! There he is!" Quincy shouted, pointing in the opposite direction from where Merona had been searching, and the two raced after the killer, following him out into the open street. Bursting outside, they looked up and down the vacant alley, sighting their target just in time to spot him raise his gun.

"Merona, get down!" Quincy bellowed, shoving her to the ground as three shots whizzed overhead.

In the next second Quincy had pulled his revolver and was exchanging fire with the gunman as Merona scrambled for cover, regretting her decision not to bring a gun of her own.

"And here I thought getting off that island would make life easier!" Merona snarled.

"Didn't you bring a gun?" Quincy shouted, exchanging another shot with the gunman.

"Of course not! I *thought* I was back in civilization!"

In the next moment, Quincy pulled a secondary firearm from one of his many holsters and tossed it to his ill-prepared niece.

"No such thing as civilization these days, my dear."

"Noted."

With that, Merona rushed for the other side of the alley to duck behind a hefty dumpster, drawing the gunman's fire as Quincy took another shot, wounding the shooter.

But just as they thought they were gaining the ground over their opponent, three more men swarmed in, pulling the wounded gunman out of harm's way and returning fire upon the Grants with a vengeance.

"Who are these guys?" Merona spat.

"Can't you guess? It's Copperhead's men!"

Merona exchanged fire, only managing to graze one of the men. "But why?"

"Severing loose ends is my guess!"

"Well, I don't care for the sound of being severed!"

"Neither do I! What do you say we retreat?"

With a nod of agreement, Merona leapt for the bar door, falling back inside as her uncle gave cover fire and followed swiftly after her. Shoving an empty table in front of the door, they raced back for Sasha, who had been busy wrapping his grazed arm.

"Time to go, Sash!" Merona called as she raced by.

Following after his companions, Sasha pocketed the envelope of money their deceased contact no longer needed.

Slipping out of the bar with the last remaining fleeing patrons, the three companions rushed down the winding streets, regrouping in a dark corner several blocks from the scene of the shootout.

"Well, this is swell!" Merona fumed. "Our only lead in months, and he gets taken out by a mystery assassin right in front of us! Now we have nothing to go on!"

Quincy looked up from tending Sasha's wounds. "Not nothing, we know Copperhead was interested in the fountain of youth, immortality, Egyptian mythology, and something to do with a sphinx... or *the* sphinx. I can't remember. Did anyone write down exactly what he said?"

"Well, seeing as I didn't think those were about to be our only lead's very last words… no, I didn't think to make any notes."

"But that still something," said Sasha, trying to be hopeful through the pain in his shoulder.

"Hardly anything!" Merona spat. "Besides the fact that good-old-Copperhead is silencing anyone who knows even a shred of info about where he's going!"

"Merona!" Quincy barked. "We *will* find her."

"How? We've got no leads left!"

"Because we are Grants! You, me, your sister… and Grants don't give up. They don't just crumble at the first setback and throw in the towel. They tighten their boot laces and get on with whatever has to be done… I have a conviction of that now, more than I ever used to."

"Why now more than ever?"

"Because *you* are standing here in front of me… after everything you just went through, you're here, determined to find Liora, just like I am, and with just as much bite as I've ever seen in you… if not a bit more."

Merona straightened up and breathed in deep. "Alright, where do we start next?"

"We start by getting your friend here a little medical attention, and then we start looking into anyone who ever worked with that Copperhead devil."

"And if everyone is too scared or paid off to talk? Then what?"

"We *make* them talk," Quincy said, his jaw tensing in resolution.

That night they were each able to find rest in the hope that their determination would not fail them… but it would be over a decade before their efforts would bear fruit…

~

Hot wind gusted across the open desert, kicking up sand that stung as it hit Liora's face and eyes. Pulling her scarf up over her nose, she turned against the wind, looking out toward the setting sun as it drifted low behind the last hints of wispy clouds remaining in the sky. Liora bounced atop her camel, sitting tall among her fellow travelers as they headed out across the Sahara, toward their still unknown destination.

Copperhead had assured Liora that they had more than sufficient supplies for the journey, but just like her sister, Liora didn't much like her own survival being out of her hands, especially when she was putting it in the hands of men she didn't fully trust... or in this case, men she didn't trust at all. They were now several weeks out on their journey deep into the desert, with said supplies rapidly dwindling, Liora felt her initial apprehensions on the subject were more than reasonable.

And she was definitely not alone in her feelings. Nearly all of the other men were beginning to have mutters of rebellion over the handling of the expedition, and the irresponsible rationing of food and water. Which might have been a comfort to know she wasn't alone, except for the ever-growing threat of violence it brought with it.

A couple camels just behind Liora, she could hear two of the men muttering to each other of how much longer they were willing to put up with this ill-fated expedition.

"At this rate, we won't even have enough food for the return trip," one man snarled.

"What about the excavation? How will we have enough supplies to even begin an excavation of this place? *If* we ever even find it!"

"So, how much more of this madness are we going to put up with? Are we just going to be led to our deaths?

We should have turned back ages ago!"

"Maybe it's time we *make* him turn back."

"Now, now, lads," Liora broke in, slowing her camel to drift back and join them. "I don't think things are as dire as all that. I'm sure Copperhead has a plan. I don't believe he would risk all our lives, his own included, if he wasn't sure of our having at least a chance of success."

"Oh, wouldn't he? Come now, Miss Grant, you were one of the first of us to voice your concerns. Now you are trying to say all will be well?"

Liora hesitated for a moment to answer. She fully agreed with every concern raised by the men, but she also knew things would get far worse if they didn't keep their head out in the wild. From her and Merona's time working with their uncle, they knew that the moment vigilante justice became an option to solving a problem, even if it seemed justifiable at the time, it would mark the moment the whole expedition began to spiral into madness and disorder. She could not allow the men's minds to descend into the mindset that out here, the strongest among them could force his will upon the rest without fear of repercussions.

And so, she swallowed back her hesitance and replied. "I have my reservations, same as anyone else, but I also know one very important thing… that Copperhead *knows* things the rest of us do not. And with how far out we've come already, it would be ill-advised to think we are better equipped to run things than he is. Let alone force ourselves into a leadership position when none of us have all the information."

The men grumbled, but couldn't help agreeing with her logic.

"And don't you just know that was his very intention in keeping us all in the dark," one of the men grumbled.

"Maybe…" said Liora. "But it doesn't make our reliance on him any less real."

With the current seeds of uprising successfully stamped out, at least for the present, Liora could breathe again as they rode on. She had to remind herself that if the expedition failed, or even worse, Copperhead was killed, she would have no hope of seeing another dime of payment from him, and it was a need of money that drove her on.

The expedition's outlook did not improve with the days that followed, and grumblings among the men soon returned. This time, leaving little room for diplomacy from Liora to stamp them out. Night after night, their plans to overthrow Copperhead, and the few men who were still loyal to him, grew more serious in nature and Liora began to fear the worst was imminent. But as a new day dawned, and they mounted their camels once again to take up their long trek, Dr. Strenburg called out from the front of the caravan.

"Copperhead! I think I see something."

"What? What do you see?" Copperhead called back, riding up to join Strenburg at the front.

"There's an anomaly... do you see it? Up there..." Strenburg pointed ahead, indicating the discovery to Copperhead.

Curious what all the fuss was about, Liora pressed her camel to hasten its pace, but as she joined the other two men, she could see nothing at all in the vast sands which stretched out before them.

Glancing at the two men with a hint of worry that they were beginning to hallucinate, Liora politely asked to have the discovery pointed out to her.

"It's hard to spot if you don't know what to look for," was Copperhead's simple reply before kicking his camel to ride on.

Following after him, Liora squinted ahead to spot whatever they had, as soon as it came more clearly into view, but after riding on for a moment more,

Copperhead called for everyone to halt and dismount, and still she could see nothing near nor far around them, save the expansive sands.

Copperhead strode out with purpose, pulling out his water canteen and swallowing the last of its contents. Liora looked on as he then placed his now empty water canteen down in the sand and stood back, waiting, for what she did not know...

To everyone's disbelief, a moment passed before all at once fresh liquid began to spill from the canteen's spout and Copperhead snatched it up from off the ground. It was then that Liora noticed it, as Copperhead's hand slipped inside the anomaly, that the air in that solitary location rippled, like the surface of a pool, reflecting colors out across the sand as it was disturbed.

"What... what is that?" one of the men sputtered.

"That, gentlemen, is just a sliver... which means we are getting close... very close."

"Close to what?" Liora sputtered. "What is it that we are hunting after?"

"Don't worry, I'll explain everything very soon. Now make sure to replenish all our food and water supplies in it before we set off again. We are going to need them."

The other men rushed forward to make use of the strange, unnatural anomaly, their faith in the expedition restored from witnessing Copperhead preform this almost godlike feat of creating water from nothing, but Liora found her confidence in the expedition no more reassured after what she had witnessed. What was it they were hunting after? And what source was this unnatural power drawn from?

~THE END~

ABOUT THE AUTHOR

A mad scribbler of art and fiction, Brina Williamson spends her days hunched over a drawing table or keyboard, developing her skills and habitual bad posture.

Her stories always seem to end up finding their way to a 1920s – 1940s setting or theme, and Brina has happily embraced the vintage genre, primarily writing cozy mysteries and pulp adventures.

Her not-as-loyal-as-in-fiction dog likes to find awkward and cramped places near Brina's feet to nap whenever she is working, but also enjoys fetch, walks, and discovering new ways to give her owner mini heart attacks whenever the doorbell rings.